From the 200___
for Best Time-Travel comes . . .

THE SEEDS OF LOVE

"This isn't about dignity, your highness. It's about saving our butts. I don't have to remember him to know that Torcall Cameron isn't a patient man. He gets what he wants, and right now what he wants is you and me doing the horizontal mambo. And that"—Marjory's husband's voice was so low she could barely hear it—"my dear, means *this.*"

She started to retort, but before a word could leave her lips, he covered her mouth with his. The touch threatened to suck the breath right out of her. His lips were hard and soft all at once, stroking, caressing.

Marjory froze for a minute, not certain how to respond; then something deep inside her clenched and released, and a wave of ecstasy shimmered through her body. Pressing closer, she reached up until her hands tangled in his hair and her breasts pressed tightly against his chest. Their kiss deepened.

Ewen's tongue traced the line of her lips, and Marjory shivered with desire. She'd never been this close to a man before—at least, not by choice. Before with Ewen it had always been over almost before it started. Quick and painful it had been—as if she were a vessel not a human, as if she were something to be filled and then discarded.

This was completely different. It was a coming-together, a bonding.

WILD
HIGHLAND
ROSE

DEE DAVIS

LOVE SPELL   NEW YORK CITY

To Julie, Kathleen, Barbara and Chris.

LOVE SPELL®

December 2003

Published by

Dorchester Publishing Co., Inc.
200 Madison Avenue
New York, NY 10016

ISBN 0-505-52570-4

Printed in the United States of America.

Visit us on the web at www.dorchesterpub.com.

WILD HIGHLAND ROSE

O my Luve's like a red, red rose,
That's newly sprung in June:
O my Luve's like the melodie,
That's sweetly play'd in tune.

As fair art thou, my bonie lass,
So deep in luve am I;
And I will luve thee still, my dear,
Till a' the seas gang dry.

—Robert Burns, 1794

Prologue

He was floating in darkness—deep, impenetrable darkness. He tried to open his eyes, to see. But there was nothing. Only the dark, its blackness surrounding him like a living thing. Moving. Breathing.

He lay still, focusing on the sound, listening to the rhythm. A beep, sharp and high-pitched, provided counterpoint for the hissing, a fractured melody of sorts. The sounds washed over him, their hypnotic tempo soothing, seductive.

Whoosh beep beep, whoosh beep beep.

He tried to move an arm, his brain telegraphing frantic messages to limbs that couldn't or wouldn't respond, but there was nothing. No pain. No sensation at all. Only the hollow ring of his thoughts as he floated through the darkness, adrift in a syncopated sea. He tried to remember where he was, who he was, but his mind stubbornly remained blank. He concentrated harder, and then harder still. Pain broke through the darkness, hot and crimson.

Panic rose, almost unbearable. He fought against it, sinking back into the soothing sound of the mechanical music, the pain receding with each throbbing beat.

The rhythm was familiar, but he couldn't quite place it. He struggled for memory, but there was only blackness. God, what he wouldn't give for light. The darkness was claustrophobic, closing around him like velvet, filling his eyes and his mouth—smothering him in softness.

As if in answer to his prayer, a flare of light pierced the darkness, its brilliance almost blinding. The sounds around him faded as he concentrated on the light. Slowly it widened until it resembled a luminous doorway and he felt himself being drawn forward, its cool beacon compelling him. His fear faded.

Whoosh beep beep, whoosh beep beep.

The noise intervened, pulling him back, the resplendent portal disappearing as suddenly as it had come. Frustrated, he tried anxiously to see through the darkness. Anything. But there was nothing, only endless black and the pulsing rhythm.

Mentally, at least, he closed his eyes, trying to imagine color and texture where there was none. To shut out the darkness and recapture the light. It began as a pinpoint, growing steadily larger until the doorway reappeared, this time in glorious color.

He could see through it now, greens and blues and yellows so bright they almost hurt his eyes. The light grew, embracing him, surrounding him, his senses springing to life. There was grass, silky and soft beneath his cheek, and sky—azure, dotted with wisps of cloud. Wind kissed his cheek, crisp and cold, and in the distance he could hear the bubbling of a small stream, its music blessedly devoid of rhythm.

Sighing with relief, certain that the nightmare had ended, he rolled onto his side, the warmth of the sun lulling him to sleep.

Chapter One

"Hold your tongue." Marjory Macpherson shot a look at the door to the solar, expecting the worst. When the shadows remained unchanged, she allowed herself to breathe but kept her voice a whisper. "The walls have ears, and well you know it."

"Allen is far into his cups by now." Fingal worked to speak softly, but his growl carried easily across the room. Her captain was not a subtle man, preferring confrontation to diplomacy no matter the cost. "He'll no' act until his father arrives."

"Then we canna wait that long." Marjory crossed her arms with a firmness she didn't feel, but there was no time for hesitation. Torcall Cameron would arrive before the next se'nnight, and she intended to be ready. "You're certain Ewen's dead?"

"I saw it with my own eyes." Fingal frowned. "There was a rockslide. The entire cliff collapsed. Before I could reach him, he was gone. No one could have survived."

3

"Where was Allen?" The two brothers had gone hunting, Fingal accompanying them to make certain that it was game they sought and naught else.

"He'd gone ahead, around the bend. By the time he got back it was all over." Fingal tightened his hand on the dirk at his waist. "He blamed me. But there were witnesses, some of his own men. It took some convincing, but eventually he backed down."

"For now." Marjory exhaled slowly, her brain still trying to grasp the concept that her husband was dead. "Once his father arrives, there will be more accusations."

"Then they'll come to naught. Make no mistake—were it no' for your grandfather, I would have cheerfully skewered the man long before now, but the rock slide was an accident."

"How many Camerons are within our walls?" Since the marriage, despite her protest, Torcall had insisted upon leaving a force of men at Crannag Mhór. Most times they numbered less than her own clan, but with the recent return of Ewen there were more.

"No more than fifty." Fingal scratched his chin. "But Torcall will bring more. And even were we to be matched in number, there's the question of age. Torcall's kin are young and well trained."

"Aye." Marjory nodded. "But Macpherson men are wily."

Fingal allowed himself a smile, the gesture only making his warrior's countenance fiercer. Long ago, Fingal Macgillivray had fought for Chattan alongside Marjory's father, and then followed him deep into the mountains, helping to build Crannag Mhór.

He had stayed to rebuild it after Torcall Cameron had destroyed her family. Hate curled in Marjory's belly, white hot, twisting her gut into a tighter knot. Part of her relished the fact that Ewen was dead. An eye for an eye.

Yet, even as she rejoiced she was filled with fear. Crannag Mhór was her home, its inhabitants her people. She was responsible for their well-being, and that meant protecting them. Her grandfather, head of Clan Chattan, would eventually sort out the situation. There would be meetings between the Camerons and Macphersons, the outcome carefully orchestrated to maintain peace. But Torcall Cameron wouldn't wait, preferring justice with a claymore, his hatred burning as brightly as her own.

Nay, long before Marjory's grandfather ever learned of the day's events Torcall would exact his revenge. And, truth be told, she wasn't at all sure she could stop him.

Tears filled her eyes. Marjory angrily brushed them away, lifting her chin to meet Fingal's somber gaze. "I will protect Crannag Mhór. And if that means groveling before the likes of Torcall Cameron, then so be it."

"You can grovel before me." Allen Cameron appeared in the doorway to the solar, a tankard in his hand, a licentious smirk on his face. "Now that Ewen is dead, perhaps you'd prefer a real man in your bed."

Marjory took an involuntary step backward as Allen moved forward with a grace that belied his bulk. She forced herself to stop, to hold her ground. She'd not bend to the will of this Cameron. "Your brother is dead, Allen." She made no effort to contain her scorn. "And here you are already claiming what was his. Have you no honor?"

The man clenched his fist, red staining the parts of his face not covered by beard.

Fingal drew his dirk, its deadly blade shining in the sunlight. "Ye've no business here, Cameron."

"And you do?" Allen's eyes narrowed before he, too, drew the knife at his waist. "Are ye bedding the wench then? I'd have no' thought it possible." His lips curled into a sneer, and Fingal took a menacing step forward.

"This isna the time." Marjory's voice cut through the tension in the room. "We need to find Ewen's body and bring it back. As much as I loathed your brother, Allen, I'd no' leave him to the predators of the mountain." Actually, were it not for Torcall, that's exactly what she'd do. But there was no sense in adding fuel to an already raging fire.

Fingal's stance relaxed. "The lass is right. And we've only a few hours left before nightfall."

Allen eyed them both, as if doubting their sincerity. Apparently satisfied with what he saw, he sheathed his weapon. "I'll gather my men."

Marjory nodded once, and watched him leave with something akin to giddy relief. There was so much at stake, so much to lose. It was like walking across a vast chasm on nothing more than a fine linen thread.

"Well played." Fingal's words were high praise, but Marjory took no comfort. Ewen's death had upset a delicate balance, one she wasn't entirely certain could be repaired. Had she the forces, she'd see to it that Ewen Cameron wasn't the only member of his clan to die this day.

But she hadn't that luxury. Torcall was coming and, even without proof, there would be hell to pay. Ewen had been his father's cherished son, the pride of the man's existence, and Marjory had no illusion as to what would happen. Torcall would want blood: Hers and the rest of her kin.

A Cameron had died this day, and in so doing, had unleashed the wrath of her enemies.

But Torcall Cameron would be wise to consider that her hatred was as strong as his own. And as long as she had breath, she would not surrender Crannag Mhór.

Aye, today an enemy had fallen. An enemy—and a husband. The carefully woven strands of her grandfather's whimsy unraveled with a single fall of rock.

There was a rock biting into his ass, the sensation something less than pleasant, and it pulled him awake with a sharp tug. Sunlight peeked through a preponderance of clouds, the smell of rain heavy in the air.

Carefully, moving an inch at a time, he sat up, the movement making him dizzy. When he was sure the spinning had subsided, he opened first one eye and then the other. The world blurred, then swam into focus—the colors muted, then vibrant. Green, yellow, blue.

Something tugged at the back of his brain, a memory, but before he could grasp the thought it was gone, the drummers in his head pounding it away. With a sigh he leaned back against a scrubby tree, gingerly exploring his scalp. There was dried blood and a couple of huge knots: one toward the back and a larger one above his left eye. Hematomas. Serious, but probably not life threatening.

Still, something had caused the injuries, and it seemed prudent to establish what. He willed his mind to yield answers, but stubbornly it remained blank. Glancing down he took in the homespun antiquity of his outfit— a linen shirt and woolen skirt. The plaid pattern was vaguely familiar, and he realized upon further examination that he was, in fact, wearing a kilt.

The only problem was that he was fairly certain he wasn't Scottish. And, even if he was, there was the surety that he would favor briefs regardless of his outerwear. All of which left a disturbing puzzle.

What the hell was he doing in the middle of nowhere

in a get-up only William Wallace could love?

Somewhere beyond incredulity a modicum of alarm surfaced, but he quashed it ruthlessly, certain that whatever was happening there was no time for fear. He was a rational man. At least he assumed he was. And somewhere in all of this was a reasonable explanation.

Using the tree as a brace and trying to ignore the pain in his head, he pulled himself to a standing position. The effort cost a lot, but it was nice to be on his feet. He glanced down again, eyeing the strips of leather that passed for his boots. Thong-type lacings held them together and bound them to his legs.

His foggy brain struggled for a rational explanation. He was evidently standing on the side of a mountain, in what amounted to a skirt, without BVDs, in shoes that would make a gladiator proud.

He grimaced, sinking back against the tree. The truth was he had no concept of where he was. Hell, he wasn't even sure who he was. An actor, maybe. That would explain the garb, but not the knots on his head.

Perhaps he'd fallen. Rising again, he forced himself to concentrate on his surroundings. The area where he'd awoken was indeed covered with rocks and debris. Looking up, he could just see the top of a cliff, the rock jagged and raw, discolored where it had collapsed.

He looked again at the scree surrounding him. Some of the rocks qualified as boulders. A fall like that would have killed a man, his mind whispered. And yet, here he stood.

At least the evidence seemed to support an accident of some kind. Perhaps someone would be looking for him—someone who could tell him who he was, explain what had happened. The thought should have brought comfort, but it didn't; a part deep inside him was certain that the truth wasn't something he wanted to know.

He struggled to remember something, anything, but his mind still refused. He slammed his hand against the tree, surprised at the force of the action, reveling in the additional pain. At least it proved he was alive.

He closed his eyes, forcing himself to turn inward, to concentrate. Surely, if nothing else, he could remember his name.

Cameron.

He smiled. It wasn't much. For all he knew it wasn't even his name. But for now it would do. It was a tether to reality. A way to move forward.

Opening his eyes, he took a tottering step, the sound of a stream forcing its way front and center. Obediently his mind filled with a picture of cool, shimmering water, the idea beyond enticing.

Cocking his head to one side, Cameron concentrated on the musical sound, forcing his feet to move toward it, one slow step after another. Around a little stand of birch trees he saw the creek. It wasn't big, but a couple of rocks had blocked the water's progress and made a small pool.

Moving gingerly, he managed to skirt the rocks and kneel by the stream's edge. Cupping his hands, he filled them with water and drank deeply, the cool liquid soothing more than his parched throat. Below him, the water sparkled in the dappled light, something at the bottom of the stream catching his eye. Curiosity got the better of him, and he reached in and pulled it out, balancing the tiny knife in the palm of his hand.

The handle was ivory in color and striated with gray and black. Animal horn, the still functioning part of his brain whispered. The blade itself was brass or some similar metal. It was flat on one side and intricately carved on the other, sort of loopy curls and circles.

Cameron looked around for its owner, but the clearing remained empty. Upon closer examination of the knife, he realized it had been in its watery home for more than a few days. Its edges were worn smooth by rushing water, and mineral deposits had begun to mar its intricate design. He started to throw it back, then hesitated.

Perhaps it would come in useful.

Not certain what to do with it, he searched his body, rejecting the belt in favor of what appeared to be a purse. Lifting the flap, he eyed its contents dubiously, discarding what looked to be a hunk of petrified oatmeal. He hated oatmeal.

Dropping the little knife in the now empty pouch, he flipped it closed, feeling as if the effort had cost him the last of his strength. The drummers in his head, abated momentarily by the water, had returned in full force. He fought nausea, dropping down on a large rock and closing his eyes, the enormity of the situation suddenly overwhelming him.

An eagle screamed in the distance. Cameron marveled at the fact that he knew it was an eagle. Certain parts of his mind seemed to be working quite well. Which meant the injury to his brain was localized. Specific to only his memory.

Forcing his eyes open, he checked his hypothesis by naming the items around him: birch trees, river rocks— granite and sandstone. Across the stream he recognized wild roses mixed with the purple of thistles, as well as the waxy green leaves of a rhododendron.

He knew that the material of this kilt was wool, and that he'd suffered hematomas. Obviously, the blows to his head had caused some sort of trauma. He hoped it was temporary trauma, but the little voice in his head

10

whispered that there was no such thing. Lying back against the lichen-covered rock he ignored the voice, preferring for the moment the sanctuary of ignorance.

Eventually he'd have to get up and face the music. Try and figure out what had happened to him and why, but right now the rock was warm and, if he held very still, the drums were only a faint staccato.

He closed his eyes, letting his mind drift.

What he needed was a little shut-eye. Just a few minutes, and then he'd be on his way.

Marjory walked through the gorse, damning Ewen Cameron. The man was the devil himself, or at least the spawn of the same, and if she'd had her way she'd not be trekking through the mountains trying to find his body.

The sky threatened rain, the clouds so close to the ground she could almost touch them. The weather in the mountains was fluid, calm one moment, stormy the next, without so much as a by-your-leave. Pulling her plaid close around her, Marjory stopped for a moment on an outcropping of rock, letting her eyes drink in the valley.

The lands of Crannag Mhór stretched below. The tower itself, situated on its islet in the loch, glistened white against the blue black of the lake, its turrets already disappearing into the gathering mist. She breathed deeply, letting the cool mountain air fill her lungs.

This was her home, and she'd not let a Cameron take it away. Living in hell had always been a small price to pay for preserving her heritage.

Fingal stopped beside her, his large hand heavy on her shoulder. "We'll find a way, Marjory. We always do."

She nodded, comfortable with the fact that he could read her mind. Since her father's death, it was Fingal to whom she turned. Fingal in whom she confided. At least, about most things.

She forced a smile, looking up, and was comforted by the fierceness in his eyes. Fingal would protect her with his life, and she'd return the favor without pause. But, even so, there were things she could not share with him. Things she kept locked away tight in a dark corner of her heart.

"It's no' far now." He moved back, his gruffness meant to hide his emotion, but she knew him too well. "Just round the bend."

As if to underscore the point, Allen appeared from behind a jutting spray of rocks, his face twisted in anger. "He's no' there."

Fingal frowned, his hand automatically reaching for his claymore. Marjory laid a hand on his arm, leaving it there until she felt him relax.

"Maybe this is no' the place," she said. She and Fingal moved forward, flanked by two more Macpherson men. "Sometimes the mountain plays tricks." Crannag Mhór was an isolated place, many of its crannies and crags inaccessible to those who didn't know it well.

Fingal shook his head as they came to the foot of the cliff, rocks and debris clearly indicating a recent landslide. "This is where he fell."

Allen growled low in his throat, eyeing the older man. "What have ye done with him, then?"

"I've done naught," Fingal roared. "I left him here same as you."

Again Marjory stepped between the two men. There was hell enough to pay already. No sense letting things get any more out of hand. She glared at Allen. "You know as well as I that there are wolves in these mountains. Anything could have happened to him." She narrowed her eyes, daring Allen to argue.

He glowered, holding her gaze for one beat and then another, and then with a snort, turned away, walking over to his men, the division between the two groups, Cameron and Macpherson, symbolic of the ever-widening gulf between the clans.

Ignoring all the men, Marjory walked away. Let them deal with the disappearance of Ewen's body. Solitude was always the best for thinking. Fingal was always saying she lacked the sensibilities of a lady; she'd use the fact to her advantage.

The flowers of summer were in fierce bloom, their color vibrant against the mist. If it weren't that her dead husband had gone missing, Marjory would have stopped to revel in the beauty of the mountains. *Her* mountains. But there was no time for idling. She had to come up with a plan, and without a body it was going to be that much more difficult.

Moving through a small stand of birch she walked toward a stream and a large rock—a favorite thinking place since she was a child, which afforded the perfect view across the valley. Except, of course, when mist hugged the ground. Then it was more like a cloister. Silent and safe.

As if in answer to her thoughts, a breeze rose, its gentle touch lifting the fog, revealing something lying across the rock. Something bulky. With bated breath, Marjory crept forward, using the undergrowth to quiet her steps and shield her from view.

The mound began to take shape, and she recognized it for what it was: a body. She'd been right about the wolves. Steeling herself she crept forward, torn between

13

a desire to run back to Fingal and the macabre need to know for certain this was Ewen.

With a trembling hand, she pulled back a tree branch for a clearer view. The body was indeed Ewen's. Relieved, she released the branch and stepped into the clearing.

Suddenly, the body shifted. Marjory stopped midstep, her heart jumping into her throat. She screamed as the body rose, the face all but obliterated by crusted blood. Flinching, she held out a hand and shut her eyes tightly, certain that she was in the presence of the dead.

"What the hell?"

The voice was garbled but definitely human. Alive. Marjory braced herself and opened her eyes. Her husband stood there, staring at her as if she were the ghost, his left hand fumbling to open his sporran.

Involuntarily she took a step backward, her head spinning, her hand out as if to ward him off. It seemed the devil had alluded death yet again. She fainted.

Cameron closed his eyes then opened them, stupidly staring at the young woman at his feet. She was still there, and still out like a light. She was a tiny thing, her features as delicate as her frame. Ethereal.

He knelt beside her, trying not to jar his aching head, and lifted her wrist, automatically feeling for her pulse. It was rapid but strong. Releasing her hand, he pushed the hair back from her face, surprised at how soft it was.

"Unhand her, or I'll slit your throat." The voice came from off to his left, and Cameron was certain that the owner meant every word.

He rose quickly, his head spinning with the action, hands raised in what he hoped was still the universal gesture of surrender. Pivoting slowly, he turned to face the voice, and immediately felt a shudder of alarm. The man before him was roughly the size of an oak, built every bit as solid, and he held the largest sword Cameron had ever seen.

Their eyes met, and the man blanched, his sword wavering. "Ye're a dead mon." His tone held a mixture of fear and awe, and with his free hand he managed the sign of the cross.

Cameron, hands still held high, took a step forward. The man swallowed, but to his credit he held his ground, his sword steady now.

"Be gone, spirit." The man waved his weapon threateningly.

Cameron, more than aware of his mortality, stepped back. "Your friend needs help," he said. He spoke slowly, as if to a child. The swordsman's English was garbled at best, and although Cameron understood him, it was obviously not his native language.

The sound of his own voice startled Cameron, the tone deeper than he remembered, more guttural—almost as if he, too, were speaking something other than English.

Ridiculous thought.

"Move away from her, Cameron."

The man knew his name. The thought was somewhat less than comforting, and Cameron searched his memory for some hint as to who this might be. He lowered his gaze to the man's sword. Obviously not a friend.

"I said move," the giant barked again, edging forward slowly, his narrow-eyed gaze fierce.

Cameron did as suggested, then watched as the man inched toward the woman. "She's only fainted," he volunteered. "I checked her pulse and she's fine."

"Ye've no right to touch her." This last was hissed

between gritted teeth. The big man bent down to touch the woman, who was beginning to stir.

"Holy Mary, Mother of God." Another giant rounded the corner, crossing himself in the same way as the first. The tangle of red hair, both on his head and face, left only a white swatch of face visible.

Again Cameron searched for recognition, but there was nothing. Enemy or friend, these people were strangers to him—which was far more frightening than the monstrous swords they held.

The woman was sitting up now, her gaze locked on him, her expression guarded. Pushing aside the first giant's offer of help, she scrambled to her feet and moved toward Cameron, tipping her head first to one side and then the other, studying him.

"You're supposed to be dead." Her voice was low, its timbre velvety. It raked across him like a warm breeze, sending his senses reeling.

"That seems to be the consensus." Cameron glanced toward the two men, noticing they'd been joined by others, all sporting swords and kilts. Apparently he'd fallen down the rabbit hole and landed in the middle of *Braveheart*. The only thing missing was the blue war paint.

Not a comforting thought, and not something he wanted to examine right now. The situation was puzzling at best, downright frightening at worst. And the truth was, this wasn't the time for a meltdown. As if in contradiction to his thoughts, his head spun, black spots swimming across his line of vision.

"I saw you fall." The first giant moved closer. "There's no way you could have survived." He looked toward the other giant for confirmation. Though it looked as if agreement was not in his nature, the man gave a brief nod, his gaze still locked on Cameron.

"Fingal, 'tis obvious that he survived," the woman said. "And nothing we wish to the contrary will make it less than so."

Another vote of confidence. It was pretty obvious he wasn't going to be voted Mr. Popular by this crowd. Cameron opened his mouth to tell them he wasn't who they thought he was. That, in fact, as far as he could tell, he wasn't anyone at all. But another look at the still drawn swords changed his mind. Best to find out the lay of the land before committing to anything. Maybe there was a way out of this Scottish version of *Deliverance*, a hospital around the corner, or a nice cold beer. Something that fit into his concept of reality.

"We'd best get you back to the holding. It'll be dark soon." The first giant, the one called Fingal, took a step forward and involuntarily Cameron stepped back. "Allen, he's your brother, perhaps you should help him."

Brother.

The word washed over Cameron and he waited for emotion, some connection to the big man striding toward him. But he felt no sense of belonging or recognition. The man was a stranger. Again he moved backward, this time following his instincts. The other man's expression changed, his eyes narrowing in confusion and something else. Wariness possibly. It seemed there was intelligence under all that hair.

"Marjory," Fingal said. "Perhaps you should be the one to help your husband."

Her eyebrows shot up in surprise, a look of loathing crossing her face. "I'm sure he has no need of me." Yet, despite her words, she moved to take Cameron's arm.

Her skin against his set his senses ablaze. *Husband?* Yet another revelation. He should have been put off. After all, he had no memory of this woman and she certainly hadn't bothered to hide her disdain for him. But Cameron's body wasn't listening to reason, and an absurd sense of elation swirled through his head.

He turned to say something—to explain that he had no brother, and certainly no wife—but before he could open his mouth the ground rushed up to meet him with a thud. The world went suddenly black.

Chapter Two

"According to Grania, he's no' anywhere close to dead."
Marjory paced back and forth in front of the fireplace,
waving her hands to emphasize her words. Not only was
her husband not dead, he apparently had every intention
of living a long and full life. The man was invincible.
"With rest, she says he'll make a full recovery."

"Well, I canna say the news pleases me, but at least it
should pacify Torcall. And quite possibly it will stop
Allen's rantings about a plot on his brother's life." Fingal
lifted his tankard, shooting the younger man an angry
look.

Allen and his clansmen were seated at a table on the
far side of the great room, clearly a separate camp from
the boisterous Macpherson men sitting closer to the dais.
Their presence was a reminder that although in name
Marjory was still the mistress of her domain, in reality
it was controlled by her husband.

Husband. The word settled bitterly in Marjory's throat.
"I wish he would have died. At least we'd no' have the
sword hanging over our head."

19

"Nay." Fingal shook his head. " 'Twould be buried in our backs."

"At least then we'd have done with it." She tried but couldn't keep the anger from her voice.

"Would that I'd have secured the fact then." Fingal's face filled with remorse, and Marjory felt immediate regret for her words.

" 'Tis all right. You couldna have known he still lived. The man probably has a pact with the devil himself. And you're right, Ewen's resurrection may calm Torcall. At least until I can talk to my grandfather." Fingal exhaled slowly, the act telling. Marjory's stomach tightened. "You have news?"

"Aye, the messenger arrived an hour ago." He met Marjory's gaze, his eyes troubled. "Yer grandfather is away from Moy. A meeting with the king. It'll be at least a fortnight 'fore he returns. Probably longer. Until then, I'm afraid we're on our own. Although we could send word to your cousin Iain."

Marjory waved a hand in dismissal. "He's only just married. I canna ask him to come now. Besides, without grandfather's approval, there's no' much he can do. We're better to try and hold things on our own."

"I'll abide yer wishes." Fingal dipped his head in submission, but Marjory knew it was an empty action. Her captain loved her as a daughter, and he'd fight to the death for her, but he wasn't the kind of man to acquiesce to a woman. If he followed her wishes, it was only because he agreed with them.

"I've lived with Ewen these last two years." Marjory gave Fingal a weak smile. "I suppose I can manage a wee bit longer."

"If Torcall has his way, it'll be longer than that, and well you know it."

"One day at a time, Fingal." She forced her smile to be more sincere, aware that Allen was watching.

"Well, I still say the process could be hastened a bit if you hadna offered the man Grania's services."

Grania was the local healer. An old blind woman, she had a way with the sick that defied logic. But Marjory was grateful for her gifts. Indeed, without Grania all those years ago, many more Macphersons would have perished after Torcall's attack.

"I canna fault your wishing it so, Fingal. But 'tis one thing if a man dies in an accident and quite another if we let him die. I willna lower myself to the level of the Camerons. There is such a thing as honor. And the Macphersons are an honorable clan."

"Aye, 'tis true, more's the pity." Fingal threw himself down in one of the chairs by the fire.

Marjory smiled at him fondly. He almost overwhelmed the chair, and it was a large one. Fingal was well over forty summers, but he looked like a man half his age. His thick, russet hair was free of gray. He was a warrior through and through.

She sent a silent prayer of thanks heavenward. If God kept count of good deeds, then Fingal was certainly in line for sainthood. She flinched as he belched loudly. Not that he embodied her idea of a saint. She shook her head at her own flight of fancy and sat down on a bench.

"Did you find anything else at the site?"

"Nay, 'twas just as I suspected." The older man took another swig of ale. "The ledge collapsed. It coulda been the recent rain, or maybe just time and wind. There's no way to be certain of the cause, but I think we can safely say that it was an accident."

Marjory nodded, chewing on her bottom lip. "Thank you for taking a look. I'll rest easier knowing that I can defend myself against any accusations Torcall might make."

Fingal left his chair, moving closer to the fire to warm himself. "Aye, best we're ready for anything. Torcall Cameron is a mistrustful bastard—to say the least."

" 'Tis more than that, and well you know it." Much more. Marjory sighed, knowing that she'd probably never truly understand the depth of Torcall's hatred or the reasons for it. But she understood her own. In an instant, a vision of her parents filled her mind. She felt tears threaten as she saw them lying on the chamber floor soaked in blood.

With the fierce determination that had protected her over the years, she pushed the memory down deep within her, locking it away, and rose to join Fingal by the fire. "Torcall hates Crannag Mhór and everyone who lives here. He's made it quite clear that he'd sooner see his son married to a witch than to a Macpherson, particularly if that Macpherson is me. Nay, Torcall will no' easily be pacified. He's been looking for an excuse to break this agreement as desperately as I. And he's no' interested in peaceful solutions."

Fingal studied her carefully. Marjory avoided his gaze, afraid of what might be revealed if he looked too long or too deep. The warrior shrugged. "Well, then, I guess we've reason to be glad Ewen lives."

"I've brought ye a wee bite to eat," a voice interrupted. "Quit yer blethering and come to the table." Aimil Macgillivray placed a large wooden platter on the dais table and looked at both Fingal and Marjory expectantly. Her brother was the first to move, rubbing his hands together in anticipation of the meal.

"Ach, sister, my belly was beginning to think ye'd

forgotten us." Fingal threw a leg over a bench, straddling it as he reached for the platter.

"Stop that this instant, Fingal Macgillivray, this isna a stable. Ye'll eat like a proper gentleman or ye'll no' eat at all." She took the platter and firmly removed it from his grasp. Fingal, like most of Marjory's clansmen, wouldn't recognize genteel behavior if it leapt up and bit him on the behind.

Aimil turned to look pointedly at Marjory, still standing by the fire. "Come, child, ye've been through much these past few days. A husband dead and then no' dead," she said, adding what sounded like a mumbled slur on Ewen's heritage.

Marjory considered the notion that Aimil had blasphemed and quickly discarded it. Aimil had watched over her since her parents' death, and at no time in all those years had Aimil ever raised her voice, let alone cursed. It must have been her imagination, or more likely, an echo of her own thoughts.

"Come on, girl, the food's getting cold and ye know Aimil willna let me eat until ye're seated." Fingal stared longingly at the joint on the platter.

"Well, I obviously canna leave you to starve." She sat at the table, her back turned to the Camerons, wanting at least momentarily to put them from her mind.

For comfort she reached for her *sgian dubh*, only to realize she'd left the wee knife upstairs in the solar. Not that it mattered, the little knife was of no consequence. It could never replace the one her mother had given her.

The one Allen Cameron had taken.

Aimil put a hand on hers. "What's wrong, child? Ye look as if you've lost yer best friend."

Marjory flushed. " 'Tis nothing, Aimil. Only my . . . my *sgian dubh*." She held out her empty hand, working

23

to hide her feelings. There was nothing to be gained by reliving the past.

"You can use mine, lass." Fingal said, misunderstanding. His mouth was full of meat. "T'll use my dirk." He handed his smaller knife to Marjory, a large chunk of rabbit still skewered on it. The gravy left a greasy brown trail across the table.

Aimil cast her brother a reproving look, then clucked, "There, there, lamb." She reached over to squeeze Marjory's hand. "I know ye miss your mother. But what's done is done."

Marjory sighed. Nibbling at the meat on Fingal's knife, she counted her problems. Ewen was alive, which apparently was both a blessing and curse. But at least that would pacify his father. For the moment.

However, it reopened an issue she'd just as soon not face.

Producing an heir.

Torcall had made no secret of his desire to control Crannag Mhór. The only thing that kept him from physically taking control was the fact that Marjory had always been a favorite of her grandfather's, and at least while he lived and was head of his clan, Crannag Mhór was safe.

Which meant that there was only one way Torcall could assure his eventual control: Ewen must get her with child. Marjory shuddered, stabbing Fingal's knife into the meat so hard it wedged in the wooden trencher beneath. Aimil had saved her before, but they couldn't possibly drug Ewen every night.

At least Ewen's accident had bought her time. She was astute enough to realize that once Torcall had his heir, her life was worth little. And the only way to ensure her safety was to remove herself to her grandfather's holding at Moy. But in doing so, she would be surrendering Crannag Mhór.

Which simply wasn't an option.

Cameron struggled back to consciousness, aware that the pounding in his head had lessened considerably. He lay for a moment, letting the sounds of the room swell around him. From outside he could hear the call of a bird, the sound lonely, plaintive. It was accompanied by a syncopated popping along with a soft shushing, the latter regular, almost white noise.

Curious, he opened his eyes to be greeted by shadows. The ache in his head had dulled considerably, but the drummers were still present. Their constant rhythm was more irritating now than painful, as if they'd withdrawn to some deeper recess within his brain.

There was weak sunlight streaming in through an open window, and Cameron recognized the pink rays of sunset. They gave the room an otherworldly feel. From his vantage point he could clearly see one wall and a corner, both made of stone. The rest of the room was obscured by what appeared to be bed curtains, the brownish material heavy and ornate, reminding him of Ebenezer Scrooge's bed.

All he had to do now was wait for the Ghost of Christmas Past.

He shivered, the thought not at all comforting.

The shushing grew in tempo and pitch, the identity of the noise suddenly clear. Snoring. Someone was snoring. Probably not the Ghost of Christmas Past. But remembering the size of the swords the men he'd encountered earlier brandished, he couldn't be certain if it was the snore of a friend or foe.

Sitting up slowly, ignoring the accompanying dizziness, he searched the bedclothes for a weapon of some sort. Not surprisingly, the most lethal thing he encountered was a pillow. As a weapon, feathers lacked a great deal, but surely a pillow was better than nothing. Holding it in front of him, shieldlike, he peered out into the room, trying to locate the source of the noise. The bed curtain to his right moved with an unseen breeze. It seemed he had found his quarry.

Moving as silently as possible, he reached for the curtain, drawing the pleated material aside. Surprise accompanied a wave of relief. An elderly woman nestled quite comfortably in a chair by the bed. As she audibly breathed, a strand of white hair moved up and down against her cheek.

Releasing the pillow, Cameron leaned back, his relief quickly turning to exhaustion. Whatever was happening to him, his injuries were real; and he was grateful for the bed, and, at the moment, the woman.

Her cheeks were a ruddy red that made him think of overripe apples. She was wrinkled with age, but the lines were soft and only added character to what was still a beautiful face. Her skin was thin, almost translucent, and blue veins were apparent along her throat and hands.

Whoever she was, she'd once been a beauty.

The woman opened her eyes. They were an odd crystalline blue, the color one imagined an iceberg. They sparkled in the light. She seemed unaware of Cameron, her movements the calculated stretches of aging bones and muscles missing the elasticity of youth.

With a soft sigh, she turned toward him, drawing back suddenly when he shifted, obviously surprised. "I'm sorry, I'd no idea ye were awake."

He struggled for something to say, the myriad questions circling through his head fighting to become words.

"Where am I?" That seemed the most relevant question. One that hopefully would clear everything up. Maybe even help him remember.

"Yer safe in yer bed at Crannag Mhór."

Or maybe not.

Crannag Mhór was definitely not a name—hell, not even words—he'd heard before. It was more like gibberish. He struggled for recognition but found none. No, he'd never heard of the place. Which in and of itself would have been all right—except for the small fact that she'd said he was safe in *his* bed.

"It's not *my* bed." As statements went it probably wasn't the strongest. But it went straight to the point, and just at the moment that seemed to be the best he could do.

The woman gently pushed Cameron back down into the pillows. "There now, of course it is. Ye're just a wee bit addled. 'Twas quite a blow on the head ye had, and ye need yer rest still."

Cameron eyed her suspiciously. She still hadn't met his gaze. "I don't want to rest." He sounded like a petulant child, but sleep was the last thing on his mind. "Tell me who you are."

"I'm Grania Macpherson." Her smile was slow, comforting in an odd sort of way. "I'm here to take care of ye."

"Grania." He tried out the sound of her name. It was unusual and sounded foreign on his tongue, but that seemed the order of the day. "Shouldn't I be in a hospital, or at least see a doctor?"

Grania paused, tilting her head as if pondering his question. "I wouldna condemn ye to a physician even if there were one nearby."

Cameron felt a tingle of worry at her words. What an

27

archaic attitude. An ugly thought pushed itself front and center, combining with his observations on the mountainside, leaving a startling realization—one he simply wasn't able or willing to process at the moment.

"Tell me how ye're feeling," the woman said, her concern apparently genuine.

"Like the Kodo Drummers are rehearsing in my head."

Again she tilted her head. This time, her brows knitted in concentration. Something pulled at Cameron's brain. He tried to pull it to the forefront, something about this woman. The thought slipped away.

She reached across him and automatically adjusted the bedcovers. Then she trailed her hand up his shoulder to his face, coming to rest on his brow. Her touch was light and soothing. "Yer no' as hot as ye were. 'Tis a good sign."

She withdrew her hand, settling it in her lap. Her head never moved. He frowned. The nagging feeling was back again. There was something here he should notice. But what?

"How long have I been here?" he asked—more abruptly than he had meant, but Grania seemed to take no notice.

"Only a few hours. They brought ye in just after noontime. It's close to nightfall now." She leaned forward, offering Cameron an earthenware cup. "Try and drink some of this."

He reached for it, his hand closing around the smooth surface, grateful for the warmth it provided. Sniffing cautiously, he recognized a broth of some sort and, as he slowly began to sip it, his mind clicked and he realized what was wrong with the picture.

"You can't see, can you?"

The woman smiled, unerringly patting his arm. "Nay,

28

no' for many years. But what God takes from us, He repays with other things."

Cameron couldn't help his next question. "Like what?"

"Bits and pieces." Again she favored him with a smile. "I've a bit o' the healing touch, and I've a way about me that allows me to see things that sighted people canna."

Cameron stayed silent for a moment, absorbing her words. "Do you know me?"

She turned, followed the sound of his voice. "They say ye're Ewen Cameron."

Part of the name certainly seemed right. Still, there was something unfamiliar about it. Maybe he *was* addled. He frowned at the woman, realizing she hadn't actually answered his question. "That's not what I asked." He shook his head for emphasis, realizing almost immediately that the gesture was pointless. "I want to know if *you* know me."

It was her turn to pause. The room was silent. Then she shrugged. "I canna say for sure. Ye feel a bit like Ewen Cameron, but ye dinna sound like him and ye certainly dinna smell like him." The last was said with a smile, a small dimple appearing in the woman's cheek.

Cameron let out his breath. It wasn't exactly what he was looking for, but somehow, under the circumstances, ambiguity seemed to fit. "My name is Cameron," he said. "But I'm afraid that's all I'm certain of."

The blind woman smiled. "Dinna fash yerself, lad. 'Twill come to ye when the time is right. What's important now is that you rest." She took the cup and helped him settle back into the warmth of the bed. For a blind person, she was amazingly adept. He closed his eyes and let the darkness surround him.

Whoosh beep-beep.

The sound swelled out of the darkness. Panicked, he wrenched open his eyes. The room swam in front of him. Grania's face appeared and came into focus.

" 'Tis all right now. I'm here. Hold on to my hand." He grasped it as if holding a lifeline. "There now, yer fine. I'll stay with ye. Sleep. Nothing can harm ye as long as Grania is here."

Cameron closed his eyes again. The dark was blessedly quiet. Then, with a sigh, he let himself sleep.

Marjory stood at the open window, watching the last of the sun drop behind the mountains. Sunsets had been different when she had lived at her grandfather's. There they had lingered, caressing the landscape as the sun slowly sank into the velvety hills, leaving behind fingers of red and orange that spread through the sky, fading to a wash of pale pink. Here, at Crannag Mhór, the sun simply disappeared. One minute it was light, the next dark. The rugged mountains that ringed the little valley seemed to swallow the sun with one great gulp.

She closed her eyes, thinking of the valley, *her* valley. A narrow pass lined with birch trees gave access to Crannag Mhór. Only those who knew the way could find it. It was supposed to have been a sanctuary, a place set apart from the turbulence that surrounded it, a place for love to flourish. Marjory shook her head, sweeping away her foolish thoughts. It hadn't been a place of peace for long. The Camerons had found it and destroyed it.

She stared at the first star as it twinkled high in the night sky. Her mother used to tell her that the stars were the lights of angels. She bit her lip, momentarily mesmerized by the tiny point of glowing light. When she was little she'd wished upon the stars for true love, the kind her mother and father had had. A ray of hope flashed deep within her.

With a deep breath, she hardened her heart. Her mother and father were dead. There were no angels. And there were no happy endings. There was nothing but Crannag Mhór and her driving need to preserve it at all costs.

No, there were no angels. If there were, how could they possibly let her be married to someone like Ewen? How could they have let her parents die? Marjory felt the anger swelling within her. She clamped down on her feelings, pushing them back into a dark corner of her soul.

Then, emotions in control, she squared her shoulders and turned her back on the stars.

It was raining cats and dogs. The driveway was slick with water. Cameron tried to hold his suit coat over his head to protect himself from the deluge, but even so he arrived at his car soaking wet. He fumbled for the key and managed, with shaking hands, to open the car door. Sliding into the leather seat, he automatically brushed away the droplets of water that accumulated there. He leaned on the steering wheel, trying to get his emotions under control. With an angry groan, he slid the key into the ignition and turned it. The powerful engine sparked to life and he flicked on the headlights.

Like the click of a camera, the picture changed. He watched through the windshield as the headlights revealed a beautiful blond woman, her hair plastered to her head by the rain. Her hands were stretched out in front of her as though she were pleading with him. Her face was washed with fear and pain. Her eyes seemed to beg him.

31

"No." She mouthed the word. He couldn't hear her, but somehow he knew she screamed.

Cameron jerked awake, sweat momentarily blinding his eyes. Panic knifed through him. It was dark. Oh, God, he was back in the darkness. He strained for the noise, the rhythmic beeping, but all was quiet and cold. He moved a hand and wiped away the sweat. The darkness lightened and he recognized the fabric of the bed curtains.

A dream. It had been a dream. He reached out with a shaking hand to move the curtain back. He needed the reassurance of light. His hand encountered another hand, and still partially locked in the terror of his nightmare he jerked back, gasping audibly.

"Be still, 'tis only me." The curtain moved, revealing moonlight and Grania.

" 'Twas naught but a dream. Try to go back to sleep now." The woman's age-worn hand clasped his, the warmth of her touch sending comfort pulsing through his body. He closed his eyes, surprised at how good it felt to know that someone was watching over him.

Chapter Three

Marjory brushed Alainn's coat with a fury that had nothing to do with the horse. Alainn shifted uncomfortably under the attack and Marjory stopped, soothing the mare with a touch of her hand.

" 'Tis sorry I am if hurt you. I wasna thinking of you, my sweet, but of that whoreson of a Cameron lying upstairs with the whole of the household waiting on him hand and foot."

"Talking to horses now, are ye?"

Marjory turned at the sound of Fingal's voice, giving her captain a wry smile and the horse a last brush. "Guilty as charged, I'm afraid. I find it quite nice to have a conversation with the beast. You see, *she* never argues with me."

"I think 'tis best to let that comment pass, as I assume some of it at least was aimed at me."

Marjory shot him a look and then bent to examine her horse's fetlock. "Could be."

Fingal leaned back against the railing of a stall, resting his arms on the wooden bar. "Come now, lass, there's no need to take yer frustrations out on me. 'Twould be better fer ye to spend some time with the claymore, I'm thinking."

Marjory had been training for battle almost since the day her parents died, preparing herself for a fight she'd no hope of winning. She sighed and released Alainn. With a pat on the rump, she shooed the mare into her stall. Closing the gate behind the beast, she reached into her pocket for a handful of oats. Alainn nuzzled her hand, greedily eating the offered treat.

"I've no time for play pretending, Fingal. No' with Torcall Cameron practically breathing down our necks." She purposely kept her back to him, her hand absently stroking the mare that nosed about her skirt in search of more grain.

"Mayhap." Fingal shrugged. "But with his son alive and well, perhaps he'll no' be quite so ready to raise a sword."

She turned around to face him, watching his eyes for signs of his true thoughts. But at the moment his gaze gave away nothing, his face remaining impassive. "I hope you're right. I've sacrificed much to keep Crannag Mhór safe."

"Aye, ye've been brave, lass. There can be no doubt o' that." Fingal stroked his beard, his eyes narrowed in thought. "Eleven years in exhile at Moy, and then four years married to that bastard." He tilted his head toward the tower where her husband lay sleeping.

" 'Twas well worth it. And as much as I'd like to see Ewen dead, I'd no' wish it at the cost of the holding. Torcall Cameron is a fearsome enemy, even in peaceful times. I wouldna want to face him over the death of his son."

"He may have caught us by surprise once, Marjory,

but I dinna think he'd be able to defeat us so easily now."

"Maybe no, but what he didna accomplish, the rest of Clan Cameron would."

Fingal opened his mouth to speak, but Marjory held up a hand to stop him. "I know what you're thinking and I agree—if Clan Cameron were to attack us, my grandfather would certainly retaliate. But, the truth of the matter is, by that time we'd be long dead and no' care who was attacking who anymore. Crannag Mhór would fall, and I'll no' risk that for anything, Fingal. You of all people should know that."

"It all comes down to that, does it no'? Ye'd protect this land and its people, but no' yer own happiness." Fingal pushed up from his reclining position and stood before her, his arms crossed over his massive chest. "Sometimes, Marjory Macpherson, I think ye have love for nothing except this tower and its lands."

Marjory started at the depth of his insight, but she met his gaze firmly with her own. "Stones and hills canna die on you, Fingal. They'll be here long after we're gone. And best I can tell you, a body has never been hurt by a piece o' ground." Marjory took a step back and turned to look out the stable door at the blue-gray of the mountains ringing the valley. " 'Tis all I have left, Fingal. And he would want me to protect it, no matter the cost."

Fingal came up to stand behind her. "Are you speaking of your father, Marjory? I dinna think you have it right, lass. I canna believe Manus Macpherson would ever want a daughter o' his to spend her life in a loveless marriage—to a Cameron no less—merely to protect a piece o' land."

Marjory straightened her shoulders, tightening her face into a mask of indifference. "Ach, foolish talk, Fingal. What's done is done. Anyway, what use have I for love?

I've got all that I need right here. And I'm doing what Father asked of me."

"And what would that be, lass?"

"I'm preserving his legacy." Marjory closed her eyes, hearing again her father's words, reciting them aloud as though saying them with him: "Protect all that I've worked to accomplish, Margie, my girl. 'Tis your birthright. Make me proud, daughter. Never forget that yer a Macpherson of Crannag Mhór." She stood in silence, lost in the memory.

"I canna speak for the dead, Marjory, but I dinna believe this is what he meant." She felt Fingal's hands tighten around her shoulders and then, just as quickly, release her. She heard his retreating footsteps, but didn't turn to watch him go.

Instead, she found herself wondering what would have happened if things had been different. If her father had been here to protect her. If her mother had been right about angels, and her wish upon the stars had come true. What if there had was someone out there just for her. Someone who'd love her. Cherish her . . .

How foolish to want something completely unobtainable. Her parents were dead, and she was a married woman. What hope for love was there from a Cameron, and a half-witted one at that? Marjory laughed at herself, and with a last pat for Alainn, headed for the tower. It was time to face her ailing husband.

"Truth be told, ye were dirty enough to warrant ten baths." Grania reached out to steady Cameron's elbow as he stepped from the oak cask that served as a bathtub. Even though he knew the woman couldn't see him, he was relieved when she handed him a length of cloth meant for drying.

"I feel like a new man." The comment was nothing more than a polite response, but the minute the words were out, he realized just how accurate they really were. More than he wanted to contemplate actually, and certainly more than he wanted to share with Grania.

He walked over to the bed, and sat down on the edge. Clean and shaven, he definitely felt more human, but the fact did nothing to lessen his increasing sense of unease.

The morning sunlight hadn't done anything to relieve the gothic gloom of his room. And with the cold harsh light of day there was no denying that he wasn't in Kansas anymore. Something about the world he was currently inhabiting didn't jibe with his sense of self. Or maybe more relevantly, his sense of century.

The pieces of the puzzle simply didn't add up to a logical whole. And the illogical options were a bit more than his beleaguered mind was willing to consider. Maybe there was an explanation. Something involving the relative normalcy of cults or historical reenactment. Anything that didn't involve a journey through *The Twilight Zone*.

The theme song to that TV show echoed menacingly in his head, and with a sigh he walked over to the bed, dropping onto the mattress, trying to ignore the fear clawing at his gut.

"I've let ye overdo it," Grania clucked. Her voice, though not exactly comforting, was at least a known quantity. Cameron lay back, closing his eyes, the drummers in his head returning with a vengeance.

"What ye need now is a wee bit o' sleep."

"What I need now are answers," he snapped. Immediately he regretted the anger that colored his voice. Opening his eyes, he struggled to sit up, ignoring Grania's attempt to help. The woman meant well, of that he had no doubt, but rest was the last thing he needed. It was tempting to voice his thoughts, to share his fears with her, but some inner sense of preservation urged caution.

"There's no' much I can tell you." She sat down in the chair by the bed, her expression inscrutable.

Ignoring her obvious reticence, Cameron pushed. "Well, for starters you can tell me about Ewen Cameron."

The woman paused, then sighed. "Ye're no' among friends here."

It was a cryptic answer at best, but it was a start. "Something to do with the woman who called me husband." A vivid memory of the blue-eyed beauty filled his mind, his body reacting as if she were present in the room.

"Aye," Grania conceded with a nod. "There's no love lost between the two of ye."

"And the man with her. Fingal. Is he an enemy as well?"

"He's loyal to your wife, and would see you in hell before he'd allow her to be hurt."

"And he believes I want to hurt her?"

" 'Twould not be impossible." Again she seemed purposefully vague. As if she too had secrets to keep.

"Why? What has this Ewen done to deserve such distrust?"

If she noticed his use of the third person, she made no comment. " 'Tis no' my story to tell. When you're strong enough, you can talk with Marjory herself."

"Something tells me that won't be as easy as you're making it sound."

"It's no' easy to gain her trust, I'll grant ye that." The old woman smiled. "She's kind of like the highland rose—beautiful and prickly on the outside, but if ye can get to the flower itself, 'tis sweeter than any other."

As analogies went it was kind of sappy, but Cameron had the feeling it was accurate. Marjory Macpherson was indeed easy on the eyes, and he'd already seen evidence of her thorns. Still, if breaching those thorns was his ticket to understanding what the hell was going on, he was more than game. "I'm not sure she'll talk to me, but I'll make nice with this Marjory if it means getting answers."

"I've the feeling yer more than capable of cajoling a body round to yer way of thinking, once ye put yer mind to it." There was a hint of mischief in Grania's face, as if she was orchestrating some grand scheme or another.

Despite himself, Cameron smiled. "I've the feeling it's you who gets her way more often than not. This whole thing would be a hell of a lot simpler if you'd just tell me what I need to know."

"I told ye, it's no' my story to tell." Her smile was serene and final.

Whatever the truth, he wasn't going to get it from Grania Macpherson.

Marjory pulled open the chamber door ready to do battle but stopped dead in her tracks. Ewen was sitting on the bed, his head turned toward the window, the morning sun streaming through the opening, illuminating his features and highlighting the golden perfection of his chest.

Marjory's breath caught in her throat, and she tried unsuccessfully to swallow. She'd never seen him like this before. And, despite her hatred, she couldn't deny the masculine beauty of his body. It was almost as if it had been sculpted, a living, breathing statue. Her fingers tightened reflexively as she imagined the velvety feel of his skin, the sinewy strength of his arms wrapped around her.

The thought should have been unthinkable.

But it wasn't.

It was almost as if she were looking at a stranger, a man she'd never met before. His face, now devoid of hair, was softer somehow, and breathtakingly handsome. Her heart responded by threatening to tear from her chest.

He turned, almost as if he'd known she was there, his eyes locking with hers, their bodies communicating on a level she'd no idea even existed before this moment— this man. She froze, her hand tightening on the door handle, her mind trying to make sense where there was obviously none.

This was her enemy.

"So, ye've come to see my patient," Grania said. Her voice startled Marjory back to reality.

She forced a smile, turning her gaze toward the old woman. "I'd no' intended to interrupt. And obviously"— she gestured toward Ewen without daring to glance again in his direction—"I've come at the wrong time."

All she wanted now was to escape, to avoid the man and the strange feelings the sight of him evoked. A strong chest and a clean-shaven face were only surface changes. Nothing could change the man that he was, or his kinship to her parents' killer.

"Nonsense, child. I've all but finished here. And the man is no' going to bite."

"I wouldn't be so certain." There were all kinds of ways to torture someone, and Ewen Cameron was no stranger to any of them. "I really just came to make certain he was well cared for." Despite herself she shot a glance in his direction, surprised to see the twinkle of amusement in his eyes. Jerking her gaze back to Grania, Marjory felt herself grow hot, although she took comfort in the fact that the sensation was more than likely caused as much by anger as embarrassment. Ogling a Cameron was something less than acceptable, and the mere thought that she'd fallen prey to his masculinity set her blood to boiling.

"Yer husband has need of ye, child." Grania's voice was soft, her words enigmatic as usual. Sometimes Marjory wondered if the woman was fey. " 'Twill do you good to *have a talk*."

Marjory couldn't think of a thing she wanted to talk to Ewen about, but there was steel in the old woman's voice, and Marjory knew from long experience that arguing was worthless. Better to give in. Truth was, Grania Macpherson always got her way.

Grania moved closer. Her hand touched Marjory's arm, her voice almost a whisper. "He remembers nothing of his past. Nothing at all."

Marjory stared at the old woman, trying to digest her words. "He's addled, then?"

"Nay." Grania shook her head. "He's no' simple. But the fall seems to have robbed him of his identity. He'll need someone to put things right."

"Well, it canna be me." Marjory spoke louder than she'd intended, and Ewen's eyes narrowed, his features sharpening with the gesture. All sign of vulnerability vanished, cloaked in an instant, his face becoming a blank mask.

"I can speak for myself, you know." His voice was hoarse, his speech different. As if he had trouble with the words. Marjory shot a questioning look at Grania.

"He'll be right as rain in no time. And I suspect his memory will return, eventually. But until then he's got questions, and I told him that ye were the best one to answer them."

"I've no desire to help him with anything," Marjory hissed. But she was dismayed to find that, in fact, that's exactly what she wanted.

"Well, *I* want to talk to *you*," he said. "So come over here. Grania's right, I won't bite." Ewen was frowning, exasperation coloring his voice.

She wouldn't put it past him to bite. Especially if it helped get him what he wanted. But at the moment he looked somewhat harmless, and Grania seemed determined for the two of them to talk. So, ignoring the flutter in her stomach, Marjory moved closer.

"You canna remember anything?" She tried but couldn't keep the disbelief from her voice. She'd never heard of such a thing. Except perhaps from someone very old, and Ewen was anything but frail.

He shook his head, then settled back into the bed as Grania bustled around him, straightening the bedclothes and fluffing the pillows. She was pampering him, and the idea of it rankled.

"There now, you just rest," the old woman crooned, her hand caressing Ewen's brow.

Marjory felt warm inside, as if she was watching something she shouldn't. Her hand involuntarily rose, as if to smooth her husband's cheek. The motion pulled her from her thoughts and she felt hot color wash across her face again. She deliberately slowed her breathing. By the saints, she was growing as dim-witted as Ewen.

She pulled herself back to reality only to find Ewen staring at her, eyebrows raised in amusement. Grania was nowhere in sight. She'd been so far gone, she hadn't even noticed the old woman leave. Narrowing her eyes in what she hoped was a haughty glare, she prayed silently for deliverance.

Ewen motioned her to the side of the bed, his gaze intense. She shook her head, but her feet, obviously with a mind of their own, moved forward and then deserted her, forcing her to sit beside the odious man.

"Your name is Marjory." It was a statement, but his inflection made it clear he wasn't convinced of the fact.

"Has been since I was born, and well you know it. You may have fooled Grania, but I'll have none of your games."

Something she would have sworn was disappointment crossed his face, but it disappeared before she could be certain. "This is far from a game. I have no idea who any of you are. Hell, I'm not even certain who I am." There was a hint of fear in his voice.

She'd never seen Ewen vulnerable. It touched her. Without thinking, she reached over to cover his hand. " 'Twill come right soon enough. In the meantime, you must rest."

"I've had enough coddling to last a lifetime." He pulled his hand away, frustration filling his eyes. It was amazing how easily she could read the emotion in his face. She told herself it was only because the beard was gone, but some part of her insisted it was something more. "What I need right now is a telephone."

Marjory studied his face. He seemed sane enough, disregarding his new penchant for cleanliness, but she had no idea what a telephone was. Perhaps Grania was wrong and he had gone simple. "I dinna ken what you're speaking of. I think perhaps this fall has left you a bit weak in the head, husband." She wasn't quite sure what made her add the last word. It was just that he looked so different, a far cry from the man she despised.

"I am not crazy," he roared, for the first time sounding like himself. "I just don't remember anything. Obviously the trauma of my head injuries has brought about some form of retrograde amnesia." He collapsed against the pillows and closed his eyes.

Marjory ran a hand across his brow. No fever. But still, he was speaking gibberish. He gently captured her hand with his and opened his eyes, the amber turning dark, intense.

"I am not losing my mind. I swear it," he said softly. The vulnerability was back, tugging at her heart, making her want to help him. A trick, her mind urged. Cameron skullduggery. This man was not to be trusted.

"Well, you canna prove it by me. First you're dead, and now you're touched. I dinna ken how all of this came to be, but I can promise you once your father arrives there'll be hell for someone to pay, and that someone will no doubt be me."

His brows drew together in a frown. "You?"

"Aye." Marjory stood up, crossing her arms as if to create a barrier between them. "There's no love lost between your father and me."

"And you hate me as well." Again it was a statement, not a question, but this time he seemed to understand.

"I thought you couldna remember anything." She'd been right. This was nothing more than a trick. "I should know better than to believe a Cameron. If my grandfather wasna away serving the king, I'd have him dismember the lot of you. As it is, I should have left you to die on the mountain."

"King? What king?" The color drained from his face, leaving only his eyes—dark and burning.

"James, of course. Surely you can't be so addled you've forgotten your king."

His eyes widened; then he slowly released a breath, as if something more was draining out of him. "Tell me what year this is." The words were no more than a whisper.

She frowned at him, trying to understand what possibly caused his pain. " 'Tis the spring of fourteen hundred and sixty-eight."

It was as though she'd struck him with a claymore or stabbed him with her dirk. What little color remained was gone in an instant, and she feared his very life was draining away. Without thinking of the consequences she rushed to his side, her warm hand clasping his cold one. "You're no' well."

"Fourteen-sixty-eight?" The question was pitched so low, she had to lean close to hear. "Are you sure?"

"Of course I'm sure." She spoke slowly, enunciating each word.

His eyes locked with hers, the naked anguish there tearing at her heart. "It's seems, then, that I was right. I'm a long way from home."

Chapter Four

1468.

Cameron closed his eyes and then opened them again, taking in the stone room, the chamber pot peeking out from under the bed, the open window with its wooden shutters, and the woman standing by the bed.

1468.

His head swirled, reality twisting in on itself, the truth slamming home with a finality that left him breathless. He wasn't just inexplicably in Scotland. He was inexplicably in *fifteenth-century* Scotland. And this woman thought he was her husband.

Terror flooded through him, his mind desperately wanting to reject the facts but categorically unable to dismiss them. He wasn't just a man without identity. He was a man with the wrong identity. A stranger in body and time. Or perhaps Marjory was right. Maybe he was just crazy.

In some ways the latter was more comforting. At least it was quantifiable. Scientifically possible. But he knew it wasn't the truth. He was sane. It was the world around him that was certifiable, a madhouse worse than anything Lewis Carroll could possibly have imagined.

Another horrifying thought occurred to him, and he closed his eyes again, trying to envision his likeness. A picture popped automatically into his head, and he was flooded with relief, but only for a moment. If he was right, then *his* face existed only in his mind.

"I need a mirror." The words came out as a croak, and he swallowed, his eyes meeting Marjory's. She stared back at him, his horror reflected in her eyes.

Obviously, she thought him unbalanced, or maybe possessed—which unfortunately was all too close to the truth. "I've no notion of what it is you want." She, too, whispered—as if their discussion needed to remain private.

He scrambled for another word, something that would explain to her what he required. "A looking glass." Her face was still blank. "Something that will reflect my face. Marjory, I need to see myself."

She raised an eyebrow but nodded, turning to a chest in the corner. Opening it, she pulled out a flat piece of metal polished to a high shine. A shield of some sort. Still silent, she handed it to him.

He held the improvised mirror out from his face and, heart pounding, he took a look. The man in the mirror was sun-bronzed and heavily muscled. His hair was long, somewhere between blond and brown. His face was hard, his skin toughened by life in the outdoors. The face was young and old at the same time. There weren't any wrinkles, but there also were no laugh lines.

The faint white pucker of a scar ran across one cheek, tracing a thin line from his ear to his chin. Even with the imperfection of the reflection, Cameron could see that his eyes were the same color as his hair. A lion, the man in the mirror was a lion—and a perfect stranger.

This, then, was Ewen Cameron.

Cameron stared at the face in the mirror, his mind recoiling at the enormity of what was happening. He was looking at himself, and yet it wasn't his reflection. Not his face, not his century. He was certain of the fact. His life, if he still had one, belonged with dream-induced memories of rainy nights and a car with a leather interior, and a blonde.

But if all that was true, then there were some pretty overwhelming questions to be answered. Like how the hell he'd gotten here and how in the world was he going to get back? For that matter, what had happened to the real Ewen Cameron? Was he dead? Was he roaming around in someone else's body? Cameron's body?

The questions built up one after another until Cameron felt as if his head would explode. God, he wished his memory would return.

He blanched as another unwanted thought planted itself firmly in his brain. What if he never remembered? What if that was part of the nightmare? What if he was always caught in some sort of limbo between glimpses of who he really was and tales of who he was not?

No.

He simply could not, would not accept that. His memory would come back. Amnesia was seldom permanent. He latched on to that thought, forcing himself to ignore the accompanying thought that traumatic head injury didn't send its victim five hundred years into the past.

"I shouldna be at all surprised that you'd spend the better part of the day admiring yourself. But I've work to do and no time for lollygaggin' about with you."

Marjory's voice drew him sharply back to the present—the past, actually. He grimaced and lowered the mirror, trying to hide his turmoil. Until he knew whom he could trust, he wasn't about to share his thoughts. Especially with Marjory.

"I thought it might trigger memories." He shrugged. "But there's nothing." He handed her the shield, forcing himself to breathe normally. There was no sense in panicking. If he was going to make sense of this nightmare, he had to get out of this bed, and to do that he had to hold his cards close to the vest.

Marjory was staring at him through narrowed eyes, her expression somewhere between pity and contempt. "Grania says they'll come back."

They'd covered this territory before, but this time Cameron was determined to get more information. "Until then, I have some questions." He tried to make his tone pleasant, to keep at least a semblance of normalcy. "Please stay." He patted the bed next to him in what he hoped was an inviting manner. In truth, his head was pounding and what he wanted most was to be alone—but that wouldn't get him answers.

Marjory glared at him suspiciously and then, apparently making up her mind, ignored the spot he'd indicated. She sat instead in the chair vacated by Grania. Cameron sighed. The woman had a will of her own.

"What do you wish to speak about?" She sat perfectly straight in the chair, poised on the edge, obviously ready to make a hasty retreat if necessary.

He wondered what Ewen had done to make her so wary of him. "Maybe we should start with why you hate me so much."

She flinched, obviously not expecting the question. " 'Tis mutual."

It wasn't an answer, but it spoke volumes just the same. "Whatever I felt before, I don't feel it now. You're a stranger to me. And I can't move forward with my life until I at least have a rudimentary understanding of who I was before I fell."

She looked as though she didn't believe him, which given the circumstances was perfectly reasonable, but he was oddly disappointed nevertheless.

"So, if we hate each other, why the marriage?"

She eyed him distrustfully. "You're a Cameron and I'm a Macpherson. Our families are enemies and, in their infinite wisdom, they decided a marriage between our clans would lessen tensions."

"You—I mean, *we*," he amended, "were the sacrificial lambs, I take it?"

"Aye."

"Did it work?" The situation sounded like something out of a macabre fairy tale. "Did your marriage to Ewen ease the tension between your clans?"

"You speak as if you are not he." Her expression held both fear and puzzlement.

He cursed his choice of words. He'd have to be more careful. If these people perceived him as insane, his chances for escape were nil. "I'm sorry, it's just that hearing all this is like listening to a story. Someone else's life."

She sighed, her expression softening. "I can imagine the way of it."

"So, did the marriage solve the problems between our clans?" He pulled the focus of the conversation back to the past—his past in some weirdly twisted way.

"Nay." She shook her head. "The sacrifice, as you call it, was for naught."

"I see." He paused, looking down at his hands—or more relevantly, Ewen's hands.

She followed his gaze, staring for a moment, then looked away in seeming embarrassment. Without thinking, he reached out and touched her hand. Electricity burned them both.

She pulled her hand away, anger sparking in her eyes. "I've no more time for blethering," she snapped, jumping up from the chair. "There's work to be done and it won't take care of itself. Your *father*"—she spat the word as if it were a curse—"will be here soon. Whatever it is you need to know, you can learn it from him."

Without giving him time to answer, she fled, leaving Cameron with the uncomfortable feeling that she'd taken the sunshine with her.

"I dinna know what it is, Aimil, but he is no' the same." Marjory raised the linen to her lips and snapped the embroidery thread.

Aimil frowned. "Not with yer teeth. Ye were raised to be a lady, no' a stable boy. And change or no' the mon is still a Cameron, and in my book that makes him the enemy. Have ye forgotten then what his family did to yours?"

Marjory bit her lip in concentration as she tried to thread the small needle. Finally, in frustration, she handed it to Aimil, who deftly threaded it and handed it back. Marjory sighed, failing to see the importance of doing such a task. There were far more critical things to worry about. And best she could tell, there was no one at Crannag Mhór who cared at all if she could embroider tapestry. Well, no one except Aimil.

She picked up the linen and earnestly began again to stitch. "Of course I haven't forgotten, Aimil. I live with that legacy every day of my life. I was only saying that I think Ewen has changed." Her body fairly sang at the thought of the physical changes. But that wasn't all of it. There was something more, something she couldn't put her finger on. Something she was hesitant to even think about, let alone believe.

"Ye sound as if ye're taking an interest in the man." Aimil shot her a concerned look over the top of her tapestry frame.

"I couldna do such a thing." Marjory felt heat rising in her cheeks. She bent her head to her work, hoping Aimil wouldn't notice. "No' with all that lies between us." And she meant the words. At least on most levels. Still, she couldn't deny that there was something about Ewen now that was more than what he'd been before— something that called to her in the age-old way of men and women.

If she'd felt anything at all for the old Ewen, it was revulsion, but try as she might she couldn't seem to recapture that feeling. It was almost as if he truly was another man. Saints preserve her, now she was one who was daft.

"Marjory Macpherson, I've known ye since ye were a bairn and I know when ye're no' telling me the truth. Ye *are* feeling something fer him."

Marjory met Aimil's eyes, her own gaze clear and strong. "Only pity, Aimil. Ewen has clearly gone a wee bit soft in the head. And the least I can do is make sure he's well taken care of until Torcall Cameron comes to take him home."

"And what if Torcall doesna want him the way he is?"

"Then he'll just have to stay here at Crannag Mhór." Aimil remained silent, but Marjory knew she was holding her tongue. "Out with it, Aimil. I know you've something to say to me."

Aimil smiled. "Ah, child, ye know me too well. 'Tis just that I dinna want ye to get any more involved with the man than ye already are."

Marjory laughed, but the sound held little humor. "I married him. I dinna know how much more involved I can get."

"Aye, but when ye married him, he wasna injured and he didna want to be here. He only came now and again in the hopes o' getting ye with child, and when that failed, he hightailed it back to his father's house and his mistress."

Marjory opened her mouth to speak, but Aimil cut her off with a wave of her hand. "Nay, I'll no' dance around the fact that he has a mistress—maybe scores of them for all we know. And it'll do ye good to remember that fact. A cat canna change his ways, Marjory. He will always roam, and this one is worse than most. He's a Cameron. Dinna let yerself care fer him, child. It canna bring ye anything but heartache. And more than likely, it'll bring ye harm."

They sat in silence, sewing almost in rhythm. Aimil was right. Marjory knew it in her mind, and her heart had long been closed to anything that even resembled feeling. She ought to be safe from the charms of her half-brained husband.

But she wasn't. Marjory touched the back of her hand, feeling again the strange warmth his fingers against her skin had invoked. No matter what her practical mind said, her body would not, could not deny that his touch had woken a part of her she had long thought dead.

She shook her head. She knew better than to open herself up to someone, and particularly to a Cameron.

With a strength of will built from the pain of a destroyed childhood, she forced herself to picture her parents' bodies. The horror of the image washed over her like icy water. The man upstairs was an enemy. No matter what he said or did, he was still a Cameron. And she hated the lot.

Cameron shifted in the bed so that he was closer to the window. From this vantage point, he could look down into the courtyard of Crannag Mhór, the people below going about their daily chores, scurrying here and there, each intent upon his or her task.

One girl, wrapped in a brightly colored plaid, looked up at his window. He waved. She blushed a bright crimson, quickly averted her eyes, and continued on her way without an answering gesture. Obviously she had been warned about the infamous Ewen.

There were several outbuildings directly across from him. He had no idea what purpose they served. One billowed smoke and so he figured it was probably a blacksmith of some kind. His knowledge of fifteenth-century craftsmanship was limited to television and movies—and everyone knew how accurate those usually were.

Adjacent to the front of the tower was another structure. This one was surrounded by a pen of some kind. A barn, he figured. At least it looked like a barn. He frowned in frustration. A horse whinnied from within. *A barn.* He smiled with relief.

Funny, how even the slightest shift in a man's sense of reality left him questioning even the most mundane observations. Not long ago, he'd had an ordinary life in the twenty-first century—or more precisely he thought he'd had such a life. Now . . . well, now he seemed to be a man without a memory, stuck in some crazy time warp.

He felt frustration rising again and tried to push it back down. It was only a matter of time, he reassured himself. His memories were already starting to come back. He'd remembered his car in the dream. And then there was the girl. The blonde. It was clear that she was important somehow—that she needed him. But why?

He told himself that it would all come back. He just had to be patient and get well. Once that was accomplished he'd find his way back to the rock slide. Surely there he'd find a way home. The little voice in his head insisted that it was a long shot at best, but he ignored it. If sheer will would get him home, he'd soon be on his way.

"Are ye all right?" Grania stood at the foot of the bed. He'd been so deep in thought, he hadn't heard her come in. He automatically reached for the sheet to cover himself, realizing as he did so that the gesture was unnecessary. Grania couldn't see him.

"I think, even were I no' blind, I would be too old for ye to have to worry about modesty—but I thank ye for the thought." Her voice was full of laughter. Somehow she must have guessed his actions. Her tone grew more solemn. "I passed Marjory outside yer chamber a bit ago. Did the two of ye have words?"

Cameron winced. If only it were that simple. "Believe me, words had nothing to do with it."

"Cameron, ye see what ye want to see and naught more." Then, with that enigmatic comment, she moved to open another window. " 'Tis time ye were up and about, lad. 'Tis a beautiful morning." She handed him his shirt. "Dinna fash yerself about things ye canna change."

Easy for her to say. Her life was ordered and as it should be. His was falling down around his ears. "I don't have the faintest idea what to do, Grania. I don't remember the person she thinks I am." He didn't allow himself to stop and examine why it was Marjory in particular that he worried about. "To listen to her tell it, I'm at best a self-centered bastard and, at worst, a hideous fiend with the devil for a father." He shifted uncomfortably on the bed and pulled on his shirt.

Grania sat patiently in the chair, her hands folded neatly in her lap. Cameron was amazed at her ability for stillness. She said, "I canna see, Cameron. By necessity I must sit for long periods of time. I find 'tis easier to bear if I find a peace within."

With uncanny accuracy, she had read his thoughts again. "How do you do that?"

She smiled at him. "Marjory would say I'm fey, but I think it's more to do with observation."

"Without your eyes?"

"There's far more to the world, lad, than what you can see. Tell me what ye remember of yerself."

"Nothing significant. Only everyday things." He didn't mention that they were everyday things that hadn't been invented yet. That would surely throw even the unflappable Grania. Then again, maybe not.

There was something about her that made him feel as if she could see through him, even without conventional sight. He shook his head at the ridiculous notion. She was nothing more than she appeared: an old lady with good instincts.

"Well, I wouldna worry o'ermuch. It will all come to ye in time. Besides, the past is ne'er as important as the present. And I've the feeling ye've something important to do here."

"Me? I hardly think so. Even I can tell I'm not wanted here. Hell, without your help, I'm fairly certain they'd have left me to die. The one named Fingal would probably have helped me on my way, if you know what I mean."

"Ach, lad, dinna go making things worse than they are. Marjory has had a rough time of it, and because o' that, she's closed off her heart—but she is no' a bad person and I dinna think she'd actually let any real harm befall ye."

"Maybe not, but I'm still glad you're here. I don't think I like the idea of putting your theory to the test." He eased his legs off the side of the bed.

"There now, what do ye think ye're doing?"

"You said it was time I was up and about." He slowly eased himself into a standing position. For a minute, the room whirled about him and his stomach did flip-flops, but he held on to the bed frame and the room soon took on its regular proportions. "There, see? I managed all right." He winced at his choice of words, but Grania didn't seem to notice.

"Are you standing, then?" She held out a hand, and Cameron took it.

"Yup. I feel a bit wobbly, but that's to be expected. I haven't had anything but broth since I got here."

"Aye, and lucky ye were to get that, ye ungrateful oaf."

"Oh, Grania, I'm sorry. I wasn't complaining. Honestly." Great, he'd managed to insult his only friend.

"Dinna fash yerself, lad, I was but teasin'. Perhaps tonight we'll dig up a wee bit o' meat for you to gnaw on."

They laughed together, their camaraderie restored.

After a second the old woman said, "She needs ye, lad. Ye must know that."

Cameron sobered and sat on the edge of the bed. "She?

You mean Marjory. I hardly think so. Besides, I don't think I'll be here long enough to help anyone. Sooner or later, I'm bound to remember everything, and when I do, I expect I'll be heading back where I belong." He sincerely hoped it would be that simple.

"And how do you know this isna where ye belong?"

"Because it isn't home, Grania. Even I know that much. Somewhere out there, I have a home, an identity. All I have to do is remember."

"Maybe 'tis best if ye dinna."

"No, I can't accept that. I will remember. Which means that making attachments here would be foolhardy."

"I've the feeling, lad, that ye've trouble making attachments no matter where ye are."

"Nonsense." The single word put an end to the conversation. But it was a lie. Unfortunately, he was afraid Grania's comment was right on the mark. Which left him somewhere to the left of nowhere.

Chapter Five

The plan was to get out of the bed, head down the stairs, and out to the courtyard. Grania had said that fresh air would do him wonders, and the idea had taken hold. Unfortunately, the progress wasn't matching the motivation.

Part of the problem was the damn skirt. Kilts seemed simple in theory, but in reality he'd take a pair of 501s any day. Untangling himself for about the twenty-fourth time, Cameron sat on the bed wondering what in the hell he'd done to deserve all of this. Maybe he'd been a bastard in his previous life and this was the punishment.

"Having a little trouble, are ye?" Allen Cameron stood in the doorway, leaning against the frame, an amused smile on his face. "Ye never did have the patience for the thing."

Cameron looked at the man who called him brother, searching his mind for a memory, an emotion, but there was nothing. Allen was as much a stranger as Marjory. Wrapping the wool around his waist one last time, he fumbled with the tail, grateful when Allen moved forward to pull it up across the shoulder.

"Thanks," he mumbled, embarrassed at his ineptitude. "I can take it from here."

Allen moved back, hands in the air. "Have it yer own way."

"I haven't really had much time to practice. Grania has been helping me." He almost kicked himself for the words. Memory loss or not, he should surely remember how to wrap himself in a plaid.

Allen's eyes narrowed. "I dinna fash how ye can let that woman touch ye. She's a witch, that one."

"I asked for a doctor."

"What did ye say?" Allen's frown deepened, and Cameron knew he'd made another mistake. "Ye hate the crazy buggers more than I do. When ye broke yer arm, ye practically skewered the mon who tried to fix it."

Cameron shook his head, fumbling for something to right his mistake. "I only meant that a doctor would be better than a crazy woman." He smiled at his brother in what he hoped was a conspiratorial manner, and was rewarded with a skeptical look. Allen obviously wasn't buying. There was shrewdness under all that hair.

"Aye, I suppose it's a bit like being stuck between the devil and a banshee."

"And the point is, I've survived." Cameron said, still struggling with the damn plaid.

Allen tugged at the top, then deftly pinned it into place. "Ye should have brought Aida. She's got a sure hand when it comes to dressing a body."

There was subtext here he was missing, but there was no way for Cameron to decipher it. "Who's Aida?"

"Yer mistress." Allen frowned. "Dinna ye remember anything?"

"That seems to be the question of the day." Cameron tried but couldn't keep the anger from his voice. "And unfortunately the answer is always the same. I can't remember anything." Not about his life, not about Ewen's. It was as if he'd been dropped into the second act of a play without knowing his lines. Hell, without knowing the story.

Allen slammed a beefy fist against the wall. "*They've* done this to you. And by the saints, I'll see that they pay for it."

"Who are you talking about? Marjory? She had nothing to with what happened."

Allen moved closer, his eyes narrowing to slits. "I wouldna be so quick to let her off the hook, brother. I saw the place where you fell. Had our men examine it carefully. I'm convinced it wasna an accident, Ewen."

He fought a wave of dizziness. "You're sure?"

Allen nodded. "I canna say who was behind it for certain, but ye know as well as I who would best benefit from yer death."

"Marjory?" He was more than aware of the fact she despised him, but the idea that she'd try to kill him seemed ludicrous. "I can't believe she'd stoop to that."

"She's a Macpherson," Allen spat, as if it explained everything. But of course it didn't.

"And we hate each other," Cameron lifted a hand in exasperation. "That's already been made abundantly clear. What I don't know is why."

"Because Manus Macpherson killed our mother." Allen's features locked into harsh lines, his hatred radiating off him with almost palpable heat.

"Marjory's father?" Cameron let the news settle. It certainly explained a lot. The forced marriage for instance. But somehow it didn't sync with what he'd observed about the Macpherson household. There was obviously more to the story.

"Aye. I canna believe you dinna remember." Allen's frown was fierce.

"Look, Allen, I wish I remembered too. It's not like I haven't tried."

Again his look was skeptical. As if he didn't believe a word. And Cameron wondered just exactly what the brothers' relationship had been. Cordial certainly. United against common enemies, but still a far cry from friendly.

"If I were you," Allen was saying, "I'd trust no one."

An apt sentiment. Cameron studied the man before him, wishing he could read minds.

Allen met his gaze, his own hardened. "Father would no' forgive me if anything happened to you. I'll deliver ye safe and sound or die trying. And I'll no' let a bit o' skirt like Marjory Macpherson get in the way."

"Father's close?" Cameron chose to ignore the implication of Allen's words, concentrating instead on applying a name to the menace that seemed to surround them all. *Torcall Cameron*. To hear Marjory talk, the man was next in line to the devil himself, but, in truth, Cameron hadn't any idea who he should believe. His brother or his wife.

Like most things he suspected the answer was somewhere in the middle, and until he knew the whole truth, he wasn't making any judgments.

"I've just had a message. He's through the pass and should be here on the morrow."

"Does Marjory know?"

"No' from me." Allen shrugged. " 'Tis no' my place to tell her. Although her kinfolk will no doubt send word that he's near."

"And when he arrives?" Ewen's father's arrival

seemed to represent some sort of catalyst. A cataclysmic one, if Cameron had to call it.

"When he arrives," Allen said, his expression grim, "Marjory Macpherson will pay for all that she's done."

Cameron sat on the bench, eyes closed, leaning back against the cool stone tower wall, letting the afternoon sun warm his face. Allen had helped him down the stairs, then gone off to check on his men. It was a beautiful day, but it was hard to enjoy it. Not with all the information swirling around in his head. It seemed that not only had he woken up to find himself inside another man's body, he'd also landed into the middle of a feudal war—Ewen Cameron at the heart of it.

And *Marjory*. The thought of her made Cameron's blood heat, despite the things Allen had said of her. It was difficult to believe she'd try to kill him, no matter how much she despised him. Yet, Allen was his brother, and had been certain the landslide was intentional.

A conundrum if ever there was one. Add to that the fact that Cameron couldn't remember who the hell he really was, and it increased from conundrum to calamity. Possibly a deadly one.

Which of course left Cameron with the primary question: Who the hell did he trust?

What he needed was a way out. Or, more realistically, a way home. But was that even possible?

He was feeling much better, the lumps on his head greatly reduced in size and the drummers seemingly departed for their next concert stop. But that didn't mean he was up to the trek back to the mountain. If he even could find the place again.

Still, the little voice in his head insisted, leaving was worth any risk, wasn't it—if he got back where he belonged? The blonde's face flashed through his mind as if underscoring the thought. He had a life, and it wasn't here.

He couldn't let these people and their problems get to him. Not Grania, not Allen, and certainly not Marjory. He had nothing to offer any of them. And even if he did, he wasn't certain he'd offer it.

A cold thought, surely, but a man had to protect himself. People weren't to be trusted.

He frowned, wondering where the hell that thought had come from. Not exactly a Pollyanna moment. He laughed at himself, surprised how bitter he sounded, and for the first time it occurred to him that maybe he hadn't been all that happy in his old life.

As quickly as the thought came, he pushed it away. Good or bad, he needed his own life—his own identity. Any thoughts to the contrary were the result of listening to Grania with her endless predictions and enigmatic ways.

If he believed in such things, he'd have to agree with Marjory's assessment that Grania was touched in some way. Or maybe they were all enchanted. A Grimm's fairy tale run amok.

Definitely not his style.

With a sigh he opened his eyes, surprised to find Marjory Macpherson perched precariously on a rickety-looking wooden ladder in front of a shed just across the way. She was obviously content to ignore him, and just at the moment the fact suited him just fine.

He couldn't help admiring the soft curve of her backside. It was something just this side of mouthwatering, and he was happy to note that his borrowed body responded like any red-blooded male to the sight of a beautiful woman.

Even a deceitful one.

Marjory barked something at a man standing below her at the foot of the ladder, and, with a fatalistic shrug, he passed her what looked to be a handful of straw. As she reached for it, the ladder shook ominously, but held, and Marjory began to weave the straw into a hole in the shed's roof.

An accident waiting to happen, if ever there was one. But far be it from him to try and share the information with Marjory. The woman was prickly at best, and since the moment in his room when they'd practically electrified the tower, she hadn't so much as acknowledged his presence. Besides, if Allen was right, she was more than cantankerous. She was an enemy. Possibly a deadly one.

He blew out a breath and dismissed all ideas of intervening. The building wasn't high, and he didn't think a fall would result in serious injury as long as someone was there to catch her. She'd be just fine without him. And he'd be better off without getting involved. Entanglements only resulted in pain.

And he'd had enough pain for a lifetime.

Again he frowned, wondering what it was he was remembering—or not remembering. Frustration crested, then died as he slowly forced a breath. He had to remain calm, hold on to his wits.

"I see you're up and about." Fingal Macgillivray towered over him, eyes narrowed and assessing.

Cameron struggled to remember what Grania had said about the man. A captain, she'd called him. Marjory's right-hand man. Which meant he wasn't a friend of Ewen's. "More or less." Cameron looked up at the Scotsman, holding his gaze, striving for a nonchalance he didn't feel.

To his surprise, the man sat down next to him, his

expression still guarded. "Ye really dinna know me?"

"Only what Grania has told me."

The man shifted uncomfortably. "Ach, the old woman is more daft than no'. I dinna trust her ways or her wisdom."

Cameron shrugged, not willing to comment, any chance for a peaceful moment alone evaporating before it could begin.

"I honestly thought you were dead." The man's tone was neither apologetic nor gloating, neutrality sitting well with him. Fingal might be a warrior, but it seemed he had a diplomatic side as well. "I wouldna have left ye there had I thought ye alive."

"Really?" Cameron studied him. "I sort of got the feeling you would have done more than that if you hadn't thought I was dead." It was a risky thing to say, but he had a feeling honesty was the right currency with this man. Friend or foe.

Fingal's lips curled into a faint smile. "But since I thought ye were dead, the thought canna have occurred to me."

Nicely sidestepped. "Well, why don't we suffice it to agree that I'm alive and that I'm not exactly the man I was?"

"I can see that ye're breathing, but as to the change, I'll no' believe it until I've proof."

"That I'm different?"

"That ye're not using circumstances to try and play Marjory for a fool."

Cameron laughed. "I doubt that anyone could play Marjory Macpherson."

Fingal crossed his arms over his massive chest. "Mayhap, but that wouldna stop some from trying."

There was a warning there, and Cameron wasn't fool

enough to ignore it. "I've no interest in hurting her, Fingal." There was truth in that. Unless Allen's accusations proved true.

The older man looked sharply at him. "Maybe no' now. But when you remember."

The words hung between them, leaving Cameron uncomfortable. It was tempting to tell the man he wasn't Ewen Cameron, that his memories if they returned would have nothing to do with Crannag Mhór or Marjory Macpherson, but he couldn't take the chance. Not yet. Maybe never. This world was a harsh one, and they didn't suffer fools lightly. A man claiming to be from the future would certainly not inspire confidence, let alone trust.

"Maybe I won't remember."

"Nay." Fingal shook his head slowly. "Torcall Cameron will no' allow it. Ye'll remember. Of that I'm certain. It's what ye choose to do with the memories that remains to be seen."

It seemed Grania had competition in the enigma department. Wonderful. Cameron leaned back against the stone wall, and he and Fingal sat in silence for a while, each left to his own thoughts, until a commotion off to the left caught their attention.

"Get out of here right now, ye wicked beasties. Out, I say. Out!"

The female voice carried from around the corner of the tower, the screech followed by a caterwauling that could only come from enraged bovines.

Cameron turned to Fingal, eyebrows raised in question.

"My sister, Aimil."

Cameron inclined his head. The commotion continued.

"Angus Macpherson, come get these animals out of my garden before they destroy it completely!" The disembodied voice carried through the courtyard to the man by the ladder. He yelled something up at Marjory and ran toward the garden.

Fingal and Cameron both rose from the bench, swallowing back their mirth, momentarily joined in camaraderie.

"An-gus." The single word came out as an indignant wail.

"Sounds to me like Angus may need rescuing more than the animals."

With a terse nod, Fingal headed off in the direction of the ruckus. Cameron was just thinking of following when he heard a cracking sound from the other direction. Spinning, he turned just in time to see the ancient ladder split in two as Marjory tried to climb down.

Adrenaline kicked in and Cameron raced to the building, ignoring the jarring pain in his head. Marjory struggled for a handhold on the roof, managing finally to dig her hands into the sod, leaving her precariously swinging back and forth from the edge of the thatch. Cameron was torn between genuine concern and amusement. He choked back a laugh.

Marjory glared angrily down at him. "Dinna just stand there gawking. Do something."

"Is there another ladder?"

"Nay—"

The word broke off abruptly as her hand slipped from the roof, broken pieces of sod raining down on his head.

Cameron reacted instinctively, reaching out with both arms to catch her as she tumbled downward. Given his current condition, even her slight weight was almost more than he could handle, but he held his ground and pulled her safely against his chest.

The reaction was instantaneous, pheromones and

chemistry causing an ignition so strong it threatened to rob him of breath—which was ridiculous considering he wasn't even certain he liked the woman.

Their eyes locked, her breathing timed with his, almost as if they shared one heart.

"Are you all right?" he whispered, fighting to control the emotions raging through him. There was just something about her, something that touched him on an intrinsic level he couldn't control.

She nodded her head, her eyes searching his face, almost as if she were memorizing its lines and planes. Or maybe she was learning them.

Either way the idea was insane. He didn't know her, she didn't know him. And more pertinent was the fact that she believed he was a man she despised, possibly enough to kill him. Loosening his grip, he broke eye contact, breaking the spell.

Marjory frowned, as if surprised to find herself in his arms. "I'll thank you to put me down now." The breathless note in her voice assured him that he hadn't imagined the combustion, although it couldn't negate the sharp regality of her order.

"Look, *Your Highness,*" he said, his voice dripping with sarcasm, the tone as much a reaction to the way she made him feel as to her words. "If I hadn't caught you, you'd have fallen right on your lovely little ass, which unless I'm badly mistaken would have hurt like hell."

"Well, I'm perfectly fine now, as you can plainly see. So, I ask you again to unhand me."

"Fine by me." He opened his arms, unceremoniously dumping her onto the ground. She scowled up at him. He smiled benignly. "Next time, I'll let you break your neck."

He walked away without looking back. Maybe Allen

was right and Marjory Macpherson deserved whatever she got.

The man was impossible. Despite her best efforts to stay away from him, she'd wound up in his arms. Although, she had to admit, it had been good to have him there. The distance from roof to ground was not that high, but still, as much as it rankled to admit it, he was right: she might have been hurt if he hadn't been there to catch her.

Her body tightened at the memory of his arms locked around her. She closed her eyes and let her imagination have free rein, remembering their eyes locked together, imagining . . .

"Are ye finished lollygagging about on the ground?"

Marjory jerked out of her reverie to find Fingal towering over her, a look of amusement playing across his usually stern features.

"I fell."

Fingal laughed. "Well, I wouldna say ye fell so much as ye were dropped. And, from the little bit o' the conversation I managed to overhear, I canna say that ye dinna deserve it."

"Dinna tell me you're taking his side!"

Fingal visibly fought to control his mirth. "Nay, lass, I willna ever side with anyone over you. But the man did manage to save ye from falling and all he got for his efforts was the sharp side o' yer tongue."

Marjory hauled herself to her feet, pulling bits of sod from her hair and dress. "Maybe I was a wee bit harsh, but I canna be too careful where he's concerned." Satisfied that she was reasonably clean again, she gave Fingal her full attention. "Did Angus save Aimil from the beastie invasion?"

"Aye, with my help, her garden is now cattle-free. There was a wee hole in the backside of the fence. I've already set some o' the lads to fixing it."

They walked together toward the tower, increasing their pace at the sound of a commotion in the courtyard. Rounding the corner, they were in time to see a young boy, his face as red as his hair, bent over at the waist with his hands on his knees, trying to catch his breath.

Seeing Marjory, he straightened and staggered over to her. "Me mother said I was to come straight here and report to no one but you." He paused for breath. "I ran all the way."

"You've done well, Thomas, but what is it you were supposed to tell me?"

The youngster fought for a breath, his words coming in short bursts. "Camerons . . . at the . . . border. Said . . . to tell ye . . . be here . . . on the morrow." He beamed at Marjory, his message completed.

Marjory frowned. She'd expected this, but the knowledge that Torcall Cameron was actually on Crannag Mhór land again was almost more than she could bear. She felt Fingal's hand on her shoulder and was glad of the connection.

"Thomas, there's gingerbread in the kitchen. Maybe Cook will give you some milk to go with it."

The boy's face was split by an ear-to-ear grin. Without further conversation, he loped off in pursuit of the promised treat.

"Well, lass, ye knew he was coming. At least now ye know when."

Marjory stared at the tower gate almost as if she expected to see Torcall Cameron come roaring through it, claymore raised for battle. "Aye, now I do."

"I canna imagine he'll want to stay long. I suspect

he'll want nothing more than to take his boy home to Tyndrum. Dinna fash yerself about it. 'Twill be over before ye know it."

"I'm sure you're right." She smiled reassuringly at Fingal. "I just need some time to get used to the idea. I think I'll take a walk."

"Do ye want me to go with you?"

"Nay, I've a need to be alone."

Fingal turned to go and then stopped, calling back to her over his shoulder. "Dinna go outside the walls without one of the lads. Ye canna be too careful with Camerons afoot."

Marjory nodded absently, already moving away toward the gate. She'd feel better after a walk.

Chapter Six

Marjory headed toward the pool. It was a good place for thinking, and at the moment that's just what she needed to do. She cut across the meadow, trying to keep her mind off the fact that Torcall Cameron was out here somewhere. Tomorrow he'd be at Crannag Mhór. Tomorrow, she would have to face him. And tomorrow, he would probably take Ewen back to Tyndrum.

Her stomach tightened at the thought. What in heaven's name had happened to her? She couldn't get him off of her mind. It wasn't as if he hadn't touched her before. He certainly had. She shuddered at the memory. But that had been different, a stubborn little voice reminded her.

The old Ewen had been rough and uncaring and had smelled like a cesspit. Revulsion washed over her at the recollection of his hands ripping her clothing as he forced her back against a wall. It had been a mating, an unwilling and painful mating—nothing more. Certainly not like it would be now.

She stopped dead in her tracks. Saints preserve her,

what was she thinking? The man was still the same no matter how different he smelled, and she'd do well to remember the fact.

What was it Aimil said? A cat cannot change its ways. True enough. And even if Ewen Cameron had changed, he was still Torcall's son, and no amount of change could negate that fact.

She had sworn never again to allow Torcall to set foot on Crannag Mhór land, and now, here she was contemplating that very thing. Greeting the whoreson as if they were old friends. Letting him take his blethering son back to Tyndrum without so much as a whimper of protest. What she ought to do was slay the both of them. Now, that would be a fine vengeance.

But even as the thought entered her head, she could hear her father rattling on about honor. " 'Tis a special kind of man who can face an enemy with honor, lass. Ye'll do well in this life if ye can remember that. Hold on to yer honor, Margie, my girl, and ye'll always be strong." What good was honor, she wondered, if it kept you from avenging the people you loved?

Frustrated, she began walking again, curving up away from the bubbling burn, heading for an all but invisible path through the trees. She left the open grassland and stepped into the sunshaded cover of the wood. It was quiet and she walked along lost in her thoughts, her feet automatically following the faint trail.

"Well, well, well, if it isna Marjory Macpherson." Allen Cameron stepped into the path, blocking her way. "Out for a wee bit of a walk, are ye?"

Marjory started to back away, but Allen's hand snaked out, grabbing her firmly by the wrist.

"No' so fast, me girl. My brother may be too addled to see ye for what ye are, but I'm no' as easily fooled."

Allen tilted her chin with his other hand. "And I'll no' stand by and watch ye get away with murder."

"I've no idea what ye're talking about." Marjory flinched at his touch and struggled to escape his hold.

"Ach, but ye've got fire in ye. I like a woman with a bit o' spunk." He leered at her, his breath foul as it grazed her cheek.

She froze at his words, memory overwhelming her. The face had changed, aged and obscured by whiskers, but the voice was the same. And she still hated him. "Unhand me, Allen," she whispered.

"I think no'." His hand moved downward, caressing her neck and shoulder. "It's time ye learned yer place, and since my brother hasna the stomach for it, I might as well be the one to do it."

His fingers brushed across her breast. Marjory tried to clamp down on the fear rising inside her. She wasn't a helpless child anymore. Gritting her teeth, she kicked Allen as hard as she could. "Let go of me, you bastard. I'll no' have the likes of you touching me."

Allen swore vigorously, releasing his hold on her arm.

Marjory stepped back, turning to run into the shelter of the trees, but Allen was faster. His arms closed around her from behind like two iron bands. She struggled against his hold, letting out a bloodcurdling scream.

Allen laughed, rubbing his lower body against hers. "There's no one to hear ye, girl. We're all alone. Didna yer parents warn ye that it was dangerous to go walking alone in the woods?"

Marjory swallowed back tears, still fighting against his hold. "You killed my parents, remember?"

"Nay. You know as well as I, it was my father who had that honor. But make no mistake, I'd have done it had I the chance."

"Well, you should have killed me, too." She spat the words at him, her hatred momentarily overcoming her fear.

"And miss the chance to fill ye to the brim?" He tugged her closer, his member pressing against her thigh. "I think no'."

She looked frantically around the clearing, praying for help. But of course there was none. Fingal had warned her to take someone with her. She had landed herself in this awful mess; now she had to use her head and figure out a way to escape.

With one hand circling her wrists, Allen jerked her around to face him, pushing her back against the rough bark of a tree trunk. He licked his lips as though contemplating a morsel of food, and Marjory felt her stomach lurch in revulsion.

"I dinna take kindly to a *lady*"—he spat the word like a curse—"trying to run from me. If ye know what's good fer ye, ye'll no' try it again." To emphasize his point, he twisted her wrists with one hand and fondled her breast with the other. "I intend on having ye, girl. So ye can decide now how ye want it to be. Willing or unwilling, either way 'twill pleasure me."

His sneered at her, his eyes glinting with more than just lust. This was a man who enjoyed causing others pain.

Marjory swallowed a scream, her blood running cold.

Cameron followed the streambed as it curled upward. Rocks jutted out haphazardly, occasionally blocking his access to the water, forcing him into the undergrowth. Branches pulled at his kilt, scratching his legs, and he alternated between swearing and swatting at what seemed to be the world's most persistent mosquitoes.

He had stopped several times along the way, giving serious thought to throwing in the towel and going back to the tower. Determination kept winning the day, however, and he continued hacking a path through seemingly impassable vegetation.

All he had to do was find the pool. It should be simple to backtrack from there and find the place where he had arrived, so to speak. He grimaced and slapped at a particularly obnoxious insect. He figured his best bet for getting out of this insanity was where it had begun. All he wanted to do was go to sleep and wake up safely in the twenty-first century.

A nagging voice inside his head reminded him of the darkness and the beeping. He angrily pushed the thought aside. The darkness would be preferable to the animosity he faced here.

Even if there wasn't a plot against his life, there was still the fact that his supposed bride was a piece of work. One minute all honey and sugar, the next pure venom. Given her obvious dislike for anything Cameron, it wasn't a far stretch to imagine she wanted Ewen dead. But wanting and acting on that desire were two separate matters.

It didn't matter anyway. Whatever Marjory Macpherson did or didn't want, it had nothing to do with him. He had a place in his own world. He just had to find a way back to it. Pushing back a tangle of vine-laden branches, he moved back in line with the stream. Where was that damn pool? Surely if he could find it, he could find the rock slide. He knew it was probably naive to think that traveling through time was as simple as a place or location, but it was the best he could come up with at the moment, and a plan was a plan. He was nothing if not a man of action.

He forged ahead, ignoring the brush scraping his skin, his mind reviewing the few facts he knew about himself. Bits and pieces had been coming to him. Nothing concrete, mainly just random pictures. Visions from his past. Some places and things, a few people.

The blonde was a big part of it all. He felt a connection to her. She was important in his life. He was certain of it. He concentrated, trying to pull something more from the blank void of his memory.

A birch sapling slapped him in the face, forcing him to abandon his thoughts and slow his pace. Passing a level rock hanging out over the stream, he stopped and gingerly sat down, rubbing his stinging cheek.

This was a nightmare. And best he could tell, there was no waking up. Which only made him all the more determined to find a way back—or forward, depending on how you looked at it. With a sigh, he stood up, ignoring the aching protest of his muscles, but before he could start off again, a scream rang out from the woods behind him.

Startled, he splashed into the stream, crossing it in two strides, breaking into a run once he reached the other side. Someone was in trouble. The undergrowth soon gave way to trees, and he slid to a quick stop.

Narrowing his eyes, he could just make out two figures. From this distance it was hard to tell, but it looked like one of the two was struggling. Not wanting to draw attention to himself, Cameron moved slowly, using the trees for cover. Drawing closer, he could now clearly make out the couple; a man and a woman.

The man pushed the woman back against a tree, one arm holding her wrists, the other intent on exploring her body. From the look of things, the woman was not enjoying his attentions. The man shifted slightly, his back still turned to Cameron, but the woman came clearly into view, her frightened blue-eyed gaze colliding with his.

Marjory.

Stunned, Cameron signaled her to be quiet and tried to think what to do. He needed a weapon. Fumbling with the closure of his sporran, he felt inside for the little knife he'd found by the river. With relief, his hand closed over the horn handle. Not exactly a weapon inspiring great fear, but a weapon nevertheless.

He grasped the knife, amazed at how comfortable he felt holding it, almost as if it were a part of him, an extension of his hand. He was obviously no stranger to a dagger. Memory flashed. Startled, he forced himself to let it go. No time now for reminiscing. He'd deal with his memories after he'd rescued Marjory.

If he rescued Marjory.

Time was of the essence. Surprise was his single advantage. He tensed himself, preparing to launch an attack.

Everything seemed to happen at once. He sprang into the clearing, and Marjory gasped in surprise, hope flaring and then dying in her eyes. Her assailant turned, and Cameron raised the knife, praying that it would stand him in good stead.

But before he had a chance to advance, light hit his opponent's face and Cameron felt everything tilt off-kilter. "Allen."

His brother whirled, still holding Marjory. "Who's there?"

"Let her go, Allen." Cameron stepped into the dappled light of the clearing, still holding the knife.

"Or what?" Allen laughed. "You'll gut me with the wee knife?" He relaxed his hold, but didn't release Marjory. "I was only having a bit o' sport with her. Ye canna deny me a little fun. Especially no' when the bitch tried to kill ye."

Marjory's face drained of color. If she was feigning surprise, she was doing a damn good job if it. Either that or she was shocked that Allen knew. Cameron stood, torn between the two of them. Brother and wife. So much for not getting involved.

"No one has proved anything, Allen. And even if they had, don't you think I should be the one to exact my own revenge?" He shot a look at Marjory, who was glaring at them both. At least anger had brought color back to her cheeks.

"You've no' exactly been of a right mind, *mo bhràthair*." Allen shrugged, tightening his hold on Marjory. "Besides, time was we shared everything, did we no'?"

"Maybe. But I think I draw the line at wives. No matter how odious they may be." He shot a mocking smile in Marjory's direction and was rewarded with a sneer. So much for gratitude. "Come on, Allen. Enough is enough. Let her go."

Allen paused, studying him. Then, apparently satisfied with what he saw, pushed Marjory away. She stumbled, but before she could fall, Cameron caught her, the feel of her heart beating against his chest setting off a riot of emotion.

As soon as he was certain she'd found her balance, Cameron released her, stepping back, quelling his surging hormones. Ignoring her, he turned to face his brother. "I want you to leave her be."

Allen shot a venomous glance in Marjory's direction. "She's no' worth protecting. But I'll abide by yer wishes. At least until Father arrives."

It was a beginning.

Allen started toward a pathway off to the left, then

stopped to look behind him. "Aren't ye coming?"

Cameron shook his head, reaching out to capture Marjory's hand as she edged away. "I'm going to stay here. I need to have a word with my *wife*." He shot her what he hoped was a firm look, but given the mutinous expression in her eyes, he doubted it had any effect.

"Suit yerself." Allen shrugged. "But if I were you, I'd get a bigger knife. That one would nary skin a cat, let alone the vixen ye've saddled yerself with." With a last withering glance at Marjory, Allen walked into the trees.

Marjory released an audible breath and tried to pull free, but Cameron kept his hold, turning her so that she was facing him. "Are you all right? He didn't hurt you, did he?"

"Nay, not in the way you mean." She stared at the ground, refusing to meet his gaze. "I'm fine. If you'll just let me go, I should be getting back. People will be worried."

Despite the bravado of her words, he could feel her shaking. It seemed Marjory wasn't as impervious to fear as she'd like him to believe.

"I'm sorry he did that." Cameron wasn't certain why he was apologizing. After all, he hadn't done anything. "It's lucky I heard you scream."

"Well, dinna think I needed your help. I was going to get away. I just hadna found the right opportunity." Marjory lifted her chin in defiance, blue eyes flashing.

Cameron released her, stepping back to put distance between them. "Well, excuse me, Your High-and-Mightyship. I was only trying to help. From my perspective, it didn't look like you were exactly holding your own."

"I would have gotten away." Her eyes narrowed, but her lower lip trembled and he could see tears forming.

"Maybe so," he said, not certain how it was she could manage to make him feel concern and rage all at the same time. She was impossible. "But I didn't think I should take the chance. Saving your sweet behind seems to have become a habit."

He watched the heat rush to her cheeks, not certain which emotion inspired it. What was it about this woman? Every time they were together, he had to fight a desire to either beat or kiss her senseless. Under the circumstances, neither seemed a valid option.

"Where, may I ask, did you get my *sgian dubh*?" she asked suddenly, all emotion safely banished—no doubt to some far icy corner of her heart.

He struggled for comprehension, her words not making a lick of sense. "Your skeen what?"

"*Sgian dubh.*" She said it slowly, but the repetition didn't help. She sighed. "The little knife in your hand."

Cameron looked down, comprehension dawning. "This is yours? I found it in the pool."

"When?" She frowned, her look disbelieving.

"Just after I awoke in the woods. Before you found me. I wanted a drink, and when I knelt beside the water, the knife was there."

"Is no' possible," she scoffed. "Yer brother took that knife from me years ago. It couldna have been in the stream all that time."

"It looks as though it'd been there quite some time, actually. See for yourself." He held out the knife, and she snatched it from his hand, almost as if she were afraid he'd pull it away again. "I take it it's important to you."

She nodded, still staring at the tiny blade in her hand. " 'Twas my mother's."

"I see." He didn't see anything at all. But it was obvious that she wasn't of a mind to explain.

As if to emphasize the point, she sheathed the knife in a loop on her belt and gave him a frigid smile. "Not that I'm ungrateful for what you did"—her words lacked conviction—"but what were you doing wandering around out here on your own?"

"I could ask the same thing of you."

Marjory squared her shoulders, eyes flashing again. "I happen to be the mistress of this valley. As such, I come and go as I please."

"Well, as far as I can remember"—he grimaced—"and I'll grant you that's not far, I am free to come and go as I please, too. And before you so rudely interrupted my 'wandering,' as you called it, I was trying to find a way out of this valley and back to where I came from—wherever the hell that is." He paused for a breath, anger turning his face to stone. "And that, my dear wife," he added, his voice dripping with sarcasm, "would mean that I would be escaping you, permanently."

He turned and started back in the direction of the burn, frustration churning his gut. The woman was maddening. Though alluring. And not his wife. Hell, she wasn't even a friend. Which meant he had no ties to her and no reason to stay here. No reason at all. Which made it all the more confusing that a part of him wanted nothing more than just that.

Without looking back, he continued to crash through the brush with no regard for his exposed skin. He hardly felt the scrapes and scratches as he pushed forward toward the stream. Damn the woman, what was it about her that got under his skin? He should have let Allen have her.

Except, of course, that he wouldn't have done something like that. No matter how things had been between

Marjory and Ewen, and no matter what her father had done, no woman deserved that, no matter the century. A low-hanging branch gouged his head. He cursed but continued walking. At this rate, he'd be at the landslide site in no time.

"You're going the wrong way."

He turned at the sound of her voice, groaning in frustration. "Are you following me?"

Marjory stood by a small evergreen, its branches a perfect backdrop for her delicate beauty. Cameron caught his breath at the sight.

"I'm no' following you. I came after you. There's a difference. I dinna want you to get lost." She tried, in vain, to look nonchalant.

Cameron smiled, pleased for reasons he couldn't quite put a name to. "You did follow me."

"Very well, have it your way then. I followed you, but only to tell you you're going the wrong way. The pool lies over there." She pointed back the way they had come.

"And why, may I ask, should I trust you? If Allen is to be believed, you tried to kill me."

"Allen is a fool. If I'd wanted you dead, you wouldna be standing here blethering at me."

"And why should I believe that?"

"Because I've never lied to you. There is no love lost between us, but I've never told you anything less than the truth."

"I beg to differ. You're lying now."

Marjory colored furiously, anger making her eyes shoot fire. "About what?"

"About the reason you followed me."

"You really are insufferable."

Cameron gave her a mock bow. "I seemed to have learned from a master."

"So, tell me then, why do you think I followed you?"

Cameron smiled at the frustration painted across her face. "You are following me, Margie, my girl, because you don't want to be alone."

She blanched, her face suddenly devoid of all color. "What did you say?" Her voice was so soft he had to strain to hear it.

"I said that you don't want to be alone."

She stared at him. "No. I mean, what did you *call* me?"

Cameron frowned, trying to remember. "I don't know. Obviously something that upset you."

"You called me Margie." She sank to the ground, looking incredibly small against the backdrop of trees and foliage. Her face, if possible, turned even whiter. " *'Margie, my girl.'* "

He dropped to his knees beside her, reaching to rub her cold hands in his. "If I did, I certainly didn't mean anything by it." He continued rubbing her hands. "I was just being sarcastic."

"My father was the only one who ever called me that." She spoke as if she were lost in memory. Tears filled her eyes. She seemed to have forgotten he was even there. " 'Twas his special name for me. He'd laugh and ruffle my hair. 'Who loves you best, Margie, my girl?' he'd say. 'Who loves you best?' " Her tears were falling in earnest now.

She wiped them away with the back of her hand, valiantly fighting to pull herself back together. Cameron eased down beside her, keeping her hand in his, not really certain why, only knowing that he wanted to take the pain away. He waited for her to say more, but she remained silent. Taking a deep breath, he decided to risk her wrath.

"When did your father die, Marjory?" He waited for the storm to erupt again, but Marjory's answer was quiet.

" 'Twas just over fifteen summers ago." She looked up at him, her eyes full of pain. "Your father murdered him."

Chapter Seven

The sentence hung between them in the glade, the words almost tangible. It explained a great deal to Cameron—Marjory's fear of Torcall Cameron, her disdain for Ewen, and even her repressed feelings. His admiration increased. He didn't know too many women who could marry their father's murderer's son and still maintain a fairly sane existence.

Although, to be fair, if what Allen had said was true, then Ewen had married his mother's murderer's daughter. He shuddered at the thought. Two innocent victims caught up in what seemed to be a very barbaric world.

Without thinking he tightened his hand on hers, but she wrenched away, tears shimmering in her eyes, her body language signalling clearly that the conversation was over. Except that he didn't want it to be over. For the first time since he'd awoken on the side of the mountain, he felt a connection with someone, and no matter how fleeting, he wanted to preserve it.

"Talk to me, Marjory."

"About what?" She spat, anger flashing in her eyes. "Your father killing mine?"

"He's not my father." The words came out before he could stop them.

"Nay. You just dinna remember him. 'Tis no' the same." There was regret in her voice, and he watched as her anger deflated. "You're still a Cameron."

"So what, you hate me because of my name?"

"I dinna hate you." She sighed.

"You almost sound like you wish you could." He watched the emotions playing across her face and wished he could erase some of the pain.

" 'Twould be easier." Her smile was faint, her eyes still troubled.

"Yeah, but worthwhile things are seldom easy." Their gazes met and held. "Tell me what happened, Marjory. I need to understand."

She shook her head. "I canna. 'Twill surely tear me apart."

"No more than it's already doing."

She considered his words, then blew out a slow breath, her tears glistening in the dappled light. "Your father and my father had a long-standing feud. I canna say why. My father would never discuss it, but I know 'twas a bitter war between them. Torcall had been imprisoned by some Macphersons on the other side o' the mountains. I dinna know how long they held him, but when he was released, my father added extra guards at the pass leading to the valley.

"I o'erheard him discussing it one night with my mother. Something about revenge, but they heard me and were careful never to talk about it in my presence again." She paused.

He reached for her hand, absurdly grateful when she didn't pull away. "Go on."

"The extra guards made no difference. Torcall managed to get into the valley anyway. He arrived at Crannag Mhór with an army of men. They stormed the tower. Father made mother and I go to our quarters. We huddled in my chamber listening to the sounds of the battle outside the door. There's a connecting door between my chamber and my parents'." Her gaze collided with his. "You're sleeping in their chamber."

"I'm sorry." He wasn't certain what he was apologizing for, but he meant the words just the same. "How old were you?"

"Eight summers." She leaned against him slightly, staring straight forward, lost again in the past. "I was so afraid. My mother tried to reassure me, but you could hear women screaming outside in the courtyard. I don't know how long we sat like that. Hours maybe. Then we heard my father's voice in the next chamber, calling my mother's name.

"Mother pushed me back against a wall and hurried to join him. I pressed myself against the rough stones." She shivered uncontrollably, and he wrapped a protective arm around her. "They pressed through the thin fabric of my nightshift. They were cold and their dampness seeped into my body. I tried to press closer, willing myself to stay absolutely still.

"It was dark. All I could see were shadows. Everywhere shadows. The doorway was a dark patch, yawning open, leading to my parents and the battle. I wasna strong. I wished with all my heart that the door would stay closed and that the evil on the other side would go away without harming me.

"I wanted to cry, but I knew I couldna. I was a Macpherson. It wasna a time for crying. Father told me once that I was the bravest girl in all of Scotland. I was determined to make him proud.

"I had my *sgian dubh*—a birthday gift from Mother, for eating no' protection, but I knew it was the best defense I had. If the Camerons forced their way into the chamber, I would be ready. I could defend myself." She straightened as though ready to fight an imaginary foe.

"The ringing of steel grew louder. It was getting closer. I shifted into the corner, trying to fight my fear. It gnawed at my gut and made my hands sweat.

"Someone screamed. My mother. They were in the outer chamber. I tried frantically to find a place to hide, but there was nowhere. I clutched the *sgian dubh* and inched forward, trying to be brave, but shaking like a leaf in the wind. I dinna think I've ever been so afraid.

"I watched in horror as the door swung slowly inward, the flicker of torchlight from the adjoining chamber momentarily blinding me. I closed my eyes and then, after counting to ten, I opened them. There was a figure in the doorway, standing motionless, his face hidden by the shadows.

"I opened my mouth to scream, but at the last moment recognized the familiar bulk of my father. I released my breath. I dinna even know I'd been holding it. I ran toward him in relief only to stop again, watching helplessly as he fell to the floor. The light washed over his face and body. All I could see was blood. Everywhere blood. I threw myself down beside him, calling his name, running my hands across his face. His eyes were empty. He couldna see me. He was gone.

"I remember looking up and through the door at the crumpled heap of white linen that was Mother. Her lifeblood was ebbing away. I couldna move. I just sat there, holding my father's hand, rocking back and forth.

"There was a movement in the outer chamber. I wasna alone. A man, barely more than a boy, stood in the doorway, his great claymore dripping with blood. His eyes were narrowed and filled with a feral blood lust that sent shivers of panic knifing through me. I moved my hand slowly to the floor, feeling for my knife. I found it near my father's head. Using his body to hide it, I grasped the knife and slipped it into the folds of my night shift.

"The boy moved forward, sneering at me. He looked like a cat, a young and vicious mountain cat. He moved closer, close enough for me to see that blood spattered his face and hair. His eyes were filled with hatred. I dinna think I'd ever seen hatred like that before.

"He called to me. 'What have we here? A Macpherson brat?' He took another step toward me. He looked like a devil, an evil grin lighting his face. I held on to my knife. If only he would step closer. I knew in my heart I didna stand a chance against the monster, but for my parents' sake I vowed to make him pay at least in some small measure for what had been done this night.

"He advanced again. Only this time, he dropped his claymore and began to hitch up his shirt. I felt bile rising in my throat. He looked so strange, almost hungry, like he was going to devour me. Another man entered the chamber, and spoke to him. 'What are ye wasting yerself on that skinny child fer?' he said. 'There are lasses to be had in the buttery with far more to offer than this wee scrawny thing.'

"I stared at the huge man in the doorway and backed up a step. This was the man who had killed my family. Torcall Cameron. I was certain of it. I canna say exactly what happened next. I remember feeling rage burning in my gut and spreading through my body. I flung myself at him, my *sgian dubh* held high.

"But the boy grabbed my hands and, before I knew it, I was swinging in the air. He laughed at me. 'Ye're right, Father, I've no use for one as skinny as this.' I struggled to get down, but his grip was like a vise. His next words, I'll never forget. He said that for such a wee lass I had fire in me. Then he said, " 'Tis almost a shame we'll have to kill her. I'd have liked the opportunity to sample her in a few years.'

"Torcall laughed with his son. 'Have ye nothing on yer mind but wenching, lad? Leave the brat. She'll likely die anyway. There's no one left here to care for her. Come, we've work to do. Vengeance is served.' The boy wrenched the *sgian dubh* from my hand and with a shove sent me sprawling into a corner. My head hit the wall and I slid to the floor, trying with everything I had to hold on to consciousness. The last thing I remember seeing is a Cameron bending over my mother, searching her body."

Cameron leaned close, horrified at her story. "Was it me?" he whispered, caught up in the story, his mind reeling with the enormity of it all. "The boy?"

"Nay," she said, her gaze meeting his. " 'Twas Allen. You were away fostering that summer."

Suddenly it all made sense: Why Ewen had been chosen as the sacrificial lamb. He hadn't been a part of the atrocities of that day. He alone could come to Marjory with a clear conscience. Although, there would still have been blood on his hands.

Cameron tried to tell himself that Allen's story was probably equally horrifying. These were obviously barbarous times. But in the face of Marjory's agony, it was almost impossible to remain neutral. His stomach hurt, feeling physical pain for the young girl who had lost her childhood in an instant.

Marjory sat frozen in silence for a moment, then burst into gut-wrenching sobs. Cameron smoothed back a wayward strand of her hair. "It's all right now. It's all right." He pulled her onto his lap, rocking her gently in his arms.

She was a mercurial thing, one minute all spit and fire, the next a tormented child. They sat like that for what seemed an eternity. She sobbed into Cameron's shirt while he patted her ineffectually on the head and whispered nonsensical words of comfort. Finally, the sobbing slowed to a few hiccups.

"Are you feeling better?"

A nod against his chest signaled the affirmative. She pushed away, wiping her nose with the back of her sleeve. "I dinna know what came over me. I've never told anyone that. No' even Fingal."

Not meeting his eyes, she moved out of his lap and settled on the ground beside him. Cameron wasn't sure she realized it, but her hand was still linked with his.

"I shouldn't have told you," she whispered, her hands twisting in her lap. "You're a Cameron."

"Right now, just let me be a friend." He said the words and realized he meant them. He wanted her to trust him. It probably wasn't fair, considering he wasn't going to stay, but the feeling was there nevertheless.

"You really dinna remember any of it?" She searched his face, looking for answers he couldn't give.

He shook his head, hoping his assurance would be enough.

She sat for a moment, absorbing the sincerity of his words. "I see."

"You don't believe me, do you?" He couldn't say he blamed her. He didn't really believe it himself. Much easier to accept the idea that he was a murdering bastard than to accept that he was from another place and time. Still, at least with the latter, he kept his honor.

For all that was worth.

She pulled her hand from his and stood up, putting physical distance between them, her face purposefully blank of expression. "Nay, I dinna say that. I just find it hard to understand how your mind can be so gone that you canna remember anything about your life."

"I may not be able to prove I don't remember, but that doesn't mean it isn't the truth."

"So you've said." Her tone was dismissive. She was obviously regretting her lapse of control, and some part of Cameron responded with disappointment.

He stood, too, and laid a hand on her shoulder. "Please don't be angry."

She shook her head and stepped back, watching his hand fall to his side. "I'm no' angry. I've just had enough soul baring for one day." She looked up through the branches of the trees at the sky. "Whatever it is you're looking for out here, I dinna think you'll find it today. Nightfall is coming, and you dinna want to be out in these mountains after dark." With that, she turned resolutely and started walking back in the direction of Crannag Mhór.

Cameron stood for a moment in the quiet of the woods, his mind locked on visions of Marjory with her dying father, her childhood vanishing in an instant. Her hatred had carried her this far. Keeping her breathing, helping her to face each day.

Cameron knew something about hatred. Something important. Only as quickly as he realized the fact, the reasoning behind it slipped away, taunting him from the dark recesses of his mind.

Such hatred killed. Of that he was certain. And somehow the lesson pertained not just to Marjory, but to him as well.

With a sigh, he turned to follow her. There were wolves in the woods, and just for a moment, he relished the safety of Crannag Mhór. An oxymoron probably. But for the moment he'd simply have to live with the illusion.

Marjory paced the confines of her chamber, replaying the events of the afternoon in her head. She still couldn't believe she'd opened up to Ewen. No matter how addled, he was a Cameron, and her tale would no doubt become fodder for many an entertaining evening back at Tyndrum once her husband shared the story with his father.

If he shared it, a little voice whispered.

She stopped, staring out at the moonlit courtyard. Ewen seemed so different—changed somehow, as if he were a new man. Which of course was a ridiculous notion. No one could change like that.

Still, there was something between them, some link or connection that had surely never existed before. She shook her head, trying to clear the cobwebs, fight against her confusion. There was just so much to comprehend.

It had been so simple before Ewen's accident. Each day much like the other, filled with plans to keep the Camerons out of Crannag Mhór without breaking her grandfather's hard-won peace. There were days when it all seemed unfair, as if she were nothing more than chattel to be bargained away—but thoughts like those she kept sequestered in a dark corner of her heart.

She simply couldn't function if she allowed her emotions to hold sway. Which made her reaction to Ewen all the more confusing. She pressed her hand against the windowpane, wishing for someone to confide in. Someone who loved her.

She knew that Aimil would listen. Fingal, too, for that matter. But they'd not understand. Their world was as narrowly defined as hers, with no room in it for more than day-to-day existence—and struggle against the Camerons. For the first time in a long while, Marjory considered there might be something more.

Something better.

But as quickly as the thought came, she quashed it.

Life was what it was—nothing more, nothing less. And to fritter away time on foolish flights of fancy was for other women. Women without responsibility. This was her home. These were her people. They depended on her. And she would not let them down.

And nothing, not even the tingling warmth of Ewen's hand against hers, could be allowed to distract her. Squaring her shoulders, she turned to go to bed. A noise from the other side of the door between her room and Ewen's brought her up short.

He was awake.

She'd heard him before at night—pacing, restless, as if the demons that drove her were torturing him as well. Sometimes he even cried out.

As if to prove her thoughts, his anguished voice split the night. He was caught in a dream. She took a step forward, then stopped. It was not her battle. And despite his words, he was not her friend. There was nothing she could do.

Turning her back, she moved toward her bed, trying to ignore the sounds from the next room. He did not need her help. He did not. And saying the mantra over and over, she settled into bed, leaving her candle burning against the demons of the night.

*   *   *

It was the dream again. Cameron tried to tell himself it wasn't real, but he could feel the rain sliding down his neck, seeping into the cotton of his shirt. He fumbled with the lock, finally getting the key in and the door open. His hands were shaking and he felt emotions battling inside him. Sliding into the dark of the car, he laid his head on the steering wheel, turned the key, and reached to turn on the headlights, already knowing what came next.

The lights flashed on, illuminating the blonde. He wanted to get out of the car, to go to her, but his movements were already choreographed and his hand reached mechanically to the stick shift, sliding the powerful car into gear. He watched with alarm as the woman in front of him raised her hands, reaching out for him, pleading with him, her mouth forming the word "no."

A silent scream.

He tried to make himself shift again, but he couldn't and he sat, helpless, as his foot pressed down on the gas pedal.

Cameron jerked upright in the bed, his heart racing. He gulped air, trying to calm himself. Each time, the dream seemed a little more detailed, almost like his memory was taunting him, dancing maliciously just out of reach.

Clutching the bedcovers, he tried to reconstruct the dream in his mind, but already reality was crowding in and the dream was fading away, slipping back into the dark recesses of his subconscious. He groaned in frustration.

He wanted to remember. To help the blonde. To help himself. He'd remembered other things—vague memories of childhood, but nothing concrete, nothing that could clarify his identity. Or his relationship to the blonde.

Long-term memory came first, the small voice in his brain whispered. What he needed was stimuli, something to jog it all back, but that certainly wasn't going to happen here in the fifteenth century. He had to find a way back to his own time, to his own body.

His best chance was the landslide. He had no idea what to expect, but there had to be a door there or something. Wasn't there always a door in the movies, or *Star Trek* or something?

He sighed, running a hand through his hair. One thing was for sure: the only way to find out was to return.

But with Torcall's imminent arrival, it could be hard to get away. Ewen would be in much demand, and if his father's hatred ran anywhere near as deep as Marjory's, he'd want his son away from Crannag Mhór at all costs. Especially once Allen started spouting his theories about the landslide.

Cameron shot a look at the door that separated him from Marjory. He still did not believe the woman was a killer. Still, it was possible that someone else had rigged the fall. And whoever it was might indeed try again.

Cameron rubbed his head, confusion making it ache. The tangle of lives at Crannag Mhór seemed epic in proportion. The hatred the two clans shared bound them together in some sort of insane dance, tragedy repeating and repeating in the name of revenge.

But it wasn't *his* tragedy.

Yet, even as he had the thought, he knew it wasn't true. Whether he liked it or not, he was now a part of the pattern; and as much as he wanted to get home, he knew he also had to play his part, to try to avert further deterioration.

A seemingly impossible task. One he'd just as soon ignore. Again he looked at the door to Marjory's room, thinking of the woman behind it. It seemed he was uniquely equipped to protect Marjory Macpherson. Not that she'd actually appreciate anything he did on her behalf. The woman was really hard to figure out, one minute spilling her guts and the next retreating behind that icy facade of hers. It was enough to drive a man in any century crazy.

He sighed, knowing he had made up his mind. He would stay and watch over Marjory, but as soon as the Camerons made their exit, he was out of here. The decision acknowledged, he felt better. He was, after all, an honorable man. At least, he assumed so.

A picture of the screaming blonde popped into his mind. He again felt his foot pushing down on the accelerator and he broke out in a cold sweat, his mind scrambling to erase the vision.

He forced himself to concentrate instead on the imminent arrival of the Camerons. He'd have to try and convince Torcall that he was Ewen, and, more importantly, he had to convince him that Ewen was fine and not interested in returning to Tyndrum. How he was going to accomplish this feat he had no idea—but he knew that both Marjory's safety and his freedom depended on it.

Chapter Eight

"They've arrived."

Marjory jerked her head up from the plaid she was mending. "Where are they?"

Fingal strode into the chamber, a frown creasing his brow. "Downstairs in the great hall."

Cold beads of sweat broke out across her forehead. Torcall was here. The moment had come. "How many are there?"

"Four in the hall and about fifteen or so in the yard. I have the lads seeing to their horses."

"Added to the others there are more than enough to pose a threat. But hopefully, with Ewen well, Torcall will hold his men at abeyance. Tell me who's in the great hall."

"His man, Dougall." Fingal paused, his eyes searching her face.

Marjory raised a hand to her cheek, seeking a physical cause for his scrutiny. "Who else is there, Fingal? 'Tis best I know the worst of it."

"Ach, I suppose ye're right. Allen's there, of course."

Marjory forced an impassive expression, but Fingal saw right through it. "I wish ye'd let me deal with the bastard."

She'd told him about the attack, and Ewen's rescue. Although she still wasn't certain Ewen could be trusted, she'd felt it important to tell Fingal all of it. "What's done is done. And no harm befell me. 'Tis best we forget it."

Her captain nodded, but it didn't look as if he'd forgotten a thing.

"Who else is down there?" She forced her mind back to the coming confrontation.

"They've brought Aida with them."

Marjory felt her chest tighten. Ewen's whore, here. He had never hidden the fact that he had a mistress, but since their wedding night, he hadn't seen fit to bring her back to Crannag Mhór. Marjory flushed at the memory.

It hadn't been bad enough that their wedding night had been harsh and painful. No, Ewen had added insult to injury by taunting her with the fact that he much preferred the skilled arms of his lady love—so much so that he had left her alone after taking her and returned to his lover's embrace. She shuddered at the memory of lying alone in her shame, listening to the sounds of their passion from the adjoining chamber.

"They're asking for ye, lass."

Marjory put her sewing down and slowly rose, trying to steady herself on shaking legs. "Well, I suppose I'd best get it over with then."

Fingal moved forward, taking her arm, giving her needed support. "Have ye seen Ewen about?"

"Nay, I've no' seen him all morning." And not because she hadn't tried. She'd looked for him everywhere, but to no avail. She prayed that he hadn't picked today to go wandering in the woods. All she needed was to have to inform Torcall Cameron that his addled son had disappeared.

Fingal interrupted her thoughts. "Marjory, we've got to send someone to find him. If we canna produce him—"

"I know. But, unfortunately, producing him may have exactly the same effect. There's no telling how Torcall will react once he learns his son's mind is no' what it once was."

"There's nothing wrong with the lad's thinking, Marjory. 'Tis only that his memories are gone."

Marjory felt her eyebrows raise in surprise. Fingal's hatred for the Camerons was only surpassed by her own. "You almost sound as if you're defending the man."

Fingal looked uncomfortable. "I'll no' pretend I understand him, but I dinna think in his present state he would purposely put us in a dangerous position."

"That's no' enough and well you know it." It wasn't Ewen she was afraid of. "When Torcall finds out that his boy isna quite right, he'll no' take it peacefully. And if Allen goes on about how the accident was no' as it seemed, I guarantee Torcall will act."

"Then, we'll just have to convince him otherwise."

"And how, pray, do you imagine we'll do that?"

"I've no notion." Fingal shrugged. "But two days ago I'd never have thought that Ewen would protect you from his brother. Strange things are afoot, Marjory, and mayhap the tide is finally turning in our favor."

"You're placing a lot of faith in Ewen's change."

"Aye, that I am. But I trust my instincts. And right now, for whatever reason, Ewen appears to be willing to play his part in helping to keep the peace. And if that's so, then all he has to do is convince his father he's well.

That done, perhaps the old man will head back to Tyndrum and leave us in peace."

"A noble thought. But not one I'd want to stake my life on. Besides you're forgetting one important fact."

Fingal lifted bushy eyebrows in question.

"Ewen may yet get his memories back. And seeing Torcall might just be the key."

"Tell me everything you know about Ewen's family." Cameron stood at the edge of the lake, idly skipping stones across its glassy surface. He had already safely positioned Grania on a nearby log.

"There's no' much to tell, really." She paused. "The truth is, I dinna know much about the Camerons, save that they're enemies of the Macphersons. It began long before I came to Crannag Mhór."

Cameron stopped in midthrow. "I thought you were born in this valley."

"I was," Grania said, "but my home was always on the far side of the loch. So I dinna interact much in the affairs of those that lived in the tower."

"Until they took you in," Cameron swung around to look at Grania sitting calmly on her perch.

"Aye. When my husband died."

"So, what do you know about the Camerons?"

"Well, I do know that Torcall was imprisoned for a number of years—at Cluny, another Macpherson stronghold."

"I know that already. Marjory told me."

"She did?" Grania's voice rose slightly.

Cameron fought the urge to explain further. Marjory had spoken to him in confidence; the least he could do was honor her trust in him, fleeting though it may have been. "Yes, she did, but she didn't know why. Allen said

Dee Davis

something about his mother being killed. Is that it?"

"Could be. 'Tis an awful tale. The story goes that he was out riding with his wife, Cait, yer mother, and they came across a party of reivers. Macphersons they were. Anyway, they tried to outrun the invaders, but couldna, and in the process Torcall was captured."

"What happened to Cait? Was she captured, too?"

"Nay, she was killed in the struggle."

"Manus Macpherson did it." Allen's words made sense now.

"I never knew how. No one here ever talked of it. But I do know she was dead, with two sons left behind. You and Allen."

"Who took care of the boys when Torcall was gone?" Cameron watched as a stone he hurled bounced one, two, three, four times. It was a pity Grania couldn't see.

"I've no notion. I canna imagine it was a pleasant time for the lads, though. What with their own sweet mother fresh in the grave and their father imprisoned at Cluny."

"So, after Torcall was released, he came back to Tyndrum?"

"Aye, and soon after that, he attacked Crannag Mhór."

"What do you remember about the battle?"

"No' much. I wasna there. I'd gone to live across the loch. I only came back afterward. There was a need for my healing touch."

"I'd imagine so." Cameron sucked in a deep breath, trying to banish the sudden image of Marjory's butchered family from his head. "And when you got there, Torcall and his men were already gone?"

"Aye, they were gone. Leaving behind nothing but the dead and the injured, and most of them dying. 'Twas an awful sight. I willna easily forget it."

"You could see then?"

"Aye, I dinna lose my sight fer many more years."

"What happened to Marjory after the battle?"

"She was traumatized. I couldna even get her to speak at first, but slowly she returned to us. And then her cousins arrived to take her away to the safety of Moy."

"Moy?"

"Aye, 'tis the seat of the Mackintoshes. Her grandfather is the head of Clan Chattan. Everyone agreed she would be safe from Torcall if she remained there."

"I see. So, when was her marriage arranged?"

"Well, I dinna recollect precisely, but it wasna long after Marjory left. It was a repayment, of sorts, for all that Torcall had taken from her."

He nodded. "Marjory told me some of it, but I still don't understand how her being forced to marry her father's murderer's son is any kind of justice." Or for that matter the reverse, as it must have been for Ewen.

"I understand yer confusion, but 'tis the way of the Highlands. Malcolm"—she paused, then offered clarification—"Marjory's grandfather, no doubt wished to avoid further feuding with the Camerons. Macphersons and Camerons have always been enemies. There would have been desire on both sides to avert further hostilities. Anyway, Torcall had taken her father away from her. In the Highlands, 'tis the father who protects his wee daughters, then in turn hands them over to a husband for continued protection."

"I'd say that things are much the same in all cultures, Grania," Cameron said. He flipped a stone, but it sank without a single bounce.

"Aye, but here 'tis the only thing that stands between a wee lassie and the cold cruel world. Scotland is still a verra wild place." She shook her head as if lost in a personal memory. "Anyway, in effect Torcall took away

Marjory's protection. By marrying her off to Torcall's son, Malcolm ensured that the protection was restored, and at the same time, he ended the need for retaliation. Marjory regained all that she and her clan had lost."

"You've got to be kidding. An unwanted husband is supposed to make up for the loss of her family?"

Grania sighed. "Ye canna remember the way of it then?"

Cameron shook his head, cursing his loose tongue. He had sounded too much the foreigner just now. And even though he trusted Grania, now wasn't the time to reveal his secret.

The old woman sat patiently, waiting for his response, her face turned toward the pale rays of sunlight trying to peek through the dark clouds.

"I guess the concept is there somewhere, but when you put it in a personal context, it seems barbaric." His words sounded lame, but she seemed to accept them. He breathed a sigh of relief. He had to be more careful. It was so easy to say or do the wrong thing—something that would brand him as more than just a little off center.

"What about me? Was I happy with the decision?"

Grania shook her head. "I dinna know ye then. But 'twas easy to see ye were an angry lad. Angry about yer mother. Angry about the marriage. Nay, ye did no' tolerate the union well."

"I hurt her?" He hated that he had to ask the question, but he wanted to know.

"I dinna know for certain. Marjory does no' confide in me. But Aimil says it's so."

"Fingal's sister."

"Aye. She's a bitter woman, that one. She hates all things Cameron—especially Torcall. And because o' that she's no' a friend o' yers."

Cameron mentally added yet another enemy to his list. A noise from the surrounding brush pulled his thoughts back to the present, and he whipped around, searching out its source. A young boy broke from the cover of the trees, running to the edge of the lake.

"Mistress Marjory sent me," he gasped, his cheeks bright from exertion. "The Camerons are here, and they're asking fer ye."

"Help Grania," he barked as he sprinted for the tower, his mind trying to assimilate all that he knew about his supposed father. With or without memories it was time to face the old man—and hopefully convince him that all was right with the world.

Except, of course, that he wasn't Torcall's son.

And nothing, it seemed, was anything close to all right.

"I've told you, I dinna know where the man is. I'm no' his keeper." Marjory stood with her back to the fire. Hands on hips, she stood as tall as her small frame would allow. Her palms were sweating, but she'd be damned to hell before she let Torcall Cameron know he was scaring her.

"I want to see my son," Torcall and his henchman, Dougall, stood across from her. She watched as he fingered the hilt of his claymore. Why hadn't she thought to arm herself? It was happening all over again. She was alone, facing Torcall, with nothing but her *sgian dubh*. She felt her breath quicken as she met Torcall's eyes. They were golden like Ewen's, only Torcall's were flat, devoid of any emotion. She wondered briefly if it was a mask, or if, in fact, part of the man was dead inside.

"Do you think, Torcall Cameron, that I can produce

him with a wave o' my hand?" She glared back, hoping that she looked half as fierce as he.

"I dinna know what to think. First I've word that Ewen is dead." A shadow crossed his face, a flicker of pain, but just as quickly it was gone. "And then I'm told that he lives, but is no' himself. And now"—he frowned, his expression turning fierce—"it seems my son has disappeared entirely."

"Perhaps she's killed him, Father." Allen stood by the dais, casually sipping ale from a wooden cup.

"Wouldn't that be a daft thing for me to do?" Marjory shot him a murderous look. "After all, you yourself saw your brother only yesterday. I'd hardly expect to get away with murdering him at this late date, now, would I?"

"Allen, stop with your nonsense. The girl isna stupid." Torcall eyed her speculatively. "But I wouldna put it past her to have sequestered him away from us."

"I've done no such thing. You act is if the man hasna a will of his own."

Torcall searched her face. "Allen tells me the accident was no' what it seemed."

"Allen lies." She stood toe to toe with him, lifting her face to meet his gaze. He towered over her, but she held her ground, determined not to let a Cameron get the better of her.

There was a grumble from the dais, but neither Torcall nor Marjory broke their stance to look.

"And why, may I ask, should I believe you over my son?" Torcall's eyes narrowed, his hand still on his claymore.

"Because your son lives. Had I ordered his death, you can be certain I would no' have failed." She'd had this conversation before—with Ewen. Like father, like son.

Suddenly Torcall Cameron threw back his head and laughed. "Ye've spirit in ye, lass, I'll give ye that. 'Tis possible yer grandfather was no' so daft as he seemed. Ye'll give Ewen strong sons." He sobered. "Assuming he's still capable of performing the act."

This time there was laughter from the dais. "If he's no', *I'll* be more than happy to oblige."

Torcall turned to his younger son, his eyes full of warning. "I'll no' have ye taking what belongs to yer brother."

Despite herself, Marjory shot Allen a triumphant look, surprised to see resentment coloring his expression. It seemed Ewen was the favored son. "I'll thank ye to stay away from me, Allen Cameron."

Torcall reached out to grasp her chin, moving faster than she'd have imagined from so big a man. "Ye'll do what ye're told, girl. Make no mistake about it. Ye belong to the Camerons as surely as if ye'd been bought and paid fer." His fingers dug into the tender skin of her neck, and she felt a shiver of fear run down her spine. "Understand this—I canna abide ye or yer kin. The only reason ye're breathing at all is to give Ewen an heir. Once that's accomplished, we'll see who it is that has an accident."

She tried to break free, but his hold was too strong. She fumbled to draw her *sgian dubh*.

"Nay," Torcall snarled, his other hand closing on her wrist. "I'll no' fall for that again."

"Unhand her." Fingal entered the great hall, his claymore drawn, shaking his head in answer to her unasked question.

Dougall, who had so far not uttered a word, seemed to spring to life at the sight of Crannag Mhór's captain.

Sliding his own claymore from its sheath, he pivoted to face Fingal, his eyes narrowing to slits.

Three more Camerons materialized from the doorway, their swords drawn as well. All eyes were on Torcall, waiting for a command. Marjory hadn't the voice to cry out. And she knew even if help did arrive, it would be too late.

The events of fifteen years ago were unfolding again, and once more she was powerless to stop them.

"Where is my son?" Torcall hissed.

"I told ye, I dinna know."

Dougall moved into a fighting stance, his grip tightening on the hilt of his sword.

"Perhaps if yer man dies, 'twill loosen yer tongue." Torcall inclined his head toward Fingal.

Almost immediately, a ringing noise sounded through the room as Dougall thrust forward, his sword glancing off Fingal's.

"Perhaps it is your man who will die." The words were out before she had time to think better of them, anger overriding all practical thought.

Fingal circled to Dougall's left, successfully moving the fight away from Marjory, his face a tight mask of concentration. "Come on, *Cameron*," he urged. "Let's have a taste o' yer blood."

Dougall moved a step closer. "It'll take more than the likes o' you to get it, Macgillivray," he growled and lunged forward. Fingal countered, metal striking metal with a deafening clang.

"Stop!" Marjory screamed above the din, anger superseding everything else. Jerking free of Torcall, she moved forward a step, hands held out beseechingly. "I willna have it. No' in this house. No' again."

The two men stopped for an instant, stunned. But just

as quickly they turned back to each other, intent on their fight. They moved apart and then together, thrusting and parrying, two dancers in a death dance.

Dougall drew first blood. Fingal cried out in anger, his next thrust going wide of the mark. Dougall turned and caught the edge of Fingal's sword, pushing it backward until his opponent was forced to drop it. With another deft twist, the point of Dougall's claymore rested against Fingal's neck.

"What the hell is going on here?"

Silence descended. All gazes went to the man coming through the archway. Marjory exhaled slowly as Ewen walked into the great hall, his eyes locked on Dougall. The champion shot a questioning look at Torcall, but Torcall had eyes only for his son.

"Ewen?" Torcall frowned as if he wasn't sure it was, in fact, his son.

Fingal used the opportunity to move away from Dougall, and Marjory rushed to his side.

"Hello, Father," Ewen said, his eyes locked on the older man.

Marjory's heart nearly stopped. He'd remembered. Holy Mary, mother of God, he'd remembered who he was.

Chapter Nine

Cameron stood in the doorway, trying desperately to sort out the players. He knew Allen of course, and the man with the tangle of graying hair was clearly Torcall Cameron. But the man who'd almost skewered Fingal was a stranger. As were the other giants standing watch over the old man.

Marjory had rushed to Fingal, her face blanched of all color, her eyes unusually large. Fingal was brushing her aside, his claymore still drawn, the blood on his arm apparently only a scratch.

Tension in the room was tight enough to sever an artery without a scalpel, and Cameron felt himself the unintentional vortex of the whole thing. Or Ewen Cameron was. He wished desperately that the door—or whatever the hell it was that had transported him here—would open and send him home, leaving these people and their feud behind.

Except that he didn't like the idea of leaving Marjory to be hurt.

"Ye know me?" Torcall asked, his words pulling Cameron from his thoughts. "They said ye dinna remember anything. But ye know me." The old man smiled, and despite everything he had heard, Cameron smiled back. Whatever Torcall Cameron's faults, the man clearly loved his son. Unfortunately, his son was most likely dead. It was only his body that lived on—with someone else in it.

"I don't remember." Cameron shook his head regretfully. "It's just that there's a resemblance. And I assumed you were . . . my father." He'd been about to say Ewen's father, but corrected himself just in time.

Disappointment washed across Torcall's face, the emotion making him look suddenly older. Cameron immediately wished he had said something different. Something that wouldn't have taken the light from the old man's eyes.

By contrast, Marjory was breathing easier, the color returning to her cheeks. He shot her a questioning glance, but she ducked his gaze, fussing instead over Fingal. The other men had relaxed slightly. It seemed his arrival had averted the killing—at least for now.

"Come, let me have a look at ye." Torcall moved closer, his head tilted as he studied what he believed was his son. "Ye shaved yer beard."

Cameron nodded, allowing the older man to trace the side of his cheek with a finger. It was a father's touch, and despite the fact that it wasn't *his* father, he relished the contact. He'd felt so isolated here.

"I thought she'd killed ye, boy." Torcall's voice turned gruff, and he pulled Cameron into a bear hug.

Across the old man's shoulder, Cameron's eyes locked with Marjory's. Her glare was an indication that she'd heard Torcall's comment. He shook his head slightly, indicating she should keep quiet, but the action only seemed to infuriate her more.

"I did naught to endanger your son, Torcall. If you dinna believe me, ask him yourself." She marched forward, blue eyes shooting sparks.

Torcall released Cameron, stepping back so that he could see them both, his brows raised in question.

Cameron knew this was a test of some sort, a moment when he had to commit to one side or the other: Cameron or Macpherson. The warmth of his reunion with his father evaporated. He had no father. He had nothing. This was all a charade, none of it real. At least not for him. Still, he held back, both Marjory and Torcall waiting for his answer.

"I dinna think he can say anything for certain, Father," Allen interjected, his eyes knowing, judgmental, as if he'd read Cameron's thoughts. "He doesna remember falling, and he seems to have forgotten who his enemies are as well." He shot a pointed look at Marjory, and then returned his knowing gaze to Cameron.

"I remember everything that has happened since then, Allen." If his brother could play rough, so could he. Even without knowing Torcall Cameron, he was fairly certain the man would side with Ewen over Allen, and the events in the wood the previous day could certainly be played to advantage.

Allen obviously recognized his plan, because he dropped his gaze, reaching instead for a cup of ale.

Cameron turned to face Torcall. "I've been treated well here, Father. As if I were one of the household." It was a bit of an exaggeration. The lady of the house hadn't exactly welcomed him with open arms, but there *had* been moments. He smiled in Marjory's direction,

114

satisfied to see her flinch. A little guilt wouldn't hurt her.

"I'm glad to hear it." Torcall seemed to have missed all the undercurrents running through the room, or perhaps he simply chose to ignore them. Wrapping his arm around his son, he drew him close again. "And there's no worries now that I'm here. I'll make certain"—his solemn gaze met first Fingal's, then Marjory's, his eyes flashing a warning—"that no harm comes to ye."

Cameron should have been comforted, but he wasn't. Truth was, he had no idea whom to trust. Common sense favored his father, but his instincts told him that he could trust Marjory. Or maybe he just wanted it to be so. Maybe none of them were to be trusted.

Then again, perhaps they shouldn't be trusting him either. After all, he was lying too. His head ached with the enormity of everything that was happening.

"You're no' well." Marjory was instantly by his side, her arm slipping around him, her touch soothing and exciting him all at the same time.

He smiled down at her, grateful for the support.

Torcall frowned at the two of them. "I dinna ken ye'd grown to tolerate each other."

"I'll no' let a man fall just because he's my enemy's son." Marjory tightened her hold on Cameron in defiance.

"I told ye, there's more going on here than we were told." Allen moved closer, his eyes on his father.

"Nay." Torcall waved him away. "I dinna think helping a mon means anything more than just that. Besides, 'tis far easier to get a wench with child if she's no' fighting every inch o' the way."

Marjory released Cameron so suddenly he stumbled. "I'll no' be a broodmare for a Cameron."

"Ye'll do what ye're told, girl." Torcall shook a finger in her direction, and Fingal moved to stand between them, tensions rising again to battle proportion.

"Leave her be," Fingal growled.

"I'm no' afeared of ye, Fingal Macgillivray. Ye know as well as I that powers higher than either of us demand an heir. 'Tis no' my order, but the lairds of Clans Cameron and Chattan."

Fingal nodded, accepting the inevitable.

Marjory's face turned red. "I'll have a say in my own life, thank you very much, and I tell you now—I willna spread my legs just because ye say so."

Cameron reached out to soothe her, but she shook his arm off, her temper holding sway.

"Dinna threaten me, girl," Torcall barked, "or I'll see that he beds ye tonight, injury or no'."

Marjory clenched her fists and took a menacing step forward. Cameron wanted to hold her back, to try and talk some sense into her, but he knew she'd just push him away. So, instead, he shot an imploring look at Fingal, whose pulse was now beating visibly at his temple, his face turned an angry red.

Fingal took a step toward Marjory, intent on intercepting her, but before he could reach her side, a blond woman burst into the room, eyes wide with joy. "Ewen, *mo chridhe,* 'tis true, ye're really alive."

She rushed to his side, her long hair flying. At first Cameron thought it was the woman from his dream, his heart stopping at the thought, but as she drew nearer he realized the likeness was only superficial. Still, she was a beautiful woman, and it was more than obvious she cared about Ewen. Her green eyes sparkled as she approached.

Unfortunately, he had no idea who the hell she was.

He shot a quick look at Marjory, hoping for guidance. Instead, he found her narrow-eyed, practically spitting nails. No help from that corner. He racked his brain for some clue to the woman's identity.

"Aida was heartbroken to think ye gone, Ewen," Torcall said.

Aida. This was the mistress then. The one Allen had talked about. No wonder Marjory was frowning. With a whirl of petticoats, the girl closed the distance between them, her arms encircling his waist, the scent of lilac clinging to her hair. It was intoxicating. Hell, *she* was intoxicating.

"I missed ye so much, Ewen." Tears filled her lovely eyes. "And when they said ye were dead, I wished I could follow ye to the grave." Aida smothered his face with tiny kisses, her breath wet and warm on his cheek.

Cameron pulled out of her embrace, more than a little overwhelmed. Given the circumstances, he couldn't exactly blame Ewen for sleeping with the woman. She was a hell of a package. But judging from the look on Marjory's face, he also knew how much it had hurt her. Not because she cared about Ewen, of course; she quite obviously didn't. But Marjory's pain was because this infidelity had been an insult of the highest order, a rejection at a soul-deep level that would tear at a person's pride.

Cameron hated the idea of infidelity, no matter the reason. And, for a moment, he felt nothing but disgust for the man he was supposed to be. He knew the pain of broken promises only too well.

A memory flitted through his brain, tantalizing him with truth, but it dissipated before he could understand its true meaning. With a grimace, he disentangled himself from the blonde, suddenly feeling smothered by her fragrance and her presence. Oddly enough, he found that he preferred the clean smell of Marjory. Hell, he even preferred her acerbic comments to this fluff of a girl, no matter how pretty she was.

He turned to find her. She was standing alone by the window, her face even paler than usual, her eyes riveted on him and the blonde, who was now clutching at his arm, trying to regain his attention. Without a word, she pivoted and ran from the room.

Cameron fought an urge to follow. But he wasn't yet ready to choose sides. He told himself the decision was as much for Marjory as for himself, but he knew it was the coward's way out. He was not the heroic type.

Not that he owed anything to Marjory or to anyone here. But still, a part of him yearned for something more: a commitment, a sense of belonging. The idea was as frightening as it was foreign and he swallowed the thought whole, turning instead to the girl on his arm.

"Fingal, we just have to tolerate them until they're gone." Marjory sat on the edge of a rickety chair by the kitchen fire, her fingers laced so tightly together she could feel the blood pounding through them.

Fingal was pacing in front of her. "I dinna like the way things are going. First the fight with Dougall, then Torcall's threats, and now Ewen thicker than thieves with them in there."

Marjory glanced in the direction of the great hall. Both clans had settled for dinner, sitting on decidedly opposite sides of the room: Two armed camps within the confines of Crannag Mhór. And Ewen was sitting with the enemy, his mistress draped over him like a simpering cat. "Ewen is a Cameron. Even if he canna remember them."

"True enough. But I thought perhaps he'd changed."

Aimil looked up from the dish she was washing with a knowing snort. "That'd be the day."

" 'Tis true, Aimil," Marjory defended. "He saved me in the woods from Allen."

"No doubt because it suited him." Aimil looked to her brother for support. "Ye know that's the way of it."

Fingal shook his head, his expression pensive. "I'm no' so sure, sister. There's also the fact that he caught her in the courtyard when she fell."

"An instinctive act, nothing more." Aimil shrugged.

"No. 'Twas more than that." Marjory felt heat washing across her face at the memory: Ewen's strong arms around her, his scent enveloping her, teasing her senses.

"Ye see only what ye want to see." Aimil put down the rag she'd been using to clean the tabletop. "Mayhap it's a trick to get ye to breed with him."

The thought had occurred to her, but she couldn't believe Ewen—*this* Ewen—would do such a thing. He'd been so gentle in the clearing when she told him about her parents. So understanding. Never mind that it hadn't lasted long; the fact that it had been there at all meant something, surely?

Fingal growled deep in his throat. "If bedding was all he wanted, he'd no' have to go to all this trouble."

Marjory shivered, and Aimil shot her brother an angry look. "Ye're as bad as the lot of them. Thinking a man can just have his way with a lass whenever he desires."

Fingal held out a hand. "I dinna mean that and well you know it. I was merely saying that Ewen's done more for Marjory since he fell than the entire time he was with her before."

"He stopped the fighting today as well. And defended me to his father. The old Ewen wouldna have done that."

"Ye're both as addled as he is," Aimil snapped, scorn

119

coloring her voice. "A clean-shaven face is no' a rebirth. And just because he's chosen to help ye on occasion, it doesna mean that he's a new man. Only that there's something in it for him."

"I'm telling ye, I see something different in the lad. He's no' the same." Fingal stroked his beard thoughtfully.

"I see it, too. And he did save me on more than one occasion."

"Ach." Aimil threw her hands in the air. "Ewen this, Ewen that. To hear ye both talk, ye'd think he was a bloody saint."

Marjory stared in openmouthed wonder. She'd never seen Aimil angry.

"I tell ye, ye'd both do well to remember that only a few nights ago he was Ewen Cameron and ye counted him as an enemy. I've said it before, and I'll say it again—no one changes that much." With a thump, she set a full jug on the table. "Now get back out there and take this ale. Enemies or no', I willna have it said that I'm no' hospitable to guests."

Marjory watched as Fingal picked up the jug and marched out of the kitchen without another word.

Aimil turned to her, shaking a finger. "Mark my words, girl, you watch yer back tonight. 'Tis a bedding Torcall Cameron wants, and Ewen has always complied with his father's wishes."

"If I have to bed him to hold on to Crannag Mhór, then so be it." The words were out before Marjory could think about them, and she realized with dismay that a part of her actually wanted to share a bed with Ewen— the new Ewen. She felt heat rushing to her cheeks.

"Dinna be daft, girl. Once ye produce a bairn, yer life isna worth a dram o' whiskey."

"You dinna know that. Perhaps he'll protect me."

"Ye're a fool if ye think a Cameron is capable of anything but deceit. Believe me when I tell ye that." Two bright spots of color marked the centers of Aimil's cheeks, and Marjory knew they were no longer talking about Ewen. "I love ye like ye were my own, Marjory Macpherson, and I'll no' let the likes o' Ewen Cameron make a fool o' ye."

"He's no' going to do that, Aimil," she argued—unable for the life of her to imagine why she was defending the man. But here she was doing it just the same. And the truth was, she believed it. Believed that she could trust him. Just like that, her heart had made the decision without even consulting her brain.

" 'Tis too late, then," Aimil mumbled under her breath, scrubbing furiously at an iron pot.

"What did you say?"

Aimil looked up defiantly. "I said ye're more of a fool than I thought. And I predict this night will mark the end of Crannag Mhór."

Cameron shifted, trying to edge away from Aida's grasp. The woman was leechlike. She hadn't left his side all day, which meant that he hadn't been able to find time alone with Marjory.

Torcall, too, had become a permanent fixture. Cameron had to admit Ewen's family loved him. But in a way that love was smothering. As if he couldn't be trusted to breathe on his own.

To add to the confusion, Allen had become downright surly. When Ewen was present, as far as Torcall was concerned, his youngest didn't exist. At least it explained the hints of anger, the veiled hostility. Allen clearly had no love for his brother. But, thankfully, he was too afraid of his father to do anything about it.

Dysfunctional at best. Still, it was a family—something Cameron had never known. Again his memories threatened to reveal themselves, only to pull away again like the tide from the shore.

Cameron looked up as Marjory stepped through a small door near the fireplace. Accompanied by Aimil, she walked to the dais and sat down, reaching for a platter of meat. Despite the tension running through the room, she seemed calm, smiling at something Fingal said, the dimples in her cheeks making her seem softer. It occurred to him that Marjory didn't laugh enough, and unfortunately he was sitting with the people who were the cause of that.

Following his gaze, Torcall glanced at the dais. "She's comely enough fer a Macpherson. At least yer job will no' be as odious as if she were ugly."

Cameron frowned. "It's not a job I relish for any reason."

Torcall shook his head. "Yer talking daft, boy. 'Tis no' about what ye want, 'tis about what's best fer the Camerons. That, and avenging yer mother." His eyes narrowed in remembered hatred.

"My mother." Cameron said the words without any emotion. There came no picture, no memory at all. Whoever his mother had been, she was lost in the black chasm of neurons and gray matter. No longer a part of his conscious mind.

"Ye canna remember." Torcall's eyes were sad.

Cameron shook his head.

"Ye look just like her. Yer hair, yer eyes. She was the most beautiful woman that ever lived. And I loved her with every breath in my body."

"But she died." Cameron whispered, afraid to break the spell. Torcall was different somehow when he spoke of Cait, as if time had rolled backward and taken away the pain etched in the lines of his face.

"Aye. At the hand of Manus Macpherson." The man nodded toward the dais, his expression darkening again.

"Allen told me some of it. But not how it happened."

Torcall pulled his attention back to Cameron, searching his face as if trying to reassure himself he was truly looking at his son. " 'Tis hard to fathom ye could forget such a thing. But then, ye weren't present that day." He reached for his ale cup and drained it. "We were out riding. Yer mother always loved to ride." He smiled, lost in his past. " 'Twas a beautiful day, and the world was ours—until we rounded a bend and found the *reivers*."

"Reivers?"

Torcall shot him a quizzical look, and Cameron cursed his stupidity. "Cattle thieves. Macphersons, they were. Wild in their lust to capture the herd. We tried to pull back out of sight, but 'twas too late. They'd seen us. In a moment we were surrounded, outnumbered and defenseless." His fist tightened at the memory. Cameron felt his pain.

"I asked them to let Cait go. To take me fer ransom and leave her to her sons. But Manus would no' hear of it. He wanted her. I could see it in his eyes. But my Cait was a fighter, and she refused to surrender, instead moving her horse away, saying her bairns needed her and she'd no' go peacefully.

"Manus laughed. I can still hear it. Then he charged at her, his steed twice as big as the mare she rode. The wee beast took fright and reared back. Cait flew off and landed against a tree, her neck broken. I held her in my arms until she died.

"I wanted to kill him, but there were too many of them and I had you and yer brother to think about. So I let them take me." He reached for a pitcher to refill his tankard, then drank deeply. "So ye see, my son, there can be no room in yer heart for anything other than revenge."

"But wasn't that what happened here when you killed Marjory's parents?"

"How is it ye remember that and no' yer own mother?" Torcall's voice rose in anger, and Allen looked up in speculation.

"I *don't* remember. Someone told me."

Torcall studied him for a minute, then nodded. "The raid was meant as revenge. A way to honor yer mother. And for a while it was enough. But there was talk of Macpherson retaliation, with more than just our two families involved, and so the lairds came together to find a *solution*." He spat the word as if it were poison. "Yer marriage was the outcome. I've no mind telling ye that I'd as soon have seen ye marry the devil himself as Manus's spawn, but I had no choice in the matter."

"And now you think if Marjory bears a child it will be the end of it all?" Cameron wasn't sure he followed the logic.

"I'd rather run her through with a claymore, but it canna be so. And if it canna, then what better revenge than to take Crannag Mhór? Manus loved this valley more than he loved life itself. And since he took what I loved best . . ."

"You'll take what was his."

"Aye." Torcall nodded, slamming a fist upon the table. " 'Tis how it must be done."

Of that, Cameron had no doubt. But revenge came at a price, and not just to those who were on the receiving end. The Camerons and the Macphersons were living proof. One death had led to others, and they in turn would lead to more. It was a never ending cycle fed by hatred.

Hatred that couldn't be stopped unless someone with little to lose could step in and make things change.

It was a heady thought, but one he did not want to accept. He was simply in the wrong place at the wrong time. He refused to acknowledge the idea that he might have been sent here for a reason. He didn't believe in things like cosmic intervention.

He was a man of science.

And more importantly, he was a man who wanted to go home.

Chapter Ten

Cameron had had enough toasting to last his entire life. At least, he was pretty sure he had. He'd know for certain when he could think clearly again. He tried to focus on the fire in the fireplace, but its hypnotic dance made him queasy. Best he could remember, they'd drunk their way well into the night.

The Cameron contingency that is. Most of the Macpherson clan had skipped the festivities, and those in earlier attendance had been stoically silent. Marjory of course hadn't stayed. She'd finished her dinner and left with the frigid regality of a queen.

She hadn't spared him so much as a glance, making it more than clear she thought him a defector. Although, it wasn't entirely apparent why he should do anything less. She'd consistently rejected him, even when he'd tried to save her. Hell, he *had* saved her, and gotten nothing but ice in return.

Damn the woman. He burped noisily—which seemed to be the order of the day for Cameron men—and drank from his cup. In truth, he didn't need Marjory. He had

Aida. No smart mouth on that one, just plain old ado-
ration. She was up there somewhere, right now, waiting
for him. He looked toward the stairs, surprised to see
that there were two sets.

"Have some more, Ewen. We'll drink to yer health."
Torcall held up his cup, sloshing ale over the rim.

Cameron tried to shake his head, to signal that he'd
had more than enough, but the gesture was more than he
could handle. Besides, it wouldn't have stopped Torcall
anyway. The man was a bottomless pit.

"To my heir," His pseudo-father called, and the Camerons all dutifully hoisted their cups.

"To Ewen," Dougall bellowed, seeming no worse for
wear. Which was amazing considering the amount of ale
he'd personally put away.

"To my brother." Allen's toast lacked sincerity, but
Cameron had already realized that there was no love lost
between them.

Like Dougall and Torcall, Allen seemed to be in no
danger of succumbing to the effects of the alcohol. For
just a moment, Cameron wished for the man's genes. Or
at least a stouter stomach.

His father waited expectantly. Never one to disappoint,
Cameron focused on both of his cups, concentrating until
there was just one, and, with a satisfied grin, lifted it in
salute, somehow managing not to spill.

Looking around at the assembled group, he realized
there was not a Macpherson left. It was only the diehard
Camerons that remained, and evidently they intended to
stay until the keg ran dry—a practice he fervently hoped
was not a nightly routine. If so, he'd pickle his liver
before he had a chance to figure a way out of this mess.

"Are ye listening to me, boy?" Torcall asked. "I want

to know when ye're going to end this thing and get the woman with child."

Torcall wanted an heir to Crannag Mhór, and he wanted Ewen to provide one. Which meant that Cameron had to sleep with Marjory. But that was impossible, considering the woman could barely keep a civil tongue in her head when talking to him. If she couldn't stand the sight of him, she was hardly likely to allow a seduction.

"She doesn't like me." Cameron blinked his eyes slowly, trying to focus. His tongue seemed thicker than usual. Not to put too fine a point on it, but he would hazard to guess that, whoever he'd been, he wasn't a drinker. He certainly didn't have the stamina of these guys. "Don't see how I can make love to her if she's not interested." He jerked his thumb toward the stairs, dismayed to see that there were still two sets.

"Since when has a bit o' spite stopped a Cameron?" Torcall asked. "Sometimes a man has to take what he wants. Besides, all ye have to do it get the wench with child. Allen can handle the rest."

The two men exchanged glances.

"Handle what, exactly?" Cameron waited, trying to clear his mind. He sensed that this was something important.

Allen sneered. "Dinna fash yerself, brother." He bent close to Cameron's ear, his breath making Cameron want to puke. "Yer part is simple. I reckon ye can do it in yer sleep."

Cameron tried to make sense of the conversation. "What do you mean? Do what in my sleep?" He closed his eyes, the room starting to spin. He opened them, forcing himself to focus on the nearest object, which happened to be Dougall's face.

"Plant yer seed. That's the important thing." Dougall's

words had begun to slur, but Cameron couldn't figure out whether Dougall's mouth or his own ears were responsible.

The other men nodded in agreement.

"And I, fer one, am no' leaving until I'm sure ye've done just that." Torcall straddled a bench, apparently prepared to wait it out right on the spot.

Cameron sobered instantly, panic rising. Surely they weren't serious. "These things take time. You can't be away from Tyndrum that long." The minute the name of Torcall's home came out of his mouth he worried that he'd said it wrong, but his father didn't seem to notice. Cameron sighed, relief flooding through him.

"Aye, 'tis the truth, Torcall. Ye canna leave the holding unattended fer too long. Yer enemies are sure to hear o' it and take advantage," Dougall agreed.

"I've an idea, Father." Drinking had only made Allen more odious. Cameron had the feeling he wasn't going to like what was coming next.

"All right, Allen me boy, let's hear it." Torcall staggered over to his son and slapped him heartily on the back. A smaller man would have been sent sprawling.

Allen eyed Cameron, his expression veiled. "Well now, lads—I say we make sure that Ewen is doing his best to make sure there's truly a Cameron in the Macpherson's belly."

Dougall looked confused. "I dinna ken what ye're saying."

"I'm saying we should watch."

"Watch what?" Dougall's eyebrows drew together as he tried to follow the conversation.

Cameron felt a dawning of comprehension and the curl of revulsion in the pit of his stomach.

"I say . . ." Allen paused to make sure his father was

129

listening. "We go with Ewen and watch him take the slut upstairs."

"Aida?" Dougall drained his cup with a single swallow and reached for the pitcher to refill it.

Allen grabbed the earthenware jug, refilling his own cup. "Nay, man, I mean his Macpherson wife."

Cameron tried to think of something to halt the conversation, but his ale-numbed mind was too slow.

" 'Tis a grand idea." Torcall downed his ale, wiping his face with his sleeve. "Just like old times."

Cameron had no idea what that meant and, frankly, he wasn't sure he wanted to know. Allen reached for his cup and filled it to the top. Cameron sipped from it absently, trying to find a way out of this new predicament. "You know, Marjory isn't going to cooperate—"

"Since when do ye care if she cooperates? She'll do as she's told. If ye canna stomach the task, brother, I'll be glad to serve in yer place."

The thought made Cameron choke. No way would he let Allen touch Marjory again. "Thanks, Allen, but I believe I can handle my wife." He met Allen's lust-filled gaze. "And I don't need witnesses." Absolutely freaking right he didn't. There wasn't going to be a bedding.

"All right then, no witnesses. But the least we can do is walk ye to the door." Torcall started for the stairs, swaying slightly.

"Now?" Cameron felt bile rising.

"Seems as good a time as any." Torcall squinted, studying him. "Dinna worry, lad, we'll no' get in yer way. We'll stay just outside the door. Ye'll never know we're there." He laughed loudly, ending with a belch. "After all, a man deserves a little privacy, does he no'?" He cuffed his son's cheek.

Dougall and Allen laughed heartily. The whole group

headed for the stairs. Cameron swallowed convulsively. Oh, God, what had he gotten himself into? Worse still, what had he gotten Marjory into?

The stairs were narrow and circular, connecting only with the family's private rooms. Even with torches, the passageway was dark. It was a difficult trek in the daylight, sober, but in the dark, reeling from all the beer, it was close to impossible. Dougall made it about ten steps before he started retching.

"Leave him then. He can follow when he's able," Allen led the way, obviously looking forward to the coming voyeurism.

Cameron tried to still the spinning in his head long enough to come up with a way out, but his brain was on cruise control and nothing seemed to be working. The only consolation he had was that he'd bet a fortune his "equipment" was also on cruise control and, therefore, beyond what was expected.

They reached the top of the stairs and entered the passageway. Cameron half hoped to find Fingal sleeping outside Marjory's door, but the hall was empty. Allen moved back with an exaggerated bow.

"After you, *mo bhràthair.*"

Cameron stepped forward. His heart pounded in his chest, a combination of the climb and nerves. He forced himself to calm down. Now was not the time to panic. He could handle this. All he had to do was convince Marjory to go along with him and give Torcall and company a show. Maybe if it was good enough, his pseudo-father would head back for Tyndrum and leave him in peace to find the doorway out of this hellhole.

"Where is everyone?" Dougall boomed from the top of the stairs. Evidently, he'd regained control of his stomach.

"Quiet. We dinna want to wake the lass. So much better if it's a surprise," Allen whispered loudly enough to wake the dead. "Don't ye agree, Father?" They reached Marjory's door, and Allen moved to open it.

"Nay, Allen, I told ye we'll wait out here. I'd wager we'll be able to hear enough."

Allen sullenly stepped aside, and Cameron moved forward, carefully turning the heavy iron handle on the door. Nothing happened.

"The bitch has locked us out." Allen looked crestfallen. Cameron fought the urge to punch him.

"Nay, all is no' lost, lads. There's a connecting door in Ewen's room." Allen smiled triumphantly.

The three of them were acting like little boys, but they were *big* little boys and Cameron didn't want to rile them. He moved down the hallway with a sigh, pulling open his door when he came to it.

The others pushed past into the room. Cameron entered slowly, wishing himself anywhere but here. He prayed that the connecting door would be locked, too, but before he could finish the thought, Allen had swung the door open on its heavy hinges.

Torcall gave Ewen a little push. "Remember—the sooner ye get her with child, the sooner ye'll be free o' her."

Cameron paused at the doorway, looking into the black room.

"Have no fear, son, 'twill be o'er afore ye ken it. I canna blame ye fer no' wanting to bed a Macpherson, but ye've done it afore, and 'tis fer the good o' yer clan. Think o' it as yer duty." His father placed a heavy hand in the middle of Cameron's back and shoved him into the room.

The firelight was dim, but Cameron could make out

the shape of Marjory's body curled upon the bed. He reached behind him to close the door.

"Trying to rob us o' our fun, brother?" Allen's beefy hand closed around the edge of the door, preventing it from fully closing.

Cameron sighed and moved to the bed on silent feet. He stood for a moment, letting his eyes adjust to the gloom. He could barely make out Marjory's features. She slept soundly, one hand tucked under her head, the other sprawled out. She was so tiny, she barely covered one half of the massive bed.

He felt like a letch. Or worse. But the idea of facing the gang outside the door drove him onward. It wasn't as if he were going to go through with it; he just had to convince Marjory to put up a show.

Easily said. Not so easily done. And even if he could convince her, she'd probably never forgive him. Still, anything less and Torcall would see him as a traitor. Far better to endure the sharpness of Marjory's tongue than to feel a blade between his shoulder blades. Not exactly his finest moment.

He reached for the pin at his shoulder. In the past few days, he had actually become fairly adept at removing his strange garments, and in less than a minute he stood by the bed in his woolen underwear.

The key was to keep her quiet long enough to explain things, while at the same time convincing Torcall and crew that he was ravishing her. Drawing a deep breath, he placed a hand across Marjory's mouth and straddled her, using his body to pin her to the bed. She came awake in an instant, her eyes wide with fear. At that moment, he'd have gladly traded his life to erase the look on her face, but it was too late; the damage was done. She struggled beneath him, trying to free her hands, but he kept them pinned, one with his knee and the other with his free hand.

"Hold still," he whispered. "I'm not here to hurt you. Torcall and crew are outside." He tilted his head in the direction of the other room. At the sound of Torcall's name, Marjory stopped struggling, her eyes still wary. "They're waiting for a show. I think, if we give it to them, they'll go away, maybe even leave here altogether. But I need your cooperation. Nod if you understand."

She stared up at him, eyes narrowed in anger, her doubt evident even in the shadows.

"Look, Marjory, I know how this seems, but I haven't got time for long explanations. Just go along with me. Please? I promise I'll keep you safe. Okay?"

Again their eyes met and held, hers full of questions, but after what seemed an eternity, she nodded. Slowly he removed his hand. She sucked in a breath but made no other noise.

Cameron rolled onto his side, his body shielding hers from the door, keeping one arm locked around her. A noise that sounded suspiciously like a snicker rang out from behind the partially closed door.

Damned if his sex life was going to be a sideshow for a bunch of drunken Scottish yahoos. With defiance singing through his veins, Cameron left the bed and slammed the door. A muffled curse rang out from the other side. With a little luck, Allén's nose had been smashed. He reached for the bar only to realize there wasn't one.

"I gave it to Grania," Marjory whispered. She was sitting up in bed, her expression still guarded.

"You what?"

"I gave it to her. She had need for a plank o' wood. She's always building something. I never use the thing, so I gave it to her." She shrugged. "I meant to get a new one. I just never did."

He looked around the room for something to prop against the door. There was nothing. "Great." He crossed back to the bed. "Move over."

"What?"

"I said move over. It's cold. I've absolutely no intention of freezing my ass off standing out here waiting for Torcall and Allen Cameron to decide we've given them enough of a show. Move over or I'm getting in on top of you."

She slid to the far side of the bed, looking at him with a mixture of anger and amazement.

He turned back the covers and crawled underneath. It was blessedly warm. He could feel where her body had been. The warmth encircled him.

"Ewen, what's going on in there. We canna hear a thing."

The door inched open, but only a little. Evidently Torcall was being true to his word and allowing him some privacy, but it wouldn't last long if he and Marjory didn't convince their audience there was a reason for giving them privacy.

"Look, we've got to at least pretend like something's going on in here. Can you moan or something?"

Moan? What in the world did he mean by that? Marjory's experience with mating, to date, had involved a little grunting on Ewen's part, but nothing that could even remotely be considered a moan.

"I'm no' going to moan," she hissed, determined to maintain the upper hand. Just because he was in bed with her didn't mean she had to follow his orders. " 'Tis no' dignified."

"This isn't about dignity, Your Highness, it's about

saving our butts. I don't have to remember him to know that Torcall Cameron isn't a patient man. He gets what he wants no matter the cost, and right now what he wants is you and me doing the horizontal mambo. And that"— his voice was so low she could barely hear it, but it was still impossible to miss the sarcasm—"*my dear,* means moaning."

She tried to contain a shiver, but couldn't. The cold combined with the emotions roiling through her had reduced her to shuddering uncontrollably. Gently, as if she were a precious thing, Ewen reached out to pull her close. "It's going to be all right," he whispered. "I swear."

His kindness was her undoing, and despite her initial reluctance she allowed herself to settle into his warmth. It surrounded her, against all odds, soothing her.

She felt the ripple of his chest muscles against her arm as he shifted. She shivered, but not from cold. Damn the man. He'd never affected her like this before. Who'd have known a shave and a bath could incite such a riot of emotion?

"What, pray tell, is a mambo?" She stumbled over the word, wondering if she'd fallen into his madness. Lying here with him, speaking nonsensical words, dreaming of his hands on her body . . . "You canna expect me to do something I've never done before."

With a groan he pulled her so close his breathing stirred the hair around her face. "Don't you ever quit arguing, Marjory mine?"

She started to retort, but before a word could leave her lips, he covered her mouth with his, the touch threatening to suck the breath right out of her. His lips were hard and soft all at once, stroking, caressing.

Marjory froze for a minute, not certain how to respond; then something deep inside her clenched and released, a wave of ecstasy shimmering through her body. Pressing closer, she reached up until her hands tangled in his hair, her breasts pressed tightly against his chest. Their kiss deepened, his tongue tracing the line of her lips, and Marjory shivered with desire. She'd never been this close to a man before—at least, not by choice. Before with Ewen it had always been over almost before it started. Quick and painful. As if she were a vessel not a human. Something to be filled and then discarded.

This was completely different. A coming-together, a mating.

His mouth dipped lower, his tongue finding the shell of her ear, rasping against the soft skin there, making her tremble with need. She wanted him to touch her. Possess her.

And she wanted to touch him. Feel his skin beneath her fingers, memorize the hard planes of his body. Acting on the thought, she reached out, fingers spread, her hand meeting velvety ridges of muscle.

She ran her fingers through the soft mat of hair curling across the broad part of his chest, her heart beating staccato against her ribs. Ewen nibbled at her earlobe, his hand covering her breast, his thumb brushing across her nipple sending lightning streaking through her.

Allowing her hand to trail lower, Marjory caressed Ewen's abdomen and hips, feeling the rigid hardness of his member through the thin linen of her nightshift. With a groan, he rolled on top of her, his mouth finding hers, his kiss demanding, intoxicating. Sighing, she opened to him, his tongue thrusting forward, capturing hers, the heat inside her building to a fever pitch. She arched against him, her need laid bare, her hands urging him to take more, to take *her*.

Dee Davis

"I think ye're having us on, brother. There's naught going on in here but blethering!" Allen Cameron burst into the room, his presence like icy water from the loch.

Marjory rolled backward in surprise, harsh reality hitting her with the force of a highland wind. This was not for real. It was playacting, a way to placate Torcall Cameron.

She tried to push away, to escape both Ewen and his brother, but her husband followed, covering her body with his. "You have to trust me, Marjory." His whispered words held an urgency she wasn't certain she understood, but the emotion was hard to ignore. And, truth be told, she wanted to trust him.

He untied the ribbons of her shift, baring her shoulders, brushing a kiss across her already heated skin. "We have to make this look real."

Saints preserve her, she wasn't certain how much more real it could be.

"It's the only way to convince them to go."

She nodded, burying her face in the warm comfort of his neck. He pulled her gown down farther, his hand covering the soft swell of her breast. Her breath caught in her throat, her heart beating so loudly she was certain that everyone could hear it.

"Get out of here, brother," Ewen said, shifting slightly to block Allen's view. "Can't you see you're interrupting?" He bent his head to lazily trail kisses down Marjory's neck, his touch sending tremors racing through her, threatening once again to rob her of all sanity.

Marjory could feel Allen staring at them, even if she couldn't see him, and involuntarily she slid down farther underneath Ewen's big body, seeking safety in his strength.

"Allen, leave the man be," Torcall called. " 'Tis obvious he's seducing the wench. Leave him to it."

But Allen didn't move, obviously unwilling to give up his lecherous pursuit.

"This is it, Marjory," Ewen whispered against her ear. "It's all or nothing."

Marjory stiffened, not knowing what to expect. Her husband's tongue traced a path down her neck, leaving fire in its wake. She arched against him, her body recognizing something her mind could not. His lips closed on her breast and she heard a sound emanating from deep within her as the flames inside threatened to engulf her.

"Allen, I said *now*." Torcall's tone brooked no refusal. With a loud sigh, Allen shuffled from the chamber, the heavy door closing with an audible thud.

Ewen lifted his head, his gaze locking with hers, and Marjory fought for breath, her throbbing breasts matching the cadence of her heartbeat. Every fiber of her being longed for his touch. She wanted him in ways she couldn't even put words to. She sucked in a breath, willing herself to calm down, but the pressure of his manhood against the juncture of her thighs made her want to writhe against him.

She moved slightly, bringing their lips closer together, then brazenly, she tasted his lips. Heaven, pure heaven.

With a groan, Ewen shifted his weight, rolling onto his side, bringing her with him, their mouths still touching, caressing. She felt their breath mingling, and for a moment she felt as if they were one. Then she lost all thought as his mouth claimed hers. There was only sensation—rising, building deep within her, swelling in power, heading for a crescendo she had never imagined. She arched against him, every fiber of her being alive and sensitive to his gentle touch. Her tongue danced with his, circling and withdrawing, again and again, first slowly, then faster and faster. She felt as if the whole world were spinning out of control.

"Marjory?" The word broke through her ecstasy, pulling her back to reality. The kiss had ended and his hand caressed her face.

She kept her eyes closed and rolled onto her back, willing the moment to continue, not wanting it to end.

"We can't do this. You've been wonderful, but . . ."

She felt a tear slip out of the corner of her eye. There was always a but.

"There's too much to deal with right now. I don't really know you. Hell, I don't even know myself." He sounded apologetic.

She knew she should be relieved. Instead, she felt as if she'd lost something she'd only just discovered, and more than anything, she wanted it back.

"Marjory?" Ewen moved away, sitting up.

She felt the chill of the early morning air against her bare shoulder. Another tear joined the first.

He caressed her shoulder, lightly, his touch unsure. "I'm sorry. I didn't mean for this to get so out of hand. I just wanted . . . to get them to leave."

She turned her head and looked at him. His cheek was wet. She wondered absently if it was from his tears or hers. She felt his weight shift as he prepared to get up and, suddenly, she threw off her lethargy.

"*Don't.*"

He stopped and turned back to her.

"Please don't go. Stay here, with me." She swallowed her fears. "I need you. Please, just hold me?"

He pushed a stray strand of hair off of her forehead. Her body, still overly sensitized, responded at once. "Just for tonight," he agreed. He carefully pulled her night-shift back around her shoulders and tied the ribbons.

Then, settling back into the pillows, he reached for her, pulling her close.

She rested her head on his chest, comforted by the steady sound of his heartbeat. Finally, feeling safe and warm, she drifted off to sleep wondering exactly what it was that had happened to her this night. Whatever it was, it had changed her forever.

Chapter Eleven

Cameron opened his eyes with a start. The cold air against his damp skin made him shiver. He'd had the dream again. He could still see the woman scream and feel his foot press down on the accelerator. Chills ran up his spine. What was he remembering?

Closing his eyes, he tried to sort through his thoughts. He concentrated on the woman, trying to picture her face, to remember a name. He knew the dream was important, but he had no idea why.

With a sigh, he rolled over, memories of the night before crashing into his beleaguered brain. Oh, God. He sat up. What had he done? The bed beside him was empty, but that didn't negate the fact that he was here in Marjory's room. In her bed.

He struggled to remember all that had happened.

There'd been lots of drinking; the pounding in his head was testament to that. There'd been Allen's lewd suggestion and the midnight raid on Marjory's bedroom.

His mind obediently trotted out the memory of her lips pressed against his, the soft curve of her hip pressed against him, the warmth of her body. His body tightened with desire, wanting her now even more than last night. Except that he had no right—not to want her, and certainly not to take her.

At least he'd had the decency to stop. Nothing irreversible had happened. They'd played their roles for Torcall and that was it—except that he hadn't left. He'd stayed with her, slept with her. He sighed, angry at himself, at his own weakness. Somehow, by staying with her and not making love, he'd won from her a hesitant trust. A bond of sorts had been formed.

Which was a great mistake. Cameron absolutely could not let himself have feelings for this woman. He had no idea who he was. In light of the dream, it seemed entirely possible that he already had commitments. Why else would he keep dreaming of the blonde?

He had to go back. Had to find his identity. Reclaim whatever it was he'd lost. This place was not his destiny: of that he was certain. He didn't belong here and he had no business romancing anyone, especially not Marjory. Her face flashed through his mind, and he sucked in a breath at the memory of the soft smile that had curled the corners of her lips as she snuggled against him, drifting off to sleep.

He shook his head viciously, purging his mind of all thoughts of her. He would play his role, nothing more. He'd help her convince Torcall to go back to Tyndrum. Once Torcall was gone, he would find his way home or die trying.

With that thought, he threw back the covers. He needed the sanctuary of his own room. Striding across the stone floor, he threw open the door. Sunlight filled his room. He squinted, rubbing his temples, feeling the full effects of last night's ale.

What he needed was a little more sleep. He'd face the music after that, when his head had stopped its rendition of jungle drums. He slipped between the curtains and fell into his bed, grateful for the cool darkness.

"I thought ye'd ne'er arrive."

A slim, naked body rolled on top of him. Warm breath caressed his cheek. Long golden hair brushed against his shoulders. Hard nipples pressed against his chest.

"Thinking of you in there, with her, has only made me want ye more," Aida purred in his ear.

Cameron shifted, rolling away and sitting up, unceremoniously dumping his mistress back onto the bed. "What the hell are you doing here?"

Aida sat up, too, her lips curved in a calculated pout. Cameron had seen that look before, but couldn't remember where. "I told ye, I was waiting fer ye. When ye dinna come to my chamber, I decided to come to you here. But ye were in there—with her. So I decided to wait. Give ye a reward after a night with *that*."

She jerked her head in the direction of the door to Marjory's room and then smiled—a slow sultry smile meant to turn a man's bones to jelly. Arching her back, she stretched like a cat, her breasts thrust out invitingly. Aida rubbed her hands along the length of her body, a suggestive caress that ended with her hands between her thighs.

Cameron had to admit it was a provocative display, but something in him was more disgusted than enticed. "Look, Aida, I've had a long night and what I need right now is a little sleep." She ran a finger down his chest, the corner of her mouth turning up with anticipation. He groaned in frustration. "Alone, Aida."

Her eyes narrowed. "Are ye telling me ye dinna want me anymore?"

Actually, he was telling her that he had never wanted her, but that wouldn't do. No good letting word get back to Torcall that he had rejected his mistress. Even with his memory loss, that was too far out of character, a sure sign that something was wrong. "No, I'm telling you that I don't want you right now. I'm exhausted. Okay?"

She continued to watch him, but her face relaxed. She stroked his cheek. "I'll be waiting fer ye, and I promise it'll be much better than lying with that cold-hearted she-witch ye're married to." She let her hand drop to his crotch, caressing him through the thin woolen material of his underwear.

He covered her hand with his. "I said, later."

She gave one last stroke. "As ye wish, but ye canna deny that a part of ye wants me to stay."

Smiling seductively, she pushed back the bed curtains and stepped out onto the floor. The sunlight illuminated her body, and Cameron had to admit it was magnificent—but his admiration lacked desire. He simply did not want this woman.

The door to Marjory's room opened with a thump.

"Ewen, are you in there? I brought you something to eat." Marjory stood in the archway holding a tray of food. Cameron watched helplessly as she took in the scene: Aida standing by the bed in all her glory; him in bed, nearly naked. She swallowed convulsively, color draining from her face. Biting her lip, she backed up a step. "I . . . I dinna know you were . . . you had . . . I mean . . . I thought . . ." She stopped, evidently unable to say more.

Aida turned to face Marjory, defiant despite her nakedness. "Cat got yer tongue then, dearie? Ye canna be surprised to find that yer husband prefers a more experienced woman. Surely ye canna think he would give up someone like me for the likes o' you?"

The tray crashed to the ground at Marjory's feet. Tears filled her eyes as she bent and began frantically trying to pick up the scattered food.

Cameron felt sick. "Marjory, wait . . ." He leapt from the bed, surprised at the strength of his feelings, his desire to comfort her, to set things right. He pushed Aida aside and knelt beside Marjory, trying to help her. She pushed his hands away, her eyes meeting his. The pain reflected there tore at him.

"I dinna need your help." He watched as she pushed all emotion from her face, replacing it with a mask of studied calm. Slowly, with dignity, she rose, tray in hand. "And I dinna care what you do or whom you do it with." She turned to face Aida, her disdainful gaze tracing a path from golden head to bare feet. "I'll just leave this here." She put the tray on a table. "And maybe the two of you can enjoy it after . . . after you've enjoyed each other."

The ice queen was back. With a glacial nod at the two of them, Marjory turned and went into her room, quietly closing the door behind her.

"There was no need to embarrass her like that, Aida. It was bad enough that she walked in and found you here."

" 'Tis yer chamber and yer business who ye have in it," Aida snapped, tossing her head, completely unrepentant.

"Yes, but this is her house."

"And yours. Are ye taking her side against mine, then?" The woman's eyes narrowed and she glared at him in accusation.

This was too complicated. He was trying to protect Marjory, but in doing so he had hurt her himself, basically defeating the whole purpose. He sighed, sitting on the edge of the bed. "Look, Aida, I'm not taking any-one's side. I'm too tired to deal with this at all right now. So be a good girl and get dressed and get out of here. All right?"

A petulant frown marred her lovely features, but she obeyed his request, pulling an embroidered shift over her head. "Fine. I'll go. But I'm telling ye, Ewen Cameron, ye belong to me, no matter who ye're married to. Dinna forget it." She bent and kissed him, her lips lingering in the hope of an invitation to stay. When he didn't respond, she flicked her hair behind a slender shoulder and flounced from the room.

Cameron lay back on the bed, totally exhausted. Women were obviously the same in any century, and a man would basically be wise to stay clear of them all.

An hour later, Cameron stood in a corral of sorts, swing-ing a claymore. He wasn't certain how exactly to use the thing, but there had to be something to muscle memory, for instinctively he thrust and parried, sometimes hitting the straw-filled target in the middle of the pen, sometimes not.

He'd seen the practice ring from his bedroom window and, given everyone's penchant for drawing swords, it seemed a good idea to familiarize himself with the weapon. Unfortunately the damn thing weighed a ton, and even with Ewen's considerable mass, he was still listing sadly to one side or the other with each swing.

Yet, despite his ineptitude, it was as good a way as any to let off steam.

"Ye're holding it too high." Fingal Macgillivray stood at the edge of the enclosure, one foot braced on a cross-bar.

Everyone was a critic. Cameron shot the man a leave-me-the-hell-alone look, but Fingal only grinned. "It's throwin' off yer balance. Pull it in tighter to yer body, and center yer weight on the balls o' yer feet."

Instinctively, he followed Fingal's advice, surprised at the difference it made. The key here was evidently to let his body rule his brain. He took a couple more swings, then lowered his weapon, and walked over to where Fingal stood.

"You look like the devil himself this morning," Fingal said. He raised an inquiring eyebrow. "Seems an odd time for practicing with a claymore."

"I felt a need to stab something." Cameron tried but couldn't keep the bitterness from his voice.

"Looks to me like ye missed more than ye hit," Fingal observed. "Could be all the drinking last night."

"Yup." Cameron nodded. If the man guessed what else he'd been up to, he'd probably skewer Cameron for breakfast. So best to keep that part to himself. "You were wise to abandon the party when you did."

Fingal shrugged. "I'm no' against drinking, mind ye. 'Twas just the company that was no' to my liking." He studied Cameron, waiting no doubt for a sign of displeasure, a defense of Torcall and crew. Cameron was too tired to play the game. And just at the moment he didn't give a damn anyway.

"They can grate on a man's nerves, I'll grant you that," he said. Which was an understatement when he thought about what they'd asked of him last night. But he wasn't prepared to go that far in denouncing what was supposed to be his kin. "Are they up and about yet?"

"Nay, they're still sleeping it off."

Cameron looked up. Judging from the sun, he'd guess it was a little after noon. "Well, it was a late night." Actually he'd guess he'd fallen asleep closer to dawn.

Maybe if he was lucky, the other Camerons would sleep the day away—or, better yet, wake up and decide to go home.

He started toward the weapons shed to return the claymore, surprised when Fingal followed. They were hardly friends. Still, for what it was worth, it was nice to have company. They passed an outbuilding of some kind, and Cameron noticed a huge skin covered object leaning against a wall. Curiosity aroused, he stopped. "What's this?" The thing was man sized and reminded him of a turtle shell, without the turtle.

" 'Tis just a *curach*."

"A what?" Cameron turned back to Fingal in time to catch his bewildered look. "If I've ever seen one of these before"—he paused, meeting the older man's gaze—"I don't remember it now."

Fingal's eyes narrowed, but then he relaxed and shrugged. "It must be terrible no' to be able to remember things. A *curach* is a wee boat."

"You mean this thing is seaworthy?" Cameron looked at the turtle shell skeptically.

"Well, now, I'd no' say seaworthy, but it will certainly keep ye afloat in the loch."

"Is it hard to handle?" Cameron pulled the small boat away from the wall. The inside was hollow, made of wood and what looked like wicker. A wooden bench of sorts ran across the center.

"Nay, ye just use the oar." Fingal motioned to a long wooden paddle leaning against the wall. "To be honest with you, I've no' been in one since I was a lad. My brothers and I had one. We used to race it across the loch at Moy."

The thing looked like a poorly constructed canoe, and a misshapen one at that. Still, though Cameron wasn't entirely sure he could manage it, but he needed to get away from here and the *curach* provided an ideal method for escape. "Would anyone mind if I borrowed it?"

"I doubt it, but what would ye be wanting it for?"

"I'm going to go fishing." Cameron felt a release of tension at the thought. Time to get things in perspective. Time to work Marjory Macpherson out of his system. Fishing was the perfect answer. He might suck at swordplay, but he could fish.

"Fishing? Whatever for? We dinna need food, and besides, there are men here to do that. You needn't go." Fingal helped Cameron lean the boat back against the wall.

"I'm not going so that I can provide food."

Fingal looked puzzled. "Then why?"

Cameron shrugged. "For fun." He started walking toward a woodpile stacked against a storage shed, already trying to think of a way to construct a fishing pole.

"Fun? Yer going fishing for merriment? Seems to me Aimil's right. Ye are a wee bit touched in the head. Perhaps bed would be a better place fer ye." Fingal kept pace as he walked.

"Nope. Just a little relaxation, and I think fishing is just the ticket. Besides, Fingal, a man has to have his little eccentricities." Cameron handed the man the claymore, then squatted down by the pile, extracting a long thin branch and inspecting it like he would a pool cue. Satisfied that it was fairly straight, he stood up, cast it back over a shoulder, and then flicked it forward several times.

"Perfect. Now all I need is some string and a hook, and I'm set. You want to come with me?" He actually didn't want company, but Fingal looked fascinated.

"I'd love to, if for no other reason than to find out just

exactly what ye're up to." He frowned. "But I canna. I've work to do."

Cameron heaved an inward sigh of relief. "Next time, then."

Fingal nodded and set off toward the stable. Cameron watched him go, then turned to find the blacksmith. Surely he would have something that could pass for a hook.

"Marjory, are ye in there, lass?" Aimil's voice drifted through the closed door. Marjory rolled over, turning away from the sound. She frantically tried to erase signs of her tears, but she was too late. She felt the bed dip as the older woman sat on its edge.

"Come now, lamb, tell Aimil what's ailing ye."

Marjory felt a hand in her hair, smoothing it with a gentle caress. The sign of affection undid her and she sat up, throwing herself into Aimil's arms. "You were right. I should have listened to you," she sobbed.

"Right about what, love?" Aimil's voice was low, soothing.

"About him."

"Him who?"

"Ewen." Just saying his name made it all come back. She'd been so happy this morning. Waking in his arms had been wonderful. She had hurried downstairs to get his breakfast, eager to spend the day with him, to simply be with him.

"Ah. I was afraid this would happen. Has he hurt you?" Aimil pulled back, looking into her eyes. "Did he—"

"No, no, nothing like that," Marjory assured the older woman, surprised by the strength of her desire to protect him.

"What then?"

"He . . . he spent the night here. 'Twas so . . ." She released a sigh. "So beautiful. But then this morning he . . . I . . ."

"Take yer time, *mo chridhe*. Tell Aimil."

Marjory took a deep breath and forced herself to calm down. "I came to bring him the morning meal and found my chamber empty. So I took the tray in there." She pointed to the connecting door. "And he was with Aida."

Tears filled her eyes again as she relived the humiliation: Aida, naked and obviously ready to climb into Ewen's bed, and Ewen sitting there waiting for her. It was her wedding night all over again, except this time her heart was involved as well as her pride. She fought the notion but couldn't deny the truth of it.

"I wish I could tell ye the news surprises me, but it doesna. I warned ye against believing the man had truly changed. He hasna and he willna. 'Tis naught but a trick. The sooner you accept that, the sooner ye can get on with yer life."

Marjory wiped her eyes. "If only it were that easy, Aimil. The man is my husband after all. 'Tis no' as if I can get rid of him altogether."

"Dinna worry yourself, lamb, things have a way o' taking care o' themselves, just ye wait and see." She patted Marjory on the shoulder. "Come now, dry yer eyes. No use letting the man know how much he's hurt ye."

Marjory swallowed her pain, pushing it deep down. Aimil was right. She wouldn't let a man like that matter to her. She'd had a moment of weakness, that was all, nothing that couldn't be forgotten. All she had to do was put him out of her mind. She climbed out of the bed, Aimil hovering worriedly. " 'Tis all right, Aimil. I'm fine. 'Twas my pride and nothing more." Liar, her heart cried. "I'll be down directly."

"If ye're sure?"

Marjory nodded and the older woman hugged her.

"Ye're like me own child, Marjory. I'll never let the likes o' Ewen Cameron harm ye. I promise ye that, *mo chridhe*."

"Thank you, Aimil, but I can take care of myself. I'm a grown woman after all."

Aimil beamed. "That ye are, me girl, that ye are." With a final pat, she turned to go.

Marjory kept her face serene until Aimil was gone. Then, with a small cry, she sank to the floor, burying her face in her hands. It was easy to tell herself Ewen didn't matter, that he hadn't the power to hurt her, but unfortunately, her heart wasn't listening.

Chapter Twelve

Cameron leaned against the handle of the narrow wooden shovel. If there were worms in the garden, they were evidently on a coffee break. He'd been digging for what felt like an hour without locating a single slimy one. Maybe it was the wrong time of year. Maybe he wasn't digging deeply enough. Actually, he didn't seem to know a damn thing about finding worms.

One more shovelful and he was going to give up. He'd head for the kitchens. Surely there was something there fish would eat. Hell, he really didn't care if he caught anything. It was just the normalcy he sought. Something removed from the harsh reality of fifteenth-century Scotland.

He ought to be out searching for a way home, wherever the hell that was. But just at the moment, even that was too much to deal with. He needed something to ground him, something that he knew how to do in any body.

He stuck the shovel into the soft brown earth, carefully turning the dirt so he wouldn't disturb the plants. All he needed to add to an already bad morning was to incur the wrath of Aimil Macgillivray.

"And just what do ye think ye're doing, Ewen Cameron?"

Speak of the devil. He looked up from the pile of sod he'd been carefully examining. "Looking for earthworms."

"I'll no' have ye speaking yer addled gibberish to me. Say it to me plain."

"I'm looking for something to bait my fishing line."

"Yer fishing line." She repeated his words slowly, as if saying them would make them make sense.

"Yes, my fishing line. It goes with the fishing pole."

"Seamus warned me ye were talking crazy."

The blacksmith had made it clear what he thought of fishing—in fact, what he thought of all recreational endeavors. It seemed the people at Crannag Mhór weren't big on leisure-time activities.

"I'm well aware of Seamus's views." Cameron dumped a handful of soil back to the ground. No worms there. He stood up, brushing his hands against his legs to knock off the remaining dirt.

"I'll have ye know, I've no time fer yer playacting. Ye may be able to fool Marjory, but ye canna fool me." The older woman crossed her bony arms across her chest and glared at him.

"Look, Aimil, I don't know what Marjory told you, but there's been a misunderstanding. When she cools off a bit, I'll explain it to her. In the meantime, I'm going to go fishing." He walked over to the shed and replaced the shovel, only to turn and find her blocking his way, a speculative look on her face.

"Fishing, is it? Are ye sure 'tis no' a rendezvous with yer whore?"

Cameron groaned. God save him from women. "I am

going out in a boat to the center of the lake to be by myself. There will be no one with me—not Aida, not Marjory, not anyone. Do you understand?" He spoke slowly, carefully enunciating each word.

Her eyes narrowed to slits. "Oh, I understand ye all right."

"Good, then if it wouldn't be too much of an effort, would you mind telling your brother I'd like to use the *curach?* I'm going to the kitchen for a few things, and then I'll come and get the boat. Okay?"

The woman relaxed. In fact, she almost smiled. "I'll do ye better than that. I'll see that one o' the lads takes the boat down to the loch fer ye. Ye can meet him at the shore."

Startled, Cameron managed to stammer out his thanks. Aimil drew herself up to her full height and leaned in close to him. "Just stay away from Marjory. Ye've no business confusing her with yer daft talk o' changing. Ye and I both know the kind of man ye are."

Actually, he hadn't the foggiest notion what kind of man he was, but that wasn't something he intended to share with Aimil. He was curious, however, to know what she thought. "And what kind of man would that be?"

"A Cameron." She spat the word like a blasphemy. "Now go. I'll have the *curach* ready fer ye."

Not one to look a gift horse in the mouth, he hurried away, relieved to have escaped with most of his hide still intact. Yes, sir, short of returning to the twenty-first century, fishing was just what he needed right now. He only hoped Scottish fish liked oat cakes.

Men were all goats. Well, most men. Some men. One man.

.Marjory turned the crank on the quern with a vigorous hand. Each bit of grain ground to meal she pictured as a part of Ewen's body. First she'd grind his hands, then his arms, then his legs, and last—last she'd grind his head. She dumped more barley into the hand-mill. Oh, yes, she'd grind him into fine bits.

"Marjory, lass, slow down. Ye're grinding enough meal to last us a fortnight—if the weevils dinna get at it first."

Marjory looked up from the mill. Grania sat at a nearby worktable, placidly peeling carrots. "How can you possibly know how much I've ground?"

Grania smiled. "Child, I may no' be able to see, but I know the amount of time it takes to grind the wee bit o' meal we need fer the bannocks. Ye've been at it fer a good long while. 'Twould no' take a pair of eyes to know that yer no' concentrating on yer task. What ails ye?"

Marjory gathered the barley flour into a large wooden bowl. "What makes you think there's something wrong?"

"I know ye, Marjory Macpherson. Now talk to me."

Marjory sighed and sat on a bench by the table. " 'Tis Ewen. He hasna changed at all."

"I suspect that few men do what we expect o' them."

" 'Tis more than that. I truly thought he was different than before, but this morning he proved to me that he is still the old Ewen Cameron through and through." She bit her lip; then, in a quiet voice, she related the morning's humiliation.

"And ye're sure ye saw the situation as it really was?"

"I dinna follow."

Grania put the bowl with the peeled carrots on the table and leaned forward, reaching unerringly for Marjory's hand. "I mean, child, that when our pride is involved we often dinna see clearly. From the way ye tell

157

the tale it seems possible that Ewen was as surprised as you to see Aida in his chamber."

"But she was standing there in, well, in nothing."

"Aye, but a woman with no scruples will use any trick in the book to get a man. And if ever there were a woman such as that, 'tis Aida Macvail."

"But he was naked, too, save for his trews." Marjory pulled her hand away, crossing her arms over her chest.

"Aye, so he was. But tell me, lass, what was he wearing when ye left him?"

"The same. But I dinna see how—"

Grania motioned Marjory into silence. "And where did ye leave him?"

"In my chamber." She felt hot color wash across her face and was relieved Grania couldn't see it.

"So, let me see if I have this right. Ye leave a sleeping Ewen in yer bed to go and fetch some food fer the two o' you. . . ."

Marjory nodded, and then, catching herself, answered verbally. "Aye."

"How long do ye suppose ye were gone?"

"No' long at all. I went down to the kitchen, got some oatcakes and barley bannocks, and brought them back to the chamber." She leaned forward, wondering what Grania was getting at.

"So then, ye're saying in that short period of time, Ewen woke up, went to his chamber, summoned Aida, got her undressed, and was about to bed her when ye walked in?"

"Well, when you put it like that, it does sound a bit far-fetched. But I saw it myself."

"Nay, lass, ye saw Aida, naked, trying to climb into bed with Ewen, who was dressed as ye'd last seen him. And when ye add to that the fact that he ran to yer side the minute ye saw what was happening, I think ye have quite a different picture."

"He was just helping with the spilled food."

"Ah, he was helping you. Now that's certainly a trait the old Ewen Cameron was known fer."

"He wasn't," Marjory snapped.

The old woman nodded her head. "Exactly. Ye have to learn to look at things with more than just yer eyes. Ye have to view them with yer heart. Things that appear one way to yer mind often appear quite differently when viewed with a little faith."

"Faith? How can I have faith in Ewen?"

"Ye just do it. Faith is no' earned, Marjory. 'Tis instinctive. Stop listening to yer head child, and start listening to yer heart." She stood, picking up the bowl of carrots. "Now, go and find the man and see if the two of ye can make peace afore we've enough barley meal to last us till Christmastide."

Marjory sat on a boulder by the loch, tossing stones into its dark gray depths. The day had turned colder. Clouds were gathering to the east. There'd be a storm before night set in, but that was hours off yet. She sat still, her eyes closed, letting the breeze wash over her. It carried the smell of gorse and rowan.

Worry ate at her. She'd spent the better part of the early afternoon searching Crannag Mhór for Ewen. He was nowhere to be found. She was terrified that he had decided to leave her alone to face his father.

She'd only just avoided a confrontation with Torcall as it was, he and that witch Aida. Whether she believed Grania's version of the morning's events or not, Marjory knew that Aida was an adversary—and a dangerous one at that.

Praise the saints for the serving passage. Her father had built it so that food could be brought more easily from the kitchen to the great hall. The passageway wound down the tower wall without stairs, was a ramp of sorts. It started in the pantry and ended in an alcove in the wall behind the dais.

It was designed so that the entryway sat behind an elaborately carved screen. That way dinner guests wouldn't be able to see. Her father had always been proud of it. Marjory had always used it as an escape route. As a child, she had mostly escaped from imaginary enemies, but as she grew older, she'd found it useful in evading people she didn't want to see.

Today, it had been Torcall Cameron. He'd been sprawled across a bench in the main solar, bellowing for his son. Aida had been there, too, sitting beside him, wrapped around his arm like an eel Marjory had seen once at Cluny, all slippery and evil-smelling. Once out of their sight, it had been easy enough for her to sneak back up the stairs and out the front entry. Now she was safely away, but still no nearer to discovering where Ewen had gone.

A splashing noise off to her left caught her attention. Someone was struggling to get a *curach* into the loch. The man held the boat over his head with both arms. He had waded a short ways into the loch and now was trying to turn the boat over and drop it into the water without tumbling in himself. After watching for a few minutes, Marjory realized he wasn't having much success.

Curiosity aroused, she stood and hurried down the beach—just as the man managed to flip the *curach* into the water. He made a wild grab for it, snagging the edge before it could drift out into the loch. As he straightened and pulled the craft partway onto the shore, Marjory's heart began to race. It was Ewen.

"Wait," she called, beginning to run. He was loading something into the boat. He didn't hear her and began to push the *curach* out into the water again. She hiked up her skirts so that she could move faster, driven by an overpowering urge to reach him.

"Ewen, wait," she yelled again, breathlessly. He paused and looked up, shading his eyes with his hand. She skidded to a stop within a few yards of him. No sense in letting him know how anxious she was. She released her skirts and patted her hair, trying to appear nonchalant.

"What are you doing here?" she asked, trying to sound surprised.

He raised his eyebrows. "Watching you tear across the meadow like a madwoman."

Marjory dipped her head, embarrassment heating her cheeks. "I was afraid you were going to leave."

"I am leaving."

"What?" Her head snapped up.

"Not forever, princess, just for a little while. I'm going fishing."

Relief washed through her. He wasn't leaving permanently. "Fishing? Whatever for?"

He shot her an exasperated look. "For fun. Why is it you people don't know anything about fishing? You live on a lake, for God's sake."

"We know about fish." She tipped her chin up. How dare he insult her people? "They live in the loch, and sometimes, when there is a shortage of game, we actually eat fish. But I canna imagine going out in that"—she pointed at the *curach*—"for enjoyment."

"Well, you may be right on that count. This thing does

look a little rickety to me, but both Fingal and Aimil assure me it's sound." He tapped the boat, illustrating his point.

"You talked with Aimil?" Marjory felt her color rising again.

"Yeah. She had quite a bit to say." He looked at her pointedly.

"About me?"

He nodded. "She basically told me that if I ever got near you again there'd be hell to pay."

"Oh." She studied her slippers.

"Marjory?"

She looked up, her heart skipping a beat as she met his eyes.

"I'm sorry about what happened this morning. I know it was awful for you, but I didn't invite Aida to my room. I swear it. If you'd given me a chance I could have explained."

"You dinna have to explain. 'Twas nothing." She looked down again, afraid he'd see through the lie.

He lifted her chin with his fingers. "That's not true. It hurt you. I know it did. And if I could have waved a magic wand and made it all disappear, I would have. You have to believe me when I tell you, I did not ask Aida to come to my room."

He brushed a strand of hair back from her face, tucking it behind her ear. "In fact, when you came in, I was telling her to leave. Unfortunately, she isn't good at taking no for an answer." His gaze met hers and held. "I really am sorry."

Looking into his eyes, she saw nothing but concern and sincerity. "I believe you." And she was surprised to find that she actually did. Which was confusing considering whom she was talking to. But then, the truth was, for whatever reason, the man he was now was a far cry from the Ewen Cameron she had married. And she prayed to God that the change was permanent, and that he would stay at Crannag Mhór.

At least, until his father took his cohorts and went home. Beyond that she did not dare imagine. It was too new, and there were too many things that could upset the fragile feelings that were building inside her. For now at least, she'd do best to keep them at bay, locked away in some safe corner of her heart.

"Do you want to come with me?"

She broke from her reverie. "In that?"

"Well, if we're going to go out on the lake, it's best to take a boat, don't you think?"

"Aye, but I still dinna see the purpose o' going at all."

"Marjory." He sighed. "Sometimes it's good to do things for no reason at all. Come on. Let go. Live a little."

What was it Grania had said? Listen with your heart? Maybe she did let her head rule too much. "All right," Marjory said, the decision made. "I'll go. What do I do?"

"Give me your hand."

She placed it in his, shivering at the warmth of the contact. The man definitely had an effect on her. She sat on the bench in the center of the *curach*.

"All settled?"

She nodded, and he pushed the little boat clear of the shore. Then almost effortlessly, he jumped over the side and settled beside her on the bench. The *curach* rocked back and forth, but held strong.

The bench was small, with barely enough room for the two of them. Marjory settled comfortably against his side, thinking that maybe fishing wouldn't be so bad after all.

*　　*　　*

"Are you sure you're doing it right?" Marjory peered over the side of the boat into the murky water where his line disappeared.

Cameron smiled. "Yes, I'm sure."

"But you havena caught any fish. Isn't that the whole point of fishing?"

Cameron sighed. There was simply no explaining the art of doing nothing to someone who probably thought tossing a caber was recreational. "Just be patient, we'll catch something."

"Do you really think the fish will eat pieces of oat-cake?"

Better them than him. "I'm not sure, really. But they were plentiful and the cook didn't seem to mind my having them."

Marjory laughed. "I'll wager you didna tell her what you were wanting them for."

"No, I didn't." He grinned sheepishly. "She probably thinks I've developed a taste for them."

They sat in companionable silence, watching the fishing pole, waiting for something to happen. A brisk breeze had come up and the little boat rocked back and forth. Suddenly, the pole jerked and the line pulled tight. Cameron drew back on the stick, feeling the line pull in the opposite direction. "I think we've got something."

Marjory leaned over the side, trying to see. "What do we do now?"

"Good question. Normally, you use a reel to help you pull it in, but I didn't have time to figure out how to make one. So, I guess we'll just have to do it manually."

"Manually?" She looked at him in confusion.

Hell, everything they did was manual. "On our own, without the aid of the reel," he explained. She really didn't look any less confused, but at least she nodded as if she understood.

He handed her the stick. "Here, you hold on to the pole." She grasped it in both hands. "Great, now with a little luck, I'll bring this guy in." He started to pull the fishing line in, hand over hand. Fortunately, the fish wasn't very big, or it wasn't putting up much of a fight. Marjory was leaning out over the water, pole in hand.

"Where is he? I canna see him."

"Keep watching, I've almost got him here." The line hadn't seemed very long when it was empty, but now that he wanted to get to its end, it seemed to stretch on forever.

"Wait a minute, I think I see him." Marjory pointed to a flicker of silver just over the side.

Cameron leaned over the edge, allowing his line of vision to follow her pointing finger. Sure enough, there was a flash of fin. He yanked on the last of the line, sending a spray of water over Marjory and the fish flying through the air. It landed in the boat with a flop.

"You've caught him." Marjory's voice held a note of awe. Cameron felt as though he had just slain a dragon. She peered at the fish. "It looked bigger in the water." Okay, a very tiny dragon. "I think 'tis a wee babe. It looks so helpless."

Great, so much for the conquering hero stuff. "Shall we let it go?"

"Aye." She shot him a smile that warmed him all over. Back to king for a day.

"No problem." He picked up the little fish and worked the hook from its mouth. "All right, fish, this is your lucky day." With a grin at Marjory, he tossed it over the side. The fish hit the water with a smack and quickly disappeared from sight.

"Well, that's it then. We've fished."

Cameron threw back his head and laughed. "That we have, Marjory Macpherson. That we have."

The little boat rocked on the water, the motion soothing, the silence around them comfortable. Marjory seemed content for the moment to simply trail her hand through the water and watch him fish. There was something so domestic about all this: the perfect way to spend the day. The perfect woman to spend it with.

The thought brought him up short, surprising him with its tenacity. He liked Marjory—most of the time. Surely his feelings didn't go beyond that. After all, they were practically strangers.

An image of their bodies tangled together filled his mind, the memory of their passion crescendoing until he actually felt the heat between them as if it were happening now.

"Where have you gone?"

"Beg pardon?" Her words jerked him back to reality, embarrassment replacing his other emotions. "I was thinking about what a wonderful day it is."

She studied him for a moment, as if questioning the truth of his statement, then nodded in acceptance with a smile. "I was thinking how happy I am, too. How much I like being with you."

His stomach sank as the reality of her words hit him hard. They were headed down a dangerous path. One he shouldn't—couldn't—pursue.

Her eyes widened in surprise as she took in his expression. "Did I say something wrong?"

He reached for her hand, taking it firmly in his, wishing away his riotous thoughts. "No, not at all."

"Then why, may I ask, are you frowning?" she asked, worry creasing the line of her brow.

"I'm not really. See?" He grinned, praying that it was convincing but knowing from the look on her face, it was not.

"Dinna lie to me, Ewen. Tell me what's wrong."

He chewed on his upper lip a minute, trying to formulate the words. "It's hard to explain. But I guess the truth of it is that I feel like I'm taking advantage of you."

"Taking advantage? How?"

He blew out a long breath, not certain if this was the right time or place for confessions but convinced it was important she know. Important that he tell her. He wanted no secrets between them. No matter the cost.

The loch was still peaceful, the storm on the far side forming a spectacular backdrop. The dark angry clouds seemed at odds with the gently lapping water. Somehow it seemed to mirror his predicament. The peace he felt here with Marjory was a lie, nothing more than a precursor to the storm that would follow.

He was so tired of being alone. Of trusting no one. His gaze met hers, his heart heavy. "I'm not who you think I am, Marjory. I'm not Ewen Cameron."

Chapter Thirteen

"I dinna understand. Of course you're Ewen Cameron. You just dinna remember, that's all." She fought to make sense of his words. If he wasn't Ewen Cameron, then who was he? The little voice in her head insisted his words were true. That she'd known it all along. But she brushed it aside, not willing to examine the implications.

"Look, Marjory," Ewen was saying, his voice sincere, his eyes begging her to listen. "My name is Cameron. That's all I remember. But I know it isn't Ewen." He took a deep breath, and she felt herself mimicking it as she drew in her own breath, waiting for his next revelation.

"When I woke up after the fall . . ." He paused as if searching for the right words.

Marjory released her breath and pulled her hand from his, waiting for him to continue. A look of pain washed across his face as she drew away. He looked lost and alone. But she was confused and afraid, herself.

Her heart urged her to take his hand again, to keep contact, but her head was yelling that distance was much

168

better. Her head won out. It was much easier to think clearly when they were not touching.

"God, this is difficult." He buried his face in his hands, and then as if thinking better of it, he raised it again to look at her. "I think that Ewen, your Ewen, died. At least, I'm pretty sure of it."

"But you're here."

"No. That's what I'm trying to tell you. Ewen *isn't* here. He died in the landslide, and I woke up in his place. I know it sounds insane on the surface, but if you'll think about it, think about me, you'll see that I'm speaking the truth."

She raised her eyebrows, waiting for him to tell her he was speaking in jest. He shifted uncomfortably, the little boat bobbing with the motion, but his gaze was steady and he didn't look away. Merciful heaven, he wasn't jesting.

"Look, I know it sounds insane. Especially since I don't remember much about before, but, Marjory, what I do know for certain is that I'm not Ewen Cameron."

"Aye, you've made that abundantly clear. And I canna argue with the fact that you're different now than before." She paused, feeling her cheeks burn. "The old Ewen Cameron would never have . . . done what you did last night." She finished, mortified that she'd said it out loud. "But that doesna mean you're no' him. Only that the knock on your head changed you."

Ewen shook his head. "It goes deeper than that and you know it. How many times have you told me that a man can't change that much? Think about it, Marjory."

"Maybe I want it to be so." She could admit that much, but anything beyond was simply more than she could fathom.

"But you can't handle the implications." He paused,

burying his face in his hands again. "Well, neither can I—but unfortunately that doesn't change the facts."

She waited, her brain numb.

He looked up again, his amber gaze meeting hers. "There's something I haven't told you." He blew out a breath. "I do have memories, Marjory. They're disjointed and out of sequence, but they are clear on one thing. My memories are of things that haven't happened yet, things that haven't even been invented yet."

"What are you saying to me?" She felt her heart skip a beat. This was not what she'd expected at all.

"I'm saying that I think I've traveled back in time, Marjory. From my century to yours."

"And what century would that be?" She tried to keep the skepticism out of her voice, but it was difficult.

"The twenty-first."

"But that's . . . that's . . ."

"Five hundred years from now." He reached for her hand, but she jerked it away.

"That canna be. People dinna go about hopping in and out of bodies and dashing about through time."

He leaned forward, looking her full in the eyes. "A few weeks ago, I suspect I would have agreed with you. Now I can't argue the fact. It has to be possible because it's happened to me."

"I'm no' saying I believe you, but for the sake of argument, what memories exactly do you have that support this daft notion of yours?"

Ewen bit his lip again, contemplating her question. She waited for his answer, outwardly composed, inwardly reeling.

"Well, there was the mirror for one."

"Mirror?"

"The shield."

"My father's shield? What has it got to do with any of this?" Her heart pounded. Next he'd be telling her it was a magic shield.

"I wanted to see what I looked like, remember?"

She nodded, waiting.

"In my mind's eye, I can see what I looked like before I came here, Marjory. Even with the memory block, I can still see my face."

"So . . . ?"

"So, when I looked in the shield, the face that was reflected there wasn't mine. It was your husband's."

"That sounds—"

"Crazy," he finished for her. "I know, but it's true."

She struggled with the enormity of what he was telling her. "So you're saying that you're trapped in Ewen's body?"

"Yes."

"Holy mother of God." The small seeds of contentment that had been sprouting so hopefully inside her withered and died. She looked at Ewen, pushing her fragmented emotions deep inside her, focusing on his face. There was more, and she already knew she wasn't going to like it.

"And your memory loss?"

"I don't know. Maybe it was caused when I came here. Maybe I was supposed to have lost all memory of before. Hell"—he raked his hands through his hair in frustration—"I don't understand this any better than you. I've just had longer to think about it." He looked up, staring at the sky, almost as if he were pleading for answers.

She reached out and tentatively placed her hand over his. Whoever he was, he was gentle and good; she knew that in her heart and nothing her head could say could erase the knowledge.

He turned his hand over, enveloping hers with strong fingers, his tortured gaze holding hers. "I do know one thing for certain."

She held her breath, waiting.

"I have to go back."

Her belly lurched and she wondered if she was going to be sick. "Back?"

"Yes, back. I need to find out who I am."

"Who you are?" She couldn't seem to do anything but echo his words.

"Yes, Marjory. Don't you see? I have to know. I can't go through life with another man's identity. If I don't face who I really am, how can I ever be anything more?"

"But you're no' Ewen. You've just told me so. 'Tis possible others will accept that in time." She spoke quickly, her words tumbling over one another, knowing full well he was talking about more than not being Ewen. Her eyes pleaded with him. "Maybe you can remember here."

He shook his head. "Amnesia is a funny thing. When it's caused by trauma, which I think mine was, then the best way to bring memory back is to be stimulated by familiar things."

"And there are no familiar things here."

"Right." He took her other hand in his.

"And when you go, you willna be coming back, will you?"

He paused. "No."

The word hung between them. Marjory felt her heart ripping in two. How had this man come to mean so much to her in so short a span of time? Tears threatened, but she held them at bay. This was not the time for weakness. Nothing had been lost. She'd lived without him before, she'd just have to live without him again when the time came.

Her heart rebelled at the thought, and her chest tightened in unspoken agony.

"I'm sorry," he whispered. His voice breaking on the words.

"I know." And she did. He'd not meant to hurt her. What was happening must be as strange and frightening for him as it was for her. More so, really. And it certainly wasn't his fault that she had begun to open her heart to him. Only a very young or a very foolish girl threw herself at a man. Marjory could almost hear her mother saying those very words. She had no one to blame but herself.

Somehow, the knowledge helped to calm her. She closed her eyes and allowed herself a moment of regret. Then, summoning all the strength she had, she sat back, squaring her shoulders. "When will you go?"

"Not until we deal with Torcall. I won't leave you alone with him."

"I've handled him before. I'll handle him this time as well." Brave words, but she knew there was no truth in them. If Ewen disappeared, there would be hell to pay.

He reached for her hand again, his gaze steady; his eyes Ewen's, yet not. "I won't let you face him on your own."

She nodded, absurdly relieved—not so much because she feared Torcall, although she certainly did, but more because it meant that she still had time with him. Her practical mind whispered that the longer she was with him, the harder it would be to have him go, but her heart rejoiced in the knowledge that they still had time.

"I canna take it all in now. Perhaps later when I've had the chance to chew on it a bit." She forced a smile she didn't feel. "Right now, if you dinna mind, I think I'd like to try this fishing for myself."

With every passing minute Cameron admired Marjory more. He'd just told her a story that would have flummoxed the best of men, even the most educated, and here she was fishing as if she didn't have a care in the world. It was an act of course, her way of whistling in the dark. But he admired her nevertheless. She was an amazing woman. And in a different time or place, he'd have been the first in line to win her heart.

But he was here, now. And the truth stood between them as surely as if it were made of stone, separating them with more than just centuries. He sighed, wishing that things were different, accepting that they were not.

Marjory lowered her pole, studying the floor of the *curach*. "Should we be having this much water in the boat?"

Lost in his melancholy thoughts, he glanced at the bottom, but dismissed it. "It's just from the fish."

Marjory nodded, not meeting his gaze, and sat back on the bench. "There's rain coming." She pointed to the east at the rapidly building thunderheads. "We should be getting back."

Cameron looked at the storm clouds. "You're right." Grabbing an oar, he started to row, but was surprised at how much heavier the boat seemed to be. Looking down, he realized that the floor of the *curach* was indeed awash with water. It lapped at his feet.

Marjory was watching the water, too. "There's more than before, I'd swear to it."

Crouching down in the hull, Cameron scanned for holes. Nothing appeared to be amiss, but Marjory was right, the water level was definitely rising. Sticking his hand into the icy water, he felt along the bottom of the boat. The skin seemed solid enough. Marjory turned and, following his lead, began to search the back of the *curach*.

With the water level still rising, Cameron sat up. "I can't find anything."

Marjory joined him on the bench. "Nor can I. But the water is definitely getting higher."

"Okay, hang on, we'll just have to try and make it to shore." A crack of thunder sounded overhead. Cameron could feel Marjory shivering next to him. He slipped an arm around her in a brief embrace. "We'll be all right."

He shifted and grasped the oar with both hands, paddling furiously. The boat, having lost some of its buoyancy, responded slowly, twirling in circles rather than going forward, the tower beckoned enticingly in the distance.

A drop of rain landed on Cameron's forehead with a splat, and then another. The boat was about a third of the way full now, almost impossible to control. The rain had strengthened, coming in a steady, icy downpour. The only thing colder than the rain was the lake water rushing over their feet. Cameron wondered, briefly, how long it took to get hypothermia in the icy waters of a Scottish loch.

He turned to Marjory. Her hair was plastered around her face, and rivulets of rain ran down her neck. She gave him a weak smile. "Is this part of fishing, then?" Cameron grabbed her hand, giving it a squeeze. Any other girl, in any century, would be screaming or complaining, but not Marjory.

He looked at the tower. It was partially obliterated by the rain, but he could see enough to know that they had no chance of making it back in the boat. The opposite shore was much closer, but still too far for him to manage the already listing *curach*.

"Marjory." He lifted her chin with a finger, his eyes meeting hers. "It's time to abandon ship. We'll have to swim for the shore." There was a flash of lightning, followed quickly by the loud rumble of thunder. Not even time for *one-one hundred*. The storm was upon them.

"Ewen?" Her voice was tiny, almost lost in the force of the storm. He looked down at her, his heart constricting at the fear he saw. "I canna do this."

"Sure you can. I'll help you. There's no other choice." He was already unbuckling the belt at her waist, as the weight of her skirts alone would carry her straight to the bottom. The belt dropped and the plaid of her skirt unwound, falling to the floor of the boat. She stood there in her linen shift looking small and fragile. He took her hand in his. "There's nothing to be afraid of." He tried to smile reassuringly.

The water in the boat was almost to the halfway mark. The front was already tipping forward. Marjory placed her hand in his, looking up at him, her gaze steady. What had ever made him think this woman fragile?

"Cameron, you dinna understand what I'm trying to tell you." She bit her lower lip and then released it. "I canna do this because I canna swim."

Chapter Fourteen

Cameron took a moment to process her words. "All right then, I'll just have to swim for both of us."

Marjory's eyes widened for an instant, but she didn't say anything. Water sloshed around their legs. The boat was sinking fast. Cameron looked down at his plaid. There simply wasn't time to remove it. He'd just have to drag its sodden weight along with them. He released the pin at his shoulder and secured the loose end around his waist. At least that would leave his arm free. The wind bit through his shirt. He shivered with cold and anticipation.

"Wait. My sporran." Marjory reached for the soggy mass of wool that had been her skirt.

"Forget it, Marjory, there isn't time." The boat rocked violently, throwing her against him. His arm went around her as he fought for balance, gripping the side of the *curach* with his free hand. The boat steadied. Marjory bent down again, frantically searching for the pouch.

"My *sgian dubh*. I canna lose it. 'Tis in the sporran." Cameron reached past her, grabbing the wet wool.

With a shake, the sporran fell free, and Marjory quickly secured it around her waist.

Cameron grabbed her hands and bent close so that he could be heard over the howling wind. "Here's what we're going to do. We're going to stand up on the seat, and when I count to three, we're going to take a deep breath and jump over the side into the water." She swallowed, then bit her lower lip. "You'll be all right. I'm going to hold your hand." He lifted their joined left hands to demonstrate. "Whatever you do, don't let go. All right?"

She nodded and squeezed. He helped her onto the bench. The boat tipped drunkenly and then righted itself. He pushed his rain-soaked hair out of his face and stepped up onto the seat. The boat lurched.

"One . . . two . . ." He met Marjory's gaze and tightened his grip on her hand. "Three!"

The murky water closed over their heads. The noise from the storm was momentarily blocked and the silence was almost peaceful. The cold invaded his body, wrapping around him like a vise. With a conscious effort, Cameron forced his body to move, kicking furiously as he pulled them back to the surface. Marjory was dead weight and it took all of his strength to pull her with him. His head broke the surface only to be pounded with rain. He gasped for breath. Marjory surfaced beside him, coughing and sputtering. He wrapped an arm around her, pulling her close, treading water to keep them afloat.

"You okay?" She jerked her head in answer, her eyes wild with fear. "I'm going to put my arm around your neck." He was yelling so that he could be heard. "Try not to fight me. Just let yourself float. Breathe through your nose and keep your mouth closed." She nodded. He leaned closer and kissed her quickly on the lips. "Here we go."

Shifting his arm so that it circled her neck, he struck out for the shore. The icy water sapped his strength. He knew time was running out. They had to make it. He looked down at Marjory. She was sputtering, but otherwise okay. He kicked furiously, trying to make headway in the churning water.

Time passed slowly. It seemed that he had been swimming forever. His legs were numb. He could only hope that he was actually still kicking. Marjory had closed her eyes. He prayed that she was still breathing. He was afraid if he stopped to check, he would never be able to start again.

His arm moved through the water like an automaton's, pushing the cold, dark water out of the way. Stroke, stroke, stroke, his brain sang. Somewhere deep inside his mind, he heard another refrain. *Whoosh, beep-beep . . . whoosh, beep-beep.* No. His mind fought against the sound. Not now. He had to get Marjory safely to shore.

His knee scraped against something. He jerked back to full consciousness. A rock. He'd bumped a rock. They'd reached land. Swinging Marjory into both arms, he willed his legs to function. His weary limbs struggled to obey his brain's command. Red-hot pain jolted through his feet, racing along the nerve endings in his legs.

His knees buckled and he almost fell, but sheer will-power won out and he staggered through the shallow water onto the pebble-strewn beach. He gently lowered Marjory to the ground. Her lips were blue and her hands were icy, but her pulse was strong. He removed his waterlogged plaid and, after wringing it out, laid it on the ground. Carefully lifting her shoulders, he slid Marjory onto the cloth. It wasn't the best of protection, but it was all he had to offer.

The wind whipped around him and he shivered violently, dropping down wearily beside her, sleep threatening. He fought against it, knowing that if he lost consciousness he might not wake up again. Reaching for the loose end of the plaid, he wrapped it around them. It was wet, but at least it provided some protection against the wind, and their shared body heat would help to warm them.

The rain had stopped and a single star peeked from behind a cloud. Somewhere, in the heart of the storm, afternoon had melted into evening. He closed his eyes. He'd just rest for a minute. Then he'd figure out what they should do.

Marjory lay in the dark cocoon of her bed, wondering why it was so wet. She twisted, trying to find a warmer, dryer spot, then opened her eyes to a sky full of stars. She frowned, confused. There were no stars in her bedchamber. Memory flashed, vanquishing her lethargy. The *curach* . . . the water . . . *Ewen*. She tried to sit up, but something held her down.

Panicked, she tried to pull her arms free, but couldn't. She struggled, but to no avail. Something heavy was definitely pinning her down, and to make things worse, she seemed to be encased in a length of wet wool. It scratched her arms and held them immobile. She tried to calm herself by breathing deeply—in and out, in and out—but even her breathing seemed constricted.

The object on top of her shifted. An awful noise filled the air. Marjory closed her eyes, waiting for something terrible to happen. Silence. She opened one eye. Nothing, only the placid glow of the stars. She opened her other eye. Still silence. Determined to free herself, Marjory wriggled to the side as much as she could. By twisting her head to the left, and looking to the right, she could just make out locks of hair falling across her shoulder. Tawny locks of hair, attached, no doubt, to a familiar head.

The noise repeated itself, but this time she identified the rumbling for what it was: Ewen snoring. Relief brought a flash of anger.

"Get off of me at once." Nothing happened. Another deafening snore filled the air. "I said, get off of me, man. Do I look like a bed to you?" He snorted, but remained prone across her. Drawing in as much air as she could, she screamed at him. "Ewen, wake up!"

The minute she used his name, she regretted the fact. If he were to be believed it wasn't his name at all. Cameron, he'd said. Cameron was his name. Odious to be sure, yet oddly fitting. And suddenly Marjory wondered if there wasn't something good about it after all.

"Marjory?" He shifted his weight, his voice groggy.

"You're crushing the life out o' me. I canna move. Get off."

With a groan, he rolled off of her. Unfortunately, the wool cocoon kept them bound together, and Marjory flipped over to land on top of him, sliding forward so that blue eyes met gold, his breath mingling with hers. She felt her heartbeat accelerate at the feel of his body beneath her.

He blinked. "Where are we?"

"You read my mind. I was going to ask you the same question." His heat invaded her, lighting a fire somewhere below her belly. Forcing herself to ignore her burgeoning feelings, she concentrated instead on his face.

His eyes narrowed and then widened as he came fully

awake. With a jerk, he pulled an arm free. Fumbling with the plaid, he managed to untangle it so that one side flapped free.

"You can move now."

The significance of his words were slow to sink in. When the full impact hit her, she felt herself grow hot. He always seemed to rob her of sanity. She rolled off of him, shivering in the cool night air. The loch's water lapped at the shore, almost at their feet. The small clearing in which they lay was lit faintly by starlight, but it was difficult to make out details.

When she was sure she had her feelings under control, she turned back to him. "The *curach?*"

"Gone, I'm afraid."

"How did we get here, then?" She chewed on her lip, still very aware of his body close to hers.

"Don't you remember?"

Irritation flashed. "If I remembered, I wouldna be asking you, would I?" She immediately regretted her words. "I didna mean to sound so harsh. I remember jumping into the water." The memory of the icy darkness closing over her was something she'd never forget. "I also remember you pulling me to the surface, but after that, I'm afraid 'tis a blank."

"Join the club." He offered her a wry smile.

"Join the what? I dinna fash?" She frowned.

"Well, that makes two of us."

"I beg your pardon?" The man was talking nonsense. Maybe this last ordeal had robbed him of his sanity once and for all.

He grinned. "I only meant that if you can't remember what happened, you're in the same boat as me when it comes to amnesia."

"Of course I was in the same boat with you. How else

would I find myself stranded in the middle of the wilderness?" Saints above, the man was making no sense at all. "And there's naught wrong with me that a good night's sleep wouldna cure. I certainly dinna have amnee-sha."

He laughed, his even white teeth shining in the darkness. "Amnesia's just another word for memory loss, Marjory. I only meant that it was ironic that you had memory loss, too."

"Ach. Well, if you'd just said that instead of talking about clubs and boats . . ."

"I'm sorry, I'll try to speak more plainly in the future." He didn't sound at all apologetic.

"So, are you going to tell me what happened after we jumped into the water?" she asked indignantly.

"I swam to the shore, pulling you along with me."

The enormity of what he had done hit her. "You saved my life."

"I saved us both."

"Aye, but ye could have left me."

"Don't be silly, I would never have done that. Anyway, it's behind us now. We're here—somewhat worse for the wear, I'd say, but still alive, and that's what counts." He tipped back his head, rubbing his temples.

"Are you all right?" Fear laced through her. Maybe he was going away again. She wasn't certain what was more unsettling, the fact that he might just disappear or the fact that she believed it could happen.

"I'm fine. Just a little tired. It was a long swim." He opened his eyes, his face lined with exhaustion. "Tell me something though—how is it you grew up living next to a lake and never learned to swim?"

She grimaced and looked down at her hands, old wounds still painful. "No one would teach me."

His brows drew together in question. "Why?"

Marjory looked up at the night sky with a sigh. It certainly wasn't from lack of trying. She'd begged everyone she knew. Fingal, her father, and after he died, her cousin Iain. But the answer had always been the same: *"It isna ladylike. Women dinna swim."*

"But that's just plain stupid. What are you supposed to do when a boat capsizes?" Marjory met his gaze and stuck her chin out defiantly. His eyes widened with understanding. "You weren't supposed to be on a boat, were you?"

" 'Tis my holding and, in point of fact, my *curach*— so I can ride in it whenever I choose."

His eyes narrowed. "Marjory Macpherson, have you ever been on a boat before?"

She ducked her head, embarrassment welling up inside. The man made her daft with his questions. "Nay, no' until today."

"And why didn't you mention that fact to me before we took off for the middle of the lake?"

"Would you have taken me with you if I'd told you?" She looked up again, defiant.

He was silent for a moment, then smiled ruefully. "No."

"Well, then." She paused, hoping the conversation was at an end.

"I see." He studied her face until she felt squirmy under his gaze. With amazing speed, he reached for her hands, pulling her close. "I'll say one thing for you, Marjory mine, you've got guts."

She searched his eyes, trying to understand the meaning of his words. Was he insulting her? She sucked in a breath and swallowed convulsively. He was so close she could see the stubble of his beard. She wanted . . . well, she didn't know what she wanted exactly, but she was pretty sure now wasn't the time or the place for it. Jerking her hands free, she sat back.

His lips curled into a knowing smile. Damn the man, he saw entirely too much. "Do you know where we are?"

Praise the saints, a change of topic, and none too soon. She'd actually been fantasizing about throwing herself into his arms, propriety be damned. She looked around the clearing. Thick trees bordered it on one side. The sound of running water gurgled over the quiet lapping of loch water.

"I canna say for sure. 'Tis too dark, but I hear the sound o' a wee burn just o'er there." She pointed off to the right. "And if it's the burn I think it is, then there's a cottage no' far upstream from here." She shivered, suddenly aware of how cold she was.

"A cottage sounds great. We need to get inside and out of these wet clothes before we catch cold."

Marjory nodded in agreement. Looking down at herself, she realized for the first time that she was wearing only her shift. She felt the heat rise into her face and automatically covered her breasts with her arms. The thin material did little to hide her body.

He laughed, standing up and extending his hand. "Now is not the time for modesty, Marjory mi—" He cut off the endearment. She felt absurdly disappointed. She reached for his outstretched hand, allowing him to pull her to her feet. "Okay, so where is this cottage?"

Cottage was a kind word. Cameron looked at the remains of what had once been a dwelling of some kind. Gaping holes marked where walls had been and vegetation had overtaken its masonry to the point that it resembled a mangled topiary gone wild. A great tree lay drunkenly across the center of the cottage, effectively dividing into two halves what had been, in better days, a whole house. The tree, obviously the victim of some long-gone storm, straddled the structure, its gnarled roots reaching skyward in grotesque imitation of human limbs.

"This is your cottage?"

"I didna say 'twas mine. I only said I knew it was here." Marjory looked as disappointed as he felt. "I knew it had been damaged, but I'd no idea it had been destroyed. What do we do now?" Her voice sounded small and tired. The trek to the cottage had taken some of the fire out of her.

"Come on. Maybe it's not as bad inside as it looks from out here." He reached for her hand and felt her fingers curl warmly around his. Stepping carefully over debris and tree roots, they made their way to what had once been the door.

"Stay here." He released her hand, pushing her behind him.

"I willna. I'm no' a weak babe that needs protecting." She moved around him and stepped through the doorway.

"Fine. Have it your way." He held out his arm, bowing from the waist in an imitation of chivalry, but his gesture was wasted on her back as she disappeared into the gloom of the interior.

"Marjory, wait—" His words were interrupted by her exclamation of pain. He leapt through the opening, ready to battle whatever it was that threatened her. He barked his shin on something immobile and let out a sharp curse. Feminine laughter filled the air. He stared in its direction, waiting for his eyes to adjust to the shadows. Marjory stood directly in front of him, a beam of starlight from a hole in the roof lighting her face. He grimaced. At least there was a roof.

"I dinna think you need attack the chest. It willna harm you. Although as a sentry, I can say with certainty"—she rubbed her hip ruefully—"it does a good job."

He turned to find the infidel responsible for his throbbing shin. A waist-high chest partially blocked the door. Stepping gingerly around it, he surveyed their newfound shelter. There wasn't much left, but miraculously the tree had just missed the fireplace, which sat in the far corner, amazingly undamaged.

"Have a look at this."

He turned from his perusal of the hearth to find Marjory in the opposite corner, gleefully looking at what appeared to be a moldy pile of hay. He raised his eyebrows in question.

" 'Tis the bed. And it's in passable shape." To illustrate the point, she held up two raggedy blankets.

"You call that a bed?" He could just imagine what was living in there. It made his skin crawl.

"Well, I'd say we're lucky to find anything at all." She bent to examine the bed more closely, stepping back in alarm when an unidentified rodent scurried out from under the pile. She turned to Cameron with a sheepish expression. "Well, at least we have the blankets."

He eyed them with some hesitation and then nodded. She was right. Beggars couldn't be choosers. "Help me gather up some of this broken wood. We'll use it to start a fire."

How exactly, he had no idea. Gas jets wouldn't be invented for a couple of centuries yet, and unfortunately, that was the only way he'd ever started a fire. He wandered around the room, picking up scattered pieces of broken furniture and mangled tree branches. The wood was dry. That ought to help.

Arms full, he turned back to the fireplace to find Marjory kneeling in front of it, blowing gently onto growing yellow flames. "How did you do that?" People who looked down on the inhabitants of ages past had obviously not met any of them firsthand. They were a very resourceful lot.

She looked up with a pleased smile, the light from the fire illuminating her face. "I had a flint in my sporran." She held up the small bag triumphantly. "Aren't you glad now that I took the time to find it?"

Recalling the incident, he had to admit that escaping the boat had been his priority at the time, but now, feeling the heat of the flames reaching out to him, he was pleased she'd refused to abandon the sporran. But, he'd be damned before he would acknowledge that. After all, he was the one who was supposed to be taking care of her, not the other way around.

Surprised at the Neanderthal nature of his reaction, he watched as her face fell. Guilt washed over him, vanquishing his wounded pride. "I'm glad you have it—but even if you didn't, I suspect you'd have found a way to coax a flame from the wood." She brightened at the compliment and he stared at her, enchanted for a moment by her beauty.

"I'll need some bigger pieces to keep it going." She looked pointedly at the stack he carried.

"Right." He pulled his thoughts away from the lush curves of her body. "I'll just put it all down right here." He made a tidy little pile next to the hearth. Stepping back, he watched as she efficiently fed the growing fire. Turning away, he stripped off his plaid and hung it over a large branch of the dead tree. It made a perfect drying rack—close enough to the fire to allow the wool to absorb the warmth, and far enough away to keep it from catching fire. Hell, he sounded like Martha Stewart.

He pulled his shirt over his head and hung it beside the plaid. With a shiver, he moved closer to the fire. "You can hang your wet clothes over there on the tree."

She looked up at him, her eyes widening at his lack of attire. Cameron actually felt himself blush. The Scottish version of underwear resembled a pair of baggy Bermuda shorts, hardly enticing. Hell, his bathing suit was more revealing. But somehow, under her gaze, he felt naked.

"Here, give me one of the blankets." She handed it to him without a word, color washing over her face. Holding the material by two corners, he shook it, thankful when nothing living popped off. He twirled the thing around his shoulders making a cape of sorts. It was musty smelling but seemed to be bug free and was certainly warmer than nothing.

Marjory's eyes were still on him. He bent and picked up the other blanket, handing it to her. "Your turn."

She took the faded rectangle from him, jumping back when their hands met. Good. She wasn't as immune to him as she pretended. It made him feel better to know he wasn't alone in his attraction.

"Turn your back."

She looked a bit like a prim schoolmarm in an old western. With a grin, he spun around, granting her a little privacy. He could hear her movements and his unapologetic brain conjured vivid pictures to go along with them.

"All right. You can turn around."

She was covered in the blanket. She had managed to tie it somehow at one shoulder so that it hung from her body, toga style. It was an appealing sight.

"Here." She held out her shift. He hung it next to his plaid, trying to get his libido in control.

"What now?"

"I think we should try and get some rest. We've a long walk in the morning."

That was his Marjory, practical to the core. Her no-nonsense attitude effectively tamped down his rising desire. "Where do you suggest we sleep?"

She shot a look at the bed in the corner. "Maybe we can use a bit of that?"

He walked over to the pile of straw. It certainly looked more appealing than the debris-strewn floor. "All right. You clear a place by the fire, and I'll see what can be salvaged here." He stirred the pile with a stick, hoping to frighten off anything else residing there. Nothing moved. Gingerly, he reached under the straw, grabbing an armload to move to the center of the room.

Three trips later they had a place to sleep. Marjory had found an old piece of linen folded in the chest. She spread it over the top of the makeshift bed. "It could be worse." Ah, yes, that Gaelic sense of optimism.

"It'll be fine," Cameron said—with more enthusiasm than he felt.

"It'd be better if we had a blanket for the top." Marjory shot a look at his plaid.

"Not a chance. It's still too wet."

"Oh." Her face fell.

"I've got an idea, but I'm not sure you'll like it."

She bit her lip, waiting for his thoughts.

"I could take this off." He gestured to his blanket. "We could use it for cover."

She shook her head, slowly.

"Look, Marjory, it isn't like I'm naked under here.

190

Besides, we've slept in the same bed before."

She blushed. "Aye, but that was because of Torcall."

He smiled to himself, remembering her plea for him to stay after it had no longer been necessary. "Well," he said, trying to reassure her with his tone, "it's like this. Even with the fire, it's cold in here, and the best way I know to stay warm is to share our body heat. For that to work best we need insulation of some sort. And it's either mine"—he ran a hand along the blanket—"or yours."

She frowned, obviously thinking it over. Then, squaring her shoulders, she sighed. "Fine. We'll use yours."

The woman made it sound as if he were asking her to sleep with a cobra, for heaven's sake. He waited until she was lying down and then settled in beside her, tucking the blanket around them for additional warmth. She turned her back to him, snuggling against his chest. He willed himself not to respond as she wriggled against his body. Wrapping an arm around her, he pulled her closer, listening as her breathing deepened and slowed.

"Good night, Marjory." No answer. He inhaled the soft floral fragrance of her hair, marveling at the fact that she could still smell so good after all they had been through.

It was going to be a long night.

Chapter Fifteen

Marjory stood by the shell of the window and looked at the stars, thinking, as she always did, of her mother. Happiness would be all that her mother's spirit would wish for her now. No cry for vengeance would come from those long-dead lips. Gleda would only want for her daughter to find a love as rich as the union she had shared with Marjory's father.

Marjory tried to reach inside herself, to find her anger and her pain, but all she could think of was the man lying on the pallet by the fire. Heaven help her, she wanted him. As surely as there were clans in Scotland, she wanted this man—whoever he turned out to be.

She sighed and wrapped her arms around herself, trying to ward off the predawn chill. One thing was for certain: He was not the man she had been forced to marry, not the man who had taken her with the callousness of a conqueror. She shivered again, but this time it wasn't from the cold.

"You're going to catch your death."

Marjory felt the meager warmth of Cameron's blanket

wrap around her shoulders. She leaned back against him, letting her body mold to his.

"Are you wishing on the stars?" His voice curled around her, warm and alive, lighting fires deep within her.

"I dinna believe in such nonsense." But she wanted to—oh, Heavenly Father, she wanted to.

Cameron pulled her closer, his chin resting on her head. "Star light, star bright, first star I see tonight. I wish I may, I wish I might, have the wish I wish tonight." He paused for a minute, looking up at the night sky. "My mother used to recite that for me. Then I'd make a wish."

Marjory stared up at the twinkling stars and felt hope blossoming. "My mother always said they were angels."

"Maybe they are." His voice was soft, thoughtful. "If so, then one of them is my mother."

"Mine, too." She twined her fingers through his, not wanting the moment to end. "Except that I dinna believe in them anymore."

"If you did, what would you wish for, Marjory mine?"

She turned in his embrace, amazed at her own boldness. He met her gaze and she caught her breath. His face was close to hers, so close she could feel his breath as it stirred tendrils of her hair.

She swallowed convulsively. She could feel the blood coursing through her body. "I'd wish for you, Cameron."

His arms tightened as he considered her words. "You called me Cameron." He leaned closer, and she shivered as his hair brushed against her cheek.

" 'Tis your name."

"Yes, but you've never used it before." He whispered the words and they came out sounding like a caress.

"I know." She swallowed again, trying to focus on his words. "But 'twould be wrong to call you by another man's name. And you're no' Ewen Cameron, of that I'm certain."

"How can you be sure?" His eyes searched hers, the intensity there almost as dazzling as the stars.

"Ewen canna swim."

He laughed—a rich, deep sound that echoed off of the remaining walls of the cottage. She tried to pull away, unexpectedly hurt by his laughter. He pulled her back, forcing her to meet his gaze.

"Wait, Marjory. I wasn't laughing at you. It's just that after all this time and everything I've been through, I find it amazing that something as insignificant as swimming could convince you."

She looked up at him, letting his words sink in. Her heart had begun its staccato beat again. His warmth flowed into her, robbing her of strength. She leaned against him, trying to find words for what she was feeling. " 'Tis just that—"

"Hush." He placed a finger over her mouth. "There's been enough talk." With one swift movement, his lips replaced his hand. Marjory felt his tongue trace the contour of her lip, and opened her mouth in response. Her insides turned to liquid fire, their tongues thrusting and parrying almost as if they dueled. Marjory wondered briefly what they battled for, then lost the thought as his mouth left hers and strayed to the curve of her throat.

The blanket he'd given her fell to the floor. She moaned in ecstasy, feeling a place deep inside her tighten and throb with need. No one had ever made her feel this way before. She reached for his head, pressing it into the soft skin of her throat. She shivered with delight as he followed one tender wet kiss with another. Her hands curled instinctively into the soft silkiness of his hair.

She tipped back her head, offering herself to him. He

licked lightly at the swell of her breast, above where the other blanket covered it. Suddenly she wanted more. Much more. Her nipples hardened and she wondered what she was anticipating, but almost as quickly as the thought came, it fled in the wake of sensation.

She was on fire, and innately she knew that Cameron was the only one who could put it out. He tugged at the knot at her shoulder. She pushed his hand aside and slowly released the knot, allowing the blanket to fall to the floor. Skin met skin as he sighed, pulling her close, accepting her offering, letting his body heat warm her. His hands massaged the small of her back, circling lower to cup her buttocks.

His heated manhood pressed against her thigh, and a curious sense of elation filled her. This was the way it was supposed to be between a man and a woman. She didn't know how she knew, but she was certain.

He bent his head, his mouth covering her breast. All thought stopped at the rough feel of his tongue as it laved her skin. He sucked, briefly, at her nipple, releasing it and blowing softly. Marjory felt as much as heard the moan that escaped her lips, coming from somewhere deep within her. She pushed against him, wanting more.

He smiled. She could see the white of his teeth in the shadowy light. Lifting her up into his arms, he held her against his chest, and she marveled at the feel of his hot flesh.

"You're sure?" A shadow flickered across his face. "This doesn't change anything." The words came out a mere whisper, but Marjory could not mistake their meaning.

She reached up to cover his lips with her finger, to stop him from saying anything more. "I want you, Cameron." She met his gaze. She had never been more sure of anything in her life. Her body cried for his in a way older than time. Whoever he was, for tonight at least he belonged to her.

He walked to the pallet and gently laid her on the makeshift bed. She shivered as the cold air washed across her. Instinctively she raised her arms, calling to him, offering him all that she had, all that she was. He bent and stripped off his trews. She gasped at the sheer size of him. He stood before her, a warrior. *Her* warrior.

He gently laid himself over her, resting his weight on his elbows. Their eyes met and she sucked in a breath at the desire she saw reflected in the depths of his eyes. He bent to kiss her again, this time as softly as a butterfly. She felt her desire rising. She wanted more from him. So much more.

She shyly reached down and encircled his manhood, her hand relaxing at its feel. He sucked in a breath and she stroked its length, amazed at the combination of velvet and steel. He deepened his kiss, his tongue invading her mouth. She wrapped her arms around him, pulling him closer, reveling in his weight against her body.

He stroked the side of her hip, sending ripples of pleasure washing through her. His lips wandered down her shoulder, placing light nipping kisses as they passed. Reaching her breast, he pulled it deep into his mouth and began to suck. She cried out with the joy of it, sensation rocking her, pulling at her very core.

His hand stroked along her belly, inching lower, tangling in the curls at the apex of her thighs. She tightened, squeezing her legs together. He lifted his head, meeting her gaze. "Trust me."

How many times had he said this to her? And always, always he had held true to his words. A fleeting image of Aida crossed her vision. Marjory fought against it. She would not let that woman in here. Not now.

With a breath like a sigh, she relaxed her legs. Cameron's mouth again found her breast and she tipped back her head, wanting more. His hand caressed her thigh. Her body tightened in anticipation and she held her breath, waiting for his fingers to move higher.

With one finger, he parted the satiny folds that guarded her secret most place. In an instant, he was inside her, his finger stroking, stroking, stroking. Marjory arched against him, unable to control the shudders that rocked her. Her muscles clenched, and she wondered how anybody could stand this kind of pleasure.

Cameron's lips left her breast, and he trailed long tender kisses along the soft swelling of her stomach, the combination of his mouth and hands making her wild. She moaned with disappointment when he removed his finger.

"Patience, Marjory mine. Patience." His voice was rough with emotion.

She writhed against him, desperate for more. Then his mouth found the sweet soft core of her and she cried out, his tongue darting in and out, in and out, until she thought she'd explode. Sensation surrounded Marjory, driving her higher and higher until there was nothing but fire and need.

He changed his rhythm, moving higher and circling her tiny nub with featherlike strokes, faster and faster, until the world burst into shards of color. She reached for him, holding on as spasms of pure joy racked her body. Never had she ever dreamed she could feel like this.

Slowly, slowly, she began to come down, her body still trembling. She opened her eyes and found him watching her. She smiled tentatively, suddenly unsure.

He reached for her face, caressing it with the back of his hand. "You're beautiful." Her heart soared. "There's more. Can I take you there?"

She nodded numbly, unsure if she could survive any more pleasure but afraid to not take the chance. He pushed up onto his elbows and bent to kiss her, the taste of her still on his lips. His tongue ravaged her, sliding into her mouth and thrusting with a rhythm that matched her own. She felt the fire building again and marveled at the power of her need. She wanted him now more than ever.

"I want you." She hadn't realized she'd spoken until she saw the answering desire flash in his eyes.

With a quick twist, Cameron repositioned himself above her, his eyes never leaving hers, and pushed himself into her. She opened her legs, welcoming him, wanting to take him deeper and deeper, to sheathe him in her heat, to make him hers forever.

Slowly, he began to move. She felt a rhythm begin. Matching her body's movements to his thrusting, she met him stroke for stroke, feeling a burst of fire with every pulsing beat. Body against body, soul against soul, she felt them unite as they rose higher and higher on each wave of pleasure. Together they rode the wind, each stroke taking them nearer to the sun until, with a blinding white light, Marjory felt herself break into a million pieces, felt his arms tightening around her as he found his own release.

Lost in a cloud of ecstasy, Marjory drifted slowly back to earth, feeling the warm security of his embrace and knowing that, for once, the demons could not get to her. With a sigh, she snuggled into his side and allowed herself to sleep.

* * *

Waking, Cameron shifted, trying not to disturb Marjory. She was beautiful. Not in the artful, bottle-it-and-sell-it kind of way so common in his century, but in a natural, what-you-see-is-what-you-get kind of way.

He'd wanted so much to please her. To prove to her that a man and a woman coming together could be a joyous thing. It had been hard to contain his own desire. To pleasure her first. But it had been more than worth it.

Marjory was amazing. She had given him more than her body. She had gifted him with a part of her soul. It was the most precious gift he had ever received.

A niggle of guilt tugged at the back of his mind. He shouldn't have let this happen. The little voice in his head chided him for his callousness. He had taken from her, but what had he given in return? A night to remember? No, Marjory wasn't like that. Last night had been a commitment of sorts, a commitment that he couldn't afford to make.

He had to get back to his own time. He had to face himself, to discover for better or worse who he really was. Everything else was secondary. He had to find a way to make her understand that.

The little niggle of guilt blossomed into full-fledged culpability. With a sigh, he disentangled himself from her sleeping form, smoothing back a stray strand of silky black hair. She smiled in her sleep. Dear God, what had he done?

He stood, shivering in the cool air. His muscles were sore from their ordeal on the lake and he stretched, trying to work out some of the stiffness. First the swim, then the hike to the cottage, and then . . . He smiled despite his worries. The night had started on a bad note, but it had definitely ended as a perfectly orchestrated symphony. He laughed at the poetic turn of his thoughts, pulling on his trews.

He tugged his shirt over his head next, then stared at his plaid, shaking his head ruefully. It looked dry, but that didn't mean he'd be able to get the damn thing on.

"Cameron?"

Happiness rippled through him at the sound of his name on her lips. He turned to find blue eyes gazing at him sleepily. "Good morning."

She yawned, stretching like a cat, and glanced at the sky. "We should have been on our way ages ago."

"I guess we got a little sidetracked." He grinned, remembering in vivid detail the exact nature of their detour.

She sat up, smiling, pushing her hair back from her face. He felt his body react as he drank in the sight of her luscious naked curves. Suddenly aware of his scrutiny, she blushed and pulled the blanket up to her chin.

"I'm sorry. I forgot . . ." Her face grew redder. "I mean . . ."

"Hush, princess. It's all right. Here, put this on." He handed over her shift, turning his back so that she could dress. The irony of his actions didn't escape him, but he felt, perhaps absurdly under the circumstances, a powerful urge to protect her, even from himself.

Especially from himself.

"You can turn around now. I'm decent." She had not only donned the shift, but had managed to tie the blanket securely back into place. It gave her an exotic look. Not that fifteenth-century Scotland wasn't exotic. "Do you have any idea what time o' day it is?"

"No, not exactly." He glanced at the sun, wishing for his Rolex. "But I'd say it's almost noon."

"I beg your pardon?" She looked at him quizzically.

GET TWO FREE* BOOKS!

SIGN UP FOR THE LOVE SPELL ROMANCE BOOK CLUB TODAY.

LOWEST PRICES EVER!

Every month, you will receive two of the newest Love Spell titles for the low price of $8.50,* **a $4.50 savings!**

As a book club member, not only do you save **35% off the retail price**, you will receive the following special benefits:

- **30% off** all orders through our website and telecenter (plus, you still get 1 book FREE for every 5 books you buy!)

- Exclusive access to dollar sales, special discounts, and offers you won't be able to find anywhere else.

- Information about contests, author signings, and more!

- Convenient home delivery of your favorite books every month.

- A 10-day examination period. If you aren't satisfied, just return any books you don't want to keep.

There is no minimum number of books to buy, and you may cancel membership at any time.

* Please include $2.00 for shipping and handling.

NAME:_____

ADDRESS:_____

_____

_____

TELEPHONE:_____

E-MAIL:_____

_____ I want to pay by credit card.

__ Visa   __ MasterCard   __ Discover

Account Number:_____

Expiration date:_____

SIGNATURE:_____

Send this form, along with $2.00 shipping and handling for your FREE books, to:

Love Spell Romance Book Club
20 Academy Street
Norwalk, CT 06850-4032

Or fax (must include credit card information!) to: 610.995.9274.
You can also sign up on the Web at www.dorchesterpub.com.

Offer open to residents of the U.S. and Canada only. Canadian residents, please call 1.800.481.9191 for pricing information.

"I think it's nearly midday." He corrected, wondering if he'd ever get used to the language barrier. Not that it mattered. He wouldn't be here long enough to worry about adjusting his speech permanently.

Marjory made her way to the doorway, fastening her sporran around her waist as she walked. "We'd best get moving then."

"I can't go anywhere until I get this thing on." He pointed at his tartan, still hanging from the tree limb.

Marjory stood with her hands on her hips, eyebrows raised in question.

Cameron felt himself blush. He shrugged. "I can't get the damned thing on without help."

Her peal of laughter rang out across the room, punctuating his embarrassment. "Come here then, I'll give you a hand."

He grabbed his garment and held it out to her. She wrapped it around his waist, neatly gathering its bulk into pleats. At the feel of her hands, he caught his breath, his heartbeat accelerating. He tried grabbing the material from her—a mistake. Skin against skin was even more compelling. They stood holding hands, staring at each other, gasping.

The plaid fell forgotten to the floor.

Sunlight streamed through the hole in the roof, pulling Marjory from the contented lethargy of sleep. Opening her eyes, she nestled closer to Cameron's warmth. He groaned in his sleep, one arm thrown possessively across her waist.

She stretched, pointing her toes, feeling her body come fully awake. She closed her eyes against the intrusive sun and allowed herself to relive the past day's lovemaking. The second time had been even better than the first, and her body hummed at just the thought. She shivered with delight at the memory.

She probably ought to be feeling remorse, or, at the very least, regret—but the plain fact was, she didn't. Perhaps those feelings would come later. She pushed the thought aside. Right now, she simply wanted to enjoy the moment. Time enough for concern later.

She rolled slightly, turning toward Cameron. His eyes flickered open sleepily. She smiled self-consciously. It was one thing to remember their lovemaking on her own, quite another to think of it with him watching. She felt herself blush and bit the side of her lip. "We fell asleep again."

Cameron grinned, pulling her close. "Well, you have a way of wearing a man out, Marjory mine."

Her face grew even hotter. "I . . . I . . . that is . . ."

Her voice seemed to have deserted her. Fortunately, she was spared having to try and summon it. His mouth covered hers, opening for a long deep kiss. Marjory felt the heat building inside her again. She pressed against him, feeling his arms lock around her. She reveled in the hardness of him, giving and taking as the passion of the kiss intensified. He pulled back, a question burning brightly in his eyes.

But before she could answer, a loud rumble erupted from beneath the blanket.

"What was that?" Cameron sat up, holding his hand to his chest in mock terror.

" 'Twas my belly," she admitted, fighting embarrassment. Cameron reached out and ran a hand down her cheek, smiling with tenderness. Marjory felt her heart skip a beat.

"Well, I suppose if I were a true warrior I'd go and

kill something for us to eat, but I'm afraid my skill set doesn't extend that far."

Marjory had never heard the phrase, but she understood his meaning. And it again reinforced what Cameron had claimed last night. Ewen had been a great hunter. Evidently, the new—and greatly improved, she might add—Cameron, wasn't.

Not a problem. She'd been hunting since she was a wee lass. "I could try and snare a rabbit."

Cameron shot her a look of open amazement. "Beautiful and a huntress, too? What luck!"

Marjory blushed. Even after the morning's extended intimacy, she felt shy around him.

He smiled and tucked a strand of hair behind her ear. "I guess we really ought to be getting back." He looked at the sky through the roof.

She followed his gaze, shocked to discover that the day had progressed well into the afternoon. "I think perhaps 'tis too late to try and make Crannag Mhór this day. 'Tis quite a distance on foot. The loch stretches from one end o' the valley to the other, climbing up into the mountains at either end. Without horses 'twould take more than a day. We're better off waiting until the morning." She ducked her head, her mind already imagining another night spent in his arms.

"Well, I suppose we'll just have to make the best of it, then." He bent and dropped a kiss on her cheek. "But, first, I suggest we find something to eat."

Nodding in agreement, she rose from the makeshift bed, dragging one of the blankets with her. Picking up her scattered clothing, she turned her back and began to dress, imagining his amused stare boring into her backside. With a last tug at her ensemble, she turned back to face him, only to find that he was gone. "Cameron?"

"Over here." He stepped out from behind a pile of rubble, a wooden dipper held triumphantly in his hand. His plaid was slightly askew, but he had managed to secure it without her help. She smiled.

"What have you found?"

"Water."

She frowned in confusion. "Here?" She walked over and looked into the dipper. It *was* filled with water. She smelled it. It seemed fresh. He offered it to her and she drank thirstily.

"More?" He turned and gestured to an odd contraption behind him that was made of wood with a metal handle sticking out of the top. It looked like a giant urn of some kind with a spout on one side. She watched as Cameron moved the handle up and down. Water flowed from the spout. She crossed herself. What magic was this?

"Marjory, what is it? You act like you've never seen a pump before." His concerned gaze embraced her and some of her panic receded.

"What did you call it?" She took a step toward the contraption, curiosity overcoming her fear.

"A pump. You know, it brings water into the house—I'd guess from the stream we followed."

She tentatively touched the handle. The metal was cool to the touch. "I've never seen anything like it. A pump, did you say? Does it work by magic?"

"No, physics."

"Physics." She repeated the strange word and, holding her breath, pumped the handle. Water poured from the spout. With a start, she jumped backward, then stepped forward again when she was certain nothing else was going to happen.

Cameron came up behind her, turning her to face him. "Are you saying you've never seen one of these before?"

"Nay, never." She pulled away, moving the lever up and down again, fascinated with the resulting stream of water. "Will it run out, do you think?"

"No, not as long as there is a sufficient amount of water in the creek."

"How does it work?" She couldn't pull her eyes away from the magical contraption.

"I don't know that I can explain it all, but basically it forces the water from the stream through a channel of some kind to the reservoir. Moving the handle makes the whole thing work and the water comes out the spout. It's got something to do with pistons and valves."

" 'Tis no' magic?" He sounded so blasé. Surely he wouldn't be so calm in the face of sorcery.

"Absolutely not." He laughed. "It's just basic technology."

"Perhaps wherever it is that you come from, but we have no such techno—" She stumbled over the unfamiliar word. "—thing at Crannag Mhór."

He frowned. "Who did this cottage belong to, Marjory?" He stared at her, his expression intense, as if her answer held the key to a puzzle.

"Why, it belonged to Grania. She lived here until the storm took her sight. After that, she couldna manage on her own, so she came to live with us at Crannag Mhór." She waited for him to say something, watching as different emotions washed across his face: confusion, then shock, then something that looked like amazement.

"Well, I'll be damned."

Chapter Sixteen

The old girl had been holding out on him. Either she was a brilliant inventor or she wasn't a card-carrying member of the fifteenth century either. And then . . . well, the implications were almost limitless. She might know who he was. She might know the way home. Heck, she might even be able to send him home.

"Cameron, what is it?" Marjory's voice brought him sharply back to reality.

He looked at her beautiful face, concern forcing her brows together. There was no point in alarming her. He'd talk with Grania first, give her an opportunity to explain herself. "Nothing. It's just an amazing thing to find a pump here. Grania must have connections with people from London or the continent."

He flinched at the lie, knowing that pumps hadn't been put into use anywhere until well after the fifteenth century. He hated to play fast and loose with the truth, especially in the face of their newly found intimacy, but, he argued with himself, it was for the best. Really it was. When the time was right, and he had some notion of what exactly was going on, he'd tell Marjory the whole truth—or at least what tiny part of it he was privy to.

"Hmmm." She narrowed her eyes in thought. "I do seem to remember hearing something about Bertram having family outside o' Scotland. He wasn't from Crannag Mhór, you understand. He was a tinker by trade, visiting the valley only on rare occasion. But after he met Grania he came more often, eventually staying for good."

She still looked at the pump, trepidation mixed with awe, but at least for now she seemed to be buying the story. He moved to distract her. "What about that rabbit you promised me?" His stomach rumbled ominously, "Maybe you'd better try for two. I could eat a whole one by myself."

She laughed. "Well, then, you'd best come and help me or there may no' be even the one."

An hour later, as they hiked through the woods, Cameron was still trying to make heads or tails of the fact that Grania had a pump. Marjory walked ahead of him, holding a snare she'd fashioned from some rope she'd found. Unfortunately, the rabbits seemed to be way ahead of them and had all left the vicinity—and his stomach was still rumbling.

Marjory knelt suddenly, lifting a broken sapling, her eyes scanning the horizon. The sight made Cameron think of an old TV show: *Davy Crockett, King of the Wild Frontier.* The inane theme song danced through his brain.

Oh, yeah, he was Davy Crockett all right. Davy Crockett in a skirt. His warped recollections were interrupted when Marjory tugged at his hand. She held a finger to her lips and pulled him down into the tall grass of the forest undergrowth. "There's someone out there."

Listening intently, he could hear leaves rustling with the fall of footsteps. Whoever it was, he wasn't trying to be secretive. A tree branch somewhere in front of them, took on a life of its own as it bent forward and then snapped back into place.

"Bloody hell." The oath broke the silence of the glen. The figure of a man emerged from the underbrush, gingerly rubbing his cheek. Cameron couldn't help smiling. Score one for the trees. The man walked slowly forward, searching the woods on either side of the path, still too far away for Cameron to recognize.

Not so Marjory. With a cry of joy, she jumped up. "Fingal." She flew along the path, throwing herself into his arms. Cameron stood up and followed her. It seemed they'd been rescued. Perversely, he felt an absurd sense of disappointment.

"Saints be praised, ye're alive." Fingal kept hold of Marjory, his assessing eyes meeting Cameron's over the top of her head. "We feared you dead."

He meant Marjory of course, and for a moment, Cameron found himself wishing he had been included in the man's concerns. It was hard enough to feel like an outsider, but for it to be because of being someone he wasn't—well, that was almost more than a man could contemplate.

"Ye're sure ye're all right?" Fingal pushed Marjory back, his eyes searching her face.

"I'm fine. Cameron took care of me."

"Cameron?" Fingal asked, his gaze returning to Cameron.

"Aye." Marjory nodded, pulling out of his embrace. "Cameron saved me. We wouldna be here at all if it were no' for him."

"Again?" Fingal raised an eyebrow and looked at Cameron with speculative eyes.

Marjory planted her fists on her hips. " 'Tis true. When the *curach* began to sink, we had to jump o'er the side, and Cameron swam with me to the shore. Without him, I would definitely have drowned."

"Without me, you wouldn't have been in the boat at all," Cameron added dryly.

Marjory swung around to face him. "Dinna be starting that again. I chose to get into the *curach* all on my own. 'Twas no' like you forced me to do it."

"Peace, both o' you," Fingal said. "You sound like a couple of bickering children. 'Tis enough that ye're safe and unharmed, lass." He ruffled Marjory's hair. "Come on then, they'll be wondering where I've gotten off to."

"Who's with you?" Cameron suspected, of course, but he wanted to hear nevertheless.

Fingal frowned. "Some of our men, along with the Camerons. Torcall and Allen and that henchman o' his, Dougall, are here. We're making camp o'er there." He nodded in the direction of the cottage. "We'd just about given up hope o' finding you. Torcall has been raging about yer luring Ewen to his death. He'll be pleased to see his son still lives, but I've no doubt he'll still be thinking there's witchery afoot."

Cameron suddenly felt tired. There was no winning this war. Hatred would consume them all in the end. Revenge begetting more revenge. He wished he could just escape the lot. Go home. Nothing in his old life could possibly be as complicated as all of this.

As if on cue, his mind trotted out the vision of the blonde standing in the rain. Maybe she needed him. Maybe her very life depended on his return. But then Marjory needed him, too.

At the thought, he pivoted to face her, surprised to see her and Fingal huddled together, whispering. They moved apart, Fingal's expression guarded, Marjory's apologetic.

"Fingal was just telling me that we should be careful what we say to Torcall."

"What do you mean?" Cameron frowned.

Fingal sighed. "I mean that tales of you swimming to Marjory's rescue willna go o'er well with him."

"Go on. Tell him the rest o' it." Marjory poked her captain, insistent that he continue.

"Whatever is happening here"—Fingal shot another speculative look in Cameron's direction—"it canna help to share it with Torcall. He's talked o' naught but the fact that Ewen canna swim since he discovered you took the *curach*. I dinna like to think how he'll react when he finds ye swam to shore with Marjory in tow."

Fingal obviously believed Marjory's story. Which meant that he accepted the fact that Cameron had swum them both to safety. But if Ewen Cameron couldn't swim, then that also meant that Fingal must realize he wasn't Ewen. Which meant that Fingal might accept him as a potential ally. Just like that. Cameron marveled at the ability of these people to accept the seemingly impossible without batting an eye.

Fingal was right, though—Torcall Cameron was a different story. The man wanted his son, not a twenty-first-century surrogate. Telling their tale would only put them in danger. At all costs, Torcall must be made to believe that Ewen lived. Memory or no.

Marjory interrupted his thoughts. "We could tell him that the *curach* washed us ashore during the storm."

"Nay, he'd ne'er believe that," Fingal said. "We found the *curach* this afternoon. 'Twas smashed to bits."

Cameron frowned. "Maybe that could have happened after we were safely ashore."

" 'Tis possible, I suppose. But whatever ye tell him, be careful." He turned his attention to Marjory. "And no talk of heroes."

Marjory gave him a mutinous look, then sighed. "Fine."

Cameron reached for her hands. "Thanks for the vote of confidence, princess, but Fingal's right." Their eyes met. He gently squeezed her hands.

"Fingal Macgillivray, I swear, if ye're up to more of your tricks . . ." Torcall's voice rang through the woods.

Marjory tightened her grip on Cameron's hands.

"It's show time." Cameron watched as Torcall came into view and then stopped at the sight of them on the path. The man's craggy face broke into a grin, and he strode toward what he believed to be his son, a look of relief lighting his fierce countenance. Cameron drew in a breath, preparing for the inevitable.

"So the two o' ye were washed to shore?" Torcall frowned at Cameron, his eyes skeptical.

"Yeah, we were lucky. It dumped us in shallow water. All we had to do was make our way to dry land." Cameron paused, sizing up his audience. Allen sat across the fire, a sullen expression on his face, lost in his thoughts. Dougall had disappeared into the woods, presumably to heed the call of nature, and Marjory was sitting by a second fire, surrounded by her kin. Leaving Cameron on his own with Torcall.

"But ye canna swim."

Cameron sighed. This preoccupation with Ewen's water skills was getting on his nerves. Not to mention the fact that he hated lying. But in his heart he knew that this all was necessary to protect Marjory. "I told you, all we had to do was walk to shore. Crawl actually. We were pretty tired. There was no need for swimming."

Torcall grunted, obviously unsatisfied. "Even if I accept yer account of yer landing, that doesna explain what you were doing in the *curach* in the first place."

"I wanted to see what it was like to be in a boat. I never even thought about the need to swim." Weak, but plausible.

But Torcall wasn't a fool. "Ewen, you canna even ford a stream without finding the narrowest place to cross. Now ye're expecting me to believe that ye suddenly had an urge to go out on the loch in a boat no bigger than a man?" Torcall's voice rose in frustration.

Allen pulled out of his lethargy and stared intently at Cameron. "Ye're no' telling us the truth o' it. I tell you, Father, there's more here than he's willing to explain."

"Look, I'm not lying to anyone. I just wanted to go out in the damn boat. I had no idea Marjory would decide to come along, and I certainly had no idea there was going to be a storm. That's all there is to it." He took a deep breath, his anger rising. Enough was enough. "Would you rather I tell you that Ewen is dead and that I'm a traveler from another time occupying his body and that I know how to swim?"

Silence filled the campsite. Allen sat frozen in place, his mouth open, his chin resting on his chest. Marjory and her kin had obviously heard his outburst. Fingal looked bemused. Marjory looked terrified. Cameron's anger slowly drained from his body, leaving a bitter taste in his mouth. What the hell was he doing?

Blowing out a breath, he turned to face Torcall. The man stared at him, shocked, his eyes narrowed as he tried to process his son's outburst. The two men glared at each other in silence. Then, suddenly, Torcall threw back his head and laughed.

"You jest!" He pounded Cameron on the back, the power of the blow nearly knocking him forward into the fire. Torcall continued to laugh, finally calming enough to wipe his eyes with a sleeve. Still breathing hard, he threw a heavy arm around his son's shoulders. "I've missed ye, boy. 'Tis glad I am that ye've survived yet again. And I trust that, now, ye'll know better than to head out on the loch on your own."

Cameron nodded, relieved that Torcall seemed to have let the matter of the *curach* drop.

"A time traveler. Did you hear that, Allen?" Torcall looked at his son and dissolved into laughter again. Cameron ducked to the side to avoid the already flying arm, his gaze meeting Allen's.

Allen wasn't laughing. He was staring at Cameron with speculative eyes. He offered no response, nor did it seem that Torcall expected one. Cameron suppressed a shiver. Brother or not, this man was his enemy.

Cameron idly threw sticks into the fire and looked around the campsite. Men were sprawled in every direction: some sleeping, others tossing about trying to find a comfortable position. It looked like someone had drawn a line across the encampment, Camerons sleeping on one side, Macphersons on the other.

Marjory was somewhere, sleeping securely within the ranks of her men. It reminded Cameron of something out of *Romeo and Juliet*. The Montagues and Capulets. Not that he was much of a Romeo. Hell, he wasn't even a Montague.

Disturbed by the turn of his thoughts, he concentrated on the glow of the campfire. It had burned low, only shooting flames when he flicked a new twig onto the coals.

"Cameron?"

He turned at the sound of his name and smiled. Not exactly "wherefore art thou, Romeo?" but it would have to do. Marjory emerged from the shadows, her mouth open to speak again. He put a finger to his lips and motioned for her to sit by the fire.

"I couldna sleep," she whispered.

"Neither could I."

They sat for a minute in companionable silence. He could feel the warmth of her body next to his and curbed the desire to pull her into his arms. The time for intimacy of that sort was long past.

"What did you tell him?" She shot him an inquisitive look.

"Torcall?"

She nodded, her dark hair dancing in the firelight.

"You mean, besides the fact that I'm from the future?" She'd heard that part loud and clear. Hell, probably everybody in the valley had been able to hear his outburst.

"Aye."

He lifted his eyebrows in surprise. It wasn't like Marjory to miss a chance to go for the jugular. "I told him I wanted to see what it was like in a boat, and that it never occurred to me that I might need to swim."

She nodded again, this time drawing her brows together in a frown. "Do you think he believed you?"

"I don't know. Possibly." It had been a lame explanation.

" 'Twould have been nice if you could have invented a more plausible tale."

"Well, it was the best I could come up with. Next time, you be the one to try and pacify him."

Marjory flinched.

He reached out to touch her hand. A mistake. Sparks flew between them. He withdrew his hand. "I was just joking. I would never leave you alone to face him."

She relaxed. "Well, at least he thought you were merely jesting. Whatever possessed you to tell the truth?"

It was his turn to flinch. "It was crazy, I know. It's just . . . I'm so sick of everything. Especially the inquisition about my—or should I say Ewen's—inability to swim. Anyway, you're right. He thought the whole thing was a joke. Frankly, I think Torcall is willing to believe whatever I say. He wants Ewen alive so badly, he'll buy into almost anything."

"Maybe, but I dinna like the way he was looking at you. I think 'tis possible that there's a seed o' doubt now that wasna there before."

"Possibly."

"And then there's the wee matter o' Allen. He definitely didna find your explanation humorous."

He thought again about the look of animosity Allen had leveled on him. "I know. It seems we're stuck between a rock and a hard place."

"What?" Her eyes widened in confusion.

"It's just a phrase. It means we're in a difficult situation. We've got to figure out how to get Torcall back to Tyndrum and Allen with him."

She nodded, chewing on her lip—a sure sign she was worried.

"Look, I know that won't solve all your problems, but at least it will buy some time for you and Fingal to figure out what to do."

She met his gaze. "Time is exactly what I need. I told

215

you I sent word to my grandfather, asking for reinforcements. But he's with the king and so he didna receive my message. Given a little more time, he'll be home, and then I've no doubt he'll come help me put Torcall Cameron in his place."

"So, as long as we can get Torcall to go home, you'll be all right?"

She nodded, tears welling in her eyes.

"Then why are you crying?"

"You." She angrily brushed her tears on the linen of her sleeve.

"Me?"

"Dinna act daft, man. Of course I'm worried about you. You've got the here and now of Allen to deal with and then you've got to find . . ." She stumbled over the last words, beginning to cry in earnest. He resisted the urge to kiss the tears away. She took a deep breath, regaining control. "You've got to find your way home. It may no' be as easy as you think. It may no' even be possible."

He hoped she was wrong, that Grania would be able to help him, but he had to admit there was truth in what she said. "I'll find my way. I have to believe that."

"So you can find yourself."

"Right." Somehow when she said it, it sounded trite—but knowing who he truly was important. Somewhere out there he already had a life, and he couldn't just desert it because he'd landed somewhere else. Surely he owed himself better than that? He simply couldn't go on living the life of another man. He had to have answers and those answers lay in the twenty-first century.

"I understand." Marjory rose, wrapping her arms around herself.

"Look, Marjory, if it could be any other way . . ." He

moved to stand behind her, resting his hands lightly on her shoulders.

She shook him off. "I said, I understand." She walked away then, her slight form fading into the night. He watched until she disappeared; then sat back on the log, fighting the desire to go after her, to swear he'd never leave.

Shaking his head, he broke the spell. He had no choice in the matter. He had to remember who he was. Had to get back to his life, to the blonde. He'd had the dream for a reason, and he simply couldn't ignore the fact—no matter how much he might want to.

Chapter Seventeen

Marjory shifted uncomfortably in her saddle. They had been riding since dawn. The sun-silvered walls of Crannag Mhór gleamed in the distance. Just an hour or so more and they would be home. She twisted around to look behind her.

Cameron and Fingal rode together, their heads bent close in conversation. It seemed odd, the older man with Ewen. But then, it wasn't really Ewen. She felt an unreasonable stab of jealousy watching the two of them. There wasn't much time left and she wanted Cameron to spend it all with her.

As if sensing her eyes on him, he looked up and grinned. Her heart turned over and joy washed through her. With conscious effort, she forced herself to turn back to watching the trail. She was behaving like a ninny. She was the head of her clan and she had to act accordingly. People depended on her. She sighed, thinking how much easier it all would be with someone to love by her side—but that was impossible.

"We're almost home."

Marjory jumped at the words. Fingal had pulled forward his mount riding alongside hers. "What did you say?"

Her captain shot her a concerned look. "I said that we're almost home. Are ye sure ye're feeling all right?"

"I'm fine, really. Just a little tired." She gave him a bright smile.

Fingal nodded, his eyes still questioning. "Aimil will be o'erjoyed to see you. She was practically inconsolable when she first heard ye'd gone out in the *curach* with Ewen."

"He prefers Cameron." She spoke automatically, and immediately wished the words back.

Fingal merely shrugged. "Cameron it is then."

" 'Twill be good to get back home," she said, seeking to change the conversation.

Fingal nodded, not so easily put off. His face was still shadowed with concern. "There's still something ye're no' telling me, but I'll wait until ye're ready to speak o' it."

Marjory managed a smile and let her horse fall back to the rear. Fingal was entirely too observant. She hated to keep anything from him. She owed him honesty, but she wasn't ready to share her feelings. Besides, Cameron would soon be gone, and she would rather deal with the loss on her own. She couldn't bear the thought of anyone else grieving for her.

Aimil and Fingal were almost like parents. After the massacre, they had been the glue that held her together. Marjory had no doubt that without them, she would never have been able to survive. It had been Aimil who had accompanied her to Moy and held her through all the long, dark, sleepless nights; Aimil who had dried her tears and soothed away the nightmares.

Fingal, too, had devoted himself to her—staying behind and working all those years to rebuild Crannag Mhór. And then he'd stayed on after she returned, to help her run the holding and protect her from the wrath of the Camerons.

They had sacrificed their lives for her. The enormity of the thought was daunting. She had never really thought about it in that way before. Neither of them had ever married, and there had never been talk of either of them leaving Crannag Mhór to build lives of their own. They'd simply always been there. For her.

She jerked forward abruptly as her horse slowed to a stop, gripping the pommel in an effort to keep her balance. Lost in thought, she had failed to notice that the men in front of her were slowing.

She looked past them, searching for the source of their caution. She could just make out a rider approaching from the direction of the tower. She squinted into the sunlight, trying to see him more clearly. His colors were Cameron. She drew in a sharp breath, shading her eyes as she watched Torcall and Dougall pull away from the line of horses, spurring their mounts into a full gallop.

Fingal moved to follow them, but was blocked by Allen's claymore. He pulled back, drawing his own weapon, holding his position just behind Allen.

The other men shifted uneasily, Camerons eyeing Macphersons. Tension filled the air.

"What are they up to, do you think?" Marjory shivered at Cameron's whispered words. She looked up, meeting the warmth of his gaze. For a moment enemies were forgotten and there was nothing but the two of them. She fought the urge to run her hand along the strong ridge of his jaw, to trace the line of his scar.

She shifted, pulling her gaze away from his. "I dinna ken, but the rider is a Cameron."

"How can you tell?"

"The colors o' his plaid." She gestured toward the man.

"Who the hell is he, then? I thought all of Torcall's men were here with us."

" 'Twas certainly what they led us to believe." Marjory turned her attention back to Allen. He was shifting impatiently in his saddle, holding his sword at the ready. He alternated between watching Fingal and looking toward his father. It was more than obvious that he waited for a signal of some kind. Marjory reached for her sporran. She would have preferred a sword, but her *sgian dubh* would have to suffice.

Cameron glanced at her hand as she fumbled with the catch on her bag. "Do you really believe you'll need that?"

"I've no notion, but 'tis best to be prepared." She watched as Torcall and Dougall reached the other man. The three riders stopped and appeared to be earnestly talking. " 'Tis possible the man is no more than a messenger."

Torcall raised a hand in signal. Marjory drew in a breath, watching as Allen glanced at Cameron and then spurred his horse toward his father. Fingal sheathed his weapon but didn't relax his guard.

"I believe you've been summoned."

Cameron looked confused. "Me?"

Marjory smiled, feeling some of the tension ease out of her. "Well, perhaps no' *you* precisely, but certainly Ewen." She paused, waiting for his comprehension. She didn't have to wait long.

"And that puts me in the perfect position to find out what's going on."

"You're as brilliant as you are handsome." She leaned forward and their lips touched briefly. She pulled away and their eyes met and held. "Be careful."

He reached for her hands. "Don't worry. I'll be back."

She watched as he urged his horse forward, riding away. If only he'd come back to stay. She shook her head. No sense in sinking into hopeless dreams, especially not while Torcall Cameron was still on Crannag Mhór soil.

"The Maclearys have been raiding again. They've taken forty o' our best beasts and laid havoc on the cottages in the far glen. Fergus Macmartin is dead." Torcall paced as he talked, and Cameron could see the man held his anger tightly in check.

Allen fingered his claymore. "We must avenge his death."

"Aye. He's left behind a wife and three small bairns." The sentiment seemed out of place coming from Dougall's mouth. He wasn't exactly the sensitive type. Still, Cameron reminded himself, these people were real, not creations of someone's skewed view of the past. They had hopes and fears, love and loyalty. . . .

"We'll get our revenge." Torcall's voice was harsh. "Get the men ready."

Dougall mounted and rode back toward the others. Torcall turned to Cameron. "This is Eamon Macleary's doing. He's taking advantage of my absence. I must leave at once, before he takes it into his head to try and take the tower."

"Father, ye know as well as I that there is no way that

Macleary could manage to take Tyndrum." Allen spoke forcefully, his anger apparent.

"True enough, but they could do a lot of damage before Eamon accepts that fact. I need to stop him, and there's no way to do that from here."

"So you're riding back to Tyndrum?" Cameron asked. He had no idea who Eamon Macleary was, but at the moment he was willing to kiss the man if it meant Torcall was leaving.

Torcall paused before answering, searching Cameron's face. "Aye, as soon as all is readied." He turned to Allen. "Go help Dougall. I need to talk with yer brother."

Allen opened his mouth to protest, but Torcall cut him off with a single word. "Go."

Shooting a sullen look at Cameron, Allen leapt up into his saddle and turned his horse to follow Dougall.

Cameron turned to face the man who called him son. The older man looked concerned and perhaps a little sad, his eyes crinkled with age and sorrow. So much had been lost. This was a brutal age, one that Cameron couldn't even pretend to understand. And in that light, he wasn't about to judge either.

Torcall placed a hand on his shoulder. "I dinna think ye should try and go with us."

Cameron started to speak, but Torcall cut him off.

"Nay, I know that ye want to ride with me, but ye've only just escaped dying . . . twice, and I'll no' risk yer health. I've handled the likes o' Macleary afore and I can do it again."

Cameron nodded, completely at a loss for words. He felt relief that he didn't have to try and explain his way out of going to Tyndrum, but he also felt a vague sense of discomfort.

"You be careful and watch yer back. I dinna trust these

223

people." Torcall's stern gaze met Cameron's. "There something afoot here. First yer *accident* on the mountain . . ." Cameron opened his mouth in rebuttal, but Torcall shook his head silencing him. "I know ye dinna believe it. But ye're no' thinking straight. Besides, there's also the question o' the wee boat. I've no idea what ye were doing in the thing. But I dinna believe it went down on its own."

"But Marjory was with me."

" 'Twas no' expected, ye said. Think on it, Ewen. Who knew ye were going out?"

Fingal and Aimil were the only ones he'd talked to, but he'd made no secret of going. "Anyone could have seen me, Father." He was surprised at how naturally the name came to him.

"Aye, 'tis true. And were it no' for Macleary, I wouldna leave ye here on yer own. As it is, I'll leave some protection, but I canna leave too many. Still, ye can get word to me if need be. And make no mistake, I'll come back in a heartbeat. I'll no' lose ye again, son. Especially no' to the Macphersons."

Cameron nodded, not knowing what to say. Torcall was a brutal man, but Cameron couldn't reconcile that fact with the man's obvious devotion to his son.

"Remember, Ewen," Torcall continued. "Marjory Macpherson is only a means to an end. Never forget that. If ye start to have tender thoughts toward her, think of what happened to yer mother. That should make it clear what side ye're on." Pain washed across his face but just as quickly was gone. "I'll leave Aida with you. She'll help ye ken what a real woman is like."

"Thanks." Aida was the last thing he needed right now, but the gesture seemed to call for some sort of gratitude.

"Ewen." Torcall looked distinctly uncomfortable. "I love ye, lad." He stepped forward enveloping Cameron in his embrace. They stood like that for a moment; then he released him and turned to go.

Cameron watched Torcall ride away, strangely saddened by the fact that if he had his way, the man would never see his son again. Even without his memory, Cameron was certain that his own father had never felt as strongly about him. Whatever his other shortcomings, Torcall Cameron loved his son.

"Well. That's it, then. They're gone." Cameron watched as the riders moved off across the valley.

"For now." Marjory held a hand over her eyes, blocking the sun.

Cameron pulled his gaze from the departing men and looked down at Marjory. "Well, hopefully by the time they come back you'll have some help. When will you send for your grandfather?"

"He's no' due back at Moy for a se'nnight." She kept her eyes on the riders. "So he canna come until after you're gone."

He felt his stomach lurch. Put into words, his departure sounded so final. Placing his hands on her shoulders, he turned her toward him. "Promise that you won't wait to contact him."

" 'Tis no' your concern." She refused to look at him, but her voice was steady.

He should have been pleased that he was out of this mess, that she wasn't trying to convince him to stay. Hell, he should be euphoric, but he wasn't. Absurdly, he wanted to be the one to protect Marjory and keep her safe—but of course that was impossible. He might look like a Scottish warrior, but he certainly wasn't one.

He wasn't anything. The shell of one man and the vague memories of another. The only thing he was really certain of was that he wanted this woman more than he thought possible, that and the fact that he couldn't have her.

Almost of its own volition, his hand reached for her chin, tipping her face gently upward. Their gazes met and held. The longing in her eyes mirrored his own. Longing and pain. Pain that he was responsible for.

He traced the curve of her jaw, wanting more than anything to pull her into his arms, to erase the sadness in her eyes. Instead, he dropped his hand to his side and stepped back, breaking contact. "We should get back to the others. I'd hate for them to think we'd gone missing again."

Marjory squared her shoulders, all emotion vanishing from her face, leaving in its place a mask of civility. "Aye, 'tis getting late." She turned to go, not waiting to see if he followed.

With one last look at the party of Camerons making their way toward the woods at the base of the mountains, Cameron turned to follow Marjory. It seemed the adventure was over.

Chapter Eighteen

"I canna believe ye're here, safe and sound. I was so sure that devil husband o' yers had harmed ye in some way." Aimil fussed over Marjory, tucking a blanket around her legs then poking at the fire.

Marjory smiled tolerantly. Aimil really wasn't that far from the truth. Physically she was fine, but emotionally she'd never be the same.

"It was daft enough fer the man to go out in a boat when he couldna swim, but to take ye with him . . . Well, all I can say is that his fall definitely robbed him o' his senses."

"I wish everyone would quit blaming him. I *chose* to go in the boat." She paused, debating whether to say more. Aimil turned from the fire, meeting her gaze.

"Ye've fallen fer him haven' t ye?"

"Nay. I'll admit he's changed. And that I like what I know o' the new and improved Ewen Cameron—but that's as far as the feelings go." Marjory felt the warmth of a blush belie her words.

Aimil fisted her hands on her hips. "Marjory Macpherson, dinna lie to me. I can see that ye have feelings fer the man. I only wish I could convince ye he's up to no good."

Marjory pushed the blanket away and stood up with a sigh. "Aimil, we've covered this territory before. I know how you feel about him, but you're going to have to accept my word that he's changed." She crossed restlessly to the window and pulled back a shutter. Icy wind blew through the open window, spraying her with a fine mist of rain. She shivered.

"Close the shutter, girl. Ye'll catch yer death." Aimil reached around her and banged the plank of wood shut. The solar immediately felt warmer. With a firm but gentle shove, Aimil sent her back to the bench by the fire.

Marjory restrained a laugh. The woman was almost clucking, a mother hen if ever there was one. "I'm a grown woman, Aimil. I've enough sense no' to make myself ill."

The older woman sniffed. Sitting in a small chair, pulling a tapestry frame closer to her, with nimble fingers she deftly began to weave the silken threads into place. "I suppose ye'll want *him* at the celebration tonight."

"Of course." Marjory felt her eyes widen in exasperation. "Without him, there would be nothing to celebrate." How many times was she going to have to say it? Apparently Aimil was not of a mind to accept Cameron on any terms, no matter what he did.

She thought briefly about telling her who he really was, but stopped. Aimil would no doubt confine her to bed, certain she had a brain fever of some kind if she so much as breathed a word of the fanciful tale.

In fact, now that she thought on it safely away from the sheer magnetism of her newly changed husband, Marjory wondered how she could have accepted it as true. The man had been very convincing, but suddenly she was filled with uncertainty. What if all this was just an elaborate plot by the Camerons? Maybe she was being naive and foolish.

"Did I hear ye mention a celebration?" Marjory looked up as Grania made her way into the chamber, holding a stack of folded plaid. Moving slowly but unerringly, she made her way to the bench and sat down, patting Marjory comfortingly on the knee.

"I did." Aimil didn't look up from her sewing. "I thought in honor of Marjory's safe return we should do something special. To that end, I've ordered Cook to prepare a feast for our evening meal."

"Well done, Aimil. We've no' had a party at Crannag Mhór in ever so long," Grania said.

Marjory reached over and squeezed the blind woman's hand, and Grania turned to her, bestowing an angelic smile. Sometimes Marjory would swear the woman radiated peace and serenity—something at the moment, she seemed to be in short supply of.

"You're none the worse for yer little adventure?" Grania's voice was filled with concern.

"Nay, I'm right as rain. Just a wee bit tired. Nothing a good night's sleep won't cure."

"Well, with Torcall Cameron gone from beneath our roof, I imagine we'll all sleep a bit better," Aimil continued making neat stitches in the tapestry.

"Aye, no doubt o' that." Grania nodded in Aimil's direction.

"I'll feel better when I know that he's off Crannag Mhór land altogether." Or, better yet, dead and buried. She frowned at the violent turn of her thoughts.

"Is he no' gone then?" Grania asked, a puzzled expression on her face.

"Oh, he's gone, right enough—but it'll take him at least another day to reach the entrance to the valley."

"Well, at least he's no longer here, in the tower." Grania covered Marjory's hand with her own. "So, tell me a bit about yer adventure. I've not heard the whole of it."

Marjory smiled broadly at the old woman. It was hard not to, even if the gesture was wasted. She told Grania about the fishing expedition and the storm. She skimmed over Cameron's water exploits, hesitant to have to explain his sudden ability to swim, using instead the story he'd concocted for Torcall.

"Heavens, child, what a tale. I take it ye managed to find shelter fer the night?"

"Oh, yes, Grania. They stayed in yer cottage, or what's left o' it. To hear Marjory tell it, they wouldn't have survived without it." Aimil snapped a silken strand of thread and deftly threaded the needle with another.

"I dinna think I made it sound that dramatic, surely?" Marjory felt Grania's hand tighten slightly around hers.

"And how did ye find my cottage?" Grania's voice had lost some of its usual timbre.

"In much disrepair, I'm afraid. What damage the fallen tree didna do, the wilds of the forest are finishing. Still, it served our purposes nicely." Again, she felt herself growing hot. She had to learn to control these blushes. Thankfully Grania couldn't see her, and with a quick glance she ascertained that Aimil was still absorbed in her needlework.

"I'm delighted that it was still of some use." Grania shifted on the bench, freeing her hands from Marjory's.

"It was." She felt her blush deepening. She needed to change the subject before her body betrayed her feelings for Cameron. "Grania, did Bertrum have family in England?"

"I dinna remember. Why do ye ask?"

"Because we found the most amazing thing at your cottage."

"Amazing? I canna imagine there's anything left to call amazing."

"Well, there was."

Aimil looked up, her attention caught. "Well, dinna hold us in suspense. What was it ye found?"

"A pump." Marjory smiled triumphantly, her mouth stumbling only a little over the new word.

"A what?" Aimil looked confused.

"A *pump*. 'Tis the word Ewen used." She'd started to call him Cameron, but changed her mind. "It made water flow from its mouth like magic."

Aimil snorted and turned back to her needlework. "Ye're having us on."

"Nay, 'tis true. I saw it with my own eyes. Ewen says 'tis the newest thing. I thought maybe your husband had built it for you. They have them in England, you know, and I thought maybe Bertrum got the idea there."

"Oh, yes, the pump. I'd forgotten all about it. Bertie did make it for me."

"Did he? I dinna recall him being good with his hands." Aimil raised an eyebrow.

For the first time in Marjory's memory, Grania looked flustered. "Well, perhaps, he bought it on one of his travels. I canna remember—it's been so long since Bertie was living. 'Tis no' as exciting as Marjory would have ye believe." She waved a hand in dismissal as Marjory opened her mouth to disagree. The pump had been nothing short of a miracle, but if Grania didn't wish to discuss it, she wouldn't press the matter.

"Ye didna say what happened to the *curach*," Grania interjected, obviously trying to change the subject.

Aimil cried out as she jabbed her finger with her needle.

Grania cocked her head at the sound. "Are you all right, Aimil?"

"Aye, fine. I only stuck myself a bit. No serious damage." She sucked at the end of her finger.

Marjory stood. "Perhaps I should go for some salve."

"Nay, sit down. I'm fine. 'Tis only a wee prick. No harm done. I wasna watching what I was doing."

Marjory settled back on the bench. "We've really no idea what happened to the boat. One minute it was fine, the next it was full o' water. We looked for a hole, but there wasna time enough to find it. We had to make for shore."

"I thought ye said the *curach* was at the shore when you abandoned it."

"Did I?" Marjory shifted uncomfortably. Lying didn't come easily. "If I did, I meant to say that we were a short way out. Anyway, we weren't able to find the cause of the leak."

"Do ye think it could have been deliberate?" Grania's normally placid face was marred by a deep frown.

"Deliberate? Who would want to hurt Marjory?" Aimil looked up from the tapestry frame with widening eyes.

"Well, there's any number o' Camerons, but I dinna think the accident was meant for her. 'Twas Ewen who took the *curach* in the first place." Grania's tone was grim.

"But who would have had the time to damage it?" Aimil asked.

"Pretty much anyone, I suppose. I think everyone, from Cook to the blacksmith, knew he was setting out in it. He dinna make much of a secret about it," Grania offered.

" 'Tis true, and you canna deny there are many folks here who canna tolerate a Cameron of any kind among them." Marjory felt a shiver of concern snake down her back.

All her previous doubt fled in the face of her worry over his safety. She hadn't thought about why the *curach* had sprung a leak. She's been busy with other things. But now that Grania mentioned the idea, it took hold, filling her with fear. If someone had tried to harm him once, surely they might do so again.

"Well, I canna say that I wouldna be pleased to see the last o' him. He's brought naught but despair on this household—to say nothing o' the fact that his sire is a murderer." Aimil looked at Marjory with narrowed eyes.

Marjory took a deep breath. It was all so complicated. She felt the old wounds opening again and wondered how she could possibly have any feeling but loathing for the son of her father's murderer. And yet, whispered her heart, if he wasn't truly Ewen Cameron, then his father was somebody else altogether—someone from another century, no less. She brushed a hand through her hair in frustration.

"Dinna let it worry ye, lass. I've no doubt Ewen can take care o' himself." Grania patted her hand comfortingly.

"Ewen this and Ewen that . . . Ye'd think the man was a bloody saint." Most of Aimil's words were mumbled under her breath, but Marjory caught the gist of what she was saying.

"Speaking of the devil," Marjory said brightly, "has anyone seen him about?" She'd not seen him at all since they'd returned.

"Oh, heavens." Grania reached for the folded plaids. "I'd quite forgotten. I was bringing him something to dry himself with. He's in the bath," she added unnecessarily.

Marjory had a clear picture of him soaking his rugged frame in the little wooden tub, water caressing his body. The familiar fire leapt in her belly. She forced herself to abolish the picture and concentrate on Grania's voice.

". . . Would ye mind then, love?"

"No, of course not." Marjory struggled to discern what it was she had just agreed to.

"Wonderful. I can manage just fine, ye know, but ye'll be ever so much faster. We dinna want the man to catch cold." Grania thrust the warm wool into Marjory's hands.

Oh, Blessed Mother, she'd just agreed to take the plaid to Cameron in the bath.

Cameron sat back, letting the warm water lap at his body. It wasn't exactly a steaming hot shower, but all in all it beat the icy water of the lake. He closed his eyes and allowed himself the luxury of picturing Marjory. His vivid imagination jumped into the task with relish and soon he had her straddling him in the tub, the water gleaming against her satiny skin. He groaned, ecstasy mixed with agony.

"Grania asked me to bring this to you."

The sound of her voice broke the spell his imagination had woven. He jerked upright in the tub. Faced with the real thing, he felt his body swell. The reality of her was more an aphrodisiac than his imagined version had been.

"Thanks." Silence loomed awkwardly between them. He had an absurd desire to cover himself, even though the water was effectively doing it for him. Her eyes drifted down to the exposed part of his body, reflecting the desire he felt continuing to rise beneath the water.

She took a hesitant step toward him and then stopped. Their eyes met and held. He drew in a breath and was just getting ready to reach for her when she swore under her breath.

"Are you daft, man?" She crossed the room in three strides, flannel still in hand, and disappeared behind the bed curtains. "You've left the window open. Do you want to catch your death?"

He smiled as he waited for her to finish the task, settling back against the side of the tub. Ever his practical Marjory.

The main door swung open with a loud creak. "Welcome home, Ewen." Aida sidled into the room. She was wearing another embroidered slip. The woman evidently didn't own any proper clothing.

"Aren't ye going to invite me to join ye?" she purred, pulling her slip down to bare a shoulder.

He groaned. There was no sound from behind the bed curtains, but he knew Marjory was there, listening to every word.

"Look, Aida, now is not a good time for this. Why don't you just put your clothes back on and we'll talk later?" He emphasized the word talk, but apparently nothing he'd said got through, because she took another step forward and slid the gown lower, baring a breast.

"Ewen, *mo chridhe*, I'm ready." He turned, stunned to see Marjory emerge from the bed curtains, clad only in a plaid. It opened suggestively as she walked towards them. "Oh, Aida, I didna hear you come in. 'Tis glad I am you're here, however. Would you be a lamb and run down to the kitchens? I'm afraid we're out of wine and I'd so like some more. Wouldn't you, dear heart?"

Cameron could only nod, his voice having plummeted to some part of his anatomy heretofore unknown. He couldn't take his eyes off her. She was magnificent.

Still looking at Aida, Marjory dropped the plaid and gracefully stepped into the tub. "Do hurry on. As you can see, we've no other needs right now." She gave Aida a queenly smile and sat down. The feel of her body against his sent a tremor running down Cameron's spine.

"I'll do no such thing. Ye can fetch yer own wine. I'd like to know what this is all about, Ewen. Surely 'tis a jest. Ye canna possibly prefer a woman like her o'er a woman like me." Aida thrust out her chest, making Cameron think of a bird, strutting its plumage.

He struggled for words. His mind had deserted him entirely, his body lost in the feel of the woman in the tub with him. "This is no jest, I assure you." His voice came out a hoarse croak.

Marjory placed a gentle hand on his cheek, sending tremors of need streaking through him. "Let me tell her, *mo chridhe*." She turned her attention back to Aida. "I'm afraid there is no gentle way to say this, so listen well. Ewen belongs to me. You seem to have forgotten that he is my husband and this is my home. And since we obviously no longer have need for you, I'd like you out of here now and out of the tower at first light. I'm sure we can find someone to escort you home." She smiled sweetly, then turned her attention back to Cameron, effectively dismissing the other woman.

"Ewen, surely you're no' going to let this woman treat me like that?" Aida stood her ground, but wrapped her arms around her waist, a certain sign that she was no longer feeling as sure of herself.

"My wife has spoken, Aida. It would be best for all of us if you honored her wishes." It was all he could do to get the words out, but if Marjory could stand up to Aida, the least he could do was support her.

Aida's mouth dropped open. The scene was oddly gratifying. Something tugged at Cameron's memory, but was gone before he could identify it.

"You heard my husband. Go." Marjory waved a hand regally in the direction of the door. "And dinna forget the wine."

Aida narrowed her eyes in anger. "Ye'll regret this, Ewen Cameron. I gave ye all that I had to give and I'll no' be tossed aside fer the likes o' her." She whirled around and ran from the room, slamming the door behind her.

Marjory sagged forward and started to push herself up out of the tub. Cameron reached for her, pulling her back into the now tepid water, holding her against his chest. He stroked her hair and felt silent sobs wrack her body. "You were magnificent."

He tipped her chin up, forcing her to meet his gaze. Emotions rioted across her beautiful face: embarrassment and triumph, elation and sadness. He leaned forward, kissing her gently on the lips, tasting the salt of her tears. He ran his tongue along her bottom lip, caressing her back with his hands. He could feel every inch of her body pressed against him and delighted in the knowledge that she was as aroused as he.

She opened her mouth and their desire took flight, their kiss deepening and taking on new meaning. He felt her press against his groin, the soft silkiness of her inner thighs caressing his engorged manhood. With a moan, he gathered her in his arms and stood, stepping carefully from the tub.

He walked to the bed and laid her reverently on it. Turning back, he reached for the cloth she'd dropped. With gentle hands he began to dry her, his fingers caressing every inch of her flesh. She lay still, her eyes closed, offering no comment other than an occasional moan as his hands found a sensitive place. Drying himself hurriedly, he stretched out on the bed beside her, his heart pounding with need.

Marjory opened her eyes, revealing deep blue pools of desire. His mouth found her shoulder. With hot, wet kisses, he trailed his tongue down her arm, lingering on each of her fingers, pulling each slowly into his mouth. She shuddered and writhed against the soft linen of the sheet.

He rolled atop her, pinning her with his body. Sliding down the silky length of her, he began at her toes—caressing each one with his mouth before slowly making his way up her legs, kissing first her ankles, then her knees, then the soft flesh of her thighs. He lifted his head, meeting her fevered gaze.

She mouthed the word "please," her breath coming in harsh gasps, her legs opening for him. His body ached with his need, but he wanted only to give her pleasure: a reward for her bravery and strength, for all she had so willingly given him. He needed to please her, to make her writhe with ecstasy—needed it almost as much as he needed to be inside her.

He lowered his head to her thighs and plunged his tongue into her, tasting her sweetness, reveling in the fact, that at least for the moment, she belonged to him. He felt her fingers rake through his hair as she pressed him closer, bucking. He held her legs, holding her still, his tongue finding the tiny knot that marked the center of her desire. He flicked at it lightly with his tongue and then drew it into his mouth, sucking gently. She arched against him and he felt an uncontrollable surge of masculine pride as she screamed his name.

He kissed her once more and then moved upward until

his mouth found her lips. Her body shuddered beneath his, and his need to possess her grew to almost unbearable proportions. He framed her face with his hands, drinking in her beauty. Her blue eyes met his, still glazed with the power of her release.

She tangled a hand in his hair, pulling him close, kissing his ear, taking the soft lobe between her teeth and tugging at it. He shivered and felt the heat in his belly begin to spiral out of control. Rolling onto his back, he pulled her with him so that she lay on top of him. With a smile, she slid down his body, stopping to kiss his nipples, her tongue rubbing them to erection. The sensation surprised him, and he reached to pull her back for a kiss.

"Nay, 'tis my turn now." She laughed softly and slipped from his grasp, moving lower, her tongue finding the throbbing hardness that marked his manhood. The wet heat of her mouth against his already over-sensitized skin almost made him explode. She circled him with her tongue, tasting and exploring. When her mouth finally closed over him, he felt a cry rip from somewhere deep inside.

With shaking hands, he reached for her, pulling her against him. She arched her back, sitting up, her legs straddling him, and with a shy smile, lifted her body and then lowered herself, carefully sliding down onto his aching shaft. His body rose to meet her, plunging deep into her welcoming heat. His hands on her hips, guiding her, they found the rhythm. He closed his eyes and allowed the sensations to surround him, to surround *them,* for he could feel her heat wrapping around him, holding him secure as he flew apart, the world turning to shards of bright light.

Slowly, slowly he drifted back to the soft nest of their

bed. Marjory was draped across him, her passion spent. With a contented sigh she stroked his brow, her fingers tracing the broad planes of his face. He raised a hand and covered it with his own. His eyes met hers. "Marjory mine." His voice was hoarse, but the words and their meaning were clear. She smiled at him, her joy reaching out and touching him.

Marjory mine. The words repeated themselves in his head, echoing in his heart.

Chapter Nineteen

"Hold still. I canna do this right with you jumping about like a wee hare." Marjory shot a frustrated glance at Cameron as she tried to fold the recalcitrant pleats of his plaid into some semblance of order. It didn't help that just touching the man through the layers of wool sent her body into shivers of anticipation.

"I'm trying, but the damned thing keeps wrapping around my neck. I miss blue jeans."

"Blue jeans?"

"Yeah, denim." He sighed.

She marveled, briefly, at the thought that an article of clothing could cause such longing. "I've never heard o' such a thing." She pulled the wool tight around his waist.

"They're pants. The uniform of my century, really."

She shot him a blank look. Pants? Uniform? His words were gibberish.

He sighed again. "Never mind." He pushed at the end of the plaid hanging loose over his shoulder, threatening to undo the entire process.

She grabbed it just as it began to fall and, with a frown

in the direction of his face, pinned it neatly back at his shoulder, forcing herself to ignore the implications of his words. "All done. I'll be more than glad when you've mastered the art of this and I dinna have to do it any longer."

"Are you saying you don't enjoy touching me?" He gave her a teasing smile echoed in the amber depths of his eyes.

She caught her breath, amazed that her passions were so easily ignited. "Nay, I dinna say that at all. I merely meant that I would rather spend the next fifty years taking your plaid off, no' putting it on." She shot him a shy smile, amazed at her own boldness, but felt it quickly fade when she met his somber gaze.

She wished desperately that she could unsay the words, but they hung between them, as solid a barrier as the thick plank of wood comprising the door to the sleeping chamber. "I wasna ... I mean, I didna ..." She stopped, unsure of how to proceed.

He sighed and tried for a smile, but it was more a lopsided grimace. "I know what you meant. It's just that we don't have fifty years and I guess I feel honor-bound to keep reminding you of it." He looked pained, and she felt her heart constrict.

"Well, you needn't. I know you canna stay, and I wasna trying to convince you otherwise. 'Twas no more than a comment made in the moment. Dinna concern yourself with it."

He moved to stand in front of her, his breath stirring the tendrils of hair around her face. "But I am concerned with it, Marjory. I care about you and I don't want to see you hurt." He stopped, guilt washing across his face.

"You canna protect me, Cameron. The heart is no' something you can control. But dinna fash yourself. I'll

242

be fine. 'Tis no' new for me to lose the people I care about. And I'll handle it this time as I have before." She swallowed, forcing herself to smile. There was no sense in adding to the pain. "I'd no' trade a minute o' it, and when the time comes for you to go, I'll survive. So quit your worrying."

"Marjory . . ." He moved to take her in his arms, but she deftly sidestepped him. If he touched her now, she'd surely fall apart.

"I said I'd be fine and I meant it." She looked at the floor, unable to meet his eyes. "We'd best get a move on. They'll have expected us at the table by now and we certainly dinna want them coming to find us." She blushed, despite herself, and spun toward the door. Her eyes blurring with unshed tears.

Cameron had never been to a finer feast. The great hall was full to brimming with people. Macphersons gathered to celebrate the safe return of their mistress. He was seated at the dais with the family, Fingal on his left and Marjory on his right. It was a place of honor. For tonight, at least, he had been accepted, the husband of the mistress of Crannag Mhór.

He glanced over at her. She was smiling at something Fingal said, her long hair swaying slightly with the movement of her shoulders. She raised her eyes and met his briefly, the contact warming him as if she'd reached out to touch him.

He took a sip of wine. It was warm and flavored with spices of some kind. He hated the fact that he was going to hurt her. Hated that he'd let himself get involved. But his heart, it seemed, had a mind of its own.

And another life. He had to face the reality that there very well could be someone out there waiting for him.

The blonde from his dreams? There was something about her, something about the dream that called to him. Made him want to go back. To face himself.

If he could go back. The thought haunted him, always on the edge of his conscious mind. What if he couldn't go back? He shook his head, not ready to face the concept. He needed to get back. Needed to face whatever demons were behind the dream. Until he did, he couldn't be whole. Not in this world or any other.

He had to go home.

And Grania could help, he was certain of it.

Marjory laughed, the sound filling him with joy and sorrow. Bittersweet. She was an amazing woman. One he could easily lose his heart to. But he'd couldn't discount the notion that he might not be free to lose it. And he valued his honor.

Of that he was certain.

More laughter interrupted his thoughts, this time from Fingal, whose mouth was full of meat. Aimil had outdone herself, the tables full to bursting with every imaginable food. Joints of beef, minced pies, venison, and rabbit. There were the requisite barley and oatcakes and earthenware pitchers of ale and wine, a full one replacing each empty almost before the last drop could be drained.

Serving platters, attached to serving people, appeared continuously from behind a large carved screen. A fire burned brightly in the huge fireplace, augmented by huge iron candelabras, the flickering light adding to the magical feel of the event.

One tray, sitting in the center of the head table, contained what Cameron supposed was the culinary masterpiece of the evening. An entire bird rested on the wooden platter, its plumage arrayed as if it were merely out for a stroll in the meadow, rather than providing the main course for the people seated on the dais.

He marveled at the detail. Grain of some sort had been used to create grass, with wildflowers added for a true meadowlike effect. It would put a museum of natural history to shame, let alone a five-star chef. Perhaps he'd have to rethink his position on medieval Scottish cuisine.

Music wafted through the room. Bagpipes, he supposed, although the instruments were smaller than the ones he recalled, with a sweeter sound, more like panpipes. There was also a harp of a sort, smaller and shaped differently from its modern-day counterpart. The soft sounds filtered through the hum of conversation, filling the hall.

"Will ye have some *caboc?*" Fingal smiled at him, thrusting a small platter in his direction. Taking it, Cameron eyed it dubiously. It looked like an ice cream cone dipped in oatmeal. Seeing his look, Fingal laughed. "'Tis no just oats, mind ye. There's much more inside." Taking his *sgian dubh,* he cut a piece off the cone and held out the knife.

Sharing utensils was common among the Macphersons, and with a sigh of resignation, Cameron took the offered blade and popped the oat-covered morsel in his mouth, praying that it wasn't intestines or eyeballs or something. He held his breath, chewed, then relaxed and swallowed. *Caboc* was cheese—just cheese.

"It's good." He returned the knife and, reaching for his own, cut off more of the cone, trying to avoid the oats.

"A toast." A red-faced man at a nearby table stood, swaying slightly, his cup held aloft. Cameron groaned. He'd already had firsthand experience with Scots when they started toasting.

The room quieted somewhat and the man raised his glass higher. "To Marjory Macpherson. 'Tis glad we are to have her home."

There was much scraping and scuffling as the assemblage pushed back benches and rose to their feet echoing the toast. Cups were drained and refilled, others expressing similar sentiments. Marjory stood serenely, looking out at the members of her clan, the faint wash of color across her cheeks the only sign that she was embarrassed by all the attention. Finally, exhausting both beverage and verbiage, the assembled Macphersons settled back into their seats.

Cameron leaned over to Marjory, speaking softly. "They love you."

She flushed a deeper red and turned to meet his gaze. "Nay, no' so much me. 'Tis Crannag Mhór they love. I'm just a figurehead o' sorts, filling the role my father should rightfully have occupied."

"Or your husband."

The color drained from her face. "I've no' husband and well you know it. Ewen is dead."

He placed his hand on the gentle curve of her cheek. "I didn't mean Ewen. I meant someone new. Someone who could love you as you deserve to be loved."

Her eyes searched his, looking for something he knew he couldn't offer. "You need a man to help you here." He paused, watching hope flare in her eyes. "A man from your own century."

As quickly as it had come, the hope died. Her eyes hardened. "I dinna need a man or anyone else. I've done fine on my own all these years and I'll manage quite nicely now." She turned away, asking Fingal for a platter of meat.

Cameron looked at his food, his appetite gone. Why

couldn't he learn to keep his mouth shut? The idea of Marjory with another man was repulsive to him. So, why had he felt the need to speak to her of finding someone else?

To ease his guilt. Cameron reached for his goblet and drained it, letting the warm wine wash away his thoughts. Guilt or not, at the end of the day the facts remained the same. He had to get back to his own time, to his own life, and he couldn't let his feelings for Marjory stand in the way.

Marjory smiled at Aimil, trying to listen to what the woman was saying. This was supposed to be a celebration, but she didn't feel particularly festive.

"Are ye going to send word to yer grandfather?"

Marjory focused on the words. "If need be."

"If need be? I dinna ken. What are ye waiting for? A direct attack by Torcall?" The old woman frowned at her.

"Aimil, I'd like nothing better than to see Torcall Cameron brought to his knees, but for now he has gone, and I canna bother my grandfather with my simple fears. I'll send word to him when the time is right, and no' before."

"I dinna believe we've seen the last o' Torcall Cameron. 'Tis a trick o' some kind hatched up between the man and his son." She tilted her head toward Cameron, lowering her voice to a whisper. "I told ye before that a cat canna change his ways."

Marjory swallowed a sigh. "There is no plot between them. Of that I'm certain."

Aimil stabbed viciously into a chunk of meat. "Well, if ye ask me ye're dancing with the devil, and there's no way ye can win. A Cameron is ne'er to be trusted. And believe me, I know that better than most."

247

Marjory tilted her head, studying the woman. "You're speaking o' my parents murder?"

"Among other things," Aimil said, her face closed, memories reflected in her eyes. "The important thing is that ye mustn't trust a Cameron, no matter how comely of face. And I'd be watching my back if I were you. I tell ye, the man will be back."

Marjory nodded and sipped absently from her goblet. There was truth in Aimil's words, no matter how enigmatic. Once Cameron left, it would only be a matter of time until Torcall discovered it. And when he did . . . She shuddered involuntarily. When he did, there would be hell to pay.

"Are you all right?"

She felt Cameron's words, warm against her ear, almost before she heard them. "I'm fine." She flashed him a smile, hoping it looked sincere.

"Look." He screwed up his mouth, a look of regret in his face, "I'm sorry if I was out of line before. I just want you to be happy." He reminded her of a puppy, scolded for something it didn't understand but still honestly repentant.

"I know." She patted his hand. "Perhaps we should call a truce. Just for tonight." She smiled and raised her cup in tribute.

Deliberately he took it from her and took a sip. She felt the embers of desire inside her stir and begin to glow. Slowly, she reached for the cup herself, taking it from him and sipping slowly, her lips touching the exact spot where his had, her eyes never leaving his. She'd never thought drinking could be so provocative.

Out of the corner of her eye, she caught a flash of color. Aida. Marjory's high spirits plummeted. The woman was sitting at a table in the far corner of the hall, surrounded by men vying for her attention. Marjory knew that they didn't stand a chance. Aida Macvail had eyes for only one man.

She drained the goblet with a long swallow, reaching for the pitcher to fill it again.

Cameron took the cup from her. "Easy, princess. Don't let her get to you." He covered her hand with his. "Remember this afternoon."

"Aye, that I do." She felt her spirits buoy a little at the thought of Aida's ousting from Cameron's chamber. The woman looked in their direction, her pouty lips drawing into a beguiling smile when she realized Cameron was looking at her. She might as well have been calling his name out loud.

"Well, what do you say we continue the show?" He raised Marjory's hand to his mouth, his tongue tracing a slow, possessive path along her palm.

Aida's smile faded and her eyes narrowed. In an instant, anger marred her features, making her beauty seem only an illusion. Marjory tightened her hand on Cameron's. Aida's gaze shifted, her narrowed eyes meeting Marjory's.

The smile remained in place, but there was nothing resembling cordiality in her gaze. If a look could be a weapon, Marjory knew she would have been mortally injured.

"Look at me," Cameron whispered, his lips still caressing her skin.

With an icy smile in Aida's direction, she tipped her head in acknowledgment of the other woman. Then she turned her attention back to the warmth of Cameron's touch.

Cameron squeezed her hand and released it. "That's my girl. Just ignore her. Tomorrow she'll be gone." He poured her some more wine, holding out the goblet when it was full. Marjory took it, her gaze straying back to the table in the corner. She'd be more than glad to see the backside of Aida Macvail.

Cameron rubbed his temples, wondering if this party was ever going to end. He'd eaten until he thought he might explode. He looked around the room. No one seemed even remotely interested in winding things down.

Marjory was sitting back with her eyes closed, looking as tired as he felt. Fingal was still eating as if there were no tomorrow. A ruddy-faced young man was talking with Grania. Cameron overheard something about love potions and knew he didn't want to hear any more. First thing in the morning, he intended to get to the bottom of Grania Macpherson's stories.

A man seated at the table directly in front of the dais, belched loudly and leaned back, lighting some kind of pipe with a rush from the floor—yet another example of the sterling quality of fifteenth-century hygiene. Cameron smiled, wondering who had died and made him the king of clean.

Aimil was refilling the wine pitchers at their table. He wouldn't put it past her to add a little something extra to his. Arsenic perhaps? Thank goodness it was a community pitcher. The woman certainly wasn't overly fond of him.

Hell, whom was he kidding? She despised him. A stray thought caught in his tired mind, its exact significance alluding him. He dismissed it. The events of the past few days were catching up with him. He stifled a yawn.

"Fingal . . . Fingal!" Aimil's cry rang out through the great hall, the terror in it instantly stilling the festivities. "Someone help him please."

Chapter Twenty

At the sound of Aimil's voice, Cameron jerked from his thoughts, quickly turning toward Fingal. The man was twitching convulsively, clutching at his throat, eyes wide. Aimil was grabbing at his shoulder, trying ineffectually to slap him on the back.

Cameron reacted from instinct, his mind focusing on the problem at hand. He rose quickly to stand behind Fingal, grasping him around the chest. Aimil yelled something about stopping him, but Cameron's focus was trained completely on the choking man.

Crossing his hands, one over the other, he made a fist and felt for the diaphragm just below Fingal's ribs. With a quick motion, he pulled upward and inward, hoping to force the man to dislodge whatever was stuck in his throat. Nothing happened.

He repeated the process twice more. In the background he could hear Aimil still screaming, although her wails were slowing. Out of the corner of his eye, he realized that someone was restraining her. He turned his mind back to his patient, shutting out all outside interference.

Dee Davis

Decisions had to be made quickly if the man's life was to be saved. Obviously, the Heimlich maneuver wasn't working. The obstruction, whatever it was, was firmly lodged in place. He knew he had minutes to correct the situation or, at best, Fingal would suffer brain damage. At worst he would die.

This wasn't exactly the best place for surgical intervention, but there really wasn't any choice. Cameron didn't take the time to question his new knowledge. There would be time for that later. Right now he needed to act, and act quickly.

"I need help. We've got to get him up on the table." With a swipe of his arm, he cleared a space, shoving plates, platters, and cups aside. Marjory sprang into action and began to clear even more space. The young man who'd been talking to Grania helped Cameron lift Fingal onto the table.

"Roll him onto his back." Cameron's tone didn't allow for argument, and the other man obeyed swiftly, turning Fingal over. He was unconscious, his face beginning to turn blue. Cameron drew in a breath. There wasn't much time. He had to establish an airway.

He glanced around the room looking for something he could use as a trach tube, dismissing the feathers on the bird. A quill might work, but it could also be too small. A bagpipe bellowed as it dropped to the floor. Cameron glanced at the fallen instrument. Its owner was frozen in place, staring at the table.

It wasn't often a fifteenth-century musician got to observe a twenty-first-century surgeon. *Surgeon.* The word reverberated in his head, memories pressing hard and fast at the door to his conscious mind. He forced himself to mentally bar the door. There would be time for remembering later.

The pipe from the bagpipe was a little too large, but it might work. He felt for a pulse and couldn't find one. His time for decision-making was over. "Bring me the bagpipe." No one moved. "I said, bring me the bagpipe. *Now*." Marjory jumped, hurrying to fulfill his request.

She handed it to him, and he tried to wrench a pipe from the bellows. There was a gasp from the musician. With another tug, the piece pulled free. It was definitely bigger than he would have liked, but it would have to do. A flicker of light caught his attention. The pipe smoker was attempting again to light the bowl. The pipe. It just might work.

"The pipe. Bring me the pipe." In an instant, Marjory responded, jerking the carved instrument from the man's hand, thrusting it across the table at Cameron. He took it and twisted the base. He wasn't disappointed, the stem easily pulled free of the bowl.

"Let me help." Grania's quiet voice filled his ear.

He placed the pipe stem in her hand. "Wash it out." He turned back to Fingal, who was definitely turning blue. "And hurry."

He took a corner of his plaid and dipped it into his wine cup. Not exactly sterile, but better than nothing. "Hold his head and tip it back." The young man obeyed without question, rolling Fingal's head so that his neck was exposed.

"Marjory, hand me your knife." Marjory began to speak, but his tone of voice offered no latitude for argument. Her mouth snapped shut and she wordlessly handed him the tiny knife.

Dipping it into the wine, he palpated Fingal's neck. After visualizing the incision, he cut the skin. Aimil screamed. No one else moved. The great hall was silent, almost as if everyone collectively held his breath. Cameron cut through the subcutaneous layer, pushing the skin and muscle apart with his other hand. The thyroid, thankfully, was not in the way and, with deft hands, he located the third and fourth rings of the trachea.

Making a small vertical cut across the two rings, he automatically called for assistance. "Trach tube." Even as he realized that no one would understand his request, the pipe stem slapped into his outstretched hand.

"It should work. I tested it before I sterilized it." Grania's voice had lost its soft Scottish edge.

Cameron took the tube and inserted it into the trachea. At first, nothing happened. Cameron bit back an oath and started to breathe into the tube. A wheezing sound echoed through the room. Fingal's chest began to rise and fall. Immediately, he began to pinken.

Cameron looked at Grania, forgetting for the moment she couldn't see him. "We're halfway there. We've got to get the obstruction out."

Grania nodded. "Ye've got to help him, lad," she instructed the young man who had helped get Fingal on the table. "Pull open Fingal's jaw and hold it so that Ewen can reach into his mouth." Her voice held the same authority Cameron's had, and the man responded immediately, tipping Fingal's head back and opening his mouth. The tube wavered ominously.

"Marjory, I need you to hold the tube," Immediately she wrapped a hand around the pipe stem, holding it firmly in place. With an approving nod, he wiped off the knife. It was a dangerous retractor, but it would have to do.

"I think I can see it." Cameron looked up at the sound of his assistant's voice, meeting the other man's gaze. "I can see the edge o' a bone. 'Tis just visible. There." The man released Fingal's jaw with one hand and pointed into his mouth.

Cameron moved around until he could look down Fingal's throat. What he wouldn't give for a penlight. He peered into the cavity and carefully used the knife handle to retract the tongue. "Hold this." The young man gingerly grasped the knife blade, keeping Fingal's tongue out of the way. Just below the uvula, Cameron saw the top of the bone. Grasping it carefully between thumb and forefinger, with a quick jerk he pulled upward. Nothing happened.

Twisting the bone to the right, he tried again. Still no movement. He twisted it the other way and felt it give. With a sharp tug, the bone and gristle pulled free. Tossing it aside, he motioned for the man to let Fingal go, then returned to Fingal's side and covered the top of the pipe stem with his finger. Fingal jerked once and then began to breathe on his own.

Cameron sighed in relief and held the plug, waiting until he was certain Fingal was breathing normally. "I'm going to need a bandage of some kind."

"Done." Grania's voice was steady as she handed him a thick folded pad of linen and a longer strip to secure it.

Working quickly, he removed the tube and immediately applied the square of linen, pressing against the wound. Marjory moved next to him, her hand replacing his as he wound the strip of cloth around the neck and bandage, securing it in place with a knot. Cameron felt for a pulse and was satisfied to feel its comforting beat beneath his fingers.

Fingal's eyes flickered open. His mouth moved, but there was no sound. Panicked, he tried to sit up. Cameron signaled the man to hold him again and placed a finger across the bandage, effectively covering the stoma.

"It's okay, you should be able to talk now." He kept his voice low and comforting, his eyes never leaving Fingal's.

"What . . ." The older man paused, sucking in a breath. ". . . happened?" His voice cracked with the effort, but the words were discernable. Aimil started sobbing anew at the sound of her brother's voice.

"You swallowed a bone, but we got it out. You'll be fine." He patted the man on the arm, remembering a thousand other times he had reassured a patient in just such a way. "Don't try to talk anymore. Just rest."

He shifted his attention to the crowd. "We need to get him to his room." Two men sprang from their positions of stupefied wonder and, grasping Fingal around the feet and shoulders, carefully began to carry him from the hall. "See that the bandage isn't dislodged."

"I'll go with them." Grania followed, a wailing Aimil bringing up the rear.

Cameron sat down, his head spinning, the doors in his mind threatening to break open now that the crisis had passed.

"Will he be all right?" He looked up to see Marjory's drawn face. It was a contrast of fear and wonder.

"He should be fine. The fact that he was talking is a good sign. I expect he'll make a full recovery."

Marjory placed her hand on his. It was cold. He automatically covered it with his own. "What . . . what magic did you do tonight?" Her words were low and her voice trembled.

"It wasn't magic, Marjory—at least not the kind you're thinking of. It was a simple procedure really. It's called a tracheotomy." She bit her lip and gave him a blank look. "Look, I'm too tired to explain it now. I'm a physician, Marjory, a surgeon. And though I normally work under less primitive conditions, a first year resident could do what I did."

"You saved him." Her voice still held traces of awe.

He pushed a hand through his hair. "Probably." There was a certain satisfaction in saving a life, but right now he wasn't thinking about that. He was thinking about his memory.

It called to him, waiting for him to open the doors and let it all back into his conscious mind. He felt panicked suddenly. Too much was happening too fast. He had to think. Alone. "Marjory, I need to be alone right now." His voice came out more harshly than he'd intended.

Hurt washed across her face, but she quickly masked it. "Fine, I'll leave you then. I want to check on Fingal, anyway." She rose and, with a last worried look in his direction, hurried from the hall.

Cameron looked around. The great hall was empty, food and drink abandoned on the tables. He vaguely recalled someone telling everyone to leave. With a grateful sigh, he buried his head in his hands and waited for the memories to come.

Marjory stood in the doorway of Fingal's chamber. Firelight mixed with candle flames to cast dancing shadows across the walls, the effect making the events of the evening seem even more ominous. Grania sat on one side of the bed and Aimil on the other. Fingal lay sleeping, the rise and fall of his chest exaggerated by the blankets covering him, giving mute testimony to the miracle.

"Is he all right?"

At the sound of her voice, both women looked to the door. Aimil's features were drawn, her face ragged and harsh.

"He's resting comfortably." Grania rose as she spoke, crossing the small chamber to Marjory's side. " 'Tis naught ye can do now, child. Let's leave Aimil with her brother. Come morning I've no doubt we'll find Fingal in fine form, asking fer his porridge."

Marjory allowed the older woman to draw her from the chamber. When they returned to the great hall, it was empty, the remains of the feast seeming like the carnage of a fierce battle. She stared at it all in a daze, her mind trying to take in the miracle that had saved Fingal's life. "What . . . what happened here tonight? Cameron tried to explain, but his words were strange and his manner even more so."

"I know, I know." Grania drew her across the vast hall to the bench by the fire.

Marjory sank down on the hard wood, her eyes falling on the discarded bagpipe. "Cameron said he was a physician."

"So his name is Cameron, is it? Appropriate, in an odd sort of way." Grania frowned as she contemplated the thought. "Judging from what happened tonight I'd say that he's no' only a physician, but a verra good one."

"But, Grania—physicians canna do what he did, surely." Marjory reached for the older woman's hand, desperate for human contact.

"Well, if I remember correctly, there are some who can perform a tracheotomy, but none whc can do it with accuracy and success. 'Twill be more than four hundred years before the procedure is perfected. Another fifty or so before it is standardized."

She spoke quietly, almost to herself, "And quite truthfully, I'd probably have used that bit o' bagpipe." She pointed in the direction of the abandoned instrument. "It was too big and might have damaged the vocal cords, but I'm no' sure that I'd have thought to use the other pipe." She trailed off, turning her face to the fire.

Marjory frowned, things suddenly coming clear. "You're more than a healer, aren't you?"

Grania nodded without answering.

Marjory pressed forward. "The pump, Bertram didn't bring it from England, did he?"

"I never even knew Bertram."

Marjory felt dizzy as revelations came faster and faster. "Never knew Bertram?"

"Nay, I came after he died. Yer father found me wandering in the woods. Yer sweet mother just assumed I was Grania. I saw no need to tell her the truth."

"Are you from Cameron's time, then? Is that how you know about pumps and trach-e-o-to-mies?"

"Aye. 'Tis true," the old woman admitted in a whisper hardly loud enough to hear.

But Marjory heard, her head spinning with the impact of the words. "Then you're a physician, like Cameron."

"No' anymore. There is too much I've forgotten. But aye—once, a lifetime ago, I was a surgeon, too."

"Ye've traveled across time?"

"Aye."

"And nobody else knows?"

"Nay. Cameron has guessed, I think, but I've ne'er told a soul."

"Why no'? You must have been so confused and afraid."

Grania smiled. "All that and more, but unlike Cameron, I had my memory and so I knew without a doubt who I had been. And I knew, too, that there was no one here who would believe me. I wasna willing to take the risk of exposure. In time, I grew content with my life here. I found a peace that I'd ne'er felt before."

The women sat in silence, their hands still joined, each lost in her own thoughts. Marjory tried to make sense of it all. So many years she had lived with Grania and never even noticed that the woman was different; she'd merely thought her gifted, perhaps a bit eccentric. Seen from this new light, however, Marjory was amazed she'd never guessed.

She almost laughed. Until Cameron's confession, the thought would never have entered her mind. Now it seemed there were two time travelers at Crannag Mhór.

Unable to deal with the enormity of that thought, Marjory concentrated on Cameron. "He's remembered, hasn't he?"

" 'Twould seem so, or at least a part of it. Amnesia is a funny thing. 'Tis often the result o' the mind trying to protect itself. I think Fingal's trauma forced Cameron to remember who he was, what he can do. As to whether he remembers whate'er it was that caused him to forget in the first place, I canna say."

"Do you think . . ." Marjory began, praying for the answer she so desperately wanted. "Do you think that he might stay, now that he knows who he is?"

"I canna say, lass."

"But *you* stayed."

"Aye, that I did. But I came to realize that the woman I'd become was a far better one than the woman I had been."

"Maybe Cameron will come to the same conclusion." Marjory's words sounded empty even to herself.

"It could happen. But ye have to remember, child, that a man is very different from a woman. Cameron's identity is everything to him. In the world he comes from, the worth o' a man is often based solely on his profession. Physicians are revered, especially surgeons. 'Twould be a hard thing to let go of. Dinna be misled by my words, 'twas no' easy, even for me."

"Did you try to get back?"

"Aye, that I did." She smiled with the memory. "But I couldna remember where it was that I arrived. I wandered about for quite a while before yer dear father found me. There was no way o' knowing where it was I first awoke."

Marjory felt her stomach lurch with dread. "Cameron knows the exact spot where he arrived."

"I know." Grania turned away from the fire to face Marjory, placing her free hand over their entwined ones. "Marjory, sometimes the hardest thing to do is to let go of the ones that we love. If you really love him, then you may have to face the fact that he'd be better off in his own time. He has a life there. Perhaps even a family."

Marjory felt tears slide down her cheeks. With an angry hand, she wiped them away. " 'Twould seem 'tis my lot in life to have to let go the ones I love." She pulled back her hands and rose from the bench, intending to escape, but she stopped, seeing the older woman's face in the firelight, wet with tears. Somehow she'd never thought that blind people could cry.

"Grania?"

The woman turned.

"What was your name? I mean, your real name?"

For a moment Grania looked startled by the question. Then, with a smile that lit the chamber she answered, "My name was Eileen Donovan Even."

Chapter Twenty-one

Cameron leaned his head back against the cool stone wall and closed his eyes, letting the silence surround him. The room was dark and more than a little cold, but any discomfort was more than made up for by the serenity it afforded. He'd never thought of himself as a particularly religious man, but he'd always believed. And even in the fifteenth century, it seemed a chapel was a place of peace.

His thoughts flashed, briefly, to a trip made as a child. A trip to New York City. His father had taken him, a special holiday for a lonely little boy recovering from the loss of his mother. It had been a short train ride from Boston to New York, but to an eight-year-old boy it had been a grand adventure.

Among other places, they'd gone to a museum full of religious artifacts from the Middle Ages. Not exactly the sort of place favored by growing boys, but there had been something magical about it. He frowned, trying to remember the name.

It was one of the Rockefeller museums. The nunnery

or something like that. He struggled with the name and then smiled at the sheer joy of trying to remember something as routine as the name of a museum. The Cloisters. That was it.

It had been a surprise to him. Quiet and subdued, unlike any other museum he'd ever been to. There had been one room, an arched vault of sorts, empty save for some rustic benches. He shifted uncomfortably on the real-life version.

He'd sat in that room much as he was doing now, and more importantly, he'd found peace there. After his mother's accident, he'd felt alone, deserted in many ways. His father had tried in his own gruff way to help him, but he hadn't been a demonstrative man, and Cameron had continued to feel isolated, devastated by the loss of his mother.

Then suddenly, in that room, at the Cloisters, he had felt comforted. As though God Himself had reached down from heaven to embrace him. The moment was as real now as it had been twenty-five years ago. And here he was again, only this time the chapel was the real thing.

He waited in the dark, waited for some kind of sign, for comfort or release, but there was only silence. He sighed. He'd probably had more than enough miracles in one lifetime. He winced. Make that two lifetimes.

"I thought perhaps I'd find ye here."

Cameron turned toward the sound of the voice. The shadows of the chapel hid the owner, but he recognized it nevertheless. "You can drop the accent. I know who you are. Or should I say, who you aren't."

"The accent is real. As real as I am. Dinna forget that I've been here for many years. Whoever I was, she is only a part of the distant past now."

"Don't you mean future?" he asked dryly. She began

to make her way across the room. "You should have a light, it's dark in here."

She chuckled and he immediately recognized the error of his words. "I've no use o' a light, lad." Grania stopped in front of him, resting a hand on his shoulder. "I've been worried about ye."

"Really? And what exactly are you worrying about? The fact that all the inhabitants of Crannag Mhór think I'm a sorcerer? Or perhaps you're concerned that I now know definitely who I am. Or maybe you're worried that I've discovered who you are?" He paused, shocked at the bitterness in his voice.

Grania moved slowly around the bench and settled beside him, a hand comfortably on his arm. "I do care, ye know."

"If you cared so much, why didn't you tell me who you were?"

She sat for a moment and then answered, her voice trembling a little. "I dinna tell ye because I've never told anyone. Old habits die hard, I guess. And ye never gave me reason to believe ye knew ye were no' from this time."

What she said was true enough. He'd purposefully kept his knowledge of the twenty-first century from her. He felt some of his anger slip away.

"Do ye know who ye are then?"

He sat forward, threading his hands through his hair. "Yeah. I do."

"All of it?" Her voice was both soothing and probing. "Do ye remember what happened to bring you here?"

He sighed. "No. I have memories from as far back as when my mother died, but nothing at all about what happened to bring me here."

"Yer mother died?"

He sat back again, closing his eyes. Somehow, it seemed easier to talk that way.

"Yeah, when I was eight."

"I'm truly sorry." She patted his knee. It was comforting in an abstract sort of way.

"It was a long time ago. I've learned to live with it."

"Have ye other family?"

"No." He paused, trying to think how to frame his next words. He'd spent the past few hours dealing with his guilt, and he wasn't sure he wanted to share it with anyone else. "My father's dead, too." There, he'd given her the truth, to a point.

"Ah, no siblings I take it."

"Nope. Just me."

"I had five."

"Siblings?"

"Aye, four brothers and a sister. My folks were Irish Catholic. I'm surprised there weren't more."

"It must have been a lively family." He wondered what it would have felt like to grow up with other children. A hell of a lot less lonely, most likely.

"I think it probably was. I dinna know really. I ran away from home, you see. We were poor and there was always more work to be done. I wanted more for myself, and so, I left one day and never looked back." There was a wistful note in her voice.

"But you miss them now?"

"Aye, that I do. The folly of an old woman, no doubt." She laughed gently.

"Is that when you came here after you ran away?"

"Oh, heavens no. I went from home to college, and from there to the home of a wealthy widower." She paused, her voice tinged with embarrassment. Cameron

265

was almost glad the shadows hid her face. "He helped me get into Harvard medical school."

"And then?"

"Pretty straightforward, really. I graduated with honors and decided to be a surgeon."

"Did you specialize?"

"No. It was the fifties. I was lucky to find a general practice that would take me. Women doctors were still pretty much an oddity, and in surgery they were a definite rarity."

"Did you marry?"

"I'd call it more of a business merger. We each needed the respectability of marriage."

"Sounds like my family. My mom was a doctor, too, and my dad was a lawyer. He came from a prominent Boston family." They sat for a moment enjoying the shared intimacy. "Did you have children?"

Grania was silent for a long while, and when she finally answered, Cameron could hear the agony in her voice. "Aye, I had a son."

He wondered what it would feel like to live in a world where your son hadn't even been born yet.

"Do you miss them?"

"I dinna think of my husband much. He was a good man, but we never shared anything more than a desire to make it big in the world."

"And your son?"

She sighed, the soft sound heart-wrenching. "I miss him every day. I regret that I wasna much o' a mother to him. I was too involved with my career. I'd give my soul to have a chance to set things right."

Uncomfortable with her obvious pain, he tried to find words. "I'm sure he remembers you fondly." The words sounded trite. He wasn't good at comforting people.

She squeezed his hand. "I hope ye're right, but I imagine 'tis more likely he doesna remember me at all."

"Was he young when you . . ." He trailed off.

"Came here? Aye."

"What happened?"

"To bring me here?"

"Yeah."

"There was a terrible accident. I remember searing pain. I thought surely I would die from it." She smiled, her teeth white in the faint light. "I guess in some ways I did. Anyway, suddenly the pain was gone and there was a flash o' blinding white light. Then I was here, wandering about the countryside in another woman's body."

"Did you try to get back?" He sat forward on the bench, intent upon her answer.

"Every day at first, but when the years kept passing and I was still here, I began to realize that maybe I was meant to be in this time."

Cameron uttered a frustrated oath.

"I know 'tis no' what ye want to hear, but ye need to face the truth o' it. 'Tis possible you, too, are *meant* to be here."

"Impossible. I have a life in Atlanta. I have a practice and a house and a . . ." He stopped, letting the sentence dangle between them.

"A wife?"

"No." He hesitated, guilty. He wanted to stop there, to avoid saying it out loud, but he wasn't a man to shirk responsibility. He turned to face her. "I have a fiancée, Grania. Her name is Lindsey Bowden."

"I see. And now ye're feeling guilty o'er yer feelings fer Marjory."

Cameron groaned. The woman could read his mind.

"Yes. In a crazy kind of way I've betrayed them both." Grania's sightless eyes seemed to search his. He had a sudden urge to throw himself on her lap and sob. He blinked and pushed the thought aside, embarrassed. "I *have* betrayed them."

"Not knowingly."

"But how could I possibly have forgotten something as important as a fiancée?" The images of his dream ran through his mind, the little voice inside him saying that he hadn't forgotten, just repressed the memory. His guilt intensified. "I've got to get back there. To make things right."

"Are ye so sure that's where you belong?"

An image of Marjory, flushed from lovemaking, popped into his head. Suddenly, her dark hair faded to gold and her eyes changed from blue to green. Lindsey. He buried his head in his hands. "I've made promises there, in Atlanta. And I think . . ." Again images of the dream flashed through his mind. "I think that Lindsey needs me. What kind of man would I be if I abandoned one woman for another?"

"A human man." He felt her arm around him. He leaned into her and felt the tears begin to flow. *Stop those tears, this instant.* He could hear his father's voice, disdainful at any sign of emotion from his young son. With a gulp, he pulled away from Grania's embrace, humiliated by his display of weakness.

"Never be afraid to show ye care, lad. 'Tis the man who canna share his feelings that is to be pitied, no' the man willing to bare his soul." She paused then, apparently making up her mind about something, stood and placed both hands on his shoulders. "I never knew exactly where it was I arrived here. 'Twas somewhere in the woods on the far side o' the loch, but I never did find the exact site."

Cameron sobered instantly, all emotion gone. "What are you trying to tell me?"

"I'm telling you that just because I couldna get back doesna mean that the same will be true fer you. Ye know where ye were when ye awoke, and more importantly, ye have good reason to go home."

"I don't understand. You had good reason, too. There was your little boy."

"Aye, but that wasn't the overriding reason I wanted to return. At least no' in the beginning."

"What are you saying?"

"I'm saying that my reasons were selfish. I wanted my life back. No' my marriage or my son, but my life, with all its wealth and privilege. I'd worked so hard to get it and then, just as I was finally feeling like I'd made it, I landed here in the lap o' poverty again."

"But you said that you prefer it here, now." He stood, too. Her hands dropped to her side and she tipped her face up toward his.

"I do. God moves in mysterious ways, and I've come to realize that the things I valued then were worthless. What matters is the people you love. Here, in this time, despite everything, I'm at peace. And I wouldn't trade that fer anything in the world—except perhaps to see my son again." She sighed, then squared her shoulders, obviously pushing the past behind her. "Marjory tells me yer real name is Cameron."

"Yeah. My first name is actually Robert, but I never use it. Always preferred Cameron." He didn't add that he had started using his middle name when his mother died. Somehow he couldn't bear to be called Robert anymore. It made her death seem more real.

As if sensing his discomfort, Grania reached for his hand. "We've said enough for tonight. Ye're tired and in need o' a good night's sleep. Things will look better in the light o' a new day."

He nodded. He was tired and, frankly, bed sounded like the perfect way to escape all of this for a little while. He squeezed Grania's hand and released it, then walked away without another word.

Chapter Twenty-two

He paced around the small bedroom. Firelight danced against the walls, creating shadowy partners that writhed to an unheard rhythm. He sat on a stool by the hearth, running his hands through his hair. No, he thought—not his hair, Ewen's hair. Cameron Even had black hair, and a life far removed from the Highlands of Scotland.

His practice in Atlanta was thriving. Or at least it would be in a few hundred years. He sighed. It was all so complicated. He thought about his new house: a great big Tudor mansion. He and Lindsey had picked it out together. It was in the most exclusive part of town. Hell, he'd just bought a brand-new Porsche.

Lindsey.

The thought of her brought a smile to his face. They were suited in so many ways. He'd known the minute he'd seen her that she would make the perfect wife. He had pursued her with the precision of a surgeon, planning each move with expertise learned from his father.

And he'd won the prize. Despite being besieged by

other suitors, Lindsey had fallen in love with him. And he with her.

And now he'd betrayed her.

Thoughts of Marjory pushed themselves front and center. The opposite of Lindsey in so many ways, she was no less attractive. Perhaps in some ways even more so. Maybe it was the framing of the fifteenth century, or maybe his mind had somehow been touched by Ewen Cameron's. But as horrible as he felt about betraying Lindsey, he couldn't force himself to truly regret his time with Marjory.

Which made him feel less than honorable. He had to go home. He had to make everything right. Prove to Lindsey that she was the one. Take away the fear and pain he saw in the dream—pain he was certain somehow, he had caused.

He stood and grabbed the poker, stirring the embers of the dying fire. It leapt to life and he spread his hands out in front of the flames, seeking their warmth. Lord, it was cold in Scotland. He released the pin at his shoulder and managed to unwind the long length of his plaid. Removing his shirt, he jumped quickly into bed, pushing back the bed curtains so that he could still see the fire.

A sound from the next room caught his attention. Marjory. He shifted uncomfortably, his thoughts bringing on a physical response. Closing his eyes, he tried not to think about her, but his mind refused to listen and he felt a longing so acute that it brought actual physical pain.

As a countermeasure, he tried to think of Lindsey, to evoke a similar kind of passion at her memory. But all he saw was the vision from his dream: Lindsey standing there in the pouring rain. Guilt washed over him. He'd never thought of himself as the philandering sort. Yet here he was with thoughts of two women.

He shifted restlessly. He had to get out of here. It was the only answer. He owed it to Lindsey. Hell, he owed it to himself. He couldn't undo what he had done, but he could certainly remove himself from temptation and get his old life back on course.

At least, he thought he could. Again he heard Grania's voice. It was almost as if she were in the room. *"I know 'tis no' what ye want to hear, but ye need to face the truth o' it. 'Tis possible you, too, are meant to be here."*

No. She was wrong. He wasn't meant to be here, to live the life of another man. He had his own life and that was where he belonged. He closed his eyes and concentrated on his life in Atlanta, on Lindsey. The effort made him sleepy.

He yawned, snuggling deeper into his blankets, allowing himself to drift toward slumber, only vaguely aware that his last thoughts were not of a green-eyed blonde, but of a blue-eyed brunette.

Marjory sat in her bed, staring at the coals of her fire, her knees drawn up under her chin. She couldn't sleep. At first she'd waited to hear Cameron come to bed. It had been late when she'd finally heard him moving around in his chamber. She'd half hoped that he would come to her, but soon it had grown quiet on his side of the door and she'd realized he wasn't coming.

Feeling dejected, she'd spent the last few hours tossing and turning, trying to make some sense out of all that had happened. She'd believed Cameron when he'd told her he was from another time, believed him primarily because he had believed it so fervently himself. And yet, she realized, some part of her had not really accepted the whole truth of it until that moment in the great hall when he had cut into Fingal's throat.

273

She lay back against her pillows, pulling her blankets up to her chin. It was cold tonight. Immediately, the thought of Cameron's lithe body lying hot against hers filled her mind. Something deep inside her tightened in anticipation and she moaned, rolling to her side, bringing her knees to her chest. Oh, how she wanted him.

She tried to tell herself that there was a chance he'd stay, that now that he knew his identity he'd be satisfied to live out his life here with her—but she knew it was only wishful thinking. Grania's words came back to her, flowing through her mind, with unwanted wisdom.

"If you really love him, then you may have to face the fact that he'd be better off in his own time. He has a life there. Perhaps even a family."

She sighed. A family. That meant a wife. Another woman who held him at night. Another woman who occupied his heart. Cameron had wanted to go back from the very beginning. He'd always been honest with her about that. She'd be foolish to think that she would be enough to change his mind. She flipped onto her back and stared listlessly upward, watching the shadows move across the ceiling.

It was going to be a very long night.

Cameron knew he was dreaming, but it still seemed real. He could feel the rain on his face, see the sheen of water on the driveway. He turned the key in the lock and slid into the Porsche.

At least it was dry inside. The water from his suit coat beaded on the leather upholstery. He brushed at it reflexively. He leaned against the steering wheel, trying to get his emotions under control. He couldn't remember ever feeling so angry. He jammed the key into the ignition, the powerful engine roaring to life.

He flicked on the headlights. The harsh light illuminated the blonde, just as it always did, but this time there was a difference. He knew her. *Lindsey*. She pushed at her sodden hair, extending a hand to him, pleading with her eyes.

Ignoring her, he grasped the stick shift, feeling the car slide into gear. He watched as she opened her mouth, both hands extended now. The word *no* resounded in his brain. It was almost as if he actually heard her. She jumped back, her face reflecting her fear.

He felt his foot press down on the accelerator. He willed himself to stop, but knew he wouldn't. This was not just a dream. He was reliving the past. Nothing his mind could say or do would change the reality of whatever happened. He felt the car jerk and waited helplessly for the dream to play out, to see at last the part that had been eluding him.

Suddenly, the picture changed, as though a movie projectionist had switched reels at the wrong moment. Lindsey was gone. All he could see was blood—blood on the windshield, blood on the steering wheel, everywhere blood. He tried to get out of the car, but he couldn't move. He opened his mouth, screaming her name.

"Lindsey!"

He came awake with a start, his breath coming in harsh gasps. The reality of the dream hit him like a two-by-four. The anger, Lindsey's fear, his foot on the accelerator, the blood. He buried his head in his hands. What had he done? Oh, God, what had he done?

Marjory sat up in bed. The last echoes of Cameron's cry resounded through the room. She fumbled with the bedcovers and, finally freeing herself, ran to the connecting door. Whatever was happening, there was no mistaking the anguish in Cameron's voice.

"Are you all right?" She held her breath, waiting for an answer. Hearing none, she ran to the side of his bed. The bed curtains were open and he was sitting up, his head buried in his hands. She climbed in beside him, placing a tentative hand on his shoulder.

"What is it? Tell me?" She waited impatiently for his answer, but there was no sound except the harsh hissing of his breath. She reached for his hand and pulled it away from his face. "Cameron, 'tis Marjory. Talk to me. Let me help you."

He stared at her as if seeing someone else, then gradually relaxed, his eyes losing their haunted look. His hand tightened around hers as if it were a lifeline of some kind.

" 'Twas only a dream." She tucked a stray strand of hair behind his ear, smoothing it away from his face with her free hand.

He shook his head. "It's not a dream. It's a memory, or a premonition, or—God, I don't know."

His anguish tore at her. If she could take it from him and carry it herself she would, but that was impossible. "Do you want to tell me about it?" There was more to the question than just the dream. She held her breath, waiting.

Cameron sighed and stood up, walking over to the fire, the embers banked and glowing. "My name is Cameron Even. I live in a place called Atlanta. I'm a surgeon, Marjory. I operate on people, save their lives."

"Like with Fingal." She thought again of the magic he'd done.

He nodded, his gaze intense. "I have a fiancée."

She shot him a puzzled look. "I dinna know this word."

He frowned and then, after a moment, tried again. "I'm betrothed."

Her heart plummeted into her stomach and she thought, for a moment, she might be sick. Sucking in a breath, she strove for normalcy. "I see."

"Well, I'm glad you do. Because I don't. I don't see anything at all. I've betrayed Lindsey, I've betrayed you, and maybe worst of all I've betrayed myself."

"Lindsey." She said the name, hating the sound of it. "Is that her name?"

"Yes."

"And you love her?" She didn't want to ask the question, but the words came anyway.

"I do, Marjory. I asked her to marry me."

"Is she the one you were dreamin' of, then?" She felt tears prick her eyes. Hadn't Grania warned her?

Cameron nodded. "I don't understand it. I can't even remember it properly. Maybe it's a prophecy of some kind. Or maybe it's already happened. Either way, I'm certain that Lindsey is in trouble. Serious trouble. And I've got to help her. Don't you see, Marjory? I've got to go back." His eyes pleaded with her, his heart laid bare.

He didn't want to leave. It was there on his face. But he had to. He had obligations. And she knew better than anyone about obligations. A part of her wanted to scream, to beg, to plead with him to stay. But she knew it wouldn't change things. "Aye. You have to follow your heart."

"My heart is here with you." He said the words, then flinched as if they'd hurt him. "At least, a part of it is."

"And part of it is there, with Lindsey. And she's the one who needs you."

He nodded, the pain on his face a reflection of the turmoil in her heart. "I've made such a mess of everything."

"Nay." She crossed to him, her only thought to erase his pain. "You didna remember her, Cameron, which means that you were no' betraying her—at least no' in the way you're thinking. What happened here happened because you didn't know who you were. Now that you do, everything is clearer."

He shook his head. "But can't you see? That's just it. It *isn't* clearer."

"What I see," she said, surprised at the calm she felt, "is a man tormented by a situation that is no' of his making. Cameron, you couldna have known. You just couldna."

He reached out to trace the line of her cheek, his touch sending shivers racing through her. "You're an amazing woman, Marjory Macpherson."

She leaned forward and curled a hand around his neck, bringing his mouth to hers. Their breath mingled as their lips brushed together. With a groan, he pulled her to him, and the kiss ignited. She opened her mouth to him, her tongue reaching for his, desperate for the contact.

Her hands ran down the smooth contours of his shoulders, her body tightening with longing. He tangled his hands in her hair and tilted her head. His tongue plunged into her mouth again and again, as if he, too, were desperate for the taste of her. She felt her nipples bead into hard nubs of desire, and arched against him, a low moan escaping from her throat.

Suddenly he pushed away, setting her free. "We can't do this." He sat back, his breath coming in gasps. "I told you, everything is different now. I have another life, a fiancée . . ." He trailed off, his face reflecting his guilt.

"You're a man o' honor. I canna fault that. 'Tis one of the things I love best about you." She tried to smile, but failed.

"You humble me with your faith, Marjory. I'm just a man, and I've made my share of mistakes."

"Perhaps, but your still no' like the men o' my world." Her thoughts returned to Torcall, and the real Ewen, and she shuddered, wondering if Cameron's return would mean Ewen's as well.

"I honestly believe he's dead." Cameron reached for her, reading her mind, pulling her close, his words whispered against her ear.

"I pray that's true. But even so, there's still Torcall to be reckoned with." Just speaking the man's name aloud sent anger coursing through her. It was his fault in part that she was losing Cameron. Had she never been forced to marry Ewen, then Cameron could never have come. Twisted logic perhaps, but it was something to hold on to.

"Marjory, you can't keep holding on to this anger. It's eating you alive. You have so much to give. So much to offer. And you're wasting it all on bitter recriminations against a man who has lost as much as you."

"What has he lost?" she spat.

"His son. Whatever his faults are, Marjory, he loved Ewen. And now he'll have to lose him all over again."

"To my way o' thinking, 'tis no' much o' a loss."

"You don't mean that." He grabbed her shoulders, turning her to face him. "His loss is as real as yours. And Ewen's death on top of Cait's will no doubt fuel his hatred as well."

"Who is Cait?" She frowned, trying to remember the name.

"His wife." Cameron blew out a slow breath, as if he weren't certain if he should speak.

"And how is it I've never heard of her?"

"She died when you were quite small. Your father supposedly killed her."

In the stillness that followed his words, Marjory could hear the fire pop, and the wind whistling through a crack in the window. Everything seemed to slow down, as if frozen in time.

"That canna be. My father wouldna kill a woman."

"I don't think he meant to. But it happened just the same. The Macphersons were stealing cattle, and Torcall and Cait stumbled upon them. In the chase, your father cornered them and spooked Cait's horse. She was thrown and died."

"And Torcall never forgave him."

Cameron nodded. "And her death set off a neverending circle of hatred and revenge. And one of you is going to have to stop it. Before it destroys you both."

Marjory pulled away from him, her thoughts tumbling through her mind like sparrows in the wind. "I dinna understand why my father never told me."

"Maybe because he wanted to spare you. To protect you. To keep you from the ugliness of reality. He loved you, Marjory. Just as Torcall loves Ewen."

"It's all too much." She waved a hand through the air as if she could simply brush it all away. Cameron, Lindsey, Torcall, Ewen—everything that had been real suddenly flipped on its side, the world as she knew it changing forever.

Cameron was beside her again, this time with his arms around her. "Let me hold you, make it right for at least one more night."

She leaned against him, letting the warmth of his body

soothe her. His smell now familiar, comforting. "We shouldna be together."

"I know," he whispered, "but if things go as planned, I'll be gone tomorrow. And I want to hold you one last time. Just hold you, Marjory."

She allowed him to pull her down beside him, her cheek resting warm against his chest, the rhythm of his breathing a final link to a life she'd never know—happiness that had once more eluded her.

Within minutes, his even breathing signaled his descent into slumber, and she lay in silence—staring at the ceiling, reveling in the warmth of his body against hers, agonizing over the fact that he loved someone else.

His words bit into her heart, cutting deeply. She had to accept the fact that he had a covenant with Lindsey and she knew without a doubt that Cameron was the kind of man who honored his promises.

She swallowed back tears. He'd never made promises to her. In fact, he'd been clear from the beginning that there could never be anything permanent between them. He was going back, back to Lindsey, back to where he belonged.

It was for the best. He'd no doubt be safer there as well.

She tightened her arms around him, feeling the warmth of his breath through the thin linen of her night shift, and shivered. At least for tonight, for this moment, he belonged to her. Tomorrow . . . She sighed. Tomorrow, she'd have to let him go.

Chapter Twenty-three

Cameron groaned, trying to block the shaft of sunlight stabbing into his eyes. He'd forgotten to shut the bed curtains again. He rolled, dragging his pillow over his head. Surely, it couldn't be morning; it felt as if he'd only just fallen asleep.

Last night had been a doozy, and the memory of it made him reach out for Marjory—only to find the bed beside him empty. They'd said so much last night, yet neither had spoken the words that really mattered. He supposed it was all for the best. He needed to move forward, to think of Lindsey and his life with her.

He saw her again, standing in the rain, reaching for him. Blood everywhere. She needed him. He was certain of it. And nothing else could be allowed to matter. He had to make things right.

"Come on then, lad, are ye going to sleep the day away? I've been sitting here for quite a time, and I tell ye, I've had enough o' waiting."

The voice startled him out of his thoughts, and he rolled to find Aimil hovering over him with a tray. He closed his eyes again, certain that he was dreaming. Aimil would never come to his bedroom, and if she did, she'd much more likely be carrying a knife than a tray.

He frowned. On second thought, maybe a tray could be used as a weapon. Something along the lines of Mrs. Aimil doing it in the bedroom with the tray. Not exactly the lead pipe, but it would probably do in a pinch.

He opened his eyes to find the smiling woman still in the room. She'd moved away from the bed and was busy arranging the tray on the bedside table. "I've brought ye food to break yer fast."

He sat up blearily, eyeing her with suspicion. "Aimil, why are you here?" he asked, deciding the direct approach would be best.

She smiled cheerily. She was actually quite pretty when she wasn't scowling. "I just told ye, I've brung yer meal."

He rubbed a hand over his stubbled jaw. "I know that. But *why* have you brought it?" This was not an easy conversation. It was like trying to do bypass surgery with tweezers.

"Because ye were bound to be hungry. And, look, no oats." She removed a square of linen with a flourish. "Barley bannocks, sweetened with honey, just the way ye like them." She fidgeted with the tray.

"Aimil, why don't you sit down and tell me why you're really here? We both know it's got nothing to do with food."

She sank down onto the chair by the bed, her hands twisting nervously in her lap. "Well, truth be told, I came to thank ye."

"For what?"

"For saving my brother."

He reached for the mug of ale on the tray and took a

long swallow, wishing as he did most every morning that it would magically turn itself into a strong cup of coffee. "It was nothing, Aimil."

Maybe in his world, but, here, it ranked up as a miracle. He immediately regretted his choice of words.

She shifted uneasily in her chair. "Ye know that it was far more than nothing. Without ye, my brother would likely have died. I've no notion where ye learned to do what ye did, and I'm no' likely to be asking, but I thank ye just the same."

"Well, you're welcome." She made no move to leave. So, Cameron reached for the tray.

He was hungry and the bannocks smelled delicious. Then, remembering his thoughts about Aimil and arsenic, he hesitated, the food halfway to his mouth, another thought pushing itself front and center. The landslide, the *curach* . . .

"Ye know." She met his gaze, shifting uncomfortably on the chair.

"I guessed." *Just now.* But he didn't tell her that.

She motioned to the bannock halfway to his mouth. " 'Tis all right. I've done naught to yer food."

He hesitated a moment more, then bit off a piece and chewed. It was delicious. He swallowed, then put the bannock back on the tray. "So, you're the one who caused the landslide."

"Aye. 'Twas easy enough to do. I thought I'd kilt ye." She twisted her hands nervously, but held his gaze. "I came to apologize, and to beg yer forgiveness."

Cameron had no problem forgiving her for the landslide. After all, it was Ewen she'd wanted dead. But there was still the issue of the *curach*. "What about the boat?"

She lowered her head and stammered in the direction of her lap. "When ye told me that ye were going out on the loch in the wee *curach,* it seemed an ideal time to . . . to . . ." She broke off, her eyes filling with tears.

"Kill me?"

She swallowed uncomfortably. "Aye."

"But Marjory could have been killed."

Tears slipped down her weathered cheeks. "I dinna know that Marjory would be on the *curach!* I thought 'twould just be you. I would ne'er do anything to harm her. Ye have to know that."

"It's all right, Aimil." The woman's obvious misery deflated his anger. "It was brave of you to come and tell me this."

"I had to do it. 'Twas only right. Ye saved Fingal and Marjory. I dinna know who ye are, but ye're certainly no' a Cameron."

"Well, I am sort of a Cameron. I mean, that *is* my name. But I'm not related to Torcall, if that's what you're getting at."

She breathed a sigh of relief. "I think ye're an angel sent to watch o'er us all." She peeked at him through her lashes. "Especially Marjory."

The thought sobered him. He didn't want to be anybody's angel. And based on his actions over the last few days, he wasn't even certain he'd qualify for the job. But the thought once presented could not be pushed away. And he remembered something Grania had said about having a purpose here.

He shook his head, unwilling to allow for anything beyond what he knew he had to do. "Aimil, I appreciate your confession and your apology." He held out his hand. She looked at it, unsure of what to do.

He reached over and clasped her trembling hand in his. "Why don't we start over?" She nodded, pulling her hand back from his grasp. "How's your brother this morning?"

Her eyes brightened. "He's doing much better. He slept well last night and this morning ate a little broth. His throat's bothering him a wee bit, but I told him that was to be expected. Grania's already been in to check on him, and she seems to think with a little rest that he'll be right as rain."

Cameron smiled. "I'd trust her diagnosis any day."

Aimil frowned at his choice of words, but then smiled, obviously getting the gist. "Ye'll see him yerself?"

"Yeah, I'll check on him as soon as I'm dressed." He gave her a pointed look and she sprang up from her chair.

"I'd best be off then. I'll just leave the tray until you're finished." She headed for the door, and he watched her leave, then reached for his plaid.

It was time to go. Of course, there was still the problem of finding the way back to the landslide—and even if he found it, there was the very real possibility that he still wouldn't be able to get back to his own time. But he had to try. Lindsey needed him. Surely that was the point of his dreams.

Again he saw the blood, her terrified eyes beseeching him. He threaded his fingers through his hair, knowing he was missing something. But what? His memory seemed to be intact, but he still wasn't seeing the whole picture. He struggled to remember, but his mind remained stubbornly blank.

The only way to find out the truth was to try and get home again. To find the door to the future. His future. Maybe he'd been sent here to learn about himself. To realize that there was more to life than achievements and success. Maybe now he'd be the kind of husband Lindsey deserved.

Just for a moment he allowed himself to think of Marjory. He remembered the feel of her wrapped in his arms, their bodies moving together as one. Heart to heart, soul to soul . . .

With a curse, he cleared his thoughts. He had obligations to fulfill and they weren't here, no matter how tempting a certain Scotswoman might be. He jumped out of bed, swallowing the last of the bannocks. It was time to go home.

He stood at the gate to the garden, watching as Grania dug her hands into the warm, moist soil. The smell of the earth filled the air, the scent soothing in some intrinsic way. Grania felt carefully along a row of plants, her hands stopping when she reached a dark green, long-leafed one; then with deft hands, she harvested stems and leaves, placing them in a basket by her side.

It was peaceful watching her work, the drone of the nearby bees a musical accompaniment. It would be easy to stay here, to forget about honor and doing what was right, but Cameron knew he couldn't. So he walked into the garden preparing to say good-bye.

Grania must have recognized the sound of his footsteps, because she looked up, her wrinkled face creasing into a smile. "Ye're an early riser. I thought fer sure ye'd sleep the day away after all ye went through last night."

"I could say the same thing about you." He came closer, squatting down on the dirt beside her.

"I dinna sleep much anymore. One of the privileges of age."

"Are these herbs for healing?" He was fairly certain of the answer, but he couldn't bring himself to move to heavier topics.

"Aye. I've got quite a few of them growing here, although there are some I can only find in the woods. I thought I'd make a poultice for Fingal. Have ye seen him?"

"Yeah, I just left him. He's healing nicely. Hasn't quite got the hang of covering the stoma before he talks, but he's getting there. I imagine in a few more days he'll be talking nonstop."

"Probably." She stopped awkwardly, as if she already knew what he was here to say.

"I've come to say good-bye."

"Ye've made up yer mind, then?" She broke off another plant, adding it to the basket, a slight tremble in her hand the only evidence his announcement had affected her.

"Once I remembered, there was never really anything to decide. I belong in the twenty-first century, Grania. My life is there."

"Ye have a life here, too."

"No. Ewen had a life. I've just been prolonging it for him."

"And what about Marjory?" Grania looked up at him, her expression so intense that for a moment he forgot she couldn't see.

He sighed, his heart twisting inside him. "She'll find someone new. Someone who can love her the way she deserves to be loved."

Grania reached over and tentatively touched his hand. "I know that, but I canna be as sure that she knows it. She's given her heart to you, lad, and it'll no' be easy for her to give it to another."

He pulled away. "I wish it could be different, Grania. I'd do anything to keep from hurting her. But I have a fiancée and she needs me. If my dreams are to be believed, her very life might depend on it."

"Surely an overstatement."

"Maybe, but there's only one way to know for sure."

Grania rubbed a leaf absently, and the sharp scent of thyme filled the air. "So ye're going. Have ye told Marjory, then?"

"She knows I'm leaving. But I didn't tell her when. It's better this way. Really."

Grania nodded, but he knew she wasn't any more convinced than he was. "Ye're truly sure this is what ye want?"

"It's the only choice I have. I have to do what's right."

She sighed. "Everything is not always as it seems, Cameron. And sometimes we dinna know what it is we have until we've lost it."

"Grania, I came to say good-bye, not listen to your riddles." He hadn't meant for the words to sound so sharp, but he was tired of thinking. Tired of trying to figure out who and what he was. He needed the comfort of choosing a course of action and sticking to it. Still, he hadn't meant to hurt her. She was his friend. "Come with me."

"What?" She turned toward the sound of his voice.

"Come with me." With repetition the idea seemed plausible. "You're not from here. Maybe if you're with me, we could both get back."

She paused, as if considering, then shook her head with a smile. "I thank ye for asking me, but my life is here now. I'd no' fit in that time anymore. I've found a peace here that canna be duplicated. And I've a purpose as well. I care for these people and they care for me. I wouldna want it any other way."

"Well then, I guess this is it." Cameron stood up, a twig of lemon balm clinging to his hand.

Grania stood also, and with a trembling hand reached

out to grasp his hand firmly. They stood facing each other for a moment; then, with a mumbled oath, he drew her into his arms.

"Thank you for everything," he said, stepping back. "You've been a true friend, and I'll never forget you."

Grania reached out to touch his face. "Nor I you."

He stood for a moment more, smiling down at her. Then he turned to walk from the garden, content for the moment to know that Grania at least had found her way home.

"If he's decided to go, then I say good riddance." Marjory stabbed the piece of linen she was trying to embroider.

"Now, child, ye know ye dinna mean that." Grania's voice was patient, but somehow still managed to set Marjory's teeth on edge.

"I do mean it. Ever since he arrived here, there's been nothing but trouble. First, he brought Torcall Cameron down on our heads."

"I think ye'll have to admit that was far more yer doing than Cameron's," Grania said.

"Well, I'd no' have had to call for Torcall if Cameron hadn't gone and gotten himself killed."

"Now, Marjory. If ye'll recall, he wasn't precisely dead—and if ye're going to lay the blame fer that at anyone's feet, I'm afraid it will have to be mine. It was, after all, me who caused the landslide." Aimil looked up placidly from her needlework.

Marjory was still reeling from that revelation. Aimil had admitted it all to her that morning. She hadn't known whether to laugh or cry.

"Well, he did lure me out on the *curach*."

"Aye, but it was me, again, that caused the sinking," Aimil reminded.

"True enough—and if ye hadn't been capsized, ye might ne'er have fallen in love with the man," Grania added cheerfully.

"I am no' in love with him!" Marjory jabbed her thumb with the needle and sucked at it angrily. "What about the banquet?" She knew she was being perverse, but she couldn't seem to help herself.

"What about the banquet?" Grania asked.

"Well, if Cameron hadn't come here, there'd have been no need for a banquet and nothing would have happened to Fingal." She pulled the thread through the linen with a sharp tug, only to realize she'd come up in the wrong place.

"Ah, but the truth is that we did have the banquet, and had Cameron no' been there, my brother would most likely have died."

Marjory looked up, glaring. "Since when are you taking his side in things, Aimil? I thought you couldna stand the man."

Aimil colored. "Well, I've changed my mind, and I think Grania's right. Ye should go and find him. Say good-bye properly." She looked to Grania for support. "Or better yet, convince the man Crannag Mhór is where he belongs."

"I canna make him do something he doesna wish to do. Besides, Grania, you said yourself that he left hours ago. How am I supposed to catch up with him? Why, he's probably taking tea with Lindsey at this very moment."

Aimil looked confused. Marjory had tried to explain things to her, but the woman was having none of it. She was convinced that Cameron was an angel, and nothing

Marjory or Grania said could alter her opinion. Marjory sighed. Cameron was certainly not an angel. No angel would make her feel blissful one moment and furious the next.

She couldn't believe he had left without so much as a word in parting. Had she meant absolutely nothing to him? She pricked her finger again. Curse the man.

"Marjory." Aimil reached for her needlework. "If ye keep this up, ye'll ruin the wee thing."

She sat back, crossing her arms over her chest in defiance. "The man is gone and that's that."

"Well now. I dinna know that that's precisely true." Aimil bit her lip, looking somewhere between gleeful and guilty.

"What are ye saying, Aimil Macgillivray?" Marjory leaned forward, trying to ignore the erratic leap of her heart.

"Well, ye see, I happened to run into Cameron as he was leaving the tower." She ducked her head.

"And?"

"And he happened to ask if I knew the shortcut to the pool."

"And?" The hope began to spread outward, warming Marjory's entire middle.

Aimil shifted uncomfortably on her stool. "And, I told him he had to follow the loch and then head toward the black rock."

"But that would . . ." Marjory felt her eyes widen in amazement.

"Take him twice as long, I figure." Aimil smiled hesitantly. "I didna think ye wanted him to go. 'Twas all I could think to do on the spur o' the moment."

"I say well done." Grania was grinning broadly.

Marjory sighed. She felt slightly overwhelmed, definitely outmaneuvered, and unexpectedly joyful. "I thank you for your concern, Aimil, but I'm still no' going after him."

"Marjory, there are only so many chances in life. I canna promise that something good will come o' yer going after him. But can ye honestly tell me ye'll no' regret it fer the rest o' yer life if ye dinna go?" Grania turned in Marjory's direction, waiting for an answer.

Marjory looked at Grania and then over at Aimil, who was placidly sewing as if she didn't have a care in the world. With an exaggerated sigh, she stood up. "Fine, I'll go, but only so that the two of you will leave me alone."

Cameron struggled up the rocky side of an embankment, cursing Aimil Macgillivray all the way. She obviously still had it in for him. Shortcut, his aunt Fanny. How was he to have known the damn stream wandered all over the mountainside?

And if that wasn't bad enough, it was also nestled so close into rocks and trees that the only way he could be certain he didn't lose it was to walk down the icy, frigid, toe-numbing middle of it.

He stumbled on a rock and cursed softly, his eyes searching for something he recognized. With a sigh, he squinted into the sunlight, realizing that the rocks here formed a sort of natural dam. *The pool.* Relief surged through him, and he splashed through the water intent on the opposite bank.

If memory served, the landslide was just around the corner.

What seemed like hours later, he wasn't as certain. Truth was, the pool might as well have been located in a different country from the landslide for all the good it had done him finding it. He'd been walking in circles and there was no landslide in sight. No pile of rocks, no great tree, no embankment, nothing. It was as if the whole thing had never existed.

He moved through the brush, wearily pushing aside a clump of tall grass, and let out a groan. He was back at the pool. This place was worse than a Pavlovian maze. He started into the small clearing, heading for the rock. He needed a break.

Something moved across the stream and he froze, visions of claymore-welding wildmen filling his mind. The bank across from the rock was shadowed, and it was hard to make anything out, but he was positive he'd seen movement. Groping for the sword he'd brought, he sent a silent prayer heavenward, grateful that Aimil had insisted he take it.

Holding the thing at his side, he took a hesitant step forward, still staring at the far bank. The bushes along its edge were waving ominously. Using both hands, he lifted the claymore, relieved when his muscles took the weight. His efforts to practice hadn't made him a pro, but he was definitely better. Thank God for muscle memory.

Taking a deep breath, he waved the sword in front of him, eyeing the bushes, listening for a telltale rustle. When the noise repeated itself, he reacted instantly, swinging the weapon in a downward arc, swiping the tops off two small saplings.

Ignoring the saplings, he held his stance, trying to convince himself he was ready for anything. Anything except the pair of cobalt eyes that met his across the pool, reflecting suppressed laughter.

"You can rest easy, Cameron. I think the wee trees are dead."

Chapter Twenty-four

"I thought . . . Ah, hell, never mind what I thought. What are you doing here?" He sheathed his sword, watching as Marjory picked her way across the stream, using the rocks that dammed the pool for stepping stones.

"Well, 'tis glad I am to be seeing you, too." She hopped lightly onto the bank, letting her skirts fall back into place. "I thought you'd be gone by now."

He scowled at her, feeling his temper rise. "I would have been, but it seems Aimil's up to her old tricks. I have absolutely no idea what possessed me to trust her. She promised me she was giving me a shortcut. A wilderness survival hike would have been a more accurate description."

"She meant you no ill will. In fact, quite the opposite. She has it in her head that you should stay at Crannag Mhór. She thinks you're our resident angel."

"I'm well aware of Aimil's notions." He sat down on the big rock.

"Well, you can't blame a body for trying." Marjory sat next to him, her eyebrows lifting.

"You mean, she wanted me to get lost?"

"Aye, that she did. But you're here now, so all's well that ends well."

"Hardly. I can't find the damned landslide. I've been all over this area and there's no sign of it."

"You must have o'erlooked it. 'Tis no' far, just beyond that tree." She lifted an arm, pointing in the direction he'd swear he'd just come from.

"And why, may I ask, should I trust you?"

"Because if I had wanted to prevent you from leaving, I'd have thought up a better plan than simply misdirecting you."

"So if you don't care if I go, why are you here?"

She winced, and he cursed his insensitivity. "I dinna say I wanted you to go. Only that I'd do nothing to prevent it. I only came to say good-bye."

Their gazes met and held, his breath catching in his throat. "I shouldn't have run away."

"It doesna matter." She shrugged as if she didn't care, but he knew that she did. They stood in awkward silence, neither knowing what to say.

Finally Marjory sighed, forcing a smile. " 'Tis just as well I came. Had I no', you'd no doubt have spent the rest o' your days wandering about in search o' the landslide."

"I would have found it." He tried to sound wounded by her lack of faith, but only managed to sound defensive.

"I'm more than sure you would, given enough time, but since I happened to come along, would you like me to show you the way?"

"You don't have to come with me. Just pointing me in the right direction should be enough."

"I think you'd be better off if I took you." She stood

up, brushing off her skirts and looking out over the valley.

With a shrug, he rose to stand beside her. He could see the tower, its walls white against the blue-black waters of the lake. It looked like a John Constable painting, peaceful and serene. This was the way he would remember Crannag Mhór. "It's beautiful from here."

There was no response from Marjory. He turned and was surprised to find her frowning, her eyes riveted not on the valley below, but on something off to their right.

Cameron scanned the terrain. "What is it? What do you see?"

"Look o'er there." She pointed to a small expanse of green off to the southwest. The trees played out into a small meadow almost at the base of a craggy arm of the mountain protecting Crannag Mhór. The little clearing was a good distance away, lower down the mountain but still well above the floor of the valley. He couldn't see anything except the crooked expanse of green against the brownish gray of the rocky peak.

He narrowed his eyes, searching for something in the pastoral scene that might have alarmed her. "What am I looking for?" As he finished the sentence, a flicker of movement at the edge of the clearing caught his eye.

"Did you see that?"

"Yeah, I did."

She lifted a hand, shading her eyes from the sun. "I think there's someone at the edge of the woods."

Watching intently, Cameron began to discern shadows moving along the tree line. Riders. He glanced over at Marjory. Her brows were drawn together in a worried frown. She'd seen them, too. "Do you recognize them?"

"Nay, they're still too much in the trees, but I dinna

think they've come from the pass." She kept her eyes on the riders.

"How can you tell?"

"I canna fer sure, but they're too far into the valley to have come through the pass this morning. And if they came through yesterday, we'd have had word o' some kind. I canna shake the feeling that something is verra wrong."

As if in emphasis of her statement, the riders broke free of the trees, riding slowly into the clearing. The sun beat down upon them, highlighting the colors of their plaids.

"Holy Mother of God." The words came out in a painful whisper. Marjory had gone rigid, her eyes riveted on meadow. "Camerons."

For the first time since spotting the riders, Cameron felt a tug of worry. "Are you sure?"

"Aye, there's no mistaking the colors o' the plaid."

He watched as the riders relentlessly moved across the clearing. There were quite a few of them, enough to qualify as a small army. "Can they get down the mountain from there?"

"Aye, faster than we can." The thought seemed to agitate her. "I dinna know what Torcall is up to, but it canna be anything good."

Cameron took her by the shoulders, forcing her to look at him. "I'll admit it doesn't look good, but it still doesn't make sense to me. There's no good reason for Torcall to cause trouble."

"I pray that you have the right o' it."

"Of course I'm right." He tried to issue the statement with more enthusiasm than he felt. "He believes I'm Ewen, and he thinks I'm working overtime to get you pregnant. Which, for whatever twisted reason, seems to

be his goal at the moment. As long as he believes that,
you're safe."

"Then why is he riding back to Crannag Mhór?"

"I don't know."

They watched the riders in silence, their march across
the clearing seeming more ominous by the minute. Cameron raked a hand through his hair. It just didn't make
any sense. One minute, the man was hell-bent on getting
back to Tyndrum, the next he was making his way back
to Crannag Mhór. He struggled, trying to find logic
where there seemingly wasn't any.

Marjory sucked in a breath, grabbing his arm, her eyes
wide with alarm. "It must be Aida."

"Aida?"

"Aye. 'Tis the only explanation. Cameron, she saw
what happened last night with Fingal. And we sent her
away. You rejected her and I humiliated her. You heard
her. She threatened us both." Her eyes turned back to
meadow, the riders were disappearing once more into the
trees. "It would no' take much to convince Torcall to
destroy Crannag Mhór once and for all, if he believes
his son bewitched . . ." She trailed off, her hand tightening on his arm.

"He'll be out for vengeance."

Marjory nodded. "I canna let him destroy my home
again." She released his arm. "I have to go." She jumped
down from the rock, starting to walk away almost before
her feet hit the ground.

"Marjory, wait," he called after her, his heart beating
furiously in his chest. He had to stop her. She'd be walking into certain death.

She turned back to him, and with a halfhearted gesture,
pointed to a large tree. "You'll find the site o' the landslide just over there, beyond the tree. 'Tis only the best

I wish for you, Cameron." She swung away, again intent on reaching the tower.

He sprinted across the clearing and whirled her around to face him. "Are you crazy? You can't go down there. If he is out for revenge, he'll be waiting for you."

She pulled out of his grasp. "I have to go. If it's to my death, then so be it, but I will no' lie down and let him take Crannag Mhór without a fight." She started to move away again.

"Wait."

She stopped, her back rigid with determination.

He let out a sigh, his mind split. Lindsey needed him. But so did Marjory. And standing here on the side of a mountain, he knew what he had to do. If he lived to tell the tale, then maybe he could still help Lindsey. But in this moment, now, he wanted to help Marjory—to stand by her side and face whatever Torcall Cameron intended.

"If you're going, then so am I. After all, I'm the one with the sword."

She turned with a faint smile. "I believe there are two trees over there who'd bear witness to that, but Cameron, you dinna belong here. This is no' your fight. 'Tis time for you to go home."

His anger peaked. "Damn it, woman, I'm not going to let you face them alone. I'm coming with you."

She searched his face, the question in her eyes going well beyond Torcall Cameron. Then, with a sigh, she nodded.

Cameron reached for her hand, attempting a smile. "I don't suppose you know a shortcut?"

Her lips quirked upward in response, her fingers tightening around his; then together they began the trek back down the mountain.

* * *

Birch trees loomed on either side of them like sentries guarding the meadow beyond. Marjory leaned against a tree trunk, trying to catch her breath. They had run most of the way, fear and urgency driving them. Now, it was important to pause and consider their options before leaving the shelter of the woods for open ground.

"What next, princess?"

Cameron stood next to her, looking every inch a Scottish warrior. She bit back a stab of concern. He wasn't a warrior, no matter how he looked, and she was taking him into what could very well be a battle for their lives. Still, despite her feelings of guilt, she was glad to have him with her.

"I'm no' sure. We canna see the tower from here. But I'm fairly certain Torcall is still somewhere between it and us. Which means we can't safely leave the shelter o' the trees without risking discovery."

"Is there someplace in the woods where we can get a good look at the tower?"

She frowned, her mind spinning with worry, and she fought to calm herself. There was no time for panic. She had to think clearly. "There's a ridge no' far from here. 'Tis no' in the woods, but I think we can safely climb to the top without being seen."

"All right then, we have a plan." He reached for her hand, giving it a squeeze. "We'll find a way to stop them. I promise."

"Dinna make promises you canna keep." Pulling her hand free, she wearily pushed back a strand of hair that kept stubbornly falling in her face. "We'll follow the line o' the trees to the north until we're almost to the ridge, and then we'll break cover. The ridge itself ought to keep us out o' view."

Cameron surveyed the tree line. "Fine. What do you say we get moving?"

She nodded, trying to focus on the task at hand. It wouldn't help if she let her imagination run free. No matter what was happening inside the walls of Crannag Mhór, she had to keep her wits about her. She'd not be able to help her people if she let her fears overtake her.

They moved cautiously through the trees, trying to keep their speed without making too much noise. To their right the open meadowland beckoned. Everything was quiet, but there was no sense in taking unnecessary chances.

"Wait." The single word was whispered, but it had all the power of a shouted command. Marjory pulled up sharply, almost running into Cameron's broad back.

"What is it?" Her heart thudded as she scanned the area for danger. "What do you see?"

"Over there." He bit the words out, jerking his head in the direction of a large birch. Marjory let her eyes drift down the tree. There was a splash of white lying at the base. She started forward only to find her progress stopped, Cameron's big hand closing on her shoulder.

"It could be a trap." His whispered words drifted past her ear, no louder than a breath of air. He yanked her back behind a rhododendron bush, its glossy leaves providing cover. They crouched there, waiting and watching. Nothing moved.

Finally, convinced that no threat awaited them by the tree, they left the shelter of the bush, walking cautiously toward the patch of white. As they neared the birch, what had been abstract color began to take shape. They stopped a short distance away and Marjory felt bile rising in her throat.

Aida Macvail lay sprawled across the exposed roots

of the tree, her eyes open, staring at the branches waving dreamily in the wind. Her mouth was frozen in a scream, her golden hair tangled with leaves and twigs. Her throat had been slit.

Cameron moved forward, taking Aida's wrist, feeling for signs of life. He turned, meeting Marjory's horrified gaze, shaking his head in response to her unasked question. Turning back to the body, he gently closed her sightless eyes.

Marjory crossed herself, trying to swallow back the need to be sick. Cameron reached her side, enclosing her in the circle of his strong arms. She buried her head in his chest, allowing herself the moment of comfort. Finally, feeling calmer, she pushed away from him.

"I can only think of one person that could have done something like this."

Marjory nodded, forcing herself to spit out the name. "Allen Cameron."

"But why Aida?"

Marjory shook her head slowly in denial. "I don't know. It doesna make sense." She tried to pull out of the lethargy of shock and force herself to think.

"There's a basket over here." Cameron bent to examine it. "It's full of herbs."

Marjory felt fear clutch at her heart as she recognized the basket. It didn't belong to Aida, it belonged to Grania.

Chapter Twenty-five

They found her a few yards from Aida. She was lying on her back, one arm draped across her abdomen. Cameron dropped to his knees, his mind sending fervent prayers to heaven. Marjory, knelt, too, cradling Grania's head in her lap.

Heart pounding with fear, Cameron reached for her wrist. The skin was warm to the touch, and to his relief he felt the faint flutter of a heartbeat. "She's alive."

Marjory looked up, tears filling her eyes. "Is she going to be all right?"

"I won't know until I can see the extent of her injuries." His eyes raked over her. There was a gash above her right eye, but despite the blood, it appeared superficial. Her left arm was bent across her body at an odd angle. Probing gently, he was relieved to discover that nothing was broken, but her shoulder was dislocated. It was already quite swollen and beginning to show color. "Nothing here life threatening."

"She's no' awake." Marjory stroked the hair back from

her face and wiped away some of the blood with the hem of her skirt.

"I know, and it worries me. Help me roll her onto her side. Maybe we're missing something." Still holding the old woman's head, Marjory placed her other hand behind Grania's injured shoulder. Cameron put his hands behind her hip and lower back. "Okay—on three. One, two, *three*."

They carefully rolled her up onto her side, exposing her back. "Merciful God." Marjory's position afforded her an immediate look at Grania's back. Cameron sat back on his heels, steeling himself for the worst.

There was blood everywhere. It had soaked into the linen of Grania's dress, which now looked like a macabre tie-dye. Even the heavy wool of her plaid was stained brownish red. With fumbling hands, Cameron worked to free her from the blood-soaked cloth, resorting finally to the small knife Marjory pressed into his hands.

When he cut away the cloth, he almost wished he hadn't. The jagged edges of a stab wound glared at him, the edges an angry red. He fought to steady his hands, then carefully inspected the wound.

It was around nine inches in length and was located on her right side, neatly penetrating the rib cage. He couldn't judge the depth accurately, but he was certain it had penetrated deep enough to hit vital organs.

Marjory silently handed him a wad of cloth and a strip to bind it with. Blessing her for her practical thinking, he pressed the pad against the wound, wishing for sutures and antibiotics, and a whole host of paraphernalia he didn't have.

Grania needed surgery, and she needed it now. But that wasn't possible, so he swallowed back his frustration and bound the wound, hoping to at least prevent further blood loss.

She moaned and shifted a little as he tied the bandage in place.

"Grania? Can you hear me?" Marjory whispered anxiously. There was no response. They carefully rolled her over onto her back. "Grania? 'Tis me, Marjory. Cameron is here, too. Can you hear me?"

She waited, exchanging a worried glance with Cameron, then leaned back over the older woman, crooning soft nothings to her. Cameron ripped a strip of linen from the sleeve of his shirt. He fashioned it into a sling and was in the process of placing it carefully around her injured shoulder when Marjory's words stopped him cold.

"*Eileen,* can you hear me?"

His head jerked up. "What did you call her?"

Marjory looked up, meeting his gaze, pushing her hair impatiently back behind an ear. "Eileen. 'Twas her real name, before she came here. Eileen Even. I thought that maybe by using it I could reach her."

A wave of dizziness washed through him, and Cameron bent over, taking slow deep breaths, his mind threatening to explode. *Eileen Even?*

"Cameron, what is it?" He felt Marjory's hand on his back. "You look as if you've seen a kelpie."

He slowly raised his head, staring in wonder at the injured woman. "Not a kelpie, Marjory, a ghost. An honest-to-God ghost. You're absolutely sure that's what she said her name was?"

"Positive. In fact, there was a bit more." She screwed up her face in the effort to remember. "I have it," she said triumphantly. "She told me her name was Eileen Donovan Even. What is it about the name that upsets you so?"

Cameron paused, his mind still reeling from the enormity of what he was now certain was reality. He drew in a breath, then sighed. "Eileen Even was my mother, Marjory. She died in a plane crash when I was eight."

A soft moan from Grania brought their attention back to the injured woman. She was tossing her head back and forth, mumbling something. Cameron felt her head. It was cool but clammy.

Placing a hand at her throat, he timed her heart rate. Too fast. She was showing signs of shock. "We've got to get her to wake up."

As if on cue, Grania's head turned in Cameron's direction. "Cameron, is that you?"

"I'm here, Grania." *Mother*, his mind added silently.

"Where am I, then?"

"You're still in the woods."

"And Allen?"

Cameron met Marjory's eyes, recognizing the flash of anger there, a reflection of his own feelings. "Gone, Grania. He's gone."

She nodded, struggling to draw breath. Her lungs made a gurgling noise as she inhaled. "Aida?"

Cameron glanced at Marjory, unsure of what to say.

"She's dead, I take it." Grania guessed.

"Yeah, she is."

"Poor thing. She came back to warn us. Fer what it's worth, I think she truly loved Ewen." Grania struggled to sit up. "Torcall is marching on Crannag Mhór. To hear the girl tell it, 'twas always the plan."

"But when he discovered his son wasna dead, surely that changed his plans?" Marjory's worried gaze collided with Cameron's.

"Perhaps fer a moment, but ye know as well as I that Torcall lives for his oldest son. And despite yer efforts,

307

the man he found at Crannag Mhór was little more than a stranger." Grania coughed, her shoulders shaking with the force of it.

"Easy now. You've got to lie still." Cameron stroked her hair.

"But he left. I saw him go." Marjory's voice was carefully controlled.

"We'll ne'er know for certain what was in the man's mind, but once Aida had told him about Fingal—about what ye did, lad—Torcall was convinced ye'd been bewitched."

"And he wants someone to pay for what he believes has happened to Ewen."

Grania nodded. "Aida panicked. She'd no intention of starting a battle. And so she slipped away, planning to come back and warn ye. But Allen found her first."

"With you."

"Aye."

The word hung between them, and Cameron fought against his rage. "Was Torcall here?"

"Nay. No' at first. 'Twas only Allen, roaring about betrayal. Had Torcall no' arrived when he did, I've no doubt Allen would o' finished what he started."

Cameron clenched his jaw. "How long ago was this?"

"I'd guess no' too long, but I canna say fer sure. I'm afraid I blacked out." She paused, wincing. "Ye must go."

Marjory reached over to pat her hand. "Torcall's already well ahead o' us. A few minutes spent with you will no' make a difference."

Cameron met her eyes, willing her to understand the depth of his gratitude. He looked back at his mother. "Try not to worry about anything right now. You need to concentrate on getting better."

She struggled to lift her hand and he reached over, placing his around it, squeezing gently. She smiled faintly. "Dinna lie to me, Cameron. The sword's caused a great deal o' damage. Unless I miss my guess, 'twill no' be long before I bleed to death."

He lowered his head, grief overwhelming him.

Her hand fluttered beneath his. "Dinna take it so hard, son."

Son. The word resonated through his head. "You know?"

She nodded.

"Why didn't you tell me?"

"Because ye'd decided to go, and I knew telling ye would only add to the burden o' yer decision." She squeezed his hand. "Besides, in truth I canna say that there's much of Eileen Even left inside me. Except my love fer you."

She jerked forward as a fit of coughing wracked her body. Cameron held her, while Marjory held a square of linen against her lips. When she calmed, Cameron eased her back down, noting the pinkish fluid on the linen as Marjory drew away.

" 'Twill no' be long now." Grania's words were low but clear.

"Don't be foolish. You're going to live a long and healthy life. You've just got to hang in there." He spoke as a physician, adopting the voice he'd used thousands of times for a critical patient.

"Cameron, dinna forget I'm a surgeon, too. I know the effects of shock when I feel it."

Cameron felt Marjory slip her hand into his. He held on tightly. "Grania, you can't die now—not when we've only just found each other again."

"Hush, child. My time has come. Dinna let it grieve

ye. I've had a long and fruitful life. God gave me a second chance and I took it, never realizing what wealth it would bring. The only thing I missed was seeing you. And now that wish, too, has been granted. 'Tis God's will that I go, and ye canna argue with Him."

"What kind of God gives you back your mother only to take her away again? I lived through losing you once. How can He expect me to go through it again?"

"Trust me, Cameron. God never gives ye anything to deal with that you're not capable o' handling. He has a purpose, even in this."

"But if He brought me back here to find you—"

"I canna believe that's all He had in mind. There's something more, lad. Ye just have to find it." She stopped, struggling again for breath. The wheezing was getting louder. She jerked as more coughs shook her slender frame. Cameron released Marjory's hand, placing an arm under Grania, holding his mother upright until the coughing passed.

Helping her lie down again, he stroked her brow. "Rest now."

"I think I'll soon be getting all the rest I need." She shot him a weak smile. "I've just a few more things to say."

He glanced over at Marjory. She sat silently, wiping the tears from her face with the back of her sleeve. Their eyes met, and somehow even without a touch, he felt comforted. He leaned back over his mother.

She spoke quietly, her words for his ears alone. "Remember that there's one here who loves ye even more than I do. All ye have to do is open yer eyes to see. There is so much joy in loving. Dinna let yerself settle for anything less." She sucked air into her lungs, the sound of the effort grating against his ears.

"Most importantly, ye've got to know that a person's identity is no' made o' flesh and blood, Cameron, but heart and soul. It's not what ye accomplish that matters, but who ye *are*. It took me two lifetimes to discover that truth. 'Tis my wish fer you, that'll ye find out the truth o' my words before 'tis too late. 'Tis my legacy to you."

He felt his tears begin to fall, his heart shattering into pieces.

"Dinna cry fer me, child. I die happy, knowing what a fine man you've become. I believe that God put me here to help ye find yer way. Now, 'tis up to you what road ye take—but know, Cameron, whate'er you choose, that the best part of me goes with you."

"I love you, Grania. And I'm proud to have you as my mother."

She smiled at him, her face lighting with the ethereal beauty he'd seen when they'd first met. Then, with a sigh, she was gone. He sat holding her body, tears coursing down his face, certain that God had made a mistake, that it was he and not her who should have been taken. He leaned over and kissed her cheek. "Good-bye, Mother."

With reverent hands, he covered her with her bloody plaid. Marjory wrapped her arms around him and they sank to the ground beside her body, in silent vigil, both lost in their own grief, connected in sorrow.

Cameron placed a final stone on the cairns. It wasn't a proper burial. There wasn't time for that, but it would keep the animals away and it provided at least a sense of closure. He had no idea when, or even if, they would be able to come back to this place.

Marjory sat a little ways off, stone-faced and silent. They'd held each other until the worst of the immediate pain had subsided, but since then she hadn't said a word. One thing was for certain: They now shared a common enemy.

Cameron lowered his head over Grania's makeshift grave and tried to pray, but instead of words of comfort and hope, his mind seethed with anger and rage. What kind of God would send him here only to make him watch his mother die again? In what way could he possibly serve these people? He was a surgeon. They needed a warrior.

Not that being a surgeon had helped him all that much. He felt bitter laughter bubbling up inside him. What final irony that he would have to watch helplessly as his mother's lifeblood drained away, his skill absolutely useless without the aid of twenty-first-century technology.

He cursed the situation, knowing one thing for certain—Allen Cameron was going to pay.

Chapter Twenty-six

"I think I see something." They were lying side by side on their bellies at the top of a ridge just above the tower, a wild profusion of gorse and broom protecting them from detection. "Over there." Marjory pointed to the south slope of the meadow, along the edge of the wood.

He followed the line of her finger. The trees played out, thinning to open meadowland as the ground angled gently down toward the tower. Nothing seemed out of place. "What am I looking for?" Before she could answer, there was a sudden flash of sunlight against metal.

"There." She pointed again.

"I saw it." Something shifted within the shadows and then was still. He thought for a moment that he'd imagined the movement, but there was another telltale sparkle. "Shield?"

" 'Tis possible, or a claymore."

The riders suddenly burst out of the shadows, relentlessly approaching Crannag Mhór. "Well, they're certainly not trying to make their presence a secret."

313

" 'Twould seem so, but I thought there were more of them."

Cameron studied the men and horses. "I don't know, maybe. It's hard to tell how many there were before. The trees on the mountain obstructed the view."

Marjory nodded, her eyes never leaving the small band of men.

"How many Macpherson men are in the gate tower?"

"I canna say with certainty, but definitely no' as many as would normally be about. The feasting left many o' them abed this morning."

"How many in the tower total?"

"I'd say around eighty. Maybe a wee bit more. But there are Camerons there as well. Torcall always leaves some of his men."

"Not exactly what I wanted to hear."

"Aye, and it only gets worse. There are also women and children in there." She bit her lip nervously, then drew in a sharp breath. "Look. Over there." She pointed to the northwest side of the tower.

Cameron squinted against the sun, trying to see what had captured her attention.

She placed a hand on his arm. "There, near the edge o' the loch."

His eyes widened. A second group of men was approaching the tower, but unlike the others, they were dismounted, leading their horses. Their movements, even from this distance, looked suspicious.

"Well, well—that accounts for the missing men. I'd say there's about ten of them." They watched intently as the small group crept along the shore. "What could they possibly hope to gain by splitting up?"

"I've no idea, unless the first group is meant as a decoy."

"Possibly." Cameron ran a hand through his hair. What he wouldn't give for a pair of binoculars right now. "But what good does it do them to approach the walls? They're impregnable, aren't they?"

"Aye." Marjory frowned. "Except for the Tinker's Gate."

"The what?"

" 'Tis a gate in the west wall. It leads to a narrow causeway along the northern wall. The wee road ends in a passageway leading under the battlements, directly into a storage room near the kitchen. My father had it built along with the passage from the kitchen to the great hall."

"So why is it called the Tinker's Gate?"

"Because that's where Father would send the traveling tinkers when they came. Sometimes they'd camp on the wee bit o' ground between the wall and the loch, but we haven't used it since he died."

"How would Torcall know about it?"

"He wouldn't—unless someone at Crannag Mhór told him."

"Well, it looks as if someone did." He frowned, his gaze still on the scene below. The men to the north disappeared from view, obscured by a small rise, but he could still see the others. They had reached the gate tower and were clustered around the entrance, waiting to be admitted. "Will they be allowed in?"

"They shouldna. With Fingal injured and me out of the tower, I left word that no one was to be admitted without my leave. But as I said, there are Camerons inside the tower—" Marjory grasped his arm suddenly, her fingers digging into his skin.

The warriors to the north appeared again, still inching their way toward the tower. This time without their horses. It was hard to see them against the dark green of the meadow and the blue black of the lake, but every once in a while the sun would glint off of the metal of a blade. If Cameron shaded his eyes from the glare, he could just make out their movements.

"Damn. It looks like you called it. They're heading for the passageway. While your men are busy with the army at the gate, Torcall and son will waltz right into the tower."

Marjory's eyes widened and her grip on his arm increased. At this rate, his arm was going to be one big bruise. "We've got to stop them."

"If we just go roaring in there without a thought, we won't do anyone any good." She released her death grip on his arm. "The only thing we have on our side right now is surprise. Torcall has no idea we're seeing this."

She nodded grimly, but he could feel her body against his, her muscles knotted with tension.

"Look, I can't imagine Torcall making a move before he's certain all of his men are in place." He reached over to brush her hair back. "I'd say that buys us a little time."

"All right." He felt her relax and heard the whisper of a resigned sigh. "What do we do?"

"Well, the way I see it, there's no way we can go through the front gate. The minute someone sees us, we've tipped Torcall off and any advantage we have is gone. So that leaves the Tinker's gate. Unless there's a third way into the tower that you haven't told me about."

"Nay, there's no' another."

"Okay. Then our first step is to figure out how to get there without anyone noticing us."

"Well, the shortest route would be to cut across the meadow. But they'd see us the minute we cleared the trees." She frowned in concentration. "Which leaves us with two other options. We can go a bit farther north until we reach one of the crofters' huts. There should be a *curach* there. We could paddle out to the causeway."

"No, thanks." He shook his head. "I've had enough adventure with Scottish boats. Besides, we can't afford to lose the time it would take. What's the third option?"

" 'Tis a bit more risky, but it might work. See the trees by the edge o' the water?"

He glanced to the north. The forest thinned considerably, but there were indeed scattered clumps of birch reaching all the way to the lake.

"It will take us longer, but the trees will provide more cover than if we try to cross the meadow directly. After that, we can follow the shoreline of the loch. 'Twill take us straight to the Tinker's Gate. We'll be out in the open for a wee bit, but the loch should provide protection."

"It might work. At any rate it's our best shot. We'll head for the edge of the woods and then wait for Torcall to make his move. Agreed?"

She nodded. "Cameron?"

He kept his eyes on the group of men outside the tower. "Hmmm?"

"What are we going to do once we reach the Tinker's Gate?"

He leaned over, brushing his lips lightly against hers. "Don't worry, Marjory mine. We'll think of something."

The huge gate stood firmly in place, its iron hinges rusted in place. It was impassable. "Well, I don't think they came in this way."

Marjory nodded, her eyes narrowed in thought. "I'm surprised it hasna fallen into worse disrepair."

"Is there another way in?"

"No' that I remember."

"Well, they've got to have found some way, because they're certainly not here." He made his way to the edge of the lake. The wall extended about fifty feet into the cold, dark water, a jagged stain of green marring the stones. The line of algae was considerably higher than the water lapping placidly at the base of the wall. "Does the wall continue around the corner?" He glanced up at Marjory, who had followed him to the water's edge.

"Nay. Father always thought the loch was enough of a deterrent. The north wall runs along the inside o' the causeway starting at the far side o' the gate. This part of the wall is merely an extension, meant to keep invaders off the wee strip o' land."

"How deep is the lake here?"

"I dinna know. 'Tis impossible to tell without getting in. The water is too murky to ever see the bottom."

Squatting down, he began to methodically search the ground at the water's edge. Finally, almost hidden by a large rock, he found what he was looking for. The soft mud between the boulder and the water should have been unmarred, washed smooth by the lake. Instead, the ground was pockmarked, as though a very bad golfer had swung and missed over and over again. Or, more appropriate to the times, as though Torcall's men had walked around the rock and entered the lake, intent of making their way around the wall.

"Why do you ask?" Marjory knelt beside him, a puzzled expression on her face.

"Well, we know they didn't use the Tinker's Gate and I doubt that they headed for the main gate. So, as I see it, that would only leave one option."

Marjory's eyes widened. "You think they went into the loch?"

"I do."

"But if it's deep, how would they manage? They're heavily armed and claymores are no' something I'd want to be swimming with." She shuddered and Cameron wondered if she was thinking about her own close call with drowning.

"I don't think they had to swim."

"I dinna follow."

"Here, look at the water mark." He pointed to the algae. Her brows drew together as she tried to follow his train of thought. "It's considerably higher than the actual water. That tells me that the lake is low right now. Coupled with this," he said, pointing at the mud, "I'd say they went around the wall via the lake."

Marjory looked at the black water and then at the little stretch of mud. "So you're thinking we should follow."

"Quite honestly, I don't see an alternative."

Taking a deep breath and releasing it slowly, Marjory squared her shoulders and met his gaze. "All right, then. We'd best get to it. If Torcall and his men did go around the wall, they'll be inside Crannag Mhór by now. There's no time to lose."

As if to underscore the importance of her words, a bloodcurdling battle cry rang out from behind the main walls of the tower. Cameron felt the hairs on his neck rise as the sound crescendoed then died. Marjory was pulling up her skirts, tucking the hem in the belt at her waist. With a nod, they stepped into the lake. The battle had begun.

The water wasn't just cold, it was freezing. Marjory felt her teeth clacking together as she moved cautiously along the wall. The water came up to her breasts, but it appeared to have reached its deepest point. Looking up, she realized the slimy line of algae was far above her head.

Suddenly she was grateful for low water; she'd had enough swimming for a lifetime. Cameron tugged on her hand, and she realized they'd almost reached the end of the wall.

"We're almost around it. Hang in there," Cameron whispered, squeezing her hand as he gently pulled her forward.

Just a little bit more and they'd clear the end. Of course, there was still the walk back to shore on the other side, but somehow that didn't seem so bad. Every step would take them closer to land, not away from it.

Cameron stopped suddenly, putting a finger to his lips. Marjory almost crashed into his back. Motioning her to stay put, he flattened himself against the stones and slid forward until he could peer around the edge. She held her breath, waiting for some sort of outburst from the other side of the barrier.

Everything was quiet. Cameron stepped around the wall, disappearing from view. She waited for a few moments and then took a few cautious steps forward, her heart beating staccato against her ribs.

"The coast is clear." Cameron's voice was barely a whisper, but he might as well have screamed.

Startled, she jumped back and would have fallen if he hadn't reached for her, his strong arm wrapping securely around her waist. She gasped for breath, feeling chagrined. Some warrior she was turning out to be.

"Are you all right?" His eyes were filled with concern.

"Aye, you just startled me a wee bit. I'm fine." She shook off his arm and they rounded the end of the wall.

The shore was nearer on this side, the strip of land marking the causeway widening a bit. She scanned the area, looking for any signs of activity, but the causeway was empty. Assured that for the moment at least they were safe, she began to make her way toward shore, leaving Cameron to bring up the rear.

Stepping out of the frigid water, she stood for a moment, simply enjoying the feel of solid ground beneath her feet. Another cry rang out from behind the tower walls, this one a scream. Marjory turned, searching for Cameron, panic rising. He was just behind her, struggling to shore, shaking water off his body.

"We must hurry." Her voice sounded strained and she forced herself to take deep calming breaths. It wouldn't help anyone if she lost her head now.

Cameron squeezed her shoulder reassuringly. "Show me where the passageway is."

She nodded, grateful for something concrete to do. The causeway was short. The far end, like the gate side, was bounded by a stone wall jutting out from the tower's northern ramparts. That too, extended out into the water, protecting the little strip of land from the loch side.

Reaching the corner, Cameron released a frustrated sigh. There appeared to be nothing but grass and stone. "It's a dead end." He turned to look at her, his expression mutinous. "Hell, this was just a waste of time."

"Appearances are deceiving." With a faint smile, she moved forward. "There are actually two walls here." She demonstrated the fact by walking to an outcropping of brush, which at first glance appeared to be growing out of the wall. In actuality, the brush was behind a shorter wall whose masonry was designed to blend into the taller battlement behind it. The foliage added to the illusion, making it look, at least to the casual observer, like one solid, impenetrable wall.

Marjory walked around the shorter wall, relieved to see that the narrow stairs descending into the rocky ground were still intact. If the passageway was in a similar condition, they'd soon be safe inside the tower. She started to walk down the steps, but stopped short when Cameron closed a hand around her arm and pulled her back around the wall.

She glared at him, jerking her arm away. "What are you doing? We've no time to waste."

"I know, but we can't just go charging down there. We don't know what we're going to find. For all we know, Torcall's men are still in the passageway." He reached for her hand again. This time she let him take it. "I know you're worried, but we have to move cautiously."

She nodded, biting her lip. "You're right. I wasna thinking."

He gave her hand a squeeze and she wondered why it was that this man's touch affected her so dramatically. Even under conditions as dire as these, she felt her body respond. Gritting her teeth, she shook off the distraction. "How do you want to proceed?"

"I'll go first." She opened her mouth to argue, but he held up a hand to silence her. "I've got the claymore, remember? Wouldn't you rather it be leading the way if we run into any of Torcall's thugs?"

She didn't recognize the word he used, but she gathered it was not a complimentary term. She rather liked the sound of it. "Fine, I'll leave the handling of *thugs* to you."

Chapter Twenty-seven

The passageway was dank and dark, but fortunately it wasn't long. There was a faint light at the end, its pale glow at least partially illuminating the path. Cameron made his way forward, claymore drawn.

Marjory followed just behind him, her hand resting against the small of his back. A shadow flickered across the patch of light. Cameron stopped abruptly, pushing Marjory back against the earthen wall. "I think I saw someone." He peered at the open doorway. It was actually slightly above them, the path slanting steeply upward toward the storage room. Nothing moved except the faint waver of light.

" 'Twas naught but the torchlight."

Cameron shook his head. "It was more than that." As if to substantiate his words, the shadow moved across the opening again, and this time they were close enough to make out its distinctly human form. "Looks like Torcall left a guard. Stay here."

Cameron waited until the shadow disappeared again and started inching forward, his sword gripped tightly in his hand. He wondered, briefly, how he had managed to get himself into this position, but the memory of Grania's battered body immediately reminded him, and he clenched his jaw in determination. He would not let her death go unpunished.

Reaching the entrance to the tower, he was relieved to find the doorway empty. He crouched low in the corner of the passage, holding his breath, waiting. A slight movement in the still air surrounding him warned him he was not alone. "I told you to stay put."

"I thought you might have need for me."

He sighed with resignation. Marjory was a willful woman. "Well, at least stay here until I dispatch Torcall's henchman."

"The thug."

Cameron could detect the smile in her voice. She was actually enjoying this. Or whistling in the dark. He turned back to the light, as the man stepped into the doorway, his back to them. It was one of Torcall's soldiers; Cameron recognized the plaid. With one swift movement, he swung upward, claymore flashing in the torchlight.

The Scotsman died with a look of astonishment on his face. His lips moved as though he were trying to say something, but instead he crumpled to the floor of the storage room, his mouth open, his eyes lifeless.

One down.

Cameron grimly stepped over the body, eyes scanning for other intruders. The room was a replica of the solars on the two floors above, except that it had only tiny slits for windows.

"He's dead." Marjory announced matter-of-factly, stepping gingerly into the room.

Cameron was already in place against the wall abutting

the door leading into the kitchen. Holding a finger to his lips, he motioned her to the opposite wall. They waited in silence, Cameron straining to hear noise.

The kitchen, usually a busy place, full of people, was ominously quiet. Keeping his claymore ready, he swung into the room. Releasing a breath, he relaxed his sword arm. The kitchen was empty.

A fire burned at the hearth, licking at the bottom of a large iron pot. The smell of stewing meat filled the room. Marjory edged around the transom behind him. "Where is everyone?"

"Hiding, I assume. I think it's a good sign that there aren't any bodies." Cameron heard her sharp intake of breath. "Let's check the other rooms." The sleeping quarters adjacent to the kitchen were empty, no sign of any occupants, living or dead. The same was true of the pantry. It was as deserted as the kitchen. Abandoned trenchers were lined up on a table ready to be filled with food.

The thick stone walls and ceiling insulated the ground floor from the rooms above. It was impossible to tell what might be happening upstairs. "Where next?"

Marjory pointed to a connecting door between the pantry and another room. "The buttery, and there's another storage room."

They cautiously stepped into the buttery. Like the other rooms, there were signs of recent activity, an open keg of ale and several pitchers clustered around it, but the room was silent and empty. A door at the end of the buttery was closed, a heavy bar in place across its wooden door.

"Is that the storage room?"

Marjory nodded. "Aye, 'tis." She stared at it, her eyes wide with concern. "I've ne'er seen it barred before."

Cameron frowned and moved cautiously toward the

door. Handing his weapon to Marjory, he struggled to remove the bar. It creaked loudly as he lifted it from its brackets. Seeing Marjory's nod of encouragement, he swung open the door. The room was tiny, and jammed full of chests and crates.

Taking the claymore from Marjory, he edged cautiously into the room. She followed closely behind, her breath tickling the back of his neck. "There's no one here." Marjory's softly whispered comment seemed loud in the silence.

A woman's wail suddenly filled the room. Cameron raised his sword.

"He's got our Marjory." The fierce-faced figure of Crannag Mhór's cook emerged from the shadows, holding what looked like a rolling pin threateningly in one large hand. The other was planted firmly on her more than ample hip. "Let her go, ye fiend."

Cameron tipped back his head and laughed, as much from relief as from humor. Marjory shot him a look that clearly indicated she thought he'd gone round the bend. Pushing him aside, she rushed over to the agitated woman. "I'm fine. Cameron is here to help us, no' cause us further harm."

The woman lowered her arm, but her narrow-eyed gaze never left Cameron, and she didn't release her grip on the rolling pin. Evidently as far as she was concerned, once Torcall's son, always Torcall's son.

"Are you alone in here?"

The woman glared at him, then softened her gaze as she turned to address Marjory. "Nay, most o' the lasses who work in the tower are here as well." Several women, two holding small children, emerged from behind the crates. Their faces were pinched with fear.

"How many altogether?"

"There's nine o' us, no' counting the bairns." Cook looked over her shoulder at the gathered women, sending a terse nod in the direction of a shadowy corner. Four children emerged from behind a large chest.

Cameron frowned. "So, fifteen counting the babies?"

"Aye." This time the cook met his gaze, and he noted that some of her hostility had been replaced by guarded hope.

He nodded. "Are there other women in the tower?"

"There's only us. We're short-handed today. Some o' the girls stayed home." Cook ducked her head, avoiding Marjory's eyes, her cheeks stained a deep red. " 'Twas a late night and there was so much excitement, I told some of them to take the day fer rest."

"Dinna fash yerself. If I had thought o' it, I'd have sent them home myself."

"We've got to get them out of here." Cameron spoke to Marjory, but there was a titter of relief from the assembled women. "Do you think you can get them out through the passageway and around the wall?"

"Aye, but dinna you think I'd be o' more value here with you?" She looked at him with an expression he was beginning to recognize as mutinous.

He chose his words carefully. "Of course I'd rather have you here." Actually, he'd rather have her safe somewhere on the other side of Scotland, but to say that was a sure invitation for trouble. "But right now, it's far more important to get these ladies to safety." He glanced at the group. They were silent, hanging on his words as if their lives depended on them. Which, he realized, they probably did.

Marjory chewed her lip, then, obviously coming to a decision, nodded. "All right, then. I'll lead them out o' here. What are you going to do?"

Cameron grimaced, hoping he sounded more confident than he felt. "I'm going to find Allen and Torcall."

He leaned against the cold stone of the tower wall, listening to the sound of swordplay in the great hall. The women were on their way out of the tower. With luck, they would soon be safely outside the walls and away from danger.

He inched toward the opening of the service passage. It was just as Marjory described, a tunnel from the pantry to the great hall. He wasn't sure what he expected to do. It wasn't as if he had training for this kind of thing. But his desire to avenge Grania burned brightly, and if he could help Marjory in the process, then so much the better. He'd spent his life taking the high road, avoiding emotional commitment of any kind. But all that had changed.

With a deep breath, he tightened his grip on his claymore and cautiously stepped into the great room. A great carved screen kept him hidden from view, but allowed him to see.

There were men everywhere. The noise from their weapons was almost deafening. They battled fiercely, standing on tables and benches as well as the floor. Across the room, Fingal, bandage and all, was twisting expertly to and fro, avoiding the sharp blade of a huge man with bright red hair. Fingal faked a lunge to the left and, when the man followed the lead, shifted right and brought his sword in for the kill. His opponent died instantly.

With a grimace of satisfaction, Marjory's captain turned to help another man who had been backed into a corner. It was hard to tell who was who, but it looked like the Macphersons had the upper hand—at least for the moment.

Cameron searched the room for Allen and Torcall. There was no sign of either of them. Fingal had moved to engage Dougall in front of the fireplace. Even with his injury, he was more than holding his own. The two Scotsmen danced around the edge of the room, coming within a few yards of the screen. Dougall resembled some prehistoric reptile, his big head bobbing slightly with each jab and thrust, his body programmed to fight.

Cameron cautiously stuck his head around the screen. Fingal gave a slight nod in recognition. Cameron mouthed the word "Allen." Fingal parried a thrust and jerked his head toward the spiral stairs leading up to the family chambers. With a terse nod of thanks, Cameron headed for the stairs, keeping his back to the wall.

Dougall, seeing an opportunity, leapt at Fingal, his sword in one hand and a lethal-looking dagger in the other. Almost without thinking, Cameron swung his claymore in a high arc over his head, the force of the blow reverberating up his arm. Dougall fell to the ground.

Two down.

Fingal nodded once in thanks, then turned back to the battle.

Cameron crossed the remaining distance. The quiet of the stairwell was unnerving after the din of the great hall. He stopped for a moment, blowing out a breath in an effort to calm his jangled nerves. He felt a moment's anguish at the thought that he had actually taken two human lives, but it was short-lived. Dangerous times called for dangerous actions.

At the top of the stairs, Cameron hesitated. If Allen was up here, he wanted to be ready. There was no question who the better swordsman was. If he had a prayer, it would only be if he kept the element of surprise on his side.

Unbidden, the thought of Marjory's father's shield popped into his head. A shield would go a long way toward helping him defend himself—although he wasn't certain he could manage the claymore with one hand. Still, he thought, better to have it available than to dismiss it entirely.

All he had to do was make it across the hall undetected. Taking a deep breath, he summoned his courage and dashed across the corridor into the bedroom, immediately dropping into a low crouch, claymore at the ready.

Shifting slightly to survey the room, he relaxed his sword arm. The room was empty. Trying to keep noise to a minimum, he crossed to the chest and opened it. The shield was lying on top, wrapped in a square of plaid. Shifting the claymore to one hand, he lifted the shield reverently from the chest. Holding it aloft, he was amazed at how little it weighed.

Carefully balancing the shield in his left hand, he took a practice swing with the claymore in his right. It was heavy and more awkward than a two-handed thrust would have been, but he thought he could manage. Maybe. He practiced a few more times, shifting and dodging as though he were fighting an imaginary opponent.

"Are ye ready fer a real fight, then?"

Cameron jerked around. Allen leaned insolently against the door frame, his claymore extending from his body almost as if it were an extension of his arm. "I knew if I waited long enough ye'd come to find me." The feral gleam in Allen's eye was unsettling.

"Where's Torcall?"

Allen's mouth split into a thin-lipped imitation of a smile. "He's no' here." He advanced a step into the room. " 'Tis just you and me, *brother*."

"That's all o' them, then." Marjory stood with Cook as they watched the last of the women wade into the water. "You're next."

The older woman turned, her eyes wide with concern. "Aren't ye coming?"

"Nay, I'll be of more use here."

"But you're a woman."

Marjory smiled. "So they say, but I can wield a sword as well as most men—and at this point, I dinna think they're likely to stop the battle because I've joined the fighting." Her smile faded. "Besides, there are people I love in there. I canna just walk away and leave them."

Cook laid a hand on Marjory's arm. "But he willna thank ye fer putting yerself in danger."

Marjory shook it off. "I've no care what *he* thinks. 'Tis Aimil and Fingal I'm speaking of. They're still in there somewhere, and I owe it to them to try and make sure they're all right. And I owe it to myself to try and protect the land my father left me."

"But 'tis only land, Marjory—surely such isna worth dying fer." Cook waited anxiously.

" 'Tis my legacy. My father would expect me to keep it safe. Now, off with you. You canna change my mind, and you'll only be in the way here."

The woman hesitated, indecision marring her normally pleasant features.

"I said, be gone."

With a sigh, the cook hoisted her skirts and waded out into the water. The first of the women had already disappeared around the end of the wall. Satisfied that they were as safe as they could be, Marjory turned back to the tower.

It was time to avenge her father.

Chapter Twenty-eight

"I'm not your brother." Cameron spat the words, feeling adrenaline kick in. He tightened his grip on the claymore and held the silver shield aloft.

"I think that's been made clear enough." Allen snarled. "I suspected something when we first found ye on the mountain, but Father would no' listen. He's always had a blind spot where yer concerned. But even he couldna ignore what that witch has done to ye."

"Marjory hasn't done a thing." Cameron hissed, circling around the larger man.

"Tell it to Father," Allen laughed, the sound vile. "He'll see her dead. Which is exactly the way I want it."

Understanding dawned. "Torcall annihilates the Macphersons, and Clan Cameron takes out your father."

"Yer bright for a halfwit." His smile was cruel. "If things go as planned, I should be head of Tyndrum afore winter."

"Aren't you forgetting about me?"

"Nay, that's the best part o' it: You're a crazy man, fighting against yer father. There's no' a man in Scotland, who'll blame me for killing ye." Allen moved quickly for such a big man.

The jab came and went before Cameron even had time to blink. Looking down, he saw a fine line of blood seeping through the linen of his shirt.

"Ye bleed awfully red fer a devil," Allen taunted. "Perhaps yer no' a demon after all." He moved as he spoke, rocking back and forth on the balls of his feet. "No' that it matters, I'll see you dead either way."

Cameron forced himself to stare into the man's eyes. He'd heard somewhere that fighters often gave themselves away with their eyes. He fervently wished the same would be true for Scottish warriors—and more importantly, that he'd be able to recognize it when it happened.

He shifted to Allen's left, crouching to better balance the weight of his sword, waiting for Allen's next move. Somehow, in the movies these things always seemed to happen faster.

Before he completed the thought, Allen's eyes shifted. Reacting purely from instinct, Cameron twisted right an instant before the blow fell to his left. He could actually feel the rush of air as the blade swung by.

"No' bad. Ye move better than I would have expected." Allen grinned. Cameron felt a lot like a mouse being sized up by a very crafty cat. He pulled in a ragged breath.

"Really? And here I was just thinking you were a little slow."

The big man snarled, all humor fleeing his face.

Cameron felt his own anger rising. Focusing on Allen, he sprang forward, shoving his claymore in front of him. It wasn't an artful move, but what it lacked in dignity, it made up for in force. Allen stumbled back in surprise.

Cameron felt a surge of satisfaction as a crimson slit appeared in Allen's shirt. He swallowed the desire to yell "touché," and forced himself to concentrate. They circled around until they had reversed places. Allen now had his back to the chest and Cameron stood in front of the door.

With a harsh cry, Allen lunged. Metal rang against metal as the swords intersected. With a series of short thrusts and parries, the two men moved through the door and into the solar. Breathing hard, they watched each other warily.

The wind whistled through an open window, the sound harsh against the quiet of the solar. Cameron knew he was outmatched. He might manage a hit here and there, but in the long run Allen would win. He clenched his jaw, thinking of Grania. He might not win the battle, but he'd damn well inflict as much damage as he could.

Then Allen shifted slightly to the right, and incredibly Cameron saw an opening. He thrust his sword forward, catching the man's thigh. He felt a rush of elation, but his triumph was short-lived. Allen grimaced in pain, then with a roar came straight for him. The man was unstoppable.

Cameron stepped back, using both sword and shield to defend against Allen's blows. The room rang with the sound of the battle, the noise almost deafening. Grimly, Cameron held his own, but bit by bit Allen was forcing him back.

He stumbled over something, losing his balance and fell backward, his head slamming onto the stone floor, something sharp stabbing into his skull. Colors exploded through his head, followed by blinding pain. He tried to open his eyes, to move, but his body refused to respond to his commands.

Somewhere above him, he heard Allen's laughter. He

struggled to open his eyes, to ward off the inevitable death blow, but he couldn't.

"And now, *mo bhràthair,* 'tis time to die."

The words sounded far off, as though Allen were speaking to him from inside a tunnel.

He felt the darkness surrounding him, beckoning him. He fought against it, a part of him wanting to stay with Marjory even if it meant dying. But another part of him, the twenty-first century part, knew it was time to go home, to face his own life. To try and help Lindsey. No matter the cost to his heart.

Marjory was out of the tower, safe with her clanswomen, and Fingal and company were holding their own. He had to go. There might never be another chance. With a sigh that reached to the depths of his soul, he surrendered to the darkness.

Marjory watched in disbelief as Allen raised his claymore. Cameron lay on the floor, a pool of blood already spreading beneath his head. She took a step forward, sword raised to try and stop Allen, but before she could act Torcall Cameron stepped into the room, his eyes wide with horror.

Everything seemed to freeze. Torcall's eyes locked on one son trying to kill the other son. The pain in his face was almost palpable. Then, with one fluid motion, he grasped and threw the dagger at his waist.

The small knife arced through the air and found its mark. With a strange sense of disassociation she watched as Allen dropped the sword and turned to find his attacker. His angry eyes turned disbelieving when he saw his father. His mouth opened, but though it moved, no words came out.

Torcall's tear-filled eyes locked with those of his

youngest son, as he stepped forward to catch him as he fell. Cradling Allen in his arms, Torcall watched the life ebb away, his dagger still embedded in his son's neck. Then with great effort, he stood and crossed to Cameron, kneeling beside what he believed was his other son, reaching out to smooth the hair from his face.

"Move away from him." Marjory hardly recognized the words as her own. Fierce rage burned within her, and she moved forward, sword in hand, seeing nothing but her enemy.

Torcall stood slowly, his hand on his weapon. "This is yer fault, girl. If ye hadn't bewitched my son, none of this would have happened. I should have killed ye all those years ago. I was soft then, and look at the price I've had to pay."

Marjory's eyes were drawn, almost against her will, to Cameron's body, her heart withering and dying. With a ragged inhalation of breath, she turned back to Torcall. He was moving toward her, his claymore angled in front of him.

She met his gaze, shaken by the depth of hatred she saw reflected there. Gripping the hilt of her sword, she moved more fully into the chamber, her eyes never leaving his.

With a cry of rage, he was on her, his blade flashing in the fading light. She swiveled to the left, warding off his blow with her blade, the impact reverberating down her arm, shaking her entire body. They circled warily. " 'Twas you who started this," she hissed.

" 'Twas no' my doing. 'Twas yer father. He began this when he killed my Cait."

"He didn't murder her. It was an accident."

" 'Twas still his fault. Because o' him, my wife is dead

these twenty-one years. Just as surely as yer bewitching has caused the death o' my sons."

"I've no' killed anyone"—she spoke through clenched teeth—"until now." With a quick intake of breath she lunged, blood lust surging through her. This man had cost her everything, and she'd see him dead.

Again and again, she thrust and he parried around the room as though following the steps to a silent reel. He was stronger and bigger, but she was agile and quick and had the stamina of youth on her side.

Marjory sidestepped a tapestry frame, twisting just in time. Torcall's blade missed her, snapping the frame neatly in half. Torcall struggled to pull it from the mangled wood.

Seeing an opening, Marjory swung her claymore up and under, the edge landing neatly against Torcall's shoulder. With a twist of her wrist, the sword drew blood and Torcall jerked back; his weapon cracking the tapestry frame as it came free.

Movement at the corner of her vision momentarily distracted Marjory. Fingal and Aimil stood in the doorway. Fingal met her gaze with a question, his hand tightening on his sword. Marjory shook her head. This was her fight.

Her attention returned to her opponent in time to see his blade descending. She hit the floor and rolled, hearing a loud chang as Torcall's sword met stone. Leaping to her feet, she swung her weapon down, aiming for his back, but Torcall was faster, twisting successfully away.

Marjory backed away, her breath coming in gasps. The backs of her legs hit something solid. She looked down and stifled a scream. Allen's lifeless eyes stared up at her. Swallowing her revulsion, she looked up to find Torcall advancing, hatred contorting his face.

She waited until he was almost upon her, then, as his arm raised to strike, she dropped down, rolling over the body, then jumped to her feet again. Torcall's claymore struck Allen's body. Stunned, he stopped, the anger in his eyes replaced by unspeakable horror.

Taking advantage of the moment, she raised her blade to his throat and, with delicate pressure, forced him to his knees. One twist, and he would be gone. It would be over. Forever. She met his eyes and saw no remorse. She knew her own held no forgiveness.

"Finish what yer father started, girl. Or haven't ye the stomach fer it?"

Suddenly, Marjory felt tired. Old and tired. She had carried this hatred so long, it had become a comfortable part of her. But now, faced with the choice to let another live or die, it seemed an intolerable burden. She glanced around at the carnage, her eyes seeing not just blood spilled today, but blood spilled for fifteen years.

Looking up, she espied the night's first star shining through the open window. Angels, her mother had said. *Angels.* Marjory looked back at Torcall. Enough blood had been shed. The time for killing was over. Cameron had been right. It was time for living. Time for forgetting.

Still holding her sword to Torcall's throat, she used her other hand to pull his sword from Allen's body. She tossed it toward the door. "Get up."

Torcall sneered as he rose. "Ye canna do it."

"Nay, I haven't the taste fer it." She dropped her claymore, the sound echoing off the walls as it hit the stone floor. "Now get out o' my sight before I change my mind."

She saw Fingal draw his weapon. He'd see that Torcall was escorted off Crannag Mhór lands. It was over. With a heavy heart, she walked over and knelt beside Cameron.

"No." Aimil's scream filled the air.

Marjory turned to see Torcall grab her abandoned claymore. With a single step, he would be within striking range. Her own stupidity would be her death. *At least,* she thought, *I'll be with Cameron.*

She staggered to her feet, trying to evade the blade but suddenly Torcall arched back, his eyes widening in pain. With a whimper of exhaled breath, he crumpled to the ground. Behind him stood Aimil, Torcall's bloodied claymore in her hand.

The woman was frozen in place, her eyes riveted on Torcall. " 'Tis as it should be." Her voice was low, almost a whisper. "Ye lied to me all those years ago, saying ye loved me."

Aimil moved forward, kneeling beside the dead man, talking to him as if he could hear her. "I believed ye, ye know. I would have gone anywhere with ye. Done anything fer you." She reached out and stroked the side of his face, her hand leaving a trail of blood. Fingal took a step toward her, but Marjory shook her head.

Aimil continued talking, taking no notice of the others in the room. "I've ne'er loved another." She sat and pulled his head into her lap. " 'Twas me who helped ye past the guards, at the pass. 'Twas only a potion to make them sleep." Her voice took on a singsong quality, and she rocked the dead man in her arms, smoothing his hair as she spoke.

"And what a night o' loving we had. Ye told me that ye'd come fer me—to take me away with ye, ye said. I was such a fool." She rocked in silence, lost in the past.

Then, suddenly, she turned to Marjory, her eyes unfocused and wild. " 'Twas me ye ken. I helped Torcall that day." Tears streamed down her face. "I killed Manus and Gleda just as surely as if I'd run them through myself."

Marjory's mind went numb. She tried to think of something to say, but there weren't any words. She stared at the woman she had thought of as a mother. She ought to feel anger or rage, but instead she felt only sadness and pity. What a tangled web of emotions and deceit had led them to this place.

Aimil turned back to Torcall's body, still stroking his hair. "Ye tricked me, ye did. Ye ne'er loved me at all. 'Twas all a ruse to get ye into Crannag Mhór, and I fell fer it like the innocent that I was." She tilted her head, looking into his face. "And even after, when everyone lay dying, I wanted to go with ye, but ye laughed and said I was o' no of use to ye anymore."

She looked up, but her eyes saw only the past. "What a fool I was, what a bloody awful fool." She ran her hand over his face, tracing the curve of his jaw. "And even when I hated ye, I loved ye. Always, I loved ye. But ye've got to understand, I couldna let ye hurt Marjory. I pledged to protect her—penance fer what I'd done. I couldna let ye kill her. And so, *mo chridhe,* I had to kill you." She leaned down and kissed his lips.

"Enough, Aimil."

Marjory tore her gaze away from the tormented woman to look toward Fingal, whose face was awash in emotion. Aimil looked at her brother, her eyes pleading. "I had to do it, Fingal. He would have hurt our Marjory. I had to do it."

Fingal placed a hand on his throat. His voice was low and raspy, but clear in the silence of the chamber. "I know, *mo phiuthair,* I know. Come now, let me take ye to yer chamber. Ye need to rest. 'Tis over, love, 'tis all over." He held out a hand, but instead of taking it, Aimil pulled her *sgian dubh.*

Fingal rushed forward, but it was too late. Before anyone could stop her, Aimil plunged her dagger into her heart.

Marjory sat in stunned silence, the chamber reeking of death. Torcall, Allen, Cameron, and now Aimil. Fingal wept openly, leaning down to gather his sister's body into his arms. With nary a backward glance he carried her from the room.

So much lost this day. Cameron had been right, the cost of hatred was high. With a gentle hand, she reached out to touch his body. It was already starting to cool. She traced the muscles of his chest, stopping to lay her hand over his heart. There was nothing. No breath. No life. Tears filled her eyes, tears for all that had passed and for all that would never be.

"I love you." She whispered the words, bending low to his ear, knowing he couldn't hear her and yet needing to say it. "I love you."

Chapter Twenty-nine

Cameron listened to the darkness. The beeping was back. The whooshing noise had vanished, but this time he recognized the incessant beeping for what it was. A monitor. He was in the hospital. He'd made it home.

"Cameron, can you hear me, sweetie?"

Lindsey. He recognized her scent before her voice. He let his eyelids flutter open and waited for his eyes to adjust to the artificial brightness of the room.

"You're awake."

Lindsey's face swam into view, rich pink artfully accentuating her lips and cheeks. He thought of Marjory's unadorned face and, oddly, found it more beautiful.

He opened his mouth to say something, but Lindsey shook her head. "Don't try to talk. You've been in a coma. They just took the tube out this morning."

She laid a book she'd been reading on the bedside table. The title, *Touch Not the Cat*, was the motto of Clan Chattan. Marjory's grandfather.

Marjory. Her name resonated through his mind like sweet music.

"Cameron, honey?" Lindsey reached for his hand. "Can you hear me?"

"Coma?" he croaked, his throat raw and painful.

"Yes." She squeezed his hand and licked her lips. "They put you into a drug induced coma, to help you heal. Dr. Graham reduced your meds today. He thought you wouldn't wake up until this afternoon."

A coma. That explained the noises and the darkness, but what about his adventure in Scotland? Had it only been a fantasy? Had he dreamed it all?

He wriggled his toes and fingers. No paralysis. Whatever medications he was on, they were keeping the pain to a dull roar. His head throbbed, and he thought there might be a splint on his leg, but other than that everything seemed to be in working order. He looked at Lindsey, catching a look of guilt on her face.

"Cameron, I've got something to say." She licked her lips again. A habit, he remembered, "I've had a lot of time to think about this. And I need to tell you while I've still got the courage."

Something in her tone set off alarm bells. Memory teased him, but slipped away almost as quickly as it had come. Lindsey shifted so that she was leaning forward, the tops of her breasts just visible below the neckline of her shirt. She reminded him of Aida. He frowned, forcing himself to concentrate on what she was saying.

". . . It was all my fault. And I swear it will never happen again. Deke and I made an awful mistake, but I want to make it up to you."

His heart rate jumped. Deke and Lindsey. *Deke and Lindsey.* Suddenly, it all came crashing back, the scene replaying itself in his mind. He'd left the hospital early. He'd planned to surprise Lindsey with a night on the town, but he'd been the one surprised. He'd walked in on her in bed with his best friend.

He felt pain rocket through him, as the memory returned. He'd rushed from the house and jumped into his car, his only thought to get as far away from the scene in the bedroom as possible. It was raining, and Lindsey had followed him to the car, begging him to forgive her, to forget what he'd seen.

He'd slammed the car into reverse and backed out of the driveway, speeding away into the night. He'd rounded a curve on the interstate going too fast. The highway was slick with rain and his Porsche had lost traction. He'd spun out of control and hit an embankment, and wound up here.

An alarm went off above his head. Lindsey jumped up. "Oh, God, have I upset you? I was just trying to make things okay. You know, to get us back where we were. I'm truly sorry, Cameron." She stood by the bed, wringing her hands. He couldn't stop staring at her perfectly manicured nails.

A nurse hurried into the room and over to the monitor by the bed. Flipping a switch, she turned off the alarm. Reaching for Cameron's arm, she felt for his pulse. Then, with a firm look in the direction of his ex-fiancée, the nurse said, "Miss Bowden, you'll have to leave now." Lindsey backed through the door, her eyes wide with worry.

The nurse wrapped a blood pressure cuff around Cameron's arm and began pumping as she glanced at her watch. Ripping away the cuff, she took a capsule from her pocket and stuck it under his tongue. Verapamil, most likely.

"Your blood pressure is high, Dr. Even. This ought to bring it down."

She fussed with an IV bag, increasing the flow of fluid into his arm. Morphine sulphate, he noted. No wonder he was feeling no pain.

"Close your eyes and rest now, I'll check back in a little while. I've put in a call for Dr. Graham." Then she bustled out of the room as quickly as she had entered.

Cameron settled into his pillows and closed his eyes, amazed that he hadn't blown an artery. He couldn't remember ever having felt so angry, so betrayed. And to think that he thought it had been his fault. That he needed to prove himself to Lindsey. To come back and save her. The lying bitch. He should never have left Marjory.

Marjory. Just thinking the name was painful. He didn't even know if she really existed. Maybe she was just a coma-induced hallucination. He'd read of such things before. His heart cried out at the thought, insisting that she was real—more real than anything he'd ever had in this life.

And he'd let her go.

The realization hit him like a brick. He'd had everything he'd ever wanted, and he'd let it all slip through his hands. He'd tried to do the honorable thing, but in reality he'd simply refused to listen to his heart. Grania had told him, but he'd refused to listen.

He wondered what had happened. Had he died in the fifteenth century? Had Marjory survived? Had she mourned his loss? Suddenly, he longed to go back. To go home. The word surprised him, and he whispered it a loud. "Home." *Crannag Mhór.* It felt right, more right than anything else in his life. But it was too late.

His brain was getting foggy, the painkiller doing its job. With a sigh, he let his eyes drift shut allowing the darkness to take him.

* * *

Marjory sat up with a start, excitement making her pulse quicken. "I think he's breathing." She laid her head back on Cameron's chest. She could definitely feel a shallow movement. "Holy Mary of God. He's alive."

Cook materialized from nowhere, the kindly woman kneeling by her side, doubt written across her face. "Nay, Marjory, 'tis just your imagination. The man is dead."

"'Tis no' true." Marjory grabbed Cook's hand and forced it down on Cameron's chest. "Feel for yourself."

Cook frowned, then slowly smiled. "Dear God, ye speak the truth. The man *is* breathing." Her smile faded. "Ye canna get your hopes up, lass. Just because he's breathing now, doesna mean he'll ever wake up. He took a bad blow to the head, and there's all this blood. That canna bode well for his recovery."

Marjory ignored the woman's gloom. She had hope. Hadn't Cameron first come to her through just such an injury? She placed an arm under Cameron's shoulder. "Help me get him up. He needs to be in bed."

"Fine. I'll help ye get him to bed. But I dinna want you getting your hopes up."

"I'll think what I want." Marjory cried, surprised at her vehemence. "The man has risen from the dead before." Her heart soared.

She leaned over Cameron, whispering in his ear, "Come back to me, you stubborn man. I've need of you here. You belong to me and no one else. Come back to me."

"Come back to me." The voice echoed in his head, pulling him from sleep, darkness surrounding him. He listened to the darkness. The beeping was incessant, pounding out a steady beat. He concentrated instead on the voice. Marjory's voice. Had he dreamed it, or was he still linked with her time?

He tried to open his eyes, but couldn't. Hope shot through him. It had been like this before. He willed himself back to Crannag Mhór, to Marjory, but nothing happened. There was only the darkness and the syncopated beeping. He struggled to see something, anything, in the dark. Frustration consumed him.

"Rest easy, child."

Grania.

He relaxed at the sound of her voice, and immediately the white door appeared. He felt his heartbeat accelerate, whether from excitement or fear he couldn't say. Probably a bit of both.

"Dinna be afraid, I'm with ye."

He felt the warmth of her love surrounding him. "I can't see you." He spoke, and yet he knew he hadn't truly vocalized any words.

"I'm here. Feel me with yer heart."

Again, he felt the warmth of her love embrace him.

" 'Tis time fer you to make a decision, Cameron. Ye must decide what it is ye want, lad. Yer old identity or a new life with Marjory. Ye canna have both, and I canna hold the door open much longer."

As he watched the white door dimmed a little. "Why are you here?"

He felt her laughter. " 'Tis my job to watch o'er ye. What I couldna do in life, God has allowed me to do in death. I want only your happiness. But the decision must be yer own."

The light faded a little more, and he wondered suddenly how he could have ever thought anything was more important than love. For he loved Marjory Macpherson with all of his soul. He belonged with her, no matter what century, no matter what body.

"Ye have chosen wisely, my son, I'm proud o' ye. Remember, a part o' me is always with you."

Grania's voice faded away with the door, and the darkness shifted, black to gray. The beeping was gone. Afraid to hope, Cameron slowly opened his eyes.

Marjory sat on a chair, resting her head on the edge of the bed coverings, her hand entwined with the sleeping man's. With Cook's help, she'd managed to clean and bind his wound. Once the congealed blood had been washed away, the gash had seemed less nasty. He did have a large knot on the back of his head, but in truth, it didn't seem any worse than any he'd had before.

But he hadn't awakened, hadn't even made a sound. Once, she'd thought she heard him say her name, but she'd only imagined it. With a sigh, she raised her head, quickly sucking in a breath, as blue eyes met amber.

"Marjory mine." His words were weak, but Marjory had never heard anything more beautiful in her life.

"I'm here, love, I'm here."

Epilogue

Marjory let the merriment of the wedding feast surround her. Camerons and Macphersons alike danced and drank and toasted to the newlywed couple. It was perhaps a bit odd to repeat the vows, but her folk accepted it without question, glad enough to have peace in the valley again.

Fingal sat slightly apart from the others. His wound had healed, but his face was still lined with grief. Aimil's death had hit them all hard. Still, life continued, and with time Marjory knew that Fingal would recover. The hatred that had run their lives was gone. It had died with Torcall and Allen and Aimil—and with Ewen.

Not many knew of Cameron's true identity, but even those who still thought him Ewen Cameron knew that he was not the same man, and because of that they were here to celebrate the joining of the clans.

Cameron reached for Marjory's hand, pulling her close against his body, and she leaned back into his embrace, delighting in the even rise and fall of his breathing. It had been touch-and-go for a while, but he was finally healed.

It would take a while before Crannag Mhór did the same, but on the whole her people were recovering. Her grandfather had made certain that there was peace between the Camerons and Macphersons. Accomplished in no small part because so many believed Cameron was in fact the resurrected Ewen, and it was simpler to let people think what they would.

"Penny for your thoughts," Cameron's voice echoed through his chest, and Marjory felt the words as much as heard them.

"I was thinking about you." She tipped her head to look up at him.

He smiled down at her, his hand running softly along her back. "I love you, Marjory Macpherson."

The look in his eyes made her heart turn over, and Marjory felt tears well up inside her. He reached for her hand again, his fingers entwining with hers. "I love you too, Cameron Even. And even though the world will know me as Ewen Cameron's wife, 'tis your wife I am and always will be."

"Once and forever mine?" he whispered, his breath sending shivers of desire chasing though her.

"Once and forever yours," she repeated. "Body, heart, and soul." She stood on tiptoe to brush her lips against his, sealing the covenant. "And you, my love, are mine."

With a sigh, she settled back against him, allowing his warmth to seep into her soul, filling her with bliss, and as he pulled her tighter, she glanced out the window. A small star twinkled high in the night sky, and she smiled, certain that after all her mother had been right about the angels.

Author's Note

The premise of this book, the forced marriage between Ewen Cameron and Marjory Macpherson, is based on historical fact.

Justice in early Scottish clans was the responsibility of the laird. When a kinsman was victimized, it was the laird's duty to force the man who committed the crime to compensate the injured party—or in the case of murder, his dependents.

Although forcing a woman to marry her father's murderer may seem bizarre by twenty-first-century standards, the principle is actually sound. The murderer had deprived the woman of her natural protector, her father, and in order to redress this loss he was providing for her, as her father would have done, a husband—returning the status quo and avoiding further bloodshed.

In 1433, just such a marriage occurred between Catherine Patrick and Reginald Johnson, soon after his father murdered hers. The seeds for my story stemmed from the idea of such a union.

Acknowledgments

I'd like to thank Sharon G. Gregorcyk, M.D. and James M. Oberwetter, M.D. for helping me understand the workings of a tracheotomy. Any errors I have made, are of course my own.

CHERYL HOWE

The Pirate &
THE PURITAN

In her youth Felicity was swept off her feet by pretty words—but though that time in Boston felt so right, the man was so wrong. Now she's sworn to bury her sensuality under somber clothes and a rigid lifestyle; religion is the cure for future mistakes.

In Barbados, Felicity finds her father's cronies worse than expected. Worst is the infuriating Lord Christian Andrews—with his strong jaw; lean, muscled body; and that diabolical glint in his eye conjuring all the reasons she's renounced pleasure. But sneaking onto Drew's ship to prove his depravity, Felicity is again swept away. The man has only a heart of gold . . . and a nature bent on uncovering her own buried passion.

Connie Mason

The Laird of Stonehaven

He appears nightly in her dreams—magnificently, blatantly naked. A man whose body is sheer perfection, whose face is hardened by desire, whose voice makes it plain he will have her and no other.

Blair MacArthur is a Faery Woman, and healing is her life. But legend foretells she will lose her powers if she gives her heart to the wrong man. So the last thing she wants is an arranged marriage. Especially to the Highland laird who already haunts her midnight hours with images too tempting for any woman to resist.

Taken by You
CONNIE MASON

English nobleman Morgan Scott pillages the high seas. When he and his crew attack the *Santa Cruz*, he sees the perfect opportunity for revenge: an innocent Spanish nun whose body he can ravage to spite her people. But Morgan quickly finds himself torn between this act of vengeance and the passion incited by her fiery spirit.

Even as Luca Santiego fears her fate at the hands of the powerful privateer, she fights the feelings of desire he inspires with his sparkling eyes and muscular contours. She may be posing as a nun, but the emotions she feels in his strong arms are anything but pious, and she soon longs to be taken by him.

- -

Lionheart
Connie Mason

Lionheart has been ordered to take Cragdon Castle, but the slim young warrior on the pure white steed leads the defending forces with a skill and daring that challenges his own prowess. No man can defeat the renowned Lionheart; he will soon have the White Knight beneath his sword and at his mercy.

But storming through the portcullis, Lionheart finds no trace of his mysterious foe. Instead a beautiful maiden awaits him, and a different battle is joined. She will bathe him, she will bed him; he will take his fill of her. But his heart is taken hostage by an opponent with more power than any mere man can possess—the power of love.

- -

THE PLEASURE MASTER

NINA BANGS

Stranded by the side of a New York highway on Christmas Eve, hairdresser Kathy Bartlett wishes herself somewhere warm and peaceful with a subservient male at her side. She finds herself transported all right, but to Scotland in 1542 with the last man she would have chosen.

With the face of a dark god or a fallen angel, and the reputation of being able to seduce any woman, Ian Ross is the kind of sexual expert Kathy avoids like the plague. So when she learns that the men in his family are competing to prove their prowess, she sprays hair mousse on his brothers' "love guns" and swears she will never succumb to the explosive attraction she feels for Ian. But as the competition heats up, neither Kathy nor Ian reckon the most powerful aphrodisiac of all: love.

___52445-7 $5.50 US/$6.50 CAN

The
Very Virile Viking
Sandra Hill

Magnus Ericsson is a simple man. He loves the smell of fresh-turned dirt after springtime plowing. He loves the heft of a good sword in his fighting arm. But, Holy Thor, what he does not relish is the bothersome brood of children he's been saddled with. Or the mysterious happenstance that strands him and his longship full of maddening offspring in a strange new land—the kingdom of *Holly Wood*. Here is a place where the blazing sun seems to bake his already befuddled brain, where the folks think he is an act-whore (whatever that is), and the woman of his dreams fails to accept that he is her soul mate . . . a man of exceptional talents, not to mention a very virile Viking.
